ABOUT THE AUTHOR

Tracy Buchanan lives in Buckinghamshire with her husband, their little girl and their puppy, Bronte. Tracy travelled extensively while working as a travel magazine editor, and has always been drawn to the sea after spending her childhood holidays on the south coast visiting family, a fascination that inspires her writing. She now dedicates her time to writing and procrastinating on Facebook.

Sign up for Tracy's e-newsletter at http://www.tracy-buchanan.com. If you're a fan of her books, join the exclusive Facebook group she's set up with other bestselling women's fiction authors for giveaways and exclusives. Just visit www.facebook.com/groups/TheReadingSnug and request to join.

Also by Tracy Buchanan

THE ATLAS OF US
MY SISTER'S SECRET
NO TURNING BACK
HER LAST BREATH

TRACY BUCHANAN

The Lost
Sister

avon.

Avon.
A division of HarperCollins*Publishers*
1 London Bridge Street,
London SE1 9GF

www.harpercollins.co.uk

A Paperback Original 2018
1

A catalogue record for this book is
available from the British Library

ISBN 978-0-00-826464-2

Typeset in Minion Std by Palimpsest Book Production Ltd,
Falkirk, Stirlingshire

Printed and bound in Great Britain by
CPI Group (UK) Ltd, Croydon CR0 4YY

MIX
Paper from
responsible sources
FSC **FSC C007454**
www.fsc.org

For Archie. We miss you, boy.

Chapter One

Selma

Kent, UK
18 July 1991

It all started when the boy nearly drowned.

Queensbay was experiencing one of those summer evenings where strangers smile at each other as they pass on the street, everyone in awe that the temperature could be that warm in grey old Britain. Flip-flops and sandals abounded, the slip-slap of soles on the wooden path and the bark of small dogs a familiar reprise. The seafront café was full to bursting, especially the outside area, with children excited at being out so late on a school night, and parents trying to drink wine and smile with friends in between reprimanding hyper and sunburnt toddlers. On the sandy beach, older couples strolled through the shallow water, shoes dangling from their fingertips as their dogs ran in and out of the caves nearby. And beyond it all, the sun as it set, a fierce orange in the sky, fringing people's heads with fire.

I watched it all through my sunglasses, the gin I'd drunk blurring the edges of my mind, just the way I liked it. The curved sandy bay looked particularly pretty that night, bookended by the café on one side and three towering chalk stacks on the other. People could walk beyond the stacks and there they'd find a secluded bay of caves overlooked by an abandoned hotel . . . the same hotel I once dreamed of buying. I sighed. Not looking likely now.

My daughter Becky chased her friend around the busy tables and I kept half an eye on her, ready to pounce at the sound of breaking glass, a sob, a crash. Next to me, my husband Mike kept a casual hand on my bare knee, smiling as his friend Greg recounted a difficult client he'd had to deal with. Why did people feel the need to discuss something as banal as *work* on evenings like this?

I yawned and stretched, noticing Greg's eyes slide over my breasts, which strained against the thin material of my floral wrap dress.

So predictable. So *wrong* too, considering his wife Julie was sitting right next to me trying desperately to feed their newborn, his crumpled little red face squashed against her bare nipple as she fanned her hot, freckled cheeks with a menu.

I narrowed my eyes at Greg and he turned away. He was what my mum would call 'trouble'. I even remember the way my mum said it, sprawled across her sofa, drink in hand as she gossiped with her friend. 'He was *trouble*, darling,' the *r* stretched out in that deep throaty voice of hers. When I asked what she meant over dinner that evening, she shot me one of her withering looks. 'What does it matter to *you*?'

A week later, I got my answer when I met the man who was

2

to become my stepfather. He was the worst of them. The others – three in total since she told my father to sling his hook when I was eight – had their faults too. Luckily I was well gone by the time the third one came along.

No, Greg was nothing like that first horrid stepfather. Well, maybe he *looked* like him with his slicked-back dark hair and wickedly handsome face. But I couldn't see him raising a hand to his wife and child like my stepfather had. I shouldn't be too harsh on Greg. The flirting, the sneaky glances . . . they were all just a little titillation for him to make the humdrum of life in that godforsaken town more bearable.

People came to Queensbay for a slower pace of life. A beautiful stretch of sand on the Kent coast, once a hidden gem favoured by retired couples and families looking to escape the rat race. The problem was, it had got *too* slow thanks to the country plunging into recession, boards covering the windows of the shops I once loved; For Sale signs up for too long outside usually desirable houses. You could barely see the words on those signs through the layer of seagull mess. Love's young dream well and truly faded.

It was the same for me and Mike too. It hadn't been that way when we'd driven through the town on the way to Margate for an old friend's wedding after we got married ten years prior. I'd been so blown away with the pretty bay, we'd impulsively booked a room in one of its hotels, staying on for a further week after the wedding. When I'd spotted the abandoned hotel sitting in an elevated position above the caves nearby, a tatty For Sale sign outside its front, I'd been in awe. Sure, the white weatherboard that adorned its exterior walls was blackened with moss, the wraparound glass windows at the front grimy with dirt. But it was still beautiful.

'I'd love to live somewhere like that,' I remember saying to Mike during that impulsive weekend away.

But he'd laughed. 'You have to be kidding. Look at the state of it!'

That was the problem with Mike. He'd never had the imagination I did, I should have known the moment he refused to play a drinking game on the first night we met in that university bar.

Anyway, back to the evening. *That* evening.

'Oh, come *on*, Finn,' Julie moaned next to me as she looked down at the baby.

I tipped my large sunglasses down to the end of my nose, peering over them at the newborn. 'Not feeding again?' I asked.

'Latching on, I *think*,' Julie replied, the dark circles under her eyes pronounced, her red hair flat and frizzy.

'Good for you, persevering.'

'Did you?'

I let out a dramatic sigh. 'Sadly, these old things couldn't produce enough milk,' I said, gesturing towards my own breasts. I caught Greg's eye and he held my gaze. 'Had no choice but to bottle feed,' I added.

Mike shot me a look. Okay, *maybe* that was a little white lie. Truth was, I'd produced plenty of milk – so much it dribbled out at night, wetting my silk camisole. But I'd hated the *act* of breast-feeding, especially the smell of my own milk. I couldn't say that out loud though, could I? It would be frowned upon, especially in Queensbay with its penchant for yoga and earth mummies.

I yawned again, peering at my gold watch. It was past eight now.

'Sorry, I'm boring you,' Julie said, frowning.

I gently touched her arm. Yes, the woman was boring me. But that wasn't her fault.

'Not at all!' I said. 'I'm just tired from the heat. You're doing great, really darling.'

'Do you think you'll have another?' Julie asked.

Mike caught my eye. He was desperate for another. But I couldn't think of anything worse, shuddering as I remembered that sticky, confusing, sick-infested time of Becky's newborn months. The emotions. The tears. I adored Becky, my perfect *one*. It would be like going back to *square one* if I had another. Plus, there was the slight problem of Mike and I barely touching any more. Maybe that should have worried me, but the truth was, I didn't want to touch or be touched. On the rare occasions when we did make love, I flinched then felt nothing, going through the motions as I turned my face away. I used to be so passionate, to love to hold and be held. But not any more.

I sighed, turning back to Julie. 'We've been told we can't,' I whispered so Mike couldn't overhear. The lie sent a thrill through me. 'We don't like to talk about it, especially Mike,' I added with a grimace. Another touch of the arm. 'You're one of the only people I've told.'

'I'm so sorry,' Julie whispered back. I could see it mixed in with the empathy in her eyes, how pleased she was to be one of the privileged few to know.

'But let's not talk about that,' I said, fanning my hand about. 'Tell me about *you*.'

As Julie launched into the details of her problems with sore nipples, I slid my sunglasses back up to hide the fact I wasn't really listening, my mind drifting off to the plot of my latest novel.

A harsh winter. A lost girl. A savage man. A world away from here.

Oh God, yes please.

'Selma!' A voice pierced my thoughts. I looked up, annoyed, as a red-faced woman in a bright pink top wove her way through the tables to get to me, waving her hands erratically, her sullen son following her.

It was Monica from work, the office manager who considered everyone her best friend, spilling the intimate details of her life to anyone who'd listen. Her husband's breakdown. Her sister-in-law's affair. The dose of thrush she'd been suffering from the past two years. I did my best to avoid her most days, unable to deal with her perpetually sunny disposition, especially on Monday mornings. But it was hard in such a compact office, just ten of us crammed into the top floor of a small barn conversion as we scribbled out copy for various clients. Thank God I only had to endure it three days a week.

'Hello, Monica,' I said with a tight smile.

Her son let out a bored sigh and crossed his arms, staring out to sea. He was ten, just a couple of years older than Becky but the same size, which always came a surprise to anyone who knew Monica, who was a tall, wide-hipped, big-breasted woman. I suppose that was one thing she and I did have in common: our curves – a contrast to the stick-thin women that seemed to grace the town.

'Oh, hasn't Becky grown!' Monica exclaimed, gazing across to Becky on the beach. Her forehead was sunburnt, freckles smattering her tiny nose, her golden hair long and tangled in the sand, ice cream smeared on her face. My heart clenched at the sight of her, my beautiful happy daughter. They tell you about the love you feel for your children and at first, for some, it doesn't come as quickly in the madness of those early newborn days. But when it does, it has a quality that supersedes all other types of love. Even I, as a writer, find it hard to describe.

I beckoned my daughter over, suddenly desperate to cuddle her. She jumped up, weaving around the tables to get to me. She smashed into my arms, putting her cheek against my neck, and I felt utterly overwhelmed with my love for her.

'She *has* grown,' I replied, leaning down to kiss Becky's head. 'Seems to every day.'

'I wish Nathan would,' Monica said with a sigh as she looked at her son. 'Amazing the amount of food he puts away and yet still, look at him!'

'Shut up, Mum,' her son hissed under his breath. Monica's face flickered with hurt and I couldn't help it, I felt sorry for the poor woman. Monica had told me – and anyone else who'd listen – of the trouble she'd had with Nathan at school, the fights he'd got into, the back-chatting too. Becky had mentioned it occasionally too.

I looked down at my own daughter and stroked her soft hair, thinking how lucky I was to have her. A challenge sometimes, yes, like many children. But she was a good girl really.

'How are the book sales going?' Monica asked, face alight with excitement.

'Fine,' I replied airily. I took a quick sip of gin, the ice clinking against my teeth. 'You don't really get told much about sales.'

'Not even two years after it's published?' Greg suddenly piped up.

I tensed. 'Nope,' I replied, taking another urgent sip of gin.

'So when's the next one out?' he asked.

All eyes turned to me and I felt my face flush. I usually loved the attention, but not when it came to talk of sales. 'Winging its way to my publisher very soon,' I replied in as cheerful a voice as I could muster.

Mike frowned. 'Really?'

'Yes, *really*, darling,' I said.

'How exciting!' Monica exclaimed. 'Give it time and you'll be the next Danielle Steel!'

Mike snorted to himself and I shot him a look. 'One day, maybe,' I said, forcing a smile. *If my husband were more bloody optimistic about my chances anyway*, I wanted to add.

'Mum, come *on*,' Nathan moaned impatiently. 'It's going to get dark soon.'

We all peered towards the sun, which was now low in the sky and would soon be dipping beneath the horizon.

'Right, better go,' Monica said. 'Nathan's insisting on an ice cream. See you at work next week!' She gave a nervous wave then wandered off, stopping again to talk to someone else as her son clenched his fists in frustration.

Becky jumped off my lap and ran to the beach to join her friend again. I took the chance to close my eyes behind my sunglasses, trying to return to that momentary period of peace I'd felt earlier. But then I felt an elbow poke me. I opened my eyes, irritated by the disturbance, and watched as Julie leaned down to get a muslin that had fallen to the ground, her baby squeezed against her blue-veined breasts.

'Here, let me,' I said, bending down to grab the cloth for her.

As I handed it back I paused, catching sight of a man standing by the chalk stacks. He was tall, over six foot, long-limbed and deeply tanned, blond hair to his shoulders, a golden beard. On his arm was a thick row of tweed bracelets, his blue shorts ripped at the pocket. He was holding a large rucksack with a sewn-in patch showing one unblinking eye.

The man turned, as though sensing me looking at him. He held my gaze and I felt my breath stutter.

Then a scream pierced the air.

Chapter Two

Selma

Kent, UK
18 July 1991

Mike stopped talking, Greg and Julie too as another scream rang out. Other people started rising from their tables, shading their eyes to look out to sea.

I followed their gazes to see a woman running to the edge of the water, bright pink top blowing about in the breeze as she flapped her sunburnt arms about.

It was Monica.

'My son!' she shouted. 'He's drowning. Someone help, I can't swim!'

I looked in the direction she was pointing to see the top of a small head poking up from the waves, before being submerged again.

'Jesus, he's in the sea,' I said.

Greg jumped up, kicking his shoes off. 'I'm going in.'

Julie grabbed at his hand. 'Be careful.'

Greg glanced over towards me then back to his wife. 'I'll be fine,' he said before jogging down to the beach. I nudged Mike and he sighed, reluctantly following his friend, the setting sun turning his balding head red.

'God, how terrifying,' Julie said as she held her newborn Finn close.

I imagined Becky out there then, her little body engulfed by the waves. The horror of it made me dizzy.

'Come here, darling,' I called over to her.

Becky jumped up and ran over to me. 'What's happening, Mummy?' she asked as I pulled her close and kissed her head.

'Just silly Nathan swimming in the sea when he shouldn't have,' I replied.

'Poor woman,' Julie said, staring at Monica as she splashed into the water, her hands to her head in horror. 'Do you know her well?'

'Just from work.' I watched Monica as she stepped forward into the waves, tears running down her cheeks, then jumped back, scared. She annoyed the hell out of me. But the way she was trying to fight her apparent fear of the water, the panic on her face . . .

'Keep an eye on Becky, will you?' I said to Julie. I stood, head suddenly swimming from the gin, then weaved my way through the tables and chairs to get to Monica.

'Oh Selma!' Monica exclaimed when I got to her, clutching at my hand. 'What if they can't get to him?'

'He'll be fine, look at all the people going to help him!'

As I said that, I noticed the man I'd seen by the chalk stacks walking towards the sea. He was calmer than the others, but his long strides somehow kept up with them. Just ahead of him, Mike followed Greg into the water, splashing into the waves clumsily, nearly falling as Greg turned to help him. But the man stepped into the sea without trouble, his outline set alight by the dying rays of the sun.

'Oh God, I can't see my boy. Can you see him?' Monica asked, fingers clutching at my arm, face paling. 'It's getting so dark!'

I stepped forward, narrowing my eyes to see better. Monica was right, it was hard to see Nathan now. The sun had disappeared beneath the horizon and the sky was an indigo blue. But I could see the man, his hair like silver in the growing darkness. While the other would-be rescuers flapped around in the water, he looked serene.

In fact, it was almost as though he were walking on the waves.

'Is that man *walking* on the water?' a woman nearby said, echoing my thoughts. Others around her laughed nervously but I could tell they were seeing the same thing.

I took a few more steps forward, heart thumping as my eyes stayed on the man, his tanned calves visible, his ankles . . . and yes, his feet. It really was like the water was ice and he was just walking across it.

'Jesus,' I whispered to myself.

A hush fell over the bay, others clearly unsure of what they were seeing too.

'Must be a trick of the light,' a man said, breaking the silence. But I could hear the waver of doubt in his voice.

The man stopped, then leaned over and lifted something into his arms.

'He's got him!' someone shouted. A nervous cheer went up among the crowds.

Monica slumped against me, crying in relief as we watched the man walk back to shore, the boy seemingly weightless in his arms. The man was clearly walking *in* the water now; clearly it had been a trick of light.

People watched him, open-mouthed, as he headed towards us.

'Mummy!' Nathan sobbed, reaching for his mum. Monica took him from the man, burying her face in her son's wet neck as she sunk to the sand.

The man looked at me. Something passed between us, something I couldn't quite get a grasp on. Then he leaned down, retrieved his rucksack and disappeared into the night, the sound of sirens filling the air.

'Did you know that man, Mummy?' Becky asked, peering up at me with those knowing blue eyes of hers.

'No, darling. He's a complete stranger.'

Chapter Three

Becky

Sussex, UK
1 June 2018

'He's a complete stranger, Kay!' Becky says as she checks the calendar for details of her next appointment. 'There is *no* chance I'm going on a date with him.'

'It's just a party. There'll be lots of people there,' Kay counters, glasses resting on the end of her nose, her white blouse stained and creased after a day fussing over puppies.

'If you're suggesting he picks me up first and takes me for a drink,' Becky says, 'it *is* a date. Anyway, Summer is still recovering from surgery. I can't leave her.'

'You have David next door! It'll have been a month by then, you know more than anyone she'll be fully recovered.' Kay's face grows serious. 'I know it's just an excuse. But no matter how much I adore those mutts of yours, three dogs are no substitute for human company, especially for an attractive thirty-four-year-old woman like yourself.'

'I politely disagree.' Becky leans forward, putting her hand on her friend's shoulder and smiling. 'I appreciate your attempts to marry me off, but I'm quite happy as I am, thank you.'

Kay crosses her arms and gives her a cynical look just as the bell above the door rings.

'Perfect timing,' Becky says with a wink as a woman walks in carrying a plastic box, a girl of about eight beside her. Becky leans down and smiles at the girl. 'You must be Jessica and this,' she says, gesturing to the box, 'must be Stanley.' The girl nods shyly. 'Come on through, we had a cancellation so we're running bang on time for once!'

Becky leads them into her small consultation room. It's a tiny practice, sitting in a red-brick building on the edge of a large field, just her, two job-sharing veterinary nurses, a part-time locum and Kay, receptionist and accountant extraordinaire. Plenty to serve the small village they live in.

The woman places the plastic box on Becky's consulting table and opens it.

Becky peers in, smiling. 'What a beauty,' she exclaims.

The girl beams with pride as her mother carefully pulls the fish tank out of the box. Becky leans down and looks at the small goldfish inside, at its transparent orange skin, globe eyes and bubbling mouth. One of the vets she'd trained with had described goldfish as a waste of his time. If he could just see the way this little girl was staring at that *waste of time* right now, he might see this goldfish – that *all* animals – are worth so much more than that.

Or maybe not. He was a bit of a shallow idiot after all.

'I'm pleased you brought him in,' Becky says.

The girl crosses her arms, frowning. 'It's a *her*.'

Becky peers at the mother who gives a little shrug.

'Ah. *Her*. Sorry,' Becky says. 'Well, I'll tell you straight off, it's not serious. You managed to bring *her* in just in time.'

'What's wrong with Stanley?' the girl asks.

Becky points to the small white spots on Stanley's fin. 'Fin rot,' she explains. The girl's big blue eyes widen. 'But no need to worry!' Becky quickly adds. 'Thanks to your vigilance, Stanley will be just fine.'

The girl smiles, lighting up her young face.

Her mother squeezes her shoulder. 'See? What did I tell you?'

Becky watches them, unable to stop herself feeling a tinge of jealousy. 'So,' she says, clearing her throat. 'Do you have some salt at home?'

The girl peers up at her mother, who nods.

'Good. That's how we'll treat Stanley. A few teaspoons of salt in her tank each day and she'll be as right as rain within the week.' Becky turns away to tap some notes into her computer. 'It's just as well Stanley has such a loving owner. Fish are *so* important. You know they were here first, way before us, even way before dinosaurs? And yet look at them,' she says, gesturing towards the tank. 'They're still here. Quite a feat.'

'They're the best pets in the world,' the girl says stoically as her mother places the tank back in the box.

'I'd agree,' Becky replies. 'But my three dogs might get a bit upset. I think that's it for Stanley today. Just call if you have any problems.'

'You've been brilliant, thank you,' the girl's mother says as they walk out to the reception area. 'Say thank you, Jess.'

'Thank you,' the girl says in a shy voice.

'A pleasure!'

When they leave, Becky returns to her consulting room and sinks down into her chair, yawning. She likes to do this at the end of the day, just close her eyes and relax for a few seconds. She's done her best to make the consulting room as homely as possible. One wall crowded with cards from grateful patients, her small, tidy desk adorned with photos of her three skinny suki whippet crosses, Summer, Womble and Danny.

Above the desk is a shelf of books lined with the usual suspects: a wide range of medical reference books. But mixed in with them are romance novels, given to Becky by patients as gifts after Kay let slip to one that Becky is a secret fan of romantic fiction. It is a running joke now, with books gifted to her by regulars each Christmas, or when an owner wants to thank her. The truth is, Becky does love the novels, devouring them whenever she is lucky enough to have a break.

But that is just about the extent of the romance in her life. It has been ten years since she was dumped by the boyfriend she'd had since school, just before their tenth anniversary. There have been a succession of bad dates since, but recently, she's begun to think a life with just her and the dogs would be perfect, *despite* what Kay thinks.

Becky's eyes stray towards the photo at the end of the row of books. It's her on the day she graduated from veterinary college five years ago. Her dad is standing stiffly beside her, a hint of pride on his face. She ought to feel pride herself when she looks at that photo but, instead, she often finds herself thinking of who *wasn't* there that day: her mum.

Becky drives thoughts of her mum away, focusing instead on her dad. God, she misses him. Even their lunches, when they would both sit and eat in complete silence, comfortable with each other after years of being in each other's company. At least he is happy now. That's what's important, even if he is many miles away in Wales with his second wife, Cynthia.

Becky smiles at her dad's proud face in the photo then grabs her pale blue rucksack and slings it over her shoulder, walking out into the reception area.

'Last patient of the day, thank God,' Kay says, standing up and stretching. 'Has seemed like a long week this week. Must be the heat. Any plans for the weekend?'

Becky shrugs. 'The usual.'

'Long walks. Dinners for one—'

'Four,' Becky says, interrupting her.

'Ah yes, the dogs. Then, let me guess, some reading?'

Becky laughs. 'You know me so well.'

'You know you can pop by any time if you find yourself getting lonely.'

'Thank you, but I honestly never feel lonely.'

Kay shoots her a cynical look. 'Either way, remember to go shopping for a new dress for my party next month.' Becky opens her mouth to say something but Kay puts her hand up. 'I refuse to hear any excuses. I'll be fifty. *Fifty!* If you really like me as much as you say, then you'll come. Plus you'll get the chance to meet the family I bitch about every day!'

Becky gives her a faint smile. She can't think of anything worse than a huge family party, even if it is for her friend. 'I'll see how Summer gets on.'

'That's a yes then,' Kay says with a wink.

They both laugh, going through their nightly routine of switching lights off and locking the place up. Then they step out into the searing evening heat, the field stretching out before them.

'Have a good weekend!' Becky calls out as Kay rushes off down the path, no doubt needing to get back to take one of her teenage kids to a football match or dance class.

But Becky doesn't need to rush. Instead, she takes a moment to stop, breathing in the warm air infused with the scent of flowers and grass. It's one of the many luxuries of not having to rush home to people like others have to, she thinks. She'll always be able to take the time to enjoy the simple things, like breathing in the beauty of a hot summer evening.

After a few moments, she heads across the fields and down a path created from grass well-trodden by dog walkers. Kay lives near the cobbled high street five minutes in the opposite direction, but Becky lives out of the way, in one of four cottages that sit in a row and overlook the field. Each of the cottages are tiny but their gardens are huge with gates that lead onto the field, ideal for the dogs. She still remembers her dad driving them through this very village on the way to their new home in Busby-on-Sea after her mum left. That was over twenty-five years ago now. 'This is a pretty village,' Becky remembers saying to him.

'Too small,' he'd replied. 'Busby-on-Sea is much better, you'll see. It even has a leisure centre! Plus, your grandparents are there.'

One shop and no leisure centre sounded perfect to her, even

then. But she knew her dad needed to be around family. She remembers asking her dad when her mum would be joining them. She knew she wouldn't be, they'd had 'the talk' just a few weeks beforehand. But she still had to ask, just to be sure.

'Mummy's not coming with us, remember?' her dad had replied, a confusing mixture of sadness and anger on his face. 'But she'll visit. I think you'll be happy in Busby-in-Sea, I really do, Becks.'

As Becky thinks of that, she gets another flash of memory. The sound of waves. Sand in between her toes. Her mum smiling down at her, nose freckled from the sun, blue eyes sparkling.

'I think you'll be happy here, Becks, I really do.'

And then beyond her, the mouth of a cave.

'Becky!' The memory trickles away as a couple in their seventies walk towards her, their golden Labrador bounding over to greet her, one of her many patients.

She stops and leans down, pressing her nose against the dog's wet one. 'Hello, Sandy!' she says. 'How's his ear today?'

'Better thanks to you, Becky,' the woman says, but she seems to already be walking away with her husband. They obviously have somewhere to be, and Sandy follows. Becky wonders where. Maybe dinner out with friends. Cinema. Or just a date with a film indoors. They had each other, whatever they had waiting for them. She feels a pang of loneliness, thinking of what Kay had said earlier.

No, Kay's wrong, she doesn't get lonely. If she ever wants company, she just needs to head out here into the fields, knowing there will always be one villager or another walking their dogs. There's such a sense of community here. Her dad hadn't seen it that way when she'd told him she'd be moving out of Busby-on-Sea four years ago, the place that had been her home since she was eight years old. But she needed the independence of living in a different town, even if it was only a twenty-minute drive away . . . and so had he. In fact, it was after she left that he got back in touch with his old friend, Cynthia. And now they were married!

Becky reaches the end of the field, stopping at the fence lining the four long gardens belonging to the cottages. Her cottage sits at the end, and looks just the same as the others with its white-washed walls and thatched roof.

In the garden next to hers, David is sitting on a chair reading a book. His Cavalier King Charles spaniel, Bronte, is lying at his feet, and Becky's three lurchers are stretched out in the evening sun on the lawn. Summer has a short chestnut coat, and big brown eyes with long lashes. Danny is as black as the night, long-haired and handsome. Womble is the longest and tallest of the three – grey, inquisitive and the fastest dog she's ever seen. Each of them had been brought into the practice for treatment after being found as strays, and each was rescued by Becky who had a soft spot for 'skinnies' as she called them. Poor Summer was the worst, brought in by the police after it was reported she had been dragged behind a car, tied to the bumper with a rope to make her run faster. She was still terrified of strangers, hiding behind Becky's legs whenever anyone but David approached her.

Summer is the first to see Becky as she opens the fence into David's garden. The dog gingerly stands up, does a quick stretch, then limps over to Becky, her leg still bound from the surgery Becky had carried out to fix a broken bone. She nudges her nose into Becky's tummy, and Becky strokes her.

'Hello, darling,' Becky says, leaning down to kiss her head as the other dogs' ears prick at the sound of her voice. They too jump up, padding over.

'Summer's been a terror today,' David says with a smile that gives away just how much he enjoyed her being a terror. He's in his sixties, and is tall with short, grey hair and a wicked smile. He moved to the area just a few months after Becky did four years ago, and they'd clicked straight away as they discussed their love of animals. They mainly talked about dogs, but David did mention once that he and his wife had split up many years before, and they had a daughter who lived abroad.

'Thanks for looking after them,' she says to him now with a smile.

'Always a pleasure.'

She occasionally took the dogs into the practice with her, but it was hard keeping three large dogs entertained in such a small space. David looked after them most days, bringing them over to see her during her breaks.

She leans down and pats Bronte on the head. She gives a soft thump of her feathery white tail then puts her little chin back on her paws. She was another rescue dog, brought in to the practice two years ago, an ex-breeding dog dumped by a local puppy farm after getting an infection. David had taken an instant liking to her after his last cocker spaniel had passed away, so he'd ended up adopting her.

'Right, let's get you all back,' Becky says, patting her thigh and heading towards the fence that divides their gardens.

'Not staying for a cuppa?' David calls out to her.

'Tomorrow,' she calls back. 'I'm so exhausted, I think I might go to bed straight after dinner.'

He laughs. 'You work too hard.'

Becky steps over the fence, the dogs leaping over with her, and lets herself into her cottage. All three dogs dart to the back of the house as soon as they get in, standing by their bowls and looking up at her with impatient eyes, ready for their dinner.

'Okay, okay, give me a minute!' Becky calls out.

She chucks her keys onto the stairs and walks down the small hallway and into the kitchen, which is surprisingly large considering the size of the rest of the cottage, and has enough room for a decent-sized pine table in the middle.

Becky feeds the dogs then sets about making her own dinner, a quick stir fry. Once she's finished cooking, she plates up and heads out onto the patio to sit down with her dinner and a book – another romance. David has gone in now. Becky leans back in her chair and blinks up at the sun. She loves this time of day; warm enough to sit outside, cool enough that she doesn't have to worry about it burning her pale skin. A bird soars above, heading east . . . maybe towards Kent, where she once lived.

The phone rings, puncturing her thoughts. She sighs. Why does this always happen when she's settling down to eat? She places her plate on a table as she stands up, then walks inside quickly to grab the phone.

'Hello?'

'Becky?'

The voice is weak, barely audible. It's a voice she hasn't heard in many years and yet she knows it in an instant. It's seared into her heart.

'Mum?'

Chapter Four

Selma

Kent, UK
19 July 1991

'Mummy?'

I nibbled on my pen while looking out towards the sea, playing over what had happened the evening before again. I'd dreamt about the man all night, hot feverish dreams, as I'm sure half the town had too.

'Mummy!'

I looked at Becky. 'Sorry, darling, I was a million miles away.'

'Did the man *really* walk on water, like everyone was saying?'

'Of course he didn't!' Mike exclaimed over his shoulder from the kitchen. 'It's just bored people imagining things.'

I smiled to myself, snapping my notepad shut. 'Yes, Daddy's right of course, very bored people making stuff up.'

Becky looked disappointed. 'Still hungry, Daddy,' she chirped, pushing her half-eaten cereal to the side.

'You've hardly eaten your cereal,' I said.

Becky shrugged. 'Don't like it.'

'You can have some strawberries then,' Mike said.

Becky frowned, crossing her arms. 'No, I want chocolate.'

I leaned in close to her ear. 'Maybe when Daddy goes,' I whispered.

Mike shot me a disapproving glance. 'Fruit or nothing,' he said, grabbing his car keys. He gave Becky a kiss on the head then waved at me before letting himself out. There was once a time when he'd kiss me before leaving for work. Not now though. Should that have made me feel sad? Well I didn't. I felt nothing.

When I was sure he was gone, I went to the cupboard and got some chocolate-flavoured cereal out, winking at a giggling Becky. 'You have to be quick though, we have to leave for school soon.'

Five minutes later, we walked to Becky's school. It was a breezy day, still warm though, the skies blue, the sun bright, the sea glimmering in the distance. People were either walking to work or coming back from dropping kids off, dressed in shorts and T-shirts, sandals and flip-flops.

The school lay at the bottom of a hill, five minutes' walk from our new-build house. As I passed the newsagent, I noticed the headline: *UK's Economy at Historic Low*. I peered towards where Mike worked with Greg at a large financial advice firm in town. There had been rumours of redundancies the year before but nothing had come of it. What if Mike was made redundant now? Would I have to go back to working full-time again?

The thought sent a dart of fear through me.

Better if they made *me* redundant from my senior copywriter job. It wasn't like I was pulling in much on my three-day salary anyway.

I put my sunglasses on, pulling up the straps of my silky red vest top to cover my bra straps, my black skirt skimming the back of my knees. Everyone else around me was wearing pastel colours, but I liked to be bold: blood reds and stark blacks, azure blues and emerald greens. I had earrings to match, necklaces sometimes too.

As I approached the small primary school, which was housed in a Victorian building, I noticed some of the parents already crowded around the gates nattering. I hated the whole school-gate drama, especially recently with all the talk of recession. Most mornings, I made up excuses to leave: lunch in London with my editor; a book signing in Canterbury; some media interview or another. I liked to make it vague, so they couldn't check whether I was telling the truth or not. Sometimes, if I was having a bad writing day or had received yet another royalty statement with minus signs on it from my agent, I'd hang around, basking in the inevitable glory of being the only published novelist in town. I suppose sometimes I needed the questions that at other times irritated me, the stories of success I weaved wiping away the disappointment.

'There she is!' a woman declared, a slim brunette called Haley. She was one of the few mums I could tolerate, plus she worked in the town library which was always a good thing as she let me take out more books then the standard eight. 'You saw it from a front row seat, didn't you?' she asked me when I got to the group.

'Saw what?' I asked. I knew perfectly well what she meant, of course. But I enjoyed this, the tease.

'The man who saved that boy last night,' one of the other mums said, a timid woman called Donna. She was wearing an oversized beige blouse and black leggings. Her shoulders were slightly slumped and she had her arms wrapped around her midriff.

'Oh, that,' I said with a bored sigh. I almost resented other people having seen it all happen. If only I'd been alone on that beach with Monica and her son so I could add embellishments to the story: a mouth-to-mouth resuscitation after, maybe?

'I hear he's a homeless man,' one of the other mothers drawled. It was Cynthia, or Gym Bunny as I referred to her. She had her blonde hair up in a high ponytail, her hip bones jutting out from the top of her Lycra leggings.

'He didn't look very homeless to me,' Haley said with a raised eyebrow. 'You have to admit it was rather exciting?'

'I suppose so. For this town, anyway,' I said as I gave Becky a kiss on the head, aware of everyone's eyes on me. As Becky ran off towards one of her little friends, I paused a moment, looking towards the sea, adding another bored sigh for effect. Then I turned back to the group of mums, shrugging. 'He's just a man who helped a kid. I think people are getting a bit carried away.'

A couple of the mums gave each other a look. But Donna looked out to the water, a wistful expression on her face as her short dark bob lifted in the breeze. She always seemed so overwhelmed by the other mums, which was surprising considering she was a midwife. Or maybe she was just used to hysterical women and had learnt to be calm and stoic in the face of dramatics.

There were times when she really should have said *something* though, like when Cynthia gave her some free passes to the gym to 'knock off those extra pounds'. Donna had just stood there in shock, eyes filling with tears. I had to do something so I'd linked my arm through Donna's and arched an eyebrow. 'Gym? With these?' I'd said, pointing to both our ample chests. 'Absolutely not! Can't risk ruining our best assets.' Cynthia, as flat-chested as her own son, just looked at me dumbfounded, Donna sneaking me a quick and grateful smile.

'Anyway, must get back,' I said now, peering at my watch. 'My book won't write itself.'

'How's it going?' Donna asked softly.

'Good,' I said, smiling at her. 'Should be finished soon.'

'And the cake preparations for next Saturday?' Haley asked. 'I hope it's still okay to do one?'

Oh bugger.

I tried to keep the smile on my face. I'd completely forgot I'd volunteered to bake a cake for Haley's son's birthday party. It had happened after Cynthia made a throwaway comment about me 'not being the domestic type', no doubt revenge for the gym pass slight the week before.

'You'd be surprised,' I'd retorted.

'Really?' Cynthia had asked, eyebrow arched.

'Yes, really.' I'd turned my best icy glare to Cynthia then. 'I'm a dab hand at baking actually.'

'You are?' Haley had said. 'We were going to find someone to make Beau's cake but if you can, wonderful! I'd pay you of course.'

'No need to pay,' I'd replied, waving my hand about as I watched Cynthia's expression out of the corner of my eye. 'It's no problem at all.'

'Can you do it in the shape of a monkey?' Haley had then asked. 'It's just that Beau's obsessed with them after our latest trip to the zoo.'

I'd nodded, trying to hide my horror. Sure, I'd made the odd chocolate cake or two. It hadn't given Mike and Becky food poisoning so that was a bonus. But that was the extent of my baking skills.

I smiled at Haley now. 'All sorted, darling. See you all next week!' Then I walked up the hill towards my house, muttering 'Bloody monkey cake' under my breath.

Before I opened my front door, I paused. I really couldn't bear the thought of returning to the house to write. I'd had to drag the words out lately. I tried to tell myself it was the house. But the fact is, I used to be able to write anywhere: on the bus in the dreary rain, sitting in a doctor's waiting room, even in my car when I was stuck in standstill traffic once. No, there was more to it than that. The past couple of years, a numbness had descended. Stopped me from wanting to be touched and touch. Stopped me from wanting to write.

Maybe I'd grown weary. It was all so far from the dreams I'd had of writing from the hotel above the cliffs all those years ago, a glass of gin by my side as Mike took up some exciting watersport. Instead, the only house we could afford when we finally decided to move from London when I was pregnant nine years ago was a good fifteen-minute walk from the sea. It wasn't much to look at either, a plain brown new-build house sitting across from a petrol station. The only bonus was it looked out to fields at the back. I'd set up an office in the spare room at the back in the hope I'd write from there, looking out over those fields, a tiny glimpse of sea in the distance.

But as soon as Becky was born, my days had mostly been filled with baby sensory classes and weigh-ins, toddler tantrums and coffees in overfilled cafés. It was only when Becky went to school

I was able to really focus on writing. But then the days went so damn fast before it was time to pick Becky up again at three. If I could only get that second book published, I could give up the job and write full-time instead of just two days a week.

That was the dream, wasn't it? It had *always* been the dream, from the moment I used to sneak glances of the novels my mother would bring back from her countless trips to local charity shops, their battered spines smelling of earth and dust. Authors became my rock stars and I'd escape into their words for hours, a place to pretend I was something other than the little girl nobody noticed.

While studying English at university, I'd been determined to come away with a novel ready to send to editors. Of course, I didn't know then how unrealistic that was. But I was so idealistic then, so full of romantic notions, attaching myself to fellow dreamers. Before I met Mike, I'd dated a beautiful Polish man with graceful hands and the softest of lips. He'd write poetry on my naked curves, inspiring me to spill words out into a notepad he'd bought me. But even then, each time I started something, I just couldn't finish it.

When I graduated, I fell into various copywriting jobs to pay the rent on the tiny flat I rented with Mike in Battersea, writing in the evenings. Then one gloomy October day, feigning an illness to stay at home, I found myself writing pages and pages of a novel that seemed to have come out of nowhere about a woman who runs a small hotel in the woods with her mother. Unable to deal with the loss when her mother passes away, she tells guests she's just resting after an illness. Sounds depressing, doesn't it? But there was a love story thrown in. *Lady Chatterley's Lover* meets *Hotel du Lac* was how my agent described it.

A year later, it was ready to submit. It had countless rejections and I nearly lost hope, but then a small publishing house took it on. I'd been so proud, I'd even called my mother to tell her, despite the fact that we rarely saw each other apart from a brief, awkward visit to her little flat in Margate over the Christmas period each year.

'I'll be able to find it in WHSmith, will I?' my mother had asked me. I'd imagined her sitting on her battered sofa with a glass of wine in her hand, her dark dyed hair in rollers.

'Yes,' I'd replied, knowing it was a lie – my editor had told me only a few independent bookshops were taking it. But I wanted so much for my mother to be proud. *Needed* so much.

A week after it was published, she'd treated me to a rare phone call. I thought it was to congratulate me on the launch of my debut. But instead, it was to berate me for 'embarrassing' her in front of her friends who thought she'd lied about her 'author daughter' seeing as they couldn't find her books in WHSmith.

'You're just one of those crappy authors, aren't you?' my mother had said. 'The ones whose books you find in the bargain bucket.'

I had slammed the phone down, resolving never to take a call from her again. That was two years ago. Two long years with only a few thousand words written of my next novel, despite having two days a week dedicated to it.

Why wouldn't the words come?

I looked up at my house, then at the petrol station across from it. It *had* to be the house. It was just so uninspiring! I impulsively turned back and headed towards the beach.

The tide was low, the sea hazy in the distance, seaweed and shells clogging the wet morning sand as people walked out of the café nearby with takeaway teas in polystyrene cups. It wasn't a built-up beach – even now it isn't – just a plain and simple sandy cove, no trendy eateries or boutique shops. Its natural beauties were enough to draw people in, the chalk stacks adorning most of the postcards in town. The bay beyond the chalk stacks with its five caves wasn't as much of a draw then; people were put off by the stories of tourists being caught out there during high tide.

I walked onto the sand that morning, taking my gold sandals off and strolling along the edge of the seaweeded area, picking up shells for Becky. I liked to do that sometimes when my mind was blocked or sad memories crowded. Breathe in the salty air, feel the sand beneath my toes and the smooth curve of shells in my palms.

After a while, I spotted a washed-up starfish, orange with black dots, its legs tangled and broken. I crouched down, staring at it, tears irrationally pricking at my eyelashes.

What the hell was wrong with me?

The wind picked strands of my dark hair up, the sound of laughter carried along with it. I stood and looked over towards the bay of caves. It was usually quiet at this time of the morning, with children at school, but there was a group of teenagers crowding around the entrance to the larger cave at the end of the bay. Four of them were girls, long hair trailing down their backs, the waistbands of their school skirts rolled up. I remembered doing the same at the struggling comprehensive I went to in Margate all those years ago. The two boys with them looked bored, their shirts hanging out, hair spiky. But the girls were enraptured as they peered into the cave at something that was out of my eye line.

I took another step forward until the focus of their attention came into view.

It was the man who'd rescued the boy the evening before.

He was sitting on a white chalk rock just inside the entrance to the cave, painting something on the cliff wall in swirling blue. His hair was up in a bun this time, exposing his long, tanned neck, the golden stubble on his cheeks. As he painted, his lean muscles flexed, the morning sun picking up the contours of his shapely arms and bare back.

'That's so cool,' I heard one of the girls say in a hushed voice.

'Totally,' another agreed.

'We should go now,' one of the boys said, looking at his watch. 'Mrs Botley will go mental if we're late.'

The blonde girl looked at the boy. 'You go,' she said, sinking to the sand and crossing her long legs beneath her. 'I'm staying.'

'Me too,' one of her friends said, joining her.

The boys rolled their eyes at each other. 'Not our issue if you get a rollocking,' one of them said before the rest of the group walked off.

I watched the two girls for a while, looking at the way they observed the man. There was clear attraction in their eyes, a calm attentiveness too.

I quickly got my notepad out, writing what I saw.

He moved his arm gracefully, slowly, like how he'd appeared to walk on water the night before. The girls watched in rapture, as though they were seeing something for the first time. Beyond them, the sea—

'The next bestselling novel?' a voice asked from behind me.

I snapped my notepad shut and looked up to see Greg smiling down at me.

'Maybe.'

A quick look at my cleavage, *quelle surprise*, then back up to my face. 'We'll have to keep an eye on him,' he said, jutting his chin towards the man painting in the cave.

I raised an eyebrow. 'And why might that be?'

'Hanging around with teenagers. Looks like we have a resident paedophile on our hands.'

I rolled my eyes. 'Honestly, Greg, talk about jumping to conclusions.'

'Really? So you'd let Becky near him? He's clearly slept in that cave overnight,' he added, pointing to a sleeping bag I hadn't noticed before, lying at the side of the cave.

'Just because he's sleeping in a cave, that doesn't make him a paedophile. There are a lot of people out of jobs thanks to this recession. Haven't you been reading the papers?' I walked past Greg and headed to the wooden path. I really wasn't in the mood for him, especially after he interrupted my rare moment of inspiration.

'Mind if I join you?' Greg asked as he fell into step beside me.

I couldn't help but sigh. 'Aren't you working today?'

'Day off. Told Julie I'm getting nappies.'

'And you're not?'

'Not now,' he said, pushing his Ray-Bans onto the top of his head and smiling at me. 'Needed to get out. All she talks about is babies, babies, babies.'

'She *has* just had one.' I peered at him sideways. 'As have you.'

'Yeah but it's different for men.'

'How?'

'You know,' he said, openly staring at my breasts.

'No, I don't actually.' I stopped, crossing my arms. 'How is it different?'

He gave me a sly grin. 'You going to make me say it?'

Here it comes . . .

'Fine,' he said with an exaggerated sigh. 'Breasts. Babies need breasts and we can't provide that, can we?'

'Ah, breasts,' I said. 'Breasts, breasts, breasts, that's all men talk about.'

'Can you blame us?' he asked playfully.

'Yes, yes I can. They are mounds of flesh, their primary function being to feed babies.'

He laughed. 'This is why I like you, fire in your belly. What do you say to a cheeky vino at the café?'

'At this time of the morning?'

'Why not?' He grabbed my shoulders in excitement. 'Seize the day! Let's do something crazy! I know you're like me, Selma, I can tell.'

I felt an overwhelming desire to slap him. But instead I pulled away from him, making my face cold. 'I'm nothing like you. And if you think drinking wine at nine in the morning is seizing the day, then you *really* need to get a life.'

His face dropped, his dark eyes flashing with anger. 'Clearly I was wrong about you. I thought you were the adventurous type.'

'I have a call with a producer who's interested in turning my book into a film,' I lied. 'I think that's a tad more adventurous than sharing a bottle of wine with a married man, don't you?' Then I stalked off.

That run-in with Greg hung over my head like a dark cloud all weekend, making me tetchy with Mike and Becky. I'd like to say it was because I felt bad for his wife, but mainly it was because he'd stopped me from writing. I hadn't felt so inspired in ages and now that sudden fizz was gone again. It wasn't much better when I walked into the office on Monday morning to get on with my copywriting day job. I only had to endure the place three days a week: Mondays, Tuesdays and Wednesdays. But it was still painful.

I walked to my desk, feeling more of a black cloud than usual hovering over my head, my lack of word count still playing on my mind. Something needed to change and quick, otherwise I'd be back to working five days a week, even if Mike *wasn't* made redundant. It had been hard enough convincing him I needed to go down to three days a week so I could write another novel. The problem was, I wasn't writing it! How could I when I was forced to have all the creativity drained out of me three days a week by this soul-destroying job?

I ignored the voice inside that told me past soul-destroying jobs hadn't stopped me from writing. The same voice that told me there had to be another reason.

I peered at my notepad in my bag, a sense of resolve filling me. I *was* going to write this novel. I had to.

'Selma!'

I looked up to see Monica waving at me from across the room, people gathered around her desk. 'Selma was there,' Monica explained to the colleagues gathered around her. 'She saw everything. Come over and tell them!'

I didn't say anything, just put my bag on my desk and switched my computer on.

'Selma!' Monica called out again.

I battled with the desire to continue ignoring her, but then I remembered the look on Monica's face as she saw her son in the ocean, that awful fear.

I sighed, making myself smile. 'Nathan okay, is he?' I called over.

'Fine. Shaken up but fine!' Monica called back. 'Come tell everyone what happened.'

'I'm sure you have given a better account than I could.' I sat at my desk, noticing my colleague Matthew smirking at me from over our divider. I smiled back at him. He was the only person in the place I could tolerate. On my first day six years ago, he'd handed me some headphones. 'You'll need these, trust me,' he'd said wryly.

'Best day of her life, her son nearly drowning,' Matthew said now in a quiet voice.

My smile deepened. 'Naughty boy,' I whispered back.

We both went quiet when our boss, Daphne, approached. 'Good weekend, Selma?' she asked.

'Lovely, thanks,' I replied. 'Apart from the barbeque catching fire,' I added.

Daphne put her hand to her mouth. 'Oh no!'

It was a lie, of course. Anything to ease the pain of the predictable Monday morning 'How was your weekend?' ritual.

'I heard your book's being made into a film,' Daphne said. 'I hope we're not going to lose you to the glitz and glam of Hollywood.'

I felt my face flush. How quickly rumours spread in this town. A mere mention to Greg and now everyone knew.

'Oh, it was just a call,' I replied. 'Might come to nothing.'

'It's exciting either way! Better get back to work, no film deal for me to pay the mortgage. Chat later!'

I narrowed my eyes at her. Was that a dig? My boss was the queen of passive aggressiveness.

As Daphne walked off, Monica strolled over.

'Oh God, she's coming over,' Matthew said, quickly putting his headphones back on.

'Did you hear the man who saved Nathan is living in one of the caves?' Monica asked, sitting on my desk, which was something I detested people doing.

'I heard something about it,' I replied as I yanked some proofs of an advert I'd written from under her bum.

'I left a bottle of wine outside to thank him with a note,' Monica said excitedly. 'He wasn't there though, so I hope nobody nicks it. There were a couple of strange characters in there. I think they'd spent the night.'

I frowned. 'How do you know that?'

'I saw sleeping bags. One of the girls was still in her nightie.'

'Girls?' Matthew asked with a raised eyebrow.

Monica turned to him, nodding. 'She looked young, maybe sixteen, seventeen.'

'I bet he's having fun,' Matthew drawled.

Was it was one of the schoolgirls from the other day?

'There was even a little table with tea and stuff on it,' Monica added. 'A few floor cushions as well. It looked rather comfy.'

'You thinking of moving in, Monica?' Matthew asked her.

'Oh gosh, no!' she said, raising her voice and getting flustered.

Daphne peered over at the sound of Monica's raised voice.

'Better go!' Monica said, waving at them both and walking off as she frowned at Daphne.

'She wants that guy's babies,' Matthew said.

'Probably. He's every frustrated housewife's dream.'

'So you like him too?'

I threw a pen at Matthew. 'You know I'm not like the rest of them.'

'Never, Selma, never,' he said, winking at me before looking back at his computer.

As I tried to write copy for a leaflet for a local gym, I found my mind drifting off towards that cave. Tea. Cushions. Teenage girls in nighties. How strange.

How wonderful.

I peered around me to check nobody was looking then discreetly pulled out my notepad and started writing, suddenly inspired again.

He smelt of tea leaves, of the forest and the snow. The girl watched him, finger flicking to her flimsy white nightie, breath heavy . . .

I crossed through the line in frustration. Too Mills & Boon.

'Right everyone, time for our weekly team meeting!' Daphne said, clapping her hands.

I squeezed my pen in frustration. Why did this have to happen just as I was all fired up to write? I watched everyone trudge into the stuffy meeting room, ready to waste an hour discussing milk being stolen from the fridge, reduced budgets due to the recession and early booking for the Christmas party. I thought of all the other meetings I'd been in, nodding my head at something someone had said while screaming inside, drawing doodles of desperate eyes and gaping mouths around the edges of the paper as I pretended to take notes.

How much longer could I endure it?

I thought of the man painting at the cave. The freedom of it. The creativity.

I shoved my notepad in my bag then slung it over my shoulder, striding over to Daphne.

'Everything okay?' she asked me.

'No actually. The school called shortly after I got to the office. Becky's ill.'

Daphne faked sympathy. 'Poor thing.' But I could see she was thinking of the deadline that day.

'I'm afraid I have to go,' I continued. 'Mike's out of town.'

'You'll miss the meeting. We're discussing the Christmas do this year.'

'I know, such a shame,' I replied with an exaggerated sigh as I backed away. Then I hurried out, breathing in the fresh air as it hit me. I truly felt as though I'd been suffocating in there. But now I felt free, even if it was just for one illicit day.

What should I do?

I looked towards the sea. What else?

When I approached the cave there were more people milling outside. A young man was strumming a guitar, with a girl dancing in circles to the music. They weren't just teenagers either. There was a tall black man who looked to be in his early forties, and a woman in her fifties too.

Monica had been right. People *were* living there with the man. Maybe they were homeless, with no choice but to live in the cave after losing their jobs. Or was there more to it than that?

I moved into the shadows of the chalk stacks and pulled a cigarette out from my bag, lighting it and drawing in the intoxicating smoke before blowing it out. I always kept a packet handy.

Officially, I gave up just before I got pregnant. But every now and again, I felt the need.

'They won't kill you, you know,' a voice said from behind me.

I turned to see a teenage girl with long, white-blonde hair watching me, a smile on her pretty face. It was one of the school-girls from the other day.

'Do you mean they *will* kill me?' I asked.

The girl shook her head. She had bare feet and I could see her nipples through her white summer dress. 'Contrary to what people say, the cigarette won't kill you. The disease will have been there for a while.'

My eyes alighted on the girl's nipples then I looked away, towards the cave. 'Thanks for that little fact.'

'You're the writer, aren't you?'

I looked back at her in surprise. 'How do you know?'

'Idris knows everything.'

'Idris?'

'Yes, Idris,' the girl said, a lazy smile on her face as she nodded over towards him as he painted on the cave walls. 'He told us you're a writer.'

I felt my heart hammer like a thunderclap. '*He* told you?'

'He says it's important that people like us – creatives – stick together.'

'Is it now?' I tapped some ash into a nook in the cliff, trying to appear casual. 'So how does Idris know I'm a writer then?'

'It's like I said, he knows everything.'

I raised an eyebrow. 'And I suppose you're going to tell me he walks on water too.'

'Of course not. But there are more interesting things than walking on water.' The girl smiled a dreamy smile as she twirled

41

her hair around her fingers. Was she stoned? 'I write poetry,' she said, 'Idris let me write a line on the cave. I live there now. My friend came too but I think she'll go home tonight, she doesn't like the fact there's no shower.'

'Can't blame her.' I looked the girl up and down. She was small-boned. Tiny. Face of a child. But something told me she wasn't as young as she looked. 'How old are you?'

'Seventeen.' She bit her lip, still smiling. 'My dad's gone ballistic.'

'I bet he has.'

'Mum's living with us in the cave now though, and my little brother too. Can I have some?' the girl asked, gesturing towards my cigarette.

I took a final drag then handed it over to the girl. 'Finish it. How old's your brother?'

'Eight.'

The same age as Becky.

The girl leaned against the rock right next to me, her arm brushing against mine. She put her bare foot up behind her and took a drag.

'Maybe I'd like to write a novel one day,' the girl said. 'Idris told me I need to grow first, mature.'

'Plenty of people publish novels at your age. Mary Shelley came up with the idea for *Frankenstein* when she was eighteen.'

The girl rolled her eyes. 'He meant spiritually, not literally. People are *so* obsessed with age, with numbers full stop. If people stopped fixating on numbers and statistics, the world would be a better place. I mean, take this recession. All this obsessing with money and numbers, and we're back to square one. All we need to do is to get into the current.'

'The current? You mean like the sea?'

The girl smiled mysteriously and shook her head. 'Nope.'

'What do you mean then?'

'You'll need to come to the cave to find out. Idris explains it best.'

I suddenly felt an irrational anger at the girl, at her dreamy expression, her big nipples and free-living. 'Might be worth you formulating some of your own thoughts before believing every word of some stranger,' I snapped.

The girl frowned.

I looked at my wrist for the time. 'The numbers on my watch are telling me I should go. But enjoy the ciggie!'

I went to walk away but the girl ran after me and grabbed my elbow. 'Why do you have to go? Come visit the cave! It's a haven for writers. Maybe you'll end up living there like me?'

'Let me think,' I said, pretending to ponder things. 'I have a mortgage to pay, a child to support. Plus my husband might have a heart attack at the prospect of no second income.'

The girl let my wrist go, looking at me with sympathy. 'All numbers. Don't you see? That sentence you just uttered is all numbers. What if you just left it behind, came to the cave with me right now?' She put her hand out to me again. 'Come.'

I hesitated; something inside me was tempted. Then I took in the girl's stained dress, the dark circles under her eyes. 'No thanks. The numbers beckon.'

A few minutes later, I was back at the office. It was time I stopped dreaming and faced reality. I was thirty-eight, for God's sake, not eighteen. I couldn't just bunk off work.

'Did you forget something?' Daphne asked as I walked into the meeting room.

'Mike turned up in the end so I could come back.'

'Wonderful!' My boss turned back to the rest of the room. 'So, about the milk that was stolen . . .'

The rest of the week was miserable; the weather was moody and the atmosphere in the house reflected it. Mike was having a tough time in his job, working long hours to prove his worth in the face of more redundancies. He was clearly growing more and more resentful of the fact I worked part-time. I usually let his irritation wash over me, but that week was different. Maybe it was the cave and the encounter with that silly girl . . . and the fact I wasn't writing much. Maybe the girl was right. Maybe that cave was a haven for writers and all I needed was a few hours there?

It was certainly attracting a lot of attention in town – in particular the mysterious Idris, with more and more rumours circulating about him. According to one woman, who I'd over-heard at the café one lunchtime, he was a millionaire from Canada who'd turned his back on his fortune after his wife died. Monica reckoned he was an Australian artist on the run after forging masterpieces. Perhaps my favourite rumour was that he was a rock star from New Zealand.

When the morning of Haley's son's party arrived, Mike took Becky out so I could focus on the cake I'd promised to bake. I stared at the recipe I'd found in a library cookbook. A cake in the shape of a monkey, for God's sake. What had possessed me to offer to do it? I looked at the clock. I had four whole hours before

Mike was due back with Becky. Four whole hours of baking . . . or four hours of writing?

'Screw this,' I said out loud.

I grabbed my keys and ran outside, jumping into the car. I'd seen a gorgeous cake shop a few towns down with lots of children's cakes on display. I headed straight down there, and when I stepped inside, I couldn't believe my eyes. The first cake to greet me was in the shape of a monkey face. No monkey body but it was close enough. In fact, it was fate!

When Mike and Becky got back, they were amazed when they saw it.

'Oh my gosh, Mummy, this looks amazing,' Becky declared.

I smoothed down my apron, the flour and chocolate I'd scattered over it earlier falling to the floor.

'It does,' Mike said, brow creased slightly. He looked at me and raised an eyebrow. 'I'm impressed.'

'It was easier than I thought actually,' I said, wiping the sides down.

'Then you'll have to do it more often,' Mike murmured, wrapping his arms around me as Becky skipped out into the garden. I froze. He rarely touched me nowadays. Clearly the domestic goddess vibe turned him on.

I peered at the clock. 'We better start getting ready, the party's in an hour.'

'Wear something sexy for me,' Mike said.

I looked at him in surprise. 'What's got into you?'

He shrugged. 'I don't know. I guess you'll find out tonight if Becky goes to sleep on time.'

I smiled but, inside, I felt nothing. Shouldn't I feel *something* for my husband? A thrill, or some millimetre of warmth? There was *nothing*.

I squeezed out from his embrace. 'I'll go and transform from domestic goddess to sexy fox then.'

Half an hour later, I stood staring at myself in the mirror. I was wearing a crimson lace dress with a plunging neckline. It wasn't quite right for a child's party but I didn't care. It would give the other parents something to talk about!

I stepped closer to my reflection, putting my fingers to my eyes and pulling at the delicate skin around them. I was getting wrinkles. The odd grey hair or two under my dye job.

I thought of the young girl I'd encountered by the cave a few days ago, so young and smooth with those pert nipples of hers. I lifted my breasts, noticing the fine lines between them. I knew I was attractive, had been told it all my life, just as my mother had. But lately, I'd been less confident of it.

I suddenly got a flash of my mother staring at herself in the mirror with the same disappointed look on her face.

No. I'm nothing like her.

I grabbed a patterned scarf, winding it around my neck to cover the fine lines on my cleavage, then I smeared some red lipstick on and twisted my long dark hair into a bun at the nape of my neck, pulling some locks down to frame the front of my face.

'Gorgeous,' Mike said as he walked into the bedroom. He wrapped his arms around me. I resisted a moment, then leaned into him. He loved me, found me attractive. Wasn't that what mattered?

'What if we just forget about the party?' I said. 'Get Julie and

Greg to look after Becky, go on an impulsive weekend away like we used to?'

Mike laughed. 'What about the cake?'

'What about it? Julie can come and collect it. We'll say we're ill. Food poisoning . . .'

Mike shook his head, unwinding his arms from my waist and turning around to check his checked shirt in the mirror. 'You're being ridiculous. Come on, we'll be late.'

I felt disappointment roar through me. 'I'll be down in a minute,' I said.

When Mike walked out, I looked at myself in the mirror again, saw the smile drop instantly from my face. For a moment, I was sure I could see the four walls of the room behind me shifting inwards.

'Trapped,' I whispered to myself. 'I feel trapped.'

'Why are you trapped, Mummy?'

I jumped, putting a hand to my chest as I noticed Becky standing in the hallway, watching me. I walked over to my daughter and pulled her into a hug, burying my nose in her soft sweet hair and drawing comfort from her.

'No, darling, Mummy's not trapped. Come on, let's go to this party.'

Ten minutes later, we were at the village hall, the monkey cake held up at my chest as Becky looked on proudly.

Haley jogged over when she saw us, blowing a wisp of hair from her eyes.

'Stressed?' I asked her.

'Organising a library event for a hundred dignitaries was less stressful than this.' She looked down at the cake in my hands, her pretty face lighting up. 'But so what, I have a monkey cake! You are a *genius*, Selma!'

'She is, isn't she?' Mike said proudly.

'My mummy's very clever!' Becky added, jumping up and down in excitement. So this was how it felt to be the wonderful mother and domestic goddess Mike wanted. Why did it make me feel so empty?

'Oh Selma, how do you do it?' I peered up to see Cynthia approach, looking at the cake in awe as she elbowed Donna out of the way. 'Working, writing . . . and cake-making! I'm pre-booking you for Elijah's first birthday.'

So now suddenly I was flavour of the month. What measures these people judged success on!

'Sorry but I'm *never* making a cake again,' I declared, forcing myself to be jolly. 'I'm still emotionally scarred from this experience.'

'So's the kitchen,' Mike said with a laugh. 'It looks like a bomb hit it.'

Other mums jogged over, cooing over the cake, but I felt numb. I was hoping I'd enjoy it, the secret deception. But I felt nothing, not even guilt. In fact, as I watched Haley carry the cake over to the large food table, I hoped she'd slip over, and that the cake would tumble through the air before landing face-down on the hard floor, sickly sweet monkey skull caving in, sugar bananas flying everywhere.

Music started blaring from some speakers as a sprightly-looking woman in a 'Monkey Fun Children's Entertainment' T-shirt bounded into the room. Behind her, Julie and Greg walked in. My stomach sank at the sight of Greg. I'd hoped he wouldn't be there. I wasn't sure I could take much more of that man.

'Gather around, children!' the entertainer cried out as the children rushed over.

I retreated with Mike to the back of the hall as the party games unfolded. Over the next hour, I gulped down warm wine, growing hot in the stifling hall. I went to unwind my scarf but Mike put his hand on my arm. 'Best keep it on.'

'But you wanted me to look sexy,' I whispered, smiling at him, the wine making my head whir.

He glanced at the fine lines between my breasts. 'It's a bit low cut.'

I felt my cheeks flush again and caught sight of Donna, who was watching from nearby with her son Tom.

I suddenly felt the urgent need to be the person she thought I was. So I yanked my scarf off.

'Well, I'm hot so I'm taking it off,' I said defiantly to Mike. 'I'm also getting another wine.'

Donna smiled.

By the end of the party, children were running around, hyper from a mixture of E numbers, exhaustion and excitement. Becky's pink tutu and white top were filthy, her cheeks red from all the fun. The party entertainer started singing an off-key version of 'Happy Birthday' and everyone joined in, including Becky, who screamed the lyrics at the top of her lungs as she bobbed up and down. I felt my heart surge as I looked at my daughter. There's never been anything fake about Becky, especially back then. It was all pure and unadulterated joy. As I watched her, I wished I could be like that.

'Pub?' Greg said to Mike as the party wrapped up. 'Few of us going to The Kingfisher next door.' I noticed he didn't look at me this time, even with my low-cut top.

'Yay, pub!' Becky said, clapping her hands.

Greg and Julie burst out laughing. 'It gets Becky's vote,' Mike said. 'That okay?' he asked me. 'Just one pint.'

I shrugged. 'Go on then.'

That one pint turned into many and one hour turned into three as several sets of parents gathered around two pub benches in the setting sun. The pub had a pretty garden surrounded by trees, with benches littered all over. As I sipped my gin, a welcome reprieve from the warm wine, I grew quiet, watching the others chat, enjoying the way the gin made my head swim.

'Right, listen up everyone,' Cynthia said dramatically, clapping her hands like a headmistress, the sun dipping into the sea behind her. 'I've started a petition to get rid of that homeless man.'

I looked at her over the top of my sunglasses. 'Idris, you mean?'

Mike frowned. 'Is that his name?'

'That's what I've heard,' I replied casually, taking a quick swig of gin and sweeping my dark fringe from my eyes.

'If we get enough signatures,' Cynthia said, 'our local councillor has agreed to look into it, get the man evicted from that cave.'

'Isn't it owned by the Petersons?' Haley asked.

'Not any more. It was taken over by someone else years ago,' Greg said.

'No one can get hold of the new owner,' Cynthia added. 'But the councillor I know says he's found a way of getting around it. He'll have the man out within the week if we add some pressure as local parents.'

'He's not doing any harm though, is he?' Donna said softly.

'Of *course* he is, Donna!' Cynthia exclaimed. 'He's dealing drugs from that cave.'

'We don't know that,' I said, irritation ticking at the core of me. 'The country's in the middle of a recession, Cynthia. He might have just lost his job.'

'But it's obvious something's going on,' Cynthia's husband Clive said, a man who held himself in that straight-backed way that suggested he wanted to let everyone know he was in charge. 'All those kids hanging around.'

'*Kids*,' Greg said. 'That's the operative word here. I don't think drugs is the real issue. The man clearly has a thing for young girls.'

Everyone nodded apart from me and Donna.

Donna frowned. 'I don't think that's very fair.'

'Speak up, love!' Clive said, Cynthia laughing.

'She said it isn't fair!' I said in a loud voice. 'Can you hear yourselves?'

Mike put a warning hand on my leg but I shoved him away.

'There's no evidence of these allegations,' I continued, feeling all the frustrations of the past few days building up inside. 'Just rumours and speculation.'

'Rumours should be enough when it comes to our children, Selma,' Cynthia said, the lines around her mouth tight. 'As a mum, you should—'

'Oh yes, as a mum,' I replied, taking another swig of gin. 'I should be perfect in every single fucking way, shouldn't I?'

Cynthia shut her mouth as Greg raised an eyebrow, everyone around the table going quiet. Only Donna smiled slightly.

'Selma,' Mike hissed, hand now painfully squeezing my knee.

I closed my eyes, felt something boiling and frothing within. Part of me wanted to contain it, but the other part wanted to let

51

it explode and roar. Mike could sense it – I felt it in the firmness of his hand on my leg.

'You *do* like defending the man, don't you?' Cynthia asked.

I opened my eyes, looking right into Cynthia's cunning green ones.

'And you like defending your husband, don't you?' I snapped back. 'Despite the fact everyone knows he fucked the nanny?'

Everyone's mouth dropped open, even Donna's. Cynthia's cheeks flushed and her husband's face went white.

'Jesus, Selma,' Mike said.

I looked at them all, at all the shocked and wounded faces around the table. I knew I'd gone too far, but I realised I didn't care. I didn't care at all.

I stood up. 'I need to get away from here.'

'Yes, I think you do,' Mike said, grabbing my arm and standing with me.

I pulled my arm away from him, glaring at him. 'No, you stay.'

I peered at Becky who was playing with her friends at the back of the pub garden. Then I walked away, my heels grappling with the gravel in the car park, my mind full of a heady mixture of emotions: guilt, embarrassment, pride and exhilaration.

'Fuck them all,' I said to myself, forcing the guilt and embarrassment away. I quickened my step, heading towards the sea, chest feeling like it might explode. The sea roared around me, the darkening skies above regarding me as though to ask: 'What next, Selma? What next?'

In response, I started running, my dark hair untangling from the high bun I'd ended up putting it into, streaming behind me. When I finally got to the sea, I grabbed onto the edge of one of

52

the chalk stacks, leaning over and gasping for breath. Then I stumbled to the water's edge, sinking to the ground, the smell of sand and seaweed clogging my nostrils.

'I can't,' I said, grabbing onto handfuls of sand. 'I can't do this any more. I just can't.'

I closed my eyes and saw the faces of all the people who'd made up my social world the past few years. And then I saw Mike . . . and Becky.

My beautiful Becky.

They were the walls with which I'd built my life lately.

They are my prison.

I imagined those walls falling one by one, a glimpse of light in the distance. Just some space, that was all I needed. A few days would give me a chance to catch my breath and get away from it all. It had worked another time, many years ago, when Becky was a newborn. Why wouldn't it work now?

I let out a sob as I thought of Becky. No! What was I thinking? I couldn't just run away, I had responsibilities . . .

Or could I?

'I can't,' I whispered.

'You can,' a voice said.

I froze. Someone had spoken, a voice carried over on the breeze. I explored the darkness behind me then noticed a figure. Of course, I knew who it was before he stepped into the moonlight.

Idris.

Chapter Five

Becky

Sussex, UK
1 June 2018

Becky has to sit down when she hears her mum's voice at the end of the phone, grasping at the arm of the chair she's in, trying to control her breathing.

Ten years.

It has been ten years since they last spoke. They'd had an argument over her mum's reluctance to send money to help Mike after a walking accident in France. Not that they'd talked much before then anyway, just the occasional awkward dinner for some birthdays, the odd letter. Of course, the cheque had arrived the next day for her dad. But the words her mum had spoken as she'd tried to defend herself, the bitterness and hatred she'd directed at Mike, the *lies*, had been the final straw.

Until now.

Her mum clears her throat. 'He said I ought to call.'

'Who said?'

'The annoying nurse standing over me right now. Honestly, you should see the look he's giving me.' There's a voice in the background, some laughter.

'You're in hospital?' Becky asks.

A sigh. 'It seems so.'

Fear bubbles at Becky's core but she swipes it away. She can never be sure with her mum. She must wait, see what she says, before she allows herself to react.

Summer pads over, nudging her nose into Becky's lap as though sensing her discomfort. She pats her dog's head, drawing strength from her.

'Are you okay?' Becky asks politely, like she's asking an acquaintance.

'I'm dying.'

Becky drops the phone. She scrambles to grab it before it hits the wooden floor. The other dogs bounce in, crowding the hallway. Becky stands, pressing the phone to her ear.

'Wait,' she says. 'Just . . . wait. What's wrong with you?' she asks, voice trembling.

'Cancer. Of course it's cancer. When *isn't* it cancer?'

'Jesus.' Becky paces up and down the hallway as the dogs trot after her. 'Have they actually told you you're dying? The doctors, I mean?'

'Yes, of course.'

Becky's medical training suddenly rushes to the fore. She grasps at it like it's an anchor stopping her from drowning. 'What type of cancer?'

'Breast cancer.'

'Have you had chemo? There are new advances, new treatments being developed. You have money, they can—'

'Oh Becky, sweetheart, I'm a lost cause.'

Becky feels tears spring to her eyes. She looks up at the ceiling. It doesn't matter what her mum has done really. She's Becky's flesh and blood. The person who gave birth to her, who had her curled up inside of her for nine months.

And now she's dying. She will be *gone*, the person she wakes each morning thinking of despite all her attempts not to.

Becky takes a deep breath, trying to calm herself. 'How long?'

'Days, they're saying.'

Becky suddenly feels sick. How could it be *days*?

'Are you still there, Becky?' Her mum's voice cracks then. The first hint of vulnerability. It strikes such sadness in Becky's heart, she can hardly breathe.

'Sorry, Mum, just trying to get a handle on things,' Becky whispers.

They're silent for a few moments. Just breathing together, mother and daughter.

'Will you come?' her mum eventually asks, her voice small like a child's. 'I don't want to die alone.'

Becky puts her hand to her mouth, stifling a sob. 'Of course. Where are you? I'll be right there.'

The ward Becky's mum is staying in isn't bleak like Becky expected. Instead, there are sunny scenes painted on the walls. Becky can even see her old hometown's quaint shops from the vast windows that line the back, including the charming little bookshop she remembers her mum doing a signing at once. It

56

was three years after her mum had left. Becky was living in Busby-in-Sea with her dad then, settled at school . . . just. It had taken time to adjust to a life without her mum's presence in it, without any *woman's* presence, especially at certain times, like when she needed to buy her first bra. A chat over the phone or a quick lunch snatched in between her mum's writing deadlines weren't quite enough for occasions like that. She'd hoped a weekend stay with her mum to attend the launch of her novel would change things, but her mum had been so busy and flustered sorting out her party, practising her speech. *Did that sound right to you, Becky? The part about writing being like the float keeping me above water? Would* boat *be better?* It meant they barely spent time together to say hello, let alone talk about shopping for bras. An eleven-year-old Becky had attended that book launch resentful and sulky, the photos after showing not one smile from her.

Now that same bookshop displays a poster of a moody-looking novel called *The Cave*, described as a 'gripping novel from debut author Thomas Delaney', a photo beneath it of a slightly overweight man in his thirties with a walking stick.

It was strange coming back to the town she'd left all those years ago, seeing the familiar chalk stacks in the distance, the sandy bay and the quaint shops. Maybe part of her had known she'd be here for this one day, her mum ill or dying.

But not so soon.

She pauses at the entrance to her mum's ward. The last time she was here would have been when she was a newborn on the maternity ward a floor down. She thinks of the photos she once pored over after her mum left, especially the one of her holding Becky in her arms, looking down at her with a frown, as though the tiny being was so confusing to her, so alien.

Becky sighs and peers at the sign at the front of the ward.

Ward 3. Oncology.

The sight of that sign makes her stomach turn. She is used to seeing that word on notes and in books. That word was for her patients, which was bad enough anyway, but now it is for her *mum*.

She takes a deep breath and walks in, past the smiling suns and fluffy clouds. She knows her mum would hate all that. Her old office in their first house was dark and brooding: an autumnal forest scene across one wall, brown paint on the others, mahogany furniture, the only sparks of colour in the form of deep purple cushions and scarlet pens. No doubt she is feeling out of sorts here in this hospital.

Maybe that's why she needs me, Becky reasons. *A familiar face.*

Is she really so familiar though? It's been ten years, after all. She catches a glimpse of her reflection in a window she passes: blonde hair pulled back into a messy ponytail, her face makeup free. Old jeans peppered with muddy paw prints. At least her light blue T-shirt is fresh, pulled on from the top of the clean laundry pile in a rush. But it's a contrast to her mum, who was always glamorous, always perfectly made-up. Would she be any different now? She was sixty-five, after all.

Becky searches the ward for her mum. There are ten beds squeezed in. People are dozing. Some have visitors. There are cards wishing them well, flowers bright and thriving as though to detract from the life seeping from their recipients' bodies.

A male nurse passes. Becky wonders if it's the nurse who was with her mum when she called.

'Excuse me,' she says, stopping him. 'I'm looking for my mum, she's—'

'Oh yeah,' he says, smiling. 'You must be Miss Rhys's daughter.'

Becky nods. It is strange that her mum has kept her married name all this time, but Becky is not surprised. It is the name her readers know her as.

'Come through. She's in the private room,' the nurse says.

Private. Of course. She is an acclaimed author, after all.

'Is it as bad as she says?' Becky asks the nurse as they walk to her mum's room.

'I'm afraid so,' he says with a sigh. 'She does a good job of looking well, but it won't be long.' He pauses and puts a hand on Becky's arm. 'I'm so sorry.'

Becky takes a deep breath. 'I just had no idea, that's all. We haven't talked in years.'

The nurse frowns. 'She told me you were at her last book launch a few months ago.'

Becky tenses. No doubt one of her mum's embellishments. 'No, she must be getting confused.'

The nurse nods sympathetically. 'It happens.'

He leads her down a small corridor lined with doors, knocking gently on one of them.

'Oh, you don't need to knock, Nigel,' Becky hears her mum call out. 'God knows you've seen it all already the past few days.'

It feels strange to hear her mum's voice again, just a metre or so away instead of over the phone. Deep and gravelly like it's scratched with sand.

The nurse laughs. 'Your daughter's here, Miss Rhys.'

Becky smooths her hair down, feeling nervous.

'Come in then,' her mum calls out. The nurse opens the door. 'I'll leave you to it,' he whispers with a raised eyebrow. Then he walks away.

Becky stands at the threshold. She can't see her mum properly, just the end of her bed and a large window that looks out to sea. Suddenly, she feels the urge to run away. Hadn't her mum once, when Becky needed her the most? She was just eight, for God's sake. And yet her mum had still turned on her heel and left, hadn't she?

But she wasn't like her mum.

She walks in, her mum gradually revealed with each step she takes. She's lying in bed, head turned towards the window, her once lush dark hair now brittle and greying in parts. Her arms that were once plump and tanned are now thin, papery and white, and her apple cheeks are sunken.

She turns towards Becky. Even her blue eyes have changed. Once vivid but now pale and watery. The only sign of her old self is a kind of fierceness in those eyes. And, of course, the vividly coloured nightdress, bright green nightingales against navy skies.

Her mum smiles slightly and, for a moment, time stops. Becky's that eight-year-old girl again, standing on a windswept beach, reaching her hand out to her mum as she smiles down at her.

'You came,' her mum says.

'Of course.' Becky walks over as her mum struggles to pull herself up, adjusting the top of her nightdress. Becky examines her mum's face. There are folds and creases there she's unused to. Her mum was never smooth-faced – a few pockmarks from childhood acne on her cheeks, crinkles around her eyes even when she was young – but they made her even more beautiful. But her age is really showing now. The torment of illness.

'Not quite how you remember me, I imagine,' her mum says as though reading Becky's thoughts.

'It has been ten years,' Becky replies. She moves a book from the chair by her mum's bed so she can sit down. *Love* by Angela Carter. She remembers her mum reading a lot of Angela Carter's books.

'Has it really been ten years?' her mum asks.

'Yes, that long.' Becky leans forward. She feels like she ought to take her mum's hand, kiss her cheek. But things feel so brittle between them, like one touch might break everything. 'How long have you known?'

'I've known about the cancer for years.'

Becky frowns. 'Why didn't you tell me?'

'I seem to recall you saying you never wanted to speak to me again the last time we talked.'

Becky's cheeks flush.

'Anyway, I've been managing fine until now.' Her mum straightens her crisp white bedsheets with her fingers and shrugs. 'Had to catch up with me sooner or later, I suppose.'

'I presume it's spread?' Becky asks.

Her mum nods. 'Brain. Bones. Liver. Cuticles and hair strands too, probably. The lot.'

Becky turns away, a tear trailing down her cheek. Out of the corner of her eye, she notices her mum reaching her hand out for her.

Then there's a knock on the door.

Her mum lowers her hand. 'Come in!' she calls out in a faux bright voice.

A doctor walks in; an Indian woman, tall and serious looking.

'Ah, you have a visitor,' the doctor says, smiling.

'Yes, this is my daughter,' Becky's mum replies.

Becky stands, putting her hand out to the doctor. 'I'm Becky.'

The doctor shakes it. 'Doctor Panchal.' She turns to her patient. 'How are you today?'

'Not dead yet,' Becky's mum replies.

Doctor Panchal gives her a stern look. She turns to Becky. 'I'm pleased you're here. Your mum may have explained that we're making preparations to move her to a hospice, a very good one. They have an excellent reputation in palliative care.'

Becky blinks. Palliative care. End of life. End of her *mum's* life.

'My daughter's one of you lot, you know,' her mum says to the doctor.

'You're a doctor too?' the doctor asks Becky.

'No, a vet,' Becky explains.

The doctor smiles. 'Wonderful. I have two cats.'

'What sort?' Becky asks, clutching onto the familiar conversation to stop her whirling down a rabbit's hole of grief.

'Siamese.'

'I had a Siamese cat in one of my novels,' her mum says.

'Oh yes,' the doctor replied. '*The Circle*, wasn't it?'

'That's right.' Becky's mum sighs. 'It's actually my least favourite novel.'

'Oh really?' the doctor says. 'I loved it!'

It still feels alien to Becky, hearing people fuss over her mum's novels. She was used to those early years, when her mum was struggling to make a success of things. But now, her mum has several million book sales and awards under her belt. Of course, she'd watched it all happen from afar, reading articles in newspapers describing her mum as the 'Sunday Times bestselling author' and 'book club favourite', the publicity photo of her staring out to sea, trademark sunglasses on, all Greta Garbo-esque. Then she'd won a major book award a few months later, and foreign deals meant she made it big in the States too.

At first, she gave interviews that Becky would read and throw away in frustration when she saw the little white lies littered throughout them: 'My divorce was amicable; I still see my husband.' Or: 'I see my daughter as much as I can.'

But the articles petered out after her mum started withdrawing from the public eye – no more inviting journalists into her home to chat. Becky had been surprised at how much she'd resented that. She was hungry for more details of her mum's life outside the brief visits they had before they became estranged, so her mum's new solitude made her angry.

And then her mum had moved to the vast house above the cave. Becky had found out about it a few years ago after reading a feature in one of the glossy Sunday magazines, a photo of the 'reclusive author' outside her new home, the cave sprawled out below it. Becky wanted to call the journalist who'd written the piece and scream: 'That cave was where she ran away to! That was what she abandoned me for.'

But she hadn't. Of course she hadn't. Instead, she tried to ignore any mention of her mum, of her growing book sales and accolades, glamour and enigma.

'I think Becky could have been a good writer actually,' her mum says now.

Becky laughs. 'Seriously?'

'You won that short story competition once, remember?'

Becky knows what she's referring to. And she hadn't won it, she'd got third place. She was still proud though, and had even brought it to one of the monthly meet-ups she'd had with her mum in those initial years after she'd left. Her mum had read the story, then peered up at her. 'You'll improve, with time.' And that was it, nothing else.

'I came third, Mum,' Becky says now.

'Oh, first or third, it doesn't matter. It was a wonderful story.'

Becky frowned. 'You didn't give that impression when you read it!'

'Probably because I was trying to hide the fact I was about to start crying.' She looks at the doctor. 'I get teary when I'm proud. What about art?' she continues. 'You were always so good at drawing, Becky. Remember that painting you did of the horse for my fortieth birthday?'

'Dog.'

'Ah yes, dog. Such a fabulous painting. If you'd just put your mind to—'

'I did put my mind to something!' Becky exclaims, her patience running out. 'I'm a vet!'

The doctor raises an eyebrow. 'Okay, I'll leave you both to catch up.' She backs out of the room, shutting the door quietly behind her.

'You're a bit tetchy this evening,' her mum says when the doctor leaves.

'Discovering your mother's dying kind of does that to a girl.'

Her mum smiles and Becky can't help but smile back. She knows how spiky her mum can be. Why get upset about it now, when they have so little time left?

'So the hospice your doctor mentioned sounds nice,' she says, sitting down again.

Her mum makes a face. 'I don't think so.'

'It'll be the best place for you, really.'

She crosses her thin arms. 'Nope. Not happening.'

'But you can't stay here,' Becky counters as gently as she can. 'Hospices like the one your doctor mentioned are there for a very specific reason. And many of them have lovely, beautiful grounds. They're peaceful places, and more spacious.'

Her mum pulls at her sheets, biting her lip. 'It doesn't matter. I'd still feel trapped.'

Trapped.

Becky has a memory then, of her mum standing in front of the mirror at home. 'Trapped, I feel trapped,' she remembers her saying.

She pushes the memory away. 'Look Mum,' Becky says gently. 'I think it's important you—'

'I said no!' her mum shouts. Her voice bounces off the walls. She leans forward, grasping Becky's hands. 'I know where I want to die and I need your help to do it.'

'Where?'

'The cave. I want to die in the cave.'

Becky moves back. 'It's out of the question.'

'Why?'

'You don't understand the care involved. Your priority soon

will be comfort. Rest and comfort. And being in a cave will *not* provide that.'

'It did once,' her mum counters.

Becky feels anger bubble up. It's so tempting to ask her mum where her eight-year-old daughter's comfort was when she was lying in bed alone at night, wondering when her mum would return. But instead, Becky forces a soft smile, squeezing her mum's hand.

'I promise you won't regret going to the hospice. Let me get more information about it, and some others too so you have options. I think you'll come to realise it's the right thing to do.'

Her mum shakes her head in frustration. 'Please, you're the only hope I have, Becky! These people here won't chance it, all obsessed with health and bloody safety. What does it matter when I'm dying anyway?'

'I'm sorry, Mum. I couldn't do that to you. Let me go and ask about those brochures. Is there anything you need me to get for you while I'm out there? Shall I go to the shop, get some chocolates, a magazine?'

Her mum's face turns glacial and she looks away. 'No. I'd like to be alone actually. Probably best if you go home. It's late.'

Becky watches her mum for a few moments. 'Are you sure? I can stay, really.'

Her mum folds the top of the bedsheet down, smoothing it. 'Absolutely.'

'Right.' Becky stands up. 'You know my number, just call if you need anything. I'll be back first thing tomorrow.'

Still no response.

Becky leans over, squeezing her mum's shoulder. 'It'll be okay,' she says softly. 'Sleep on it. Things always seem clearer in the morning.'

Her mum's forehead crinkles slightly. 'Someone else said the opposite to me once. That clarity comes with darkness.' Then she sighs and closes her eyes.

Chapter Six

Selma

Kent, UK
27 July 1991

Idris was wearing just shorts, holding a fishing line in his hands. His golden hair fell to his tanned shoulders, and his green eyes were so vivid they didn't seem real. His bare chest was bathed in moonlight and, in that light, I saw scars tapering down his chest.

'You can,' he said again, stepping towards me. 'Whatever the question in your mind is, you must answer yes.'

I looked at him in surprise. 'How did you know I even had a question?'

'You're on a precipice. I can sense it.' He placed his rod down and sat beside me, looking out to sea. He *smelt* of the sea, salty and luxurious. 'Your body screams it,' he said. 'Your posture, the expression on your face, everything.'

I crunched my hands into fists, watching as the sand squeezed out between my fingers. I wasn't sitting on this beach to be preached to by someone like him, no matter how much he fascinated me.

'I came here to be alone,' I said.

'Then I'll leave.' He went to get up.

'Wait!' I couldn't let him go before asking something. 'How do you know so much about me? My name? The fact I'm an author?'

He gestured towards the small bookshop in town. 'You did a signing there.'

'Ages ago.'

'They still have a poster up at the back.'

'Ah. I see.'

'We're all reading your book. It's wonderful.'

'The Queensbay Cave Dwellers' Bookclub, is it now?'

He laughed. 'Something like that. I'll leave you to it then.'

He went to walk away but something inside me wanted him back. I was so curious about him. Why was I sending him away?

'Wait. Stay. It's fine. Now I know you have good reading taste anyway.'

He smiled, walking over and sitting next to me again. 'Is that how you judge people, by what they read?'

'Why not?'

We sat in silence for a few moments more, then I turned to him. 'You said I should say yes to the question in my mind. What if yes means losing everything?'

He thought about it, brow creasing. 'What is everything to you?'

'My family. My husband and daughter.'

He explored my face. 'No. I don't think that's everything.'

'Excuse me?'

'If that's the case, that your family is everything, that it makes you whole, why are you looking so empty right now?'

I took in a deep breath then let it out.

'Society tells you family is everything,' he said, drawing a circle in the sand with his finger beneath the moonlight. 'But for some, it's not enough. For some, there needs to be more.' He drew an oval around the circle, turning it into an eye.

'What kind of more?' I asked, feeling my heart thump against my chest, the hair on my arms stand on end. I *did* feel I was on the precipice of something. Idris was right.

'You're a writer,' he stated. 'How do you feel when you're writing?'

I paused a few moments. 'Right,' I said eventually. 'It just feels . . . right.'

'It makes you feel whole?'

I nodded. 'Yeah.'

'We have callings in life.' I couldn't help but scoff and Idris smiled. 'I know how clichéd that sounds, but it's the truth. We each have a role to play. Our *true* callings. Anything that takes us away from that makes us unhappy.'

'That's too simplistic a view! Idealistic too. Real life means we can't dedicate all of our time to one thing.'

He looked me in the eye. 'Whose version of real life?'

'Everybody's!'

'No, it's society's view. It stifles us.'

'So you recommend we all go live in a cave and write, paint, do whatever it is you and the others in your cave do?'

He shrugged. 'Why not?'

I sighed. 'Family. It comes back to my family.'

'Bring them.'

I laughed. 'I'm not sure my husband would really be up for that.'

'Your daughter would. She'd love it.'

'I'm sure she would until it rained and her dolls got wet.'

He smiled as he peered out to sea. 'Children love a bit of rain.'

I took a moment to explore his face, to take in the golden bristles on his cheeks, the way his beard glowed white beneath the moonlight. 'I can't believe I'm even discussing this with you.'

'What's wrong with discussing it? In fact, take it a step further. Come and meet everyone.' He jutted his chin towards the direction of the cave. 'The cave is larger than it looks from the outside. We're making quite a home of it.'

'You're seriously trying to recruit me?'

He tilted his head, examining my face. '*Recruit.* That's an interesting word choice.' There was an earnestness in his green eyes, a kindness in his expression. He didn't seem deranged or weird like some said.

'Who *are* you?' I asked him.

He shrugged. 'A painter. A sculptor.'

'Where are you from?'

'Where are *you* from?'

'Ah, I see, you're a politician answering questions with more questions.'

He laughed. 'Very far from it.' His face grew serious. 'It is an interesting question though. Who are *you*, Selma Rhys? Close your eyes, really think about it. Block out the light. Clarity comes with darkness. Who *are* you?'

I tried to grapple with the question. I saw Becky, Mike . . . then my mother. Her beautiful face. Those cold, cold eyes.

'Who do you think you are, Selma?' I remembered my mother once asking. 'Just *who* do you think you are?'

Fast-forward twenty years, feeling the weight of my first novel in my hands after it arrived in the post. 'A writer, Mother. I'm a fucking writer,' I remembered saying out loud.

'A writer,' I said, snapping my eyes open. I realised tears were streaming down my face. I wiped them away, embarrassed. 'Warm wine always makes me emotional,' I said with a small laugh.

Idris stood up, putting his hand out to me. 'Come on, come meet the others.'

I looked at his hand, hesitating. Then I found myself taking it and standing with him in the darkness.

Chapter Seven

Becky

Kent, UK
2 June 2018

Becky stares into the darkness of her room. She hears the gentle snores of her dogs from the landing, trying to take comfort in the familiar sound of it. But she can't sleep. Her mind is racing. All she can see is the desperation in her mum's eyes as she pleaded to be taken to the cave. Then the bitter disappointment when Becky refused.

Becky looks at the time. Three in the morning. Not even light. *Clarity comes with darkness.*

She sighs and gets up, walking to the window and staring out over the field. Summer senses her movement, as she always does, and contemplates her from the landing, her long face resting on her paws.

'Oh Summer,' Becky says to her. 'What am I going to do?'

Summer rises and trots over, putting her face close to Becky's leg. Becky strokes her soft head.

'Clarity comes with darkness, apparently,' she says. 'So why haven't I got a clue what to do about my mum?'

In response, Summer jumps up, her paws on the window sill as she peers out, tail wagging. She lets out a low whine, which Becky knows means 'I want to go out'.

'You want to go for a walk *now*?' Becky asks.

At the mention of the word *walk*, Womble and Danny suddenly wake up, alert. Becky groans. She should have known not to use that word out loud.

'I can't believe this,' she says as they pad over, wagging their tails. 'I'm going to have to take you all out, aren't I?' They grow more excited and she laughs. 'Fine. Come on then! Maybe the darkness *will* give me some clarity.'

She pulls on some jeans and a light jumper, then heads outside. She is surprised that it's not pitch black, as the moon casts a silver light across the fields. The dogs leap ahead of her, excited at being out in the dark. Becky welcomes the cool air of night. But it doesn't clear the cobwebs inside. Her mum is wrong, darkness doesn't bring clarity.

'Ah, another person who's awake,' a voice says from the darkness. She looks up to see David. He's standing at his kitchen door, a mug in his hand. The dogs leap over the fence and bound over to him as he laughs.

'Couldn't sleep either?' Becky asks him.

'Never been a big sleeper. Not seen you out at this time of night before though.'

'I've got a lot of things on my mind.'

'Your mother?'

Becky nods. She'd told him about it as she'd hurriedly rushed to her car the evening before, asking him to let the dogs out if she wasn't back within three hours or so.

'Want to talk about it?' he asks now.

'Only if you have another one of those going,' she says, gesturing towards his mug.

'I can certainly arrange that for you.'

She smiles and lets herself into his garden through the gate, walking into the kitchen. There's a lamp on, casting a soft glow around the room. She's always liked his kitchen, full of knick-knacks picked up from his years running a pub in Ireland: ornate pint glasses, horses' shoes, framed photos of racehorses. It feels comfortable in there, a contrast to the place she used to live in with her dad in Busby-on-Sea, which was always so sparse.

'So, how is your mother?' David asks, bringing a mug of steaming hot chocolate over to her.

'Her usual defiant self. A few lies thrown in too, par the course.'

He smiles. She's told him about her mum over the years – small details, but enough to form a picture.

'I met her doctor,' Becky adds, blowing on her drink, steam spiralling up from the mug. She takes a quick sip, feeling the tears start to come. 'What she said is true. They think she only has a few days.'

David frowns, looking down at his own drink. 'I'm sorry to hear that,' he says with a heavy sigh.

'She wants to die in the cave she ran away to.'

He peers up at Becky, his frown deepening. 'Really?'

'Yep. It's impossible, of course. What with all the medication and equipment she needs.'

'Is it?' He looks into her eyes. 'Or are you just hoping it's impossible?'

'What do you mean?'

David places his mug down and drags his chair to be closer to her. Under the light of the lamp, she notices how old he looks, how tired.

'I mean maybe you don't want to do as your mother asks because she's been doing as she wants all her life. Maybe this time, *you're* in control and that feels good.'

Becky shakes her head. 'It's not like that. You know I'm not like that!'

He shrugs. 'I didn't know the little girl who got left behind by her mother. This is bringing all that back, I bet.'

Becky frowns. 'Maybe. But the fact still remains, a cave isn't a nice place to die.'

'Isn't it? Just don't rush into a decision you might regret. If she thinks she was happy there, for a while anyway, then it might be the best place for her.'

I think you'll be happy here, Becks, I really do.

A memory comes to her of her mum smiling down at her, the cave behind her. Her mum had said that to her once.

David yawns.

'Sorry, this isn't exactly the conversation to have at three in the morning,' Becky says.

'I don't mind.'

'No, really,' Becky replies, standing. 'I'm tired anyway. We both are.'

'You know I'm always here.'

'I do.' She squeezes his hand. That's the thing with David,

he is more than just a neighbour. She always finds it so easy to talk to him. It's probably because he gives such sensible, sound advice.

A few minutes later, Becky is back in bed, the dogs flat out on the landing. She closes her eyes and sleep comes instantly, but it's peppered with dreams of her mum, as she was back then. So beautiful, full of curves, those blue eyes, arms wrapping around Becky's small body. The cave again, her mum's words: *I think you'll be happy here, Becks, I really do.*

Then the scene changes. Her mum's sitting on a swing, crying. She peers up, sees Becky and smiles. 'Only you make me smile,' she hears her whisper. 'Only you, Becky.'

Scenes from a party next, loud music, a cake in the shape of a monkey. Everyone is smiling, happy, apart from her mum.

Then finally, the sight of her mum running away into the darkness, a look of freedom on her face that Becky had never seen before, the cave beckoning her . . .

Just as the sun begins to rise the next day, Becky makes her way back to the hospital. When she gets there, it's eerily quiet. The light from the sun outside the vast windows is white, blinding. She heads to her mum's room but a nurse, tired and disapproving, stops her. 'No visitors until nine.'

'It's important,' Becky says.

The nurse holds her gaze. Something in Becky's expression must make her change her mind. 'Okay, just a few minutes,' the nurse says.

Becky walks to her mum's room. Her mum is sitting up in bed, as though she's been expecting her.

77

'You wanted me to live in the cave with you, didn't you?' Becky asks her.

Her mum nods, smiling slightly. 'I left your dad, darling, not you. I wanted to take you with me. I *fought* to have you with me. Even went to court.'

Becky frowns. 'Court?' She vaguely remembers talking to official-looking people, but nothing about her mum going to court. Her dad must have kept it from her. Maybe that was a good thing. 'Why didn't I get to live with you then?'

Her mum's face darkens. She sighs and looks out of the window. 'It doesn't matter now.'

Becky walks to the chair by her bed, sitting down and taking her mum's hand. 'I'll take you to the cave.'

Her mum's face lights up. Then, for the first time in a long time, Becky sees her mum cry.

That evening, they arrive in the little car park near the cave. Becky peers behind her, anticipating a nurse chasing after them, maybe even the police. It feels so illicit, sneaking her mum out of hospital. Even more so grabbing all the medication and supplies Becky needed from the vet practice, telling Kay she'd explain everything but she needed a few days off.

She helps her mum out of the car, shrugging the large rucksack she's brought onto her back. Her mum pauses, shielding her eyes from the sun as she looks out towards the bay. A hidden treasure, as the tourist website describes it. Stretches of golden sand. White cliffs. But the biggest draw: the white chalk stacks extending towards the sky. Perfect photo fodder, especially at sunset. Becky remembers being there as a child, walking on the sand, feeling it beneath her toes. Her mum posing against one of the rocks as her dad took photos. *Click, click, click.*

And then darker memories, glaring at the cave from a distance, its opening like the mouth of a monster who'd gobbled her mum up.

'Good, the tide's out. Let's go,' Becky says. Her mum nods and they step carefully onto the wooden pathway, Becky supporting her mum's frail body.

The café is still there. Tired-looking. Quiet before the evening rush. Becky remembers they used to go there some evenings and weekends. She'd chase her friends around as her mum sat drinking gin, dark sunglasses over her eyes, Mike silent beside her. And then those times after her mum left; the awkward meet-ups that grew more and more infrequent as the months went by. The memories still cause her pain – how desperate she was to run to her mum and beg her to come back, but her childish insolence stopped her every time.

They step off the pathway and onto the sand, walking across the shadows of the chalk stacks slowly, surely. The next bay comes into view then. You don't see them at first, the caves. Like hidden entrances in a labyrinth, they're sliced into the sides of the white cliffs. The first one, smaller than the others, is strewn with rubbish, remnants of burnt-out candles. Becky wonders whether she'd have come here as a teenager if she had stayed with her mum, smoked things she shouldn't have, curled up with boys instead of reading alone. It might have been a very different life to that she'd had in the town she and her dad had eventually moved to.

She helps her mum limp past the first cave, then the second, which is larger but so low you have to duck to get in. In the distance, her mum's house, the hotel, stands grand above the last cave. Her mum's step quickens, her breath too, as they draw closer to *her* cave, as she's been calling it. It's right at the end of the bay, away from the hustle and bustle of the more popular bay, cut off by a jagged plank of white cliff.

And then, there it is, in all its glory. The cave that swallowed her mum whole.

Glimmers of recognition rush through Becky as she stares at it. She hears flashes of laughter, a dog barking. Fish, slippery in her hands. The sun twinkling above. And then her mum, as she was all those years ago, looking down at her with love.

Why are they coming back now, all the good memories? Where were they when the bad ones crashed over her? The sight of her mum, tanned and strange, when she met her in the café all those times after she left them. Her dad's anger, her mum's nonchalance. The tears she shed when she was desperate for her mum's arms around her, the hate that filled her when she realised she was never coming back.

As they draw closer to the cave, Becky sees a small one that has a notice at its front: *Do not enter. Risk of falling rock.* Her mum's face darkens when she looks at it.

'Is it safe?' Becky asks, hesitating.

'My one is.'

My one.

'Sure?' Becky asks.

'Absolutely. Come on.'

They walk up to the cave and pause, taking it in. Large chalk boulders are littered here and there, painted an assortment of colours, some smashed, one charred. The white clay of the cave is mossy in parts, ledges jutting out. Becky remembers standing on one of those ledges, looking out to sea.

Painted around the edges of the cave's entrance are different animals, and shells too. Even a child and a dog. The paint has faded slightly but it's still discernible.

Her mum raises her hand, touching the clay. 'Feel it,' she says. 'It's softer than you think.'

Becky leans her hand against it and realises her mum's right. It even crumbles beneath her palm. As she takes her hand away, she notices there are man-made dents down the length of the cave's entrance, and a black metal plate drilled into it, as if there was once something hanging there.

Her mum peers into the cave, a sense of peace spreading over her face.

Becky notices her mum's breath is laboured, her eyes hollow. 'Come on then, let's get you inside.'

She helps her mum step in, the sound and smell of the sea suddenly muffling all her senses. It's as though the cave is absorbing everything but the sea . . . even absorbing *her*. The temperature drops, and Becky notices the damp moss on the walls, the slimy vegetation. Her feet sink into the sand, wet, cold, sand flies leaping around her shoes. Rubbish congeals around the edges of the cave, cigarette butts and rotting fish bones.

How could her mum have lived here? No wonder she wasn't allowed to bring Becky to live here too. And how could she want to *die* here? But then she's never quite understood her mum.

'Look,' her mum says, pointing to the wall at the back. Her eyes are alight, as if she's seeing another place entirely.

Becky gasps. It's covered with people, sculpted from the rocks then painted. These faces smile out at her: a girl wearing a white dress with a book in her hand; a black man with a dog at his feet, a hammer in his hand. More and more people, nearly a dozen, including children – one tiny one with her eyes ominously scratched out. And then there she is, Becky's mum, her dark hair a cloud around her head as she stares into the distance, pen poised over her notepad. Next to her is a half-finished painting of a man with long, blond hair.

'Did Idris do these?' Becky asks. His name echoes around the cave, making her shiver. She often heard his name that summer her mum left, whispered first in awe then in anger by people in the town, often spat down the phone by her fuming dad.

'He did paint them. There,' her mum says as she points to the back of the cave. 'I want to be there.'

Becky helps her over. Broken wood criss-crosses the sand, pages torn from books strewn over it, a discarded soiled cup on its side. Becky sweeps it all away and unrolls the thick sleeping bag she brought with her along with a small pillow.

'I wish I'd brought more to cover the damp sand now,' she says. 'I didn't think.'

'It's fine. This is perfect.'

'How did you sleep here?'

'On wooden planks,' her mum replies, eyeing the broken panels.

'What about the damp?'

Her mum shrugged. 'We didn't mind.'

'Come, sit.' She leads her mum to the sleeping bag and helps her sit down. Her mum stares around her, a small smile on her face.

'I'll just set some things up,' Becky says, unloading the heavy rucksack from her back with relief, pulling all the items out: some fruit, water, a flask of tea, crackers, pads, flannels. And then the pain relief. Becky takes a deep breath. Will it be enough? She pops two pills out, pours some water into a plastic cup. Then she takes it all over to her mum.

'Do you want tea?' she asks her mum after she swallows the pills.

'Not right now.'

'Are you comfortable?'

Her mum closes her eyes and sighs. 'I'm very tired.'

'Why don't you lie down? It's all set up.'

Her mum looks at the sleeping bag. 'It does look rather tempting.'

'Come on,' Becky says. She unzips the sleeping bag and helps her mum into it, so aware of how thin her arms are. 'Is it okay?'

'Lovely, thank you. Though I have to admit, the pillow's a bit lumpy.'

'Here,' Becky says, lifting her mum's head and shuffling under her so she can lean on Becky's lap. 'Better?'

Her mum smiles. 'I knew the Rhys thunder thighs would come in handy one day.'

'Charming!'

Her mum laughs, but then her laugh turns into a cough. Becky gives her more water.

'I don't know how you lived here,' Becky says, looking around her. She realises she's absent-mindedly stroking her mum's hair as she says that, as she is so used to stroking her dogs as they lie on her lap. She remembers her mum doing the same when she was young, singing her a lullaby as she fell asleep.

'Oh, it was better equipped back then,' her mum says. 'There was a toilet and a makeshift shower over there,' she says, gesturing to the corner opposite to her. 'A kitchen at the front, with a huge table. Anyway, it didn't really matter. It was more about the space to write, the people. At first, anyway.'

Her eyes stray over to the half-finished painting of Idris, pain flittering across her face.

'You loved him, didn't you?' Becky says simply.

Her mum nods. 'The first time I saw him was the day the boy nearly drowned . . .'

As she begins to tell Becky about those first few days, Becky tries to find the anger she once felt at her mum for falling in love with someone else. Not just someone else, but a 'bloody hippy' as her dad referred to him. But as her mum lies with her head in Becky's lap, eyes alight with memories, Becky finds it impossible to be angry. Instead, it feels like her love for her mum has never been stronger. It swells inside her as she strokes her hair.

But as her mum continues with the story, the sound of her voice grows increasingly slurred and panic clutches at Becky's heart. It's as though coming here has made her mum feel safe enough to slowly loosen her grip on life. Becky is desperate for her to hold on a little longer, this woman who gave birth to her, who held her in her arms, who protected her despite all that came after. The past twenty-four hours have reminded her of the good memories. They crowd in, suffocating the bad that have so dominated thoughts of her mum all these years. Instead, they're replaced with the smell of her mum's warmth when Becky crept into her parents' bed at night. And the love, so much love, that she saw in her mum's eyes.

How could she have forgotten that?

One of her tears splashes onto her mum's cheek but her mum doesn't notice. She is lost in her own memories, words barely making sense now as she recounts her story, so wrapped up in her past that she is beyond caring if Becky can understand what she says.

Over the next few hours, as darkness creeps into the cave, the only light provided by a flickering candle, Becky leans against the damp wall, legs out flat, her mum's head now heavy in her lap. She watches a bird glide across the sky outside under the moonlight, another pecking at oysters that have washed up ashore with its distinctive orange beak. It peers up at her, noticing her watching, holding her gaze.

'You always had a way with animals,' her mum croaks.

The bird takes flight at the sound of her voice, its wings spread wide against the dark skies.

Then her mum closes her eyes again, mumbling something incoherent under her breath. Becky knows the end is nearing. Her mum is delirious now, breath rasping, chest rising so slowly, too slowly.

Becky holds her mum closer and silently sobs. She sobs for all the lost years, but anger starts filtering in again now too. She can't help it. Anger at her mum, the dying woman in her arms, the most important woman in her life who walked away. The woman whose lies even now might be being whispered in the dark, surrounding her, pressing into her.

As though hearing her thoughts, Becky's mum grows silent. She blinks up at Becky and Becky recognises the dimming of light she has seen so many times in the eyes of the animals she cares for.

'Are you comfortable?' she whispers, trying to keep the panic out of her voice. She doesn't want to scare her mum.

Her mum nods, clutching onto her daughter's hands which are crossed over her thin heaving chest. 'I am, darling, thank you. Will it be soon?'

Becky purses her lips, trying not to sob. She could lie. Tell her mum there will be many more hours, days, weeks. But she isn't like her mum. She can't lie.

'Yes. I think so,' she replies.

Her mum closes her eyes, tears squeezing out from the corners. When she opens them, there is a new vitality. This often happens just before death, a final fight for life. It fills Becky with terror.

Not long now . . .

'I don't think you know how much I love you, darling,' her mum says. 'Always have. Every moment of every day, you've both been in my thoughts.'

Becky frowns. 'Both? You mean Dad too?'

'No, you and your sister.'

Becky goes rigid. 'Sister?' She looks at the empty packet of pills. 'You're delirious.'

'No,' her mum says, peering towards one of the paintings of the child, the one with the eyes scratched out. 'I had another child, with Idris.'

Becky shakes her head, heart thumping so painfully against her chest she can barely breathe. Her mum's head suddenly feels like lead in her lap.

'Idris took her,' her mum whispers. She is growing weak again. She looks ahead of her, towards the wall of the cave, eyes glossy with tears. 'He took her from this very cave.'

'Are you telling the truth?' Becky asks.

A faint crinkle in her brow as her mum's eyes begin to close. 'Why would I lie about such a thing?' she whispers. And then she is gone.

Chapter Eight

Selma

Kent, UK
27 July 1991

Idris led me to the cave, his hand still wrapped around mine. A campfire flickered outside it, and the sound of guitar music, laughter, even a child giggling was carried along with the breeze. As we drew closer, I could see seven people sitting around the fire on colourful chalk boulders, listening to a young tanned man dressed in just shorts playing a soft tune on his guitar. The girl I'd met a few days before was sitting beside him with her arms wrapped around him, her fingers hungry in his hair. A tall black man sat beside her, dressed smartly in chinos and a white shirt, his fingers tapping gently on his knee, his eyes closed. A brown and white Jack Russell lay with its furry chin on the man's foot.

Behind the group sat a woman in her fifties wearing an oversized kaftan dress, paper flowers in different colours scattered around her. She was doing something I couldn't see, her arms moving erratically, her back bent over. Swaying to the music nearby was a slim, attractive woman with short, blonde hair, the flames of the fire dancing on her tanned skin. I recognised her as being a local yoga teacher, and thought it no surprise that someone like her had been drawn there. But what *was* a surprise was seeing timid Donna among the group, with her son Tom. She must have come directly from the pub just after I left. What on earth was *she* doing there?

Then there, beyond them all, was the cave and the old hotel looming dark and abandoned above it. The cave was too dark to properly see inside but I caught glimpses of colour on the walls. Idris's paintings?

When we approached the group, everyone seemed to sense him, growing quiet as they peered up. The young man even stopped strumming his guitar and Tom stopped giggling.

Weird.

'Please, continue Caden,' Idris instructed him. The young man smiled and continued playing his guitar as he glanced over me.

The girl I'd spoken to before jumped up, rushing over. 'You came!' she said, enveloping me in a hug. She smelt musty, as if she hadn't showered for a few days. It wasn't unpleasant though. 'I'm Oceane by the way.' She pronounced it *Osh-ee-anne.*

'Is that the author?' Caden asked over his music.

'Yes, the author!' Oceane exclaimed.

'That's so cool,' Caden said. He started singing. 'Sifting over the sands of my mind, trying to find treasures that never existed.'

I looked at him in surprise. 'That's a line from my book!'

'Of course,' Idris said. 'We've all been reading it. Can't ignore our local author, can we?'

'I hope you're working on something new,' the yoga teacher said, eyes sparkling as she continued to sway. 'Reading it really touched my soul.'

I opened my mouth then closed it. I didn't know what to say. Part of me was delighted. The book had barely sold so I hadn't had any feedback from readers beyond my editors and friends. But the other part thought it was bloody bizarre, all these people fawning over me.

'Come, sit with us,' Idris said, gently putting his hand on the small of my back and leading me towards the fire. I looked over my shoulder towards the town. Maybe this was a bad idea, but something propelled me forward anyway and I sat down on a straw mat, looking at the flickering orange and yellow of the flames, feeling their warmth on my skin.

I suddenly felt exhausted. I closed my eyes, breathing in the battle between the fire's ash and salt of the sea, my actions at the pub and the subsequent conversation with Idris still playing on my mind.

Something cold nudged against my bare knees and I looked down to see the Jack Russell peering up at me, its tail wagging.

Was the dog going to tell me it loved my book too?

It went to lick my hand and I leaned away from it.

Idris laughed. 'Not a dog person?'

'No, not really. Sorry,' I said. 'One of my stepdads had one. Let's just say, we didn't get on.'

'Stepdads?' the yoga teacher asked with a raised eyebrow.

'My mum got remarried a couple of times,' I replied.

'Come, Mojo,' the man in the white shirt said, patting his thigh. The dog bounded over to him, and I assumed he must be the owner.

I turned to Donna. 'Did you come from the pub?'

Donna nodded. 'I was getting fed up with the conversation. Apart from your bit anyway,' she added with a raised eyebrow.

'I think I might have gone too far.'

'It brought you here,' Idris said. 'That can only be a good thing.'

'Wine? Beer?' Donna asked, a shy look on her face.

'I don't suppose you have any gin?' I asked her.

Donna frowned. 'No, I'm afraid not.'

Caden laughed. 'There will be soon though, now you've mentioned it. Donna can't let anyone go without. She's our angel.'

'She sure is,' Idris said, walking over and putting his hand on Donna's shoulder.

Donna peered up at him, a child-like look of awe on her face. I looked between them both, trying my best not to raise an eyebrow.

'How long have you been here?' I asked Donna.

'Just a few days,' she replied.

'Long enough to make a difference,' Idris said.

Oceane smiled. 'Mum's a supercook.'

I looked between Donna and Oceane in surprise. 'Oceane's your daughter?'

Donna nodded and my eyes widened in surprise. I had no idea Donna had an older daughter . . . and they seemed so different. Or were they? Donna had come to live here, hadn't she? And she'd called her daughter *Oceane*.

I was suddenly seeing her in a very different light.

'Will wine do?' she asked me.

I shrugged. 'Sure.'

Donna stood and pulled a half-empty bottle of white wine from a cooler box, sloshing some of it into a small ceramic bowl. I took the bowl, feeling its weight and coolness.

'Interesting drinking device,' I said.

'Maggie made it,' Donna replied, gesturing to the woman by the cave with her back to us.

'What's she doing?' I asked.

Idris looked towards Maggie. 'She's in the current at the moment. Got into it quicker than most.'

'What *is* this current?' I asked. 'Oceane mentioned it to me.'

'You'll see,' Idris said mysteriously.

'I'm Anita,' the yoga teacher said, touching her hand to her chest. 'I think you might know that already? I saw you in one of my classes once.'

'Yep,' I said, taking a sip of wine. 'I learnt a valuable lesson, that lesson being I'm very unbendy.'

Everyone laughed.

'Easily remedied,' Anita said, waving her hand about. 'We'll sort it during the sunrise salute tomorrow morning.'

'Oh, I won't be here in the morning,' I said. 'Just a fleeting visit.'

Everyone exchanged knowing looks. Some sizzling chicken from the fire was passed my way. I took it without question, suddenly ravenous.

'As you know, I'm Caden,' the boy with the guitar said. 'Guitarist, song scribe, lover,' he added, wiggling his eyebrows at Oceane who laughed in response.

'I believe you know Donna,' Idris said, gesturing to her. 'And her son Tom.'

'Yes,' I said, smiling at Donna. She returned my smile, turning another chicken wing in the fire.

'And Julien,' Idris said, gesturing to the man sitting quietly on the rock with the dog. Julien examined my face then he nodded at me. I nodded back. Already I could tell there was something about him, a calmness that was slightly uncomfortable. 'That's everyone. So far, anyway,' Idris said with a contented smile.

'Tell us about your next novel,' Anita asked.

'Never ask an author that!' Oceane said.

I smiled at her. 'Oceane's right. It strikes the fear of God into us.'

'You're kidding,' Anita said. 'I thought you'd *want* to talk about writing?'

'I *adore* talking about writing,' I said. 'But I feel talking about a new idea might jinx it.'

'I get it actually,' Julien said in a cut-glass accent. 'When I start a new piece of furniture, I'd rather wait until it's finished before telling someone about it. Just in case it flops spectacularly.'

'It's fear,' Idris said.

Everyone turned to him, going very quiet. It was as if, when he spoke, everything else was wiped away.

'Fear that people won't like what you've created,' he continued, sitting down cross-legged on the sand across from me. He was looking right into my eyes. I held his gaze. 'That fear plagues artists like all of us. It's the main reason we can't get into the current,' he continued. 'We're constantly thinking of this person and that person and a dozen people, a hundred, a *thousand* people who might hate what we're working on. Numbers, when we should be looking beyond numbers.'

'What's so dreadful about numbers?' I asked.

'They cloud the judgement,' Donna said.

I looked at her. 'But they're essential to everyday living. We use them to tell the time, to take measurements, count money . . .'

Donna smiled. 'I don't use them to take measurements when I'm cooking. I use my instincts.'

'And we have no money kept here, no clocks either. In fact, watches aren't allowed,' Julien said, peering at my watch. I looked down at the watch that had once belonged to my mother.

'We wake with the sun and sleep when we're tired,' Anita added.

'Or don't sleep if we're in the current,' Caden said.

They all nodded. It was as though they were seamlessly weaving a story together . . . and yet they'd only lived with each other for a few days. Maybe it was this 'current' they all talked of. The same current they refused to tell me about.

'So how do you pay for all this if numbers aren't your thing?' I asked, gesturing to the wine and food.

'Money,' Donna said simply.

I laughed. 'That's numbers.'

'But we don't pay for it here, do we?' Julien said. 'We get money out when we're in town and use it at the shops, giving any change which remains to the charity shops.'

'Money clouds the creative juices,' Oceane said. 'All numbers do. It's impossible to get into the current if we're surrounded by them.'

'What's the bloody current?' I shouted out, the loudness of my voice surprising me.

Julien frowned but Idris laughed. 'I like your intensity.'

'Then bloody tell me what it is,' I said, leaning towards him and smiling to show him I wasn't being too serious. But the fact was, I really *did* want to know.

He stood up, putting his hand out to me. 'Come and see.'

I let him lead me to Maggie, very conscious of his warm hand around mine, intimate, soft. I felt drunk, not just from the gin and the wine but from his proximity too. It reminded me of being drunk as a teenager, night swimming with an old boyfriend, the heady freedom of it, like the night was infinite.

The dark cave unfolded before me like I was in a dream; slightly hazy, very warm. 'The infamous cave,' I whispered, suddenly feeling dizzy with the smell of salt and seaweed, ashes and barbecued chicken.

Idris came to a stop. Maggie was sitting before us, folding petals at an amazing speed, her fingers flexing and bending as she pressed the delicate flowers together. Her head was down, her brow knitted, her face in complete concentration. She seemed totally oblivious to our presence.

'Maggie is a craftswoman,' Idris explained in a quiet voice as we watched her. 'She excels at a variety of crafts, from pottery to sewing to making masks. But it's the paper flowering that she's truly able to find the current with.'

'So, being in the current is basically being in the zone?' I asked.

He thought about it. 'In a sense. But it goes deeper than that. Entering the current has a physical effect on the brain, deactivating the prefrontal cortex.' He gently tapped the bottom of my forehead. 'It controls elements like reason, logic, problem-solving . . .'

'And numbers,' I said, raising an eyebrow.

He smiled. 'Yes. When we're not dominated by those elements of our psyche, we can truly give into creativity.'

'I get it. When I'm really into writing, everything around me disappears.'

'It goes beyond that. It's hard to explain until you've experienced it. But when you do, the work you produce will be the best you ever have.'

I thought about it. That was certainly a tempting prospect considering how utterly useless I'd been at writing lately. It amazed me sometimes, how I could get lost in my writing, hours passing without me realising. And yet Idris was saying it was possible to go even deeper than that. Maybe that was just what my writing needed?

We grew silent, watching as Maggie smoothed the petals of a pink flower, examining it for imperfections before placing it with the others.

'So what's this all about?' I said after a while, gesturing to the group. 'Why are all these people here? It can't be just about getting into the current, as you call it,' I said, making quotation marks with my fingers.

'It is,' he replied. '*Everything* we do here is about getting into the current. It's our sole aim. Individually and as a group. Specifically to reach the point of being in the current together for as long as possible. Then great things will happen.'

'Like what?'

He smiled, his face lighting up. 'That's all to discover. But for you? Maybe you'll write your second novel.'

I had to admit it was appealing, even if it did sound a bit woo-woo. I peered at my wine. Clearly I'd drunk too much.

'You've achieved a lot in less than two weeks,' I said.

'Anyone can, when they put their mind to it.'

'Minus the prefrontal cortex.'

He laughed. 'Want to see inside?' he asked, gesturing towards the cave.

'Why not?'

We walked towards the cave. It was long and narrow, stretching back for what I'd imagine was over a hundred metres. Paintings dotted the entrance: blue fish; white birds, wings spread wide; starfish and shells.

'You did these?' I asked Idris.

He nodded.

'Is that what you did, before you came here?'

'I've always painted,' he replied, not really answering my question.

We stepped into the cave. At the front were two barbecues, three cooler boxes, plus two small white cupboards that appeared to have been ripped from a kitchen. Just beyond it was a long, narrow table made of thick driftwood with several mismatched chairs around it.

'Julien made that table,' Idris said.

'Nice.' And it really was nice, the kind of table I might have looked at with Mike, desperate to buy but way above our budget. The place was surprising me, making me feel strangely at home.

We stepped further into the cave and the atmosphere suddenly changed, my senses overwhelmed by the sound of the sea, as if I was holding a shell up to my ear. It felt intimate in there, like I was cut right off from it all, our own private little world apart from the rush of the sea outside.

'Quite something, isn't it?' Idris asked. 'The feeling you get?'

I nodded, overwhelmed as I looked around me. I'd visited the cave before Idris had appeared in town, of course, but it felt different at night. The walls were a mixture of black rock, white chalk and green moss. Ledges lined the cave like small shelves, and large chalk boulders were littered here and there, painted an assortment of colours.

Dotted around the cave were sleeping bags, some chairs, and small side tables made from crates. Spread across the back of the cave wall were paintings – the top half of each person residing in the cave staring out at me, doing whatever it was they loved: Maggie at an urn, Oceane curled up writing in a notepad, Donna cooking, Caden with a guitar and a pen, Julien building a table.

I walked over, putting my hand out to touch them, and I was surprised when I realised the paintings weren't flat. Idris had somehow carved everyone's features into the chalk then painted them with pigment.

'I paint anyone who joins the group,' Idris explained.

I imagined a painting of myself up there, writing my second novel.

I shook my head. How ridiculous! I stepped away, wet sand gliding across my bare toes. It felt like snow, cold to the touch. Lining the bottom of the walls was driftwood, carried in by high tides.

'Doesn't it get damp?' I asked, touching the mossy wet walls.

'It does. But we don't mind.'

'What about the sea? Does it get in during high tide?'

'It hasn't while we've been here.'

I peered up. There was vegetation growing from the walls, green leaves dotted here and there. I turned back around, looking out of the mouth of the cave towards the sea. It felt as though I was looking at a projection film of the sea.

'It doesn't feel real, does it?' Idris said, as if he knew exactly what I was thinking. 'It's as though this cave is all that exists and everything outside is fiction.' He smiled. 'Perfect for writing, don't you think?'

I smiled back. 'I know what you're trying to do.'

'Can you blame me? I'd love you to join us here.' He held my gaze and I felt my breath quicken.

'I see we have a new member,' a voice boomed out.

We looked over to see Maggie standing at the mouth of the cave, her long grey hair turned white by the moonlight. She strode in, putting a dusty hand out to me. 'I'm Maggie.'

'I'm Selma and I'm *not* a new member – just a curious visitor.'

Maggie smiled as though she didn't believe me. It irritated me. 'Oceane mentioned you,' she said, 'you're the writer. I loved your novel.'

The irritation trickled away. 'Your flowers are beautiful,' I said.

Maggie plucked a purple flower from her pocket and tucked it behind my ear. 'And now you're even more beautiful. More wine? I'm gasping for some.'

Over the next couple of hours, the group discussed their art and the importance of getting into the current, and I was surprised to find myself in a heady space of self-contentment despite my cynicism about the place. I was, quite simply, a writer here. Not in the way people like my colleague Monica perceived me, with the faraway glitzy title of 'author'. But in the real, earthy way that only those who created could understand. Nothing to do with my publishing contract, sales, literary world domination. It was just about the *craft*.

After a while, we all fell into a strange dreamy silence prompted by Idris. He simply stopped talking, stopped responding to questions. Just fell silent and still. Anita followed his lead, crossing her legs and closing her eyes and the others quickly did the same. Even Donna's son grew quiet.

I felt awkward, looking at all these people with their eyes closed. I took the chance to really take Idris in, the flames flickering on his face. His skin seemed to shine in the moonlight, as it had the night he saved Monica's boy. My eyes trailed down to his bare shoulders and chest. He was still shirtless, despite the creeping cold of night. I noticed his nipples harden as the breeze stirred around him and I felt a stirring inside me too. It surprised me. I hadn't felt any kind of stirrings for such a long time.

He opened his eyes, catching me watching him. Then he closed them again without saying anything.

God, what *was* I doing there, staring at a man's naked chest and talking about getting into the bloody current?

I jumped up and walked to the sea's edge. After a while, Idris joined me, so close I could feel the bristles on my arms buzzing from his proximity. He turned to me, green eyes taking in mine.

'I think you'll come to live here.' It wasn't a question. More a statement.

I laughed, shaking my head. 'You're asking me to come live in a cave with eight strangers.'

'Donna's not a stranger.'

'You know what I mean.'

'Why not?'

'My daughter for a start!'

'She'll come too! We have Tom living happily here already. It's warm, sheltered, with plenty of food. That's all a child needs, isn't it?'

I shook my head, laughing. 'It's ridiculous to even consider it. Utterly, utterly preposterous.'

'Preposterous to think it's possible to have a novel published. But you did it.'

'That's different!'

He cocked his head. 'Is it? You followed your heart, wrote what was in your heart, sent it off, despite everything we read telling us the chances of getting published are minimal. And yet you find it hard to believe living in a cave with eight strangers might be the best thing you could do right now?'

He held my gaze. I wanted to turn away but the look on his face was so intense, so sure, I found I couldn't.

'How's your next book coming along?' he asked, his eyes all-knowing.

'Fine.' I peered towards town. 'I have to go home.'

'What if this is home?'

'Now you're just being ridiculous.'

He smiled slightly. 'I like you. I like the way you talk.' He sighed. 'Okay, fine, go. But at least let me walk you back to the main path. It's very dark on the beach. And on the way, I can show you one more thing . . .'

'You're not going to slaughter a goat and make me drink the blood, are you?'

He laughed, touching my arm. 'You really are funny. Come.'

So I did, too curious not to. We walked along the dark beach together, the waves of the sea crashing next to us. I looked in the direction of my house, my stomach sinking. For a moment, I imagined stepping into the waves rather than going back there to Mike.

Would Idris walk on water to save me?

I rolled my eyes. I was officially going insane.

Idris paused at the small cave closest to his one and crouched down, stepping inside.

He blinked out at me from the darkness. 'Come in!' I hesitated and Idris laughed. 'Don't look so worried, there are no goats in here! You have nothing to fear, Selma. I promise. You need to trust me.'

Did I trust him? No, I barely knew him. But nonetheless, I desperately wanted to take the hand he had extended to me, and accept the thrill of stepping into the unknown. So I took his hand, then crouched down and entered the cave's tiny opening. At first, I was shrouded in complete darkness and panic set in. But then Idris's soothing deep voice reached me.

'It's okay, I'll lead you. We don't need light.'

He gently guided me down a stony tunnel and I allowed my free hand to glide along the damp bumpy walls as I bent over to stop myself from bumping my head. A buzz ran through me. How strange, to be here in this cave with a stranger as my family sat a few minutes' walk away. Strange but exciting too.

'You can stand properly now,' Idris said just as I felt a gust of air reach me, the wall disappearing from my touch.

I did as he asked, my eyes adjusting to a new quality of darkness. The tunnel had opened right up, dim light filtering down from above to reveal a huge area with trickling water in front of me.

'I didn't even know this was here,' I said, open-mouthed as I looked around me.

'Not many do,' Idris said in the semi-darkness, his hair a silver veil down his neck. 'Look,' he said, pointing upwards.

I followed his gaze towards the ceiling of the cave to see something hanging across it.

'Stalactites,' I whispered.

'No,' Idris said, shaking his head. 'Look closer. Here, I'll show you how.' He took my hand again and led me towards some large boulders, stepping up onto them. I did the same, peering upwards again when I got to the top.

The hanging objects were just a couple of metres away now, a dozen or so in different shapes and sizes, all made of stone. I frowned. The object directly above me looked like a bird. And there, was that a bat? Frozen mid-flight and somehow entangled in a long line of something.

'Are they real?' I asked Idris.

'Yes, they've been petrified. There would have been a time when this cave would have suddenly filled with sea water, rising high enough to cover the entire area. Over time, it gained an unusually high mineral content, causing these items to become petrified.' He smiled. 'Fascinating, isn't it? Some of these may have been formed centuries ago.'

I looked at the small bird, its mouth open mid-squawk, the fine details of its wings beautiful in the semi-darkness. 'I ought to be appalled. But there's a beauty to them.'

Idris nodded. 'Yes, I like that. A *beauty*. But the fact is, they're trapped in time, aren't they? Not sure there's much beauty to that. Easily done though,' he added, turning his gaze to me. 'Getting trapped, turning to stone. It's too late for them, sadly.'

'I know what you're doing,' I said, crossing my arms. 'Talking in metaphors. Trying to shine a light on what you *think* is my life.'

He tilted his head. 'So what if I am? Are you telling me it's not true? Why are you struggling so much with your next novel? I can tell you are, you know.'

I thought of how I'd felt lately. Trapped. Confined. Was I turning to stone like those animals above me?

'I feel like I'm in a philosophy lecture, to be honest,' I said, dismissing the thought.

Idris smiled. 'Sorry, I have a tendency to do that. You're not an easy student, you know.'

'I never have been.'

'But you could be. I could be too.'

'*You* could be?'

'I feel I can learn from you just as much as you could learn from me,' he said, his handsome face very serious.

I looked at him, trying to organise the thoughts swirling around my mind: the strange allure of him, of the cave, of this place too. Then the fear too, every part of my sensible mind – my *prefrontal cortex* – telling me to get the hell out before I started falling down the rabbit hole of possibility.

I stepped off the rock, the fear winning. 'My learning days are over.'

He frowned slightly.

'Thanks though,' I said. 'It's been . . . different.'

Idris was silent as we made our way out of the cave. When we got out, a cloud had passed over the moon, turning the beach pitch black, the only light from the fire outside the main cave.

'I hope you'll be back,' Idris said. 'I think you will be.'

I dragged my eyes away from the cave. 'Stop saying that. I have a child, Idris. I can't run away to live in a cave.'

As I walked into the darkness, leaving the light from the fire and distant voices behind me, I realised I was telling myself that more than Idris. The fact was, there was something about that cave that was drawing me to it.

Chapter Nine

Becky

Kent, UK
11 June 2018

Becky's mum's funeral is held in a small church not far from the cave where she passed away, sitting atop a cliff with vast views of the sea. The sound of waves whistles through the church's heavy doors, propped open to provide some solace from the intense heat of the day. There are scores of people there, all of them strangers to Becky . . . maybe to her mum too. She was a successful writer, a bestseller. People like that attracted temporary acquaintances, hangers-on. There were articles about her death in various newspapers after all.

There *are* people who care deeply for her mum though. Becky can see it in their faces, especially in the two nervous-looking women who stand up to do poetry readings during the simple service: 'Remember' by Christina Rossetti and 'You're' by Sylvia Plath. And that hurts Becky, how distant she was from her mum's life that she doesn't know who her closest friends were, and how they don't seem to know who she is either.

She sighs. She needs to stop dwelling on the 'what if's. It was just the way it was between her and her mum and she needs to accept it, just as she needs to accept the lies her mum told – the biggest one of all uttered just before she died: that Becky had a sister. Her dad had been shocked into silence on the phone when she'd told him her mum had passed away. She understood the strange clash of emotions he must have felt: grief for the woman he once loved combined with the hurt from her leaving him, even after all these years.

'She said something strange before she died,' Becky had said after breaking the news.

'Oh yes?'

'She said she had another daughter . . . with Idris.'

A pause. 'No,' her dad had said eventually. 'I'd have known.'

'Exactly.' She'd taken a deep breath, glad that her dad could reaffirm her own thoughts. 'The funeral's a week on Monday.'

'That was quick.'

'Her solicitor sorted it all. She gave him instructions. He also confirmed that no other person had been named in the will apart from me. Surely Mum would have left something to another child if I had a sister?'

'It's nonsense, Becky. I told you. You know how your mum was.'

'Yes.' But something niggled inside.

'But I'm pleased she left something to you in her will.'

More than 'something'. Becky had been surprised when the solicitor had told her it would all be left to her. Silly really, as she was her mum's only living relation after all. It meant she got the whole estate – this house, the London flat, all the items within, and her mum's savings too. Plus there were the ongoing royalties for her mum's books. She hadn't quite figured out what to do with it all yet. She loved her job so couldn't possibly think of leaving, even though she might be able to afford to now.

'I still haven't quite wrapped my head around it,' Becky had said to her dad. 'I've taken the week off after the funeral to go through all her belongings.'

'Good. At least you got something out of the relationship.' He must have regretted saying that as he sighed. 'She was a good mum, before everything.'

'Will you come to the funeral then?'

Another pause, another sigh. 'I can't, Becky. Cynthia and I have booked a holiday to see her parents in Spain, and you know how ill her father is.'

Becky had tried to hide her disappointment. 'Okay. I understand.'

Becky pulls at her starchy black dress now and follows everyone outside as the service ends, aware of the flood of bright colours around her. She clearly hadn't got the memo. She watches as people exchange kisses on cheeks. Dramatic sighs and the slow shaking of heads. Dabbing at tears with silk handkerchiefs.

'Quite a turnout,' someone says from behind her. Becky turns to see a woman with long, frizzy grey hair who looks to be in her seventies. 'You're Becky, aren't you?' the woman asks.

Becky smiles. 'I am.'

'Thought so. I recognise you from the photo your mum used to keep in the cave.'

'You knew her from the cave?'

The woman smiles and puts her hand out. 'Yes. My name's Maggie.'

Becky shakes the woman's hand, noticing grey powder when she takes it away. She wipes it on her dress, leaving a handprint on the black material.

'Oops, sorry,' Maggie says, spitting on a tissue and rubbing at the mark. 'I was in the middle of making a pot with my grand-daughter when I noticed the time and had to leave. That's what happens when you're in the current.'

'It's fine, really, I'm usually covered in dog hairs!' She frowns. 'What's the current?'

'The flow. The zone.'

Becky nods. She vaguely recalls her mum mentioning something about it. Or maybe it was from one of the school kids? Word had quickly got around about Idris and his 'followers' and their strange ways that summer, the fact her mum was part of it all bringing endless embarrassment and teasing for Becky.

'How long were you there?' she asks.

'Almost a year. It was quite something,' Maggie adds with a wistful sigh.

Becky looks in the direction of the cave. 'Mum was in the cave when she passed away. She asked me to take her there.'

Maggie puts her hand to her mouth, her grey eyes filling with tears. 'Was it peaceful?'

Becky nods, trying to contain her own tears. 'Very.'

'Poor girl,' Maggie says, clasping her hand. 'It must be so difficult for you.'

'It's been a shock.'

'Yes, I imagine.'

'Is anyone else from the cave here?' Becky asks, looking around.

'Not from what I can see. I've only kept in touch with a couple of them.'

'Like Idris?' Becky asks, voice tensing at his name.

Maggie shakes her head. 'No, not Idris. Haven't seen him since I left.'

'I'm surprised he didn't show up today.'

'Me too,' Maggie sighs. 'But then they did part rather abruptly, your mum and Idris.'

'What happened?'

'I wasn't there at the time. It's just what I heard. He upped and went, leaving your mum behind.'

Becky had never learnt the details. All she knew was that the cave's occupants had all packed up one day, leaving just her mum behind.

'They argued?' Becky asks, keen for more details now.

'I'm not sure. Something must have gone on though. They were so in love. It was hard in those last few weeks . . .' Her face darkens. 'That's why I had to leave. Though I sometimes wonder if I ever really left, if any of us did,' she adds, looking towards the cave, her smile returning. Maggie sighs. 'Oh well, it's ancient history. I'd rather not go into all that. I've worked bloody hard to leave it all behind.' She looks around her. 'So where's your sister then?'

Becky almost stops breathing. 'Sister?'

'Yes. I thought she'd be here?'

Becky tries to talk but finds she can't.

Maggie's eyes widen. 'Don't tell me you didn't know?' Becky can't say anything. She just stares into the distance, mind struggling to compute what Maggie has just said. Maggie puts her hand to her mouth. 'My God. You didn't.'

'Mum said something before she died but I presumed she was just delirious from the meds.' She closes her eyes, suddenly feeling weak.

Maggie senses it, and helps steer her to a bench. A willow tree hangs over, its leaves stirring in the summer breeze. Becky turns to Maggie. 'Did you meet my sister?'

My sister. There, just like that, another member of her family is formed.

'I was there when she was born,' Maggie replied. 'I left the cave not long after but met your mum again in this very café just before I headed off to the States. That's where I've been all these years, why your mum and I lost touch. Well, I like to blame it on that but, truth is, I simply never got a response to any of my letters to her.'

'It was definitely her baby? The one you met in the café?' Becky asks, desperate to keep on track.

'Yes, definitely. Pretty little thing.'

'Why didn't Mum tell me? Tell my *dad*?'

'Sweetheart, she'd just lost you in that court battle with your father. There was no chance she could risk social services marching her baby off. They kept her hidden away in that cave and your mum barely went out in those later stages of her pregnancy.'

'And barely saw me,' Becky adds. That would explain a lot, how suddenly her mum's visits dropped off in the months before Becky moved to Busby-on-Sea with her dad.

'Do you know what happened to the baby?' Becky asks Maggie.

Maggie shakes her head. 'Like I said, I lost touch with your mum after that. Maybe social services *did* catch up with her. Maybe the little mite was adopted?'

Becky thinks back to what her mum said before she died. 'Mum said something about Idris taking her.'

Maggie's face darkens. 'Really? That's not good. You'd think she'd try to track her daughter down if Idris took her though. She had all that money, probably contacts too.'

'Do you know where Idris is now?'

'I heard he went to Spain, to some cave encampment above the hills of Granada. I think he was hoping to start over, build up a brand new group. Maybe he'd have got his way if—'

She stops talking.

'If what?' Becky asks.

'Like I said, ancient history.' Maggie pulls an old watch from her pocket and looks at it. 'I have to go. I have a flight to catch later and I need to say my goodbyes to the family. You take care, okay?' She digs around in her bag for a paper and pen, scribbling her name and number down. 'Here's my number, in case you ever need to chat.' Then she walks from the graveyard.

Becky stays where she is, looking towards the cave where her mum died . . . and maybe gave birth to a secret child, hidden away so she wasn't taken from her as Becky had been. But in the end, someone *did* take her child away.

Idris.

Chapter Ten

Selma

Kent, UK
28 July 1991

When I got home at midnight after visiting Idris's cave, the house was dark and silent. Mike's car was in the drive so I knew he was home from the pub with Becky. I stepped inside with some trepidation but then readjusted my mind. What was wrong with taking a few hours out? I went into the kitchen and got a glass of water, drinking gulps of it down as I stared out into the garden. It was a lovely garden, one of the reasons we'd bought the house. Wide and surrounded by trees, it overlooked a field of horses at the back. I'd hoped to write my next novel looking out at that. Would it be easier in that cave with the sea as my view?

'Where were you?' a voice asked from the darkness. I turned to see Mike watching me from the doorway. He stepped into the kitchen, eyes accusing. He was in his pyjamas. 'You just disappeared,' he said, voice cold.

'That's allowed, isn't it? It was only a couple of hours.'

'Not when you have a child.'

'You were with Becky!'

'She was asking for you.'

I crossed my arms. 'Don't pull a guilt trip on me, Mike. I'm allowed to have some *me* time every now and again.'

'You get *me* time two days a week,' he threw back.

'That's work! How many times do I need to remind you?'

Mike gave me a pointed look. 'Work? Is that what you call it?' He grabbed some paper from the side and waved it in front of my face. 'According to this contract, there was no two-book deal – just one. And as for that royalty cheque you promised will arrive soon, that's bullshit too, isn't it? I found your statement. Three hundred and two units sold. I thought you said you'd sold thousands?'

I went very still. 'You went through my stuff.'

'Can you blame me? You've been acting so weird lately.'

I put my hand to my head. I already had a tension headache and I'd only been home a few minutes. I suddenly yearned for the cave again, for the crackling fire and wistful guitar music, the talk of writing and art and 'being in the current' and nurturing creativity.

'It's just numbers,' I said, surprising myself. 'What does it matter?'

'What does it matter?' Mike said, throwing the contract at me, the paper fluttering to the floor. 'We have a mortgage to pay, Selma. And you *lied* to me. Lied without batting an eyelid.'

'Because I knew you'd go on and on.'

'Jesus Christ,' he said, staring up at the ceiling in exasperation. 'You just don't get it, do you?'

'You don't get it!' I shouted back, my voice trembling. 'You don't get how bloody unhappy I am.'

Mike paused. 'Unhappy?'

As he said that, I realised just how deeply unhappy I was.

'You get everything you want,' he said. 'Two days of writing, that bloody view which we pay a premium for,' he said, flinging his hand towards the window. 'Everything you ask for.'

'This isn't what I asked for,' I said miserably.

'What do you mean by *this*? Me? Becky?'

'Of course I don't mean Becky. I *adore* her.'

'Do you really? Sometimes I wonder what you love more, your daughter or your writing.'

'How dare you say that!'

But maybe Mike was right. Wasn't my own mother the same way? All those years I had to endure her dispassion, sitting at the kitchen table and sucking on a cigarette as I silently begged her to *look* at me, *speak* to me, anything. I'd seen the desperation on my father's face too. The desire to bring his wife back into the here and now, to *look* at her family. Was Mike doing the same?

No, I wasn't like my mother. How could I think that? I *did* pay attention to Becky; I talked to her, listened to her. Becky knew I adored her. She knew I was always there for cuddles, for kisses, to hold her when she hurt herself. Or when she cried out in the night, my reflexes sent me flying to Becky's room before Mike had even registered our daughter's cry. A world away from the way my own mother had been with me.

And the fact Mike was daring to judge me in that moment made me more angry than ever. Criticise my failure as a wife, maybe. But a mum? No.

115

'Don't ever question my love for our daughter,' I said firmly.

Mike's face turned stony. 'And what about your love for me?'

My shoulders slumped. For once, I was sick of lying. 'It's changed for me, you're right.' I lifted my eyes to meet his. 'I'm sorry, Mike.'

He held my gaze, his nostrils flaring as tears gathered in his eyes. 'Then go,' he hissed.

'What?'

'You heard me, get out. You've not paid towards the mortgage for the past few months. So officially, this is my house. Pack your bags and get the fuck out.'

My heart started thumping uncontrollably. 'You can't do that.'

'I can and I will.'

I opened my mouth to protest again then I paused. Maybe it *was* time to leave, even if it was for a few days?

'Fine,' I said.

Surprise flickered on Mike's face. Then he stormed into the living room, slamming the door shut behind him.

I stayed where I was for a few moments, blinking into the moonlight-flooded kitchen, my head buzzing. Then I walked upstairs, pausing on the landing as I peered towards Becky's room. She was curled up on her side with her thumb in her mouth, something she still did when she slept. Her covers were thrown off, her face red from the night's heat, her little legs protruding from her pink shorts.

I walked in and lay next to her, watching as she breathed. When Becky stirred slightly, I almost wanted her to wake. Maybe seeing my daughter's pretty, innocent eyes blinking up at me might switch something in my brain, make me see reason instead of that cave, those knowing eyes of Idris's.

I lay like that for many hours, not sleeping, just with my arms wrapped around Becky's warm body. Mike remained downstairs, probably asleep on the sofa.

By the time sunlight started peeking through the curtains, I'd made my decision.

'I'm sorry,' I whispered to Becky, stroking her soft hair. 'Mummy's just trying to figure some things out and – and none of it's your fault, okay? I love you so much and I'll come back for you, I promise.'

I kissed her on the forehead then walked to the door. But before leaving the room, I paused. Maybe I should just take Becky with me? What could Mike say, Becky was my daughter too.

No, that wouldn't be fair on her. I just needed a couple of days, then I'd come back for her. I wouldn't leave her for good. *Couldn't*.

I packed some items then tiptoed downstairs. I knew where I was going.

When I approached the cave a few minutes later, the rising sun spread a pink hue across the sea. I paused a moment to take it in, breathing in the beauty, the simplicity. The world was so tranquil at this time. Usually I'd still be sleeping, on the brink of being woken by Becky.

Becky.

I thought of her waking to find her mum gone and I hoped Mike would explain it in a way that wouldn't sadden our daughter. I couldn't bear to think he might not, too bitter and angry. No, he wasn't like that. And anyway, hadn't *he* told *me* to leave?

As I drew closer to the cave, I saw Idris sitting outside it, cross-legged as he watched the rising sun. Beyond him, within the cave, people lay still and quiet in their sleeping bags, eyes closed. And above, the old hotel stood white and dilapidated. How ironic that I'd dreamed of buying the place when I became a published author. Instead, I was going to live in the damp cave below it. But somehow, that seemed just as exciting to me now.

When Idris turned to look at me, suddenly it all seemed very real, the weight of my overnight bag heavy on my shoulder. He stood and walked to me, barefoot on the sand.

'Here, let me take your bag,' he said, putting his hand out for it.

I shrugged the bag off, handing it over to him.

'I've set a bed up for you. I think you'll like it,' he said, as though he'd not doubted for a moment I would come.

I followed him into the cave, leaving my old life behind.

Chapter Eleven

Becky

Kent, UK
12 June 2018

Becky peers up at her mum's house, the old hotel she once used to stare at as a child from the beach below. 'When I get my big book deal,' her mum used to say, 'I'll buy this place for us. Then you can run around as much as you want, causing mischief.'

Her mum had got her wish in the end, except Becky hadn't been with her. How strange to think it is Becky's now, as the main beneficiary of her mum's fortune. That is why Becky is here – to clear out her mum's belongings, get the house on the market. What else is she to do with this vast beast of a house on her own? Plus it is a good chance to dwell on what Maggie had confirmed: that her mum *had* had another child.

Becky is still struggling to come to terms with the idea that she has a sister.

She'd tried to call her dad again on his mobile yesterday to talk

119

about it, but it had just gone to voicemail. She'd left a message, quickly trying to summarise what Maggie had said.

She looks around the house now, imagining running around it with another little girl. How different life could have been. She'd felt lonely sometimes as a child, especially after her mum left. When she'd moved to Busby-on-Sea with her dad, he'd promised her she'd always have friends to play with, her cousins not far away. But they were older than her and she rarely saw them anyway. Most weekends were spent at her grandparents' house with her dad, a bit of a miserable experience for a child as they didn't like the TV being on. She made some friends at school, but none of them particularly close ones. Maybe that was why she put so much into her first boyfriend when she was fourteen, spending most of her time with him until he dumped her ten years later.

She would have loved to have a sister, living in this place too, with her mum's beaming smile and sneaky chocolate gifts instead of her dad's quiet ways, no matter how much she loved him.

She gazes around her. The old hotel looks smarter than she remembers, the weatherboards a sparkling white, the windows new and gleaming. Her mum had clearly renovated it. Becky's dogs sniff at the overgrown grass outside, stopping to make their mark.

As she lets herself in the front door, she is instantly overwhelmed by the musky scent of her mum's perfume. Becky irrationally looks around for her mum, but no, of course she isn't here. The dogs bound in, paws sliding on the wooden floors. How would her mum feel about dogs being in her house? She'd never been a fan.

'Calm down,' Becky shouts at them. The three of them stop

where they are, peering over at her. 'Go gently,' she says, voice softer now. 'And stay by me,' she adds, patting her thigh. They all trot over, staying close to her as she looks around. It's clear it was once a hotel, the old reception desk to the right of the hallway made from the same wood used to clad the house. An ornate silver rail sits at the back of it, piled with a range of her mum's colourful jackets, coats and scarves. Maybe she found it charming, quirky, inviting people over to her empty hotel for dinner. Becky could imagine her mum doing that.

Becky places her car keys on the counter along with the dogs' leads.

She walks down the hallway and into an L-shaped bar. A long navy sofa made from plush velvet adorns it, facing out to sea. Beyond is a long dining-room table made from driftwood. It looks well used with dents and circles left behind by wine glasses and mugs. A strange-looking chandelier hangs above it and, as Becky draws closer, she sees it's made from books, beautifully arranged, with glimpses of lightbulbs between them. The books are some of her mum's favourites: Angela Carter novels, of course; a copy of *Hotel du Luc* by Anita Brookner; John Donne's poetry; a James Joyce novel or two.

Becky smiles. How typical of her mum.

She walks around the bar to the side of the room towards some French doors leading out to a large enclosed garden littered with trees and, to her surprise, swings, a treehouse with a slide, even toys discarded on the lawn. They look too new to have been there when the house was a hotel all those years ago. So why are they here now? She wonders for a moment if her sister *did* stay with her mum, hidden away in this vast hotel. But why no mention of her in the will? Why hadn't her mum told her about her sister earlier?

Either way, there must have been children here. Becky can't help but feel a dig of jealousy. Her mum couldn't stick around when she was a child but it looks like she was happy to have them here.

The dogs scratch at the French doors so Becky tries some of the keys on the bunch she was given by the solicitor, finally finding one to open them.

'Behave!' she calls to the dogs as they dart out. She pours some water into a travel bowl and leaves it on the steps for them, then heads back out to the hallway towards some dark stairs that twist upward from behind the reception area. She climbs them, finding there are two further floors, one with several rooms leading to en-suite bathrooms. Some are empty, others are lined with cardboard boxes, piles of books, and clothes draped over chairs. Some have been made into simple guest rooms, clearly recently used, with crumpled sheets and glasses of misty water on the bedside tables. Who stayed here with her mum? She thinks back to the funeral, the many faces . . . and yet her mum had been described as a recluse. It didn't make sense.

Becky goes up the next flight of stairs and knows instantly this is where her mum must have spent most of her time. The walls are papered in luxurious patterns with hummingbirds and exotic flowers. Becky walks down the hallway, fingertips gliding over the walls. She imagines her mum doing the same each day, and bites her lip to stop the tears. The grief still hasn't really hit her. It's just so much to take in. So confusing, too. She hadn't seen her mum in recent years, so the gap left behind isn't tangible. But it still somehow feels vast.

There's a large bathroom with a duck-egg-blue bath that has cast-iron feet. A towel lies discarded on the floor. Becky goes over to it, picking it up and bringing it to her nose, smelling her mum. Her tears wet the material and she gently folds it, placing it on one of the shelves.

She notices a small amount of blood on one of the double sinks, then some more on the navy blue tiles. Did her mum fall? Is that why she ended up in hospital, no longer able to care for herself?

Becky sits on the pretty wooden chair by the window, looking out to sea as she clenches her fists. Why didn't her mum just *call* her when she started to deteriorate? She would have come to help in an instant, despite all that had passed between them. But instead, she was left to spend her last weeks struggling. She may have had carers but, still, it must have been difficult.

Becky goes to the room across the hall, no doubt her mum's bedroom. Her slippers still lie on the plush patterned rug, the bed unmade. There's hair in her brush, the wardrobe left open to reveal an array of beautiful dresses. And a book, face down on the side table, spine bent, waiting to be continued. It's her mum's first novel. Was she reading it again, a step back in time as death descended?

Becky leans against the wall. It feels as though she's trekking up a hill, the torrent of grief catching up with her now. She closes her eyes, tears squeezing out between her eyelashes as she remembers her mum's last breath, and her last words too: *Why would I lie about something like that?*

Could she really have a sister out there? She looks at her phone. Still no message from her dad.

'Right,' Becky says to herself, wiping her tears away. 'Pull yourself together.' She checks on the dogs out of the window, happy to see them behaving, then heads down the hallway to the door at the end, her mum's study . . . the most important room in the house. She takes a deep breath and walks in.

The room is large, with huge windows looking out over sea views, the cave – her mum's precious cave – just a hundred or so metres below. Her mum would have written her recent books on that driftwood desk, similar to the dining table downstairs. Her presence seeps from the dark wallpapered walls and Becky can almost see her sitting there, maybe thinking of the child that was taken from her.

Why would Idris do that? Maybe her mum had threatened to leave him and this was his reaction. Parents did that, didn't they? Snatch children away as punishment?

Becky sighs. It's no good speculating. She walks around the room. There are some framed covers of her mum's books on the walls, all similar in theme: title and name in purple bold typeface, formed into a circle atop the silhouette of a woman's face. Award certificates join them too, including one for the Baileys Women's Prize for Fiction the previous year. Becky had learnt about the win from a newspaper she saw someone reading in the practice's waiting room. It had shocked her, seeing her mum's face staring out at her: one of her dark eyebrows was raised, her lips painted scarlet red, shoulders swathed in black silk, still so beautiful in her sixties. For a moment, she was tempted to call her mum and congratulate her. But then she'd remembered her mum's absence from her graduation a few years before. She'd just got a small card of congratulations for that, nothing else. Why did she deserve more? So Becky had sent her a congratulatory card too, but she'd spent ages looking for just the right one. She found one that featured a woman on a cliff, peering out to sea. When you looked closer, you could see the cliff was made from piles of books. Her mum hadn't acknowledged it. She'd thought there might be a phone call. But nothing.

Becky walks to the desk, misshapen and stretched across the corner of the room. There's a mug sitting on it, congealed milk at the bottom that's beginning to smell. Becky leans over the desk, opening the window to let fresh air in. As she does, she notices a pair of glasses on the table, a trace of foundation on the bridge. A pile of paper lies in the in-tray, some of it spilling onto the floor, contracts and invoices probably ignored. Her agent had promised to check out any paperwork. Becky reaches to gather everything up, ready to place in her bag to post the next day, then pauses.

On top of the pile is an old copy of the *National Geographic*, opened to a faded article featuring a photo of a group of people sitting on a hill, caves spread up above them, rows of houses below. *The Cave Dwellers of Sacromonte*, the headline reads. The people pictured are an eclectic mix. In the middle stands a man with long blond hair, his hand on the shoulder of a young girl of about three or four. But she can't make out their faces properly, the magazine looks pretty old after all. Could the man be Idris? She'd seen glimpses of him as a child, remembers his long white hair. But not much more, so she can't be sure.

But her mum had clearly been interested in him. His face is circled, as is the face of the young girl with him.

Becky picks the article up, heart thumping as she looks at the child, then at the date: June 1996. If her mum had given birth just before Becky left for Busby-on-Sea with her dad, then her sister would be around the same age as the little girl in the photograph then. Could it be her sister? Maggie *had* mentioned Spain.

Becky sits down on the chair, the article in her hands. Maybe they were still in Spain – the article describes the caves as 'permanent dwellings' after all.

A breeze drifts in from the window, and out of the corner of her eye, Becky sees something fluttering. She looks towards an armchair by the bookshelves, noticing a range of paper objects hanging from the ceiling there: *Birds. Bats. Shells.* She imagines them being real, frozen creatures with their lives on hold.

She walks over and reaches up, her fingers grazing one of the bird's wings. It twirls, sunlight glinting on its pink paper feathers, turning them silver. Then Becky notices something. On the back of each one are small photos, printed over and over.

She raises herself to get a better look then gasps. They are photos of Becky, lots of different ones of her as newborn and a child . . . and as an adult, too. In fact, one of them is taken from her profile page on the veterinary practice website.

Becky puts her hand to her chest. Her mum was following her progress all this time.

Then she notices another face behind the smallest bird: a baby, tiny with its eyes closed.

Her sister?

Did her mum sit here watching her daughters' faces twirl around above her? Two daughters she let slip through her fingers.

'Oh Mum,' Becky whispers, tears gathering in her eyes.

'Becky?'

Becky looks up with a start, surprised to see her dad standing at the door.

'Dad, you scared the life out of me! What are you doing here?'

'I got your message yesterday.' He steps in, looking tired. He's fair-skinned like Becky, tall and slim, blue-eyed with a bald head. Each time she sees him, she realises how old he's getting, nearly seventy now. 'I should have come to the funeral. I'm sorry, love.'

She strides towards him and hugs him, feeling him stiffen slightly in her arms. He was never one for hugs, not like her mum was. She missed that when her mum left, the way she'd always be hugging and kissing her when they lived together. Becky's dad tried his best. It wasn't that he was cold or unkind. He just didn't know how to show affection like her mum had. He *had* been there for Becky all those years though, just him. She'll always be grateful for that.

'I thought you were going away?' Becky asks him.

'I had to come back. It felt wrong you being alone at a time like this. I could hear in your voice you needed me.'

Love rushes through Becky. She gives him another hug. 'Thanks, Dad. That really means a lot.'

Her dad walks around the office, his fingers faintly gliding over everything.

'Is Cynthia here?' Becky peers into the hallway. Truth is, she hopes she isn't. She's never got on with her stepmother. Her dad had actually met her when he was still with Becky's mum. She was one of the school gate mums. They'd shared some playdates after her mum left and the two kept in touch over all those years. She clearly cared for Mike, but Becky could never warm to her.

The way she held herself all straight-backed and stiff with her glacier eyes like she was above everyone. It just didn't sit right with Becky.

'No, she's rather annoyed at me for coming here actually,' Mike replies.

Becky grimaces. 'Oops.'

Her dad smiles slightly. 'Won't do me any harm putting my foot down every now and again.' He walks over to his ex-wife's desk, placing his palm against it. 'This is just how I'd imagine your mum's office to be. The whole house, actually. She always said she'd buy this place. Good on her for doing it.' He smiles sadly. 'So,' he says, taking a deep breath. 'How was the funeral?'

He doesn't turn to look at Becky when he says that but she can tell from the slump of his shoulders he's finding it difficult. He loved her mum after all, and he hadn't wanted them to split up. Becky had caught him crying once, a few weeks after her mum left. He'd quickly recovered himself – lied and said he'd got something in his eye. But Becky had known, even at that age, how heartbreaking it was for him, for *both* of them. She wished they'd talked about it more, shared the burden.

'Shall we get some tea?' Becky says. 'I'd better let the dogs in before they dig up the garden anyway.'

'Yes, I heard them running around out there,' he comments, following her out. He pauses to look back at the study, shoulders slumping in sadness. Then he sighs and walks out.

Five minutes later, they're sitting at the large table overlooking the sea with two steaming mugs of tea. The dogs are sprawled out on the floor, Womble with his chin on Mike's feet. He was a bit like her mum, never one for dogs. But he tolerated them, had even grown to feel some affection for them. Cynthia, on the other hand, couldn't abide them. She'd kick them away from her; something Becky's mum never would have done – despite everything that had passed, hurting others was not in her nature.

'I feel bad for rushing the phone call the other week,' Mike says. 'I was in shock.'

'I know.'

'It was all rather sudden, wasn't it?'

'It was.'

'And the funeral. Was it . . . bearable?'

Becky looks down at her mug. 'It felt more like a large publishing bash, to be honest. A sombre one, anyway.'

Her dad coughs slightly. 'I feel bad you had to endure it alone.'

'Oh, it's fine Dad,' she says, shooting him a smile. 'Really. You're here now, and that's what counts.'

He frowns, his eyes fixed on the sea outside. 'I know things weren't great between me and your mum, but it still saddens me. Her death has brought back lots of memories too actually, good and bad. Especially that summer.'

'The summer she left?'

Her dad nods. 'It was a difficult summer anyway, what with the recession and people losing their jobs. Made for a strange atmosphere in the town, all the joviality of those warm months felt a bit false, you know?'

'I remember. Lots of kids at school had parents who lost jobs.'

He nods. 'I was one of the lucky ones. Until your mum left, anyway.' He looks up at the book chandelier and frowns, reaching up to touch one of the pages. 'I was so angry, so hurt. But looking back, I understand. Your mum struggled. Sometimes, she'd be fine. More than fine actually. You remember the way she was with that dry sense of humour of hers? Fun too, especially after a few gins. That's the woman I fell in love with.' The smile drops from his face. 'Other times, there was a darkness.'

'Darkness?'

'Depression, I suppose you could call it. I asked her to get help once but she said it was just the way she was, the way *writers* were.'

'What happened when she was depressed?'

'She'd go into herself. Wouldn't be very responsive.'

Becky nods. 'Yes, I remember her being like that sometimes. It never really occurred to me it might be depression.'

'It wasn't so bad when you got older actually, but I think she must have felt it returning that summer.' He sighs. 'Maybe it was the atmosphere in the town seeping into her? Looking back, I didn't understand why she ran off like she did. But I understand more now.' He scrutinises Becky's face. 'Do you remember much from then?'

'I remember how embarrassed I was.'

'Embarrassed?'

'All the cave cult stuff in the papers. It's all the kids could talk about. Then my mum leaves us to live in that cave. To make matters worse, rumours start circulating about her and Idris.'

'You were teased?'

Becky scratches at some grained-in cheese on the table. 'Mercilessly. They called me cave child but I'd only visited once.'

Her dad frowns. 'Why didn't you say?'

'We never talked about it, Dad. I didn't want to make you even more upset than you already were, so I just got on with it.'

He shakes his head, taking a sip of his tea. 'That must have been difficult, especially when the tide turned and people started getting angry with the cave dwellers.'

'Yeah, Idris started off as a saviour of sorts, didn't he? I remember all the older girls at school talking about him in hushed tones.'

Becky's dad nods. 'People rather enjoyed the strangeness of it at the beginning, a chance to talk about something other than the recession. But then the novelty wore off. It was a relief to be away from it all when we moved.'

'Yep, it was for me too.' Becky gets up and retrieves some treats from her bag for the dogs. 'I was *desperate* to start afresh at a school where people had no idea what my mum had done.'

'I was never quite sure if you wanted to go, especially as we were leaving your mum behind.'

'I'd given up on her by then. I was barely seeing her.' Becky throws the bones for the dogs and they snatch them up, settling beneath the table to chew them. Becky's brow creases. 'And now I know why I didn't see her much then. She was pregnant.'

Her dad closes his eyes, pinching the bridge of his nose. 'Yes.'

'Yes? So you *knew*?'

He opens his eyes, looking right into Becky's. 'Deep down, yes. I could see how her shape changed when I saw her, the way she was acting.'

'Acting?'

'The depression I mentioned. It got worse when she was pregnant, with all those heightened hormones. She got a bit erratic with it and she was the same those months before we moved. I suppose I was in denial. The idea that the woman I loved was pregnant with another man's child – not just another man but one some people saw as a god – was too much to endure.'

'Oh Dad.' Becky reaches over and squeezes his hand. 'So you really think she was pregnant then, that she was telling the truth when she said she had a daughter?'

'I know your mum was always a bit liberal with the truth, Becky, but why would she lie about something like that? To what end?'

Becky sighs. 'That's what she said, too.'

'So what are you going to do?'

'What do you mean?'

'Are you going to try to track the girl down?'

Becky thinks of the *National Geographic* magazine she found. 'It could be a wild goose chase.'

'But you might regret it if you don't.'

Becky frowns. She's surprised her dad wants her to try. This was the child his ex-wife had with the man she pretty much left him for.

'*I* regretted it,' her dad says.

'Regretted what?'

'I had a best friend at school, Henry Hope-Frost.' He smiles. 'We were thick as thieves. But then he moved away and we lost touch. I always thought about tracking him down again. Friends come and go but he always stuck in my mind. So last year, I decided to try to find him.'

'That's great!'

He shakes his head. 'It was too late. He passed away just a few weeks before. If I'd only done it years ago when I first started considering it, I might have had a few more years with him as my friend.'

Becky's heart goes out to her dad. 'I'm so sorry, Dad.'

'The reason I'm telling you this is I don't want you to live with the same regret. And this is bigger, this is your *sister*.' Becky has never seen him look so animated. 'I remember sitting downstairs while you hid away in your room after your mum left. You don't know how many times I thought about coming up and talking to you, really talking. But it's hard for your old dad, I'm not used to it. Your mum did all that. I knew you missed the female touch. Maybe your little sister did too? She's been without her mum all these years too, remember.'

Becky thinks back to those years after her mum left. First the confusion: why wasn't her mum living with them? Her parents had tried to explain it: Mummy and Daddy just can't live together any more, though she'd wanted to shout at them, *But what about me?* Maybe if her dad had told her how much her mum fought for her, even going to court, things would have been different. But quickly that confusion had turned to pain, tears wetting her pillow each night as she tried to figure out what she'd done wrong to drive her mum away. Anger soon took over, the teasing she got at school fuelling it. Better to blame her mum than herself, especially as everyone seemed at pains to tell her it wasn't her fault.

When she moved to Busby-on-Sea with her dad, she decided the best route was numbness. Just try not to care. So she disappeared into the romance books her mum left for her, was quiet at school, making one or two friendships but none deep enough to get invites over for dinner or to many parties. She told herself it suited her. She liked her own company, had learnt silence and calm was better than what her mum represented: chaos and erratic behaviour. But she missed female company. The softness, the giggling, the non-stop chatter. There was no way she could talk to her sweet but awkward grandmother, nor her distant aunt. Her dad coped the best he could – he'd given her a book on puberty, and even discreetly left packs of sanitary towels in her bedroom when she started her period.

But it just wasn't the same.

Becky imagines what it would have been like to have a sister to share all that with. Had her *own* sister yearned for someone to talk to when she reached those special milestones too, like bra shopping and getting her first period? Maybe there were other girls she could talk to as she travelled around with Idris, people she could turn to. But the girl in the picture, if indeed it was her sister, had looked sad, lost.

Becky remembers that feeling. She'd felt it herself so often over the years, and not just when she was younger. If her sister had come looking for her, maybe things would have been easier. Maybe they will be now, for both of them, if they find each other. There are still so many years left to share, so much opportunity to provide that much-needed female support to each other, a lifetime of milestones to come.

Becky takes a deep, determined breath. 'I think you're right, Dad. I think I need to go and find my sister.'

Her dad smiles, grasping her hand. 'Good. Your mum would be pleased. I think that's why she finally told you before she died, you know. A hope you might find the daughter she lost.'

Chapter Twelve

Selma

Kent, UK
28 July 1991

Idris led me to the back of the cave, past the sleeping people. Now I could see it in daylight, I realised it wasn't just sleeping bags that people were lying in, but there were mattresses too, slung over wooden pallets to keep them dry. Donna and her two children lay together on a double mattress, Oceane looking like a young child, curled up against her mum. They were surrounded by Maggie's paper flowers, some of which were now draped across the walls of the cave. Caden was stretched out on a single mattress nearby, his arms above his head, a book open on his chest. Julien was lying on his front, his dog in a ball beside him.

I wondered where Idris slept. *If* he slept. I shook my head.

He isn't a god!

We stopped at a clean single mattress right at the back of the cave. It was partially covered with a floral sleeping bag, a soft white pillow. There was a cheap-looking bookcase next to it adorned with several books and a comfortable-looking floor cushion, all of which I was sure hadn't been there the night before.

'Yours,' Idris said, gesturing to it all.

'How did you get all this overnight?'

'I have my ways.' He nodded towards the mattress. 'You look tired. Sleep. It's not even six yet.'

I shook my head. 'There's no way I can sleep right now.'

That smile again. 'You will. Sleep is essential, unless you're in the current of course.'

'The current. Always about the current,' I said with a smile.

'You'll see. The bathroom is there,' he said, gesturing to a dark corner of the cave with a shower curtain concealing it. 'It's just a portable camping toilet for now, and there's a jug of clean water to wash with. We're working on getting a bath, and a better toilet too. I'll wake you for breakfast. You'll enjoy it, it's a proper feast. Before you sleep though, can I ask something?'

'Sure.'

He looked at my watch. 'Please can you remove that? We don't allow watches or clocks here.'

I frowned. I only ever took off my mother's watch at night-time or when swimming. But Idris was giving me this look like I had no choice in the matter, so I unbuckled it and placed it in a pocket in my overnight bag.

'Happy?' I said as I zipped the pocket up.

Idris smiled. 'Thank you. See you at breakfast.'

I watched as he padded quietly through the cave, his body casting a huge shadow over the walls and the sleeping people around him. Then I quickly took the watch out again, slipping it into my pocket. It was a silly rule. How on earth would I be able to tell the time, there were no clocks there? I had the right to know the time, if I wanted to!

And how on earth was I going to sleep after everything that had happened with Mike? I leaned back on the bed anyway and was surprised when a feeling of exhaustion overwhelmed me. Before I knew it, I was fast asleep.

I woke to the smell of sizzling fish and the sound of laughter. I stayed where I was for a moment, taking a few seconds to drink it in. The cave looked surreal in the daylight, a strange mixture of earthy chalk, green vegetation and black rock set against the pastel paper flowers hanging from the walls. I looked above me at the ceiling which sloped up towards the entrance. It had holes carved into it by time and weather, looking like a dark ancient map of the world. I breathed in, smelling moss and the sea all mingling with the food that was being barbecued.

Was I really here?

I pulled myself up, looking around me. There were indents in the walls, turned into shelves by the occupants, filled with various framed photos, vases, books, dots of colour against the mossy clay. Maggie was working at her urn nearby, Julien shaving using a mirror by his bed with a towel around his waist, his dog at his feet. At the front of the cave, Donna was cooking at the barbecue, the long narrow table beside her adorned with food: heaps of fresh fruit, large bowls of what looked like granola and jugs of orange juice. Caden sat at one of the chairs, bleary eyed as he sipped a mug of coffee, his guitar propped on the side.

Outside, the sun was shining bright. Tom traced patterns in

the sand, completely naked. By him was Anita, stretching her lithe body into yoga positions as she looked up at the sun.

I wiped the sleep from my eyes and slipped out from the sleeping bag.

'Good morning.' I looked over to the wall opposite me to see Idris standing on a ladder, watching me. He smiled and turned his attention back to painting.

I dragged myself up and walked over to him, raking my fingers through my hair. People nodded in greeting, but didn't make a fuss, as though I'd been there forever. When I got to Idris, I realised he was painting the outline of a woman with soft curves wearing a summer dress like mine. In her hands she held a notepad and a beautiful pen, just like the one I had.

'It's me,' I said.

'Yep.'

It felt irritatingly presumptuous of him. 'What if I don't stay?'

He turned to look over his shoulder at me. 'What if you do?'

'Questions being answered with questions again.' He smiled at this, the white of the morning sunlight highlighting the crinkles around his eyes and the bristles on his cheeks. I couldn't help but smile back. 'You're very talented. You must have done this before you came here.'

'What does it matter what came before? All that matters is now.'

'Mysterious. So how do you make sure the paint doesn't come off? It can get pretty damp in here.'

He gestured towards a small paint-splattered table filled with colourful bottles. 'Weather-proof liquid pigments.'

'You seem to know your stuff. You painted stone in your previous life then?'

He shot me a wicked grin. 'There you go again, asking more questions.'

'Okay everyone, breakfast!' Donna called out, bringing a huge platter of barbecued fish to the table.

But Idris and I held each other's gazes. He was the first to break away, stepping down from the ladder he'd been using to paint and cleaning his hands in a bowl of water.

'Come on, you must be hungry,' he said.

'Ravenous.'

We walked to the table along with the others, each taking one of the mismatched seats. Tom took the seat next to me, gazing up at me with a smile. He was wearing shorts now, his face grimy with sand. I imagined Becky sharing breakfast here with us all and felt a pang. I missed her.

'This looks amazing,' I said, admiring the feast before me.

'Donna is a culinary genius,' Maggie said.

I went to grab some fruit but Donna gently put her hand on my arm. 'Not yet. We have to do the morning prayer first.'

My stomach sank. 'Prayer?'

Caden laughed. 'Don't worry, it's not what you think.'

'Your caution is understandable,' Idris said. 'Religions have hijacked the word prayer. But in its simplest form, it means to ask.' Everyone nodded. 'I'll start. As you know, yesterday I asked for Selma and – well, you can see for yourself she's here.'

I looked at him quizzically. 'You asked for *me*?'

'I asked for someone who would enlighten me, teach me something new. That turned out to be you. Thank you for coming, Selma.'

'Thank you,' everyone murmured, smiling at me.

I tried to smile back but I imagine it was an awkward smile that displayed how overwhelmed I was. It all still felt surreal.

'I sense Selma has crossed paths with us for a wonderful reason,' Idris said. 'She's on the brink of producing a masterpiece and, by teaching her to enter the current, we can help her do that.'

'Masterpiece? No pressure then,' I said with a raised eyebrow.

'You *will* do it though,' Oceane said. 'Honestly. I've been producing the best work I ever have since learning to be in the current.'

'Me too,' Caden said.

Others nodded in agreement.

'And we can't wait to see what our famous author has in store,' Anita said. More nods, eager looks in their eyes.

'As you can see, we're all really excited to have you here,' Idris said with a laugh.

'Wow, that's quite a welcome,' I said, not quite sure what else to say. 'Thank you, all of you.'

'So, let's start with the morning prayer,' Idris said. 'Any volunteers?'

Maggie put her hand up.

'Maggie,' Idris said.

'Today I plan to finish three vases,' Maggie said. 'Oceane will pick some sweet-smelling flowers she's seen nearby, make the cave smell *and* look delicious.'

'That's great. I love to hear about collaboration,' Idris said.

As everyone else went through their 'asks' for the day – the composition of a new song for Caden, a new recipe for Donna, a poem and flower picking for Oceane, a new yoga inversion for Anita, the creation of a driftwood desk for Julien . . . and an 'awesome sandcastle' for Tom – I found myself drawn into their creative ambitions, despite how weird the whole set-up was. The fact was, it was refreshing to be surrounded by creatives, and so early in the day too. I was so used to starting the morning in a rush, with Becky moaning about her 'boring breakfast' and Mike reeling off a list of tasks for me if I was writing from home, as if I didn't have work to do myself.

As I thought that, I felt a rush of guilt, imagining Becky asking Mike where her mum was right in that moment.

'Selma?' Idris asked. 'What about you? What's your ask for the day?'

Everyone looked at me. I shrugged. 'I don't know. I guess I usually set myself daily word counts so—'

Idris shook his head. 'No numbers.'

I couldn't help but laugh. 'Okay, fine, no numbers. Then I guess my ask is to *really* get into my writing, no interruptions.'

As I said that, I felt a surge inside. I could have gone to a hotel when Mike told me to leave, but I went to the cave. Deep down, I knew why.

To write.

I wanted to try it out, to see if what they all said about 'getting into the current' proved true. God knows I had to try *something* to get my writing going again. It wasn't just about the writing though. It was more than that. I needed to *feel* something again. I'd felt so numb lately.

'Good ask,' Idris said. 'Right, tuck in everyone!'

Everyone started piling their plates high with food. 'Make the most of this,' Oceane said to me, spooning granola into her bowl. 'We won't get to eat again until this evening.'

'What?' I asked in surprise.

'Idris says lunch isn't conducive to getting into the current,' Caden explained. 'Tea and water are fine, even wine. But no food until six in the evening.'

'I can't survive without eating that long, seriously . . .' I said, reaching for some more fish. It certainly wasn't what I was used to eating for breakfast but it was delicious and that was what counted.

'You will,' Donna said, brown eyes sparkling. 'Wait and see.'

I looked at her. She was really falling for all this, wasn't she? I peered around the table. They *all* were. Was it just Idris? He had something about him, there was no doubt about it. But there had to be more than that to drive what seemed like reasonably normal people to live in a cave.

'Well, I'd better make the most of breakfast then.' I bit into a forkful of fish, its meaty goodness filling my mouth. 'This is delicious, Donna,' I said in between mouthfuls.

'Thank you. I try to make everything while in the current.'

I tried not to roll my eyes.

'That way it seeps into the food and helps everyone else get into the current,' Donna continued.

'She's even started a vegetable patch,' Maggie said, pointing to a small squared-off area outside the cave, soil mixed in with sand and a scattering of green buds.

'Pulling veg out of sand,' I said. 'What next? Five thousand fish from two? You really are Jesus, aren't you?' I said to Idris.

But he didn't smile back. I bit my lip. Maybe I'd taken it too far? I resolved to keep my quips to myself a bit more before I got kicked out. They were all clearly taking it *very* seriously.

'Everything we're going to cook here will be aimed at getting the creative juices flowing, Selma,' Idris explained in a serious voice. 'So yes, in a way, you are right. A multitude of creativity from just one fish,' he said, gesturing to the fish I was eating. 'Cold-water fish like salmon and mackerel are known to enhance one's creative thinking, as does lots of fresh fruit and veg. And coffee, of course. Lots of it!' he added with a smile as he lifted his mug. 'Caffeine gets bad press but the truth is, it's wonderful for pushing the mind to think creatively.'

'It's quite the set-up here already,' I said, taking a sip of my own coffee. 'How long's it been now? Just over a week? And all this established, including the routine, in that short time?'

'That's what Idris does,' Julien said. 'It's his talent, making things happen quickly. No point wasting time.' That was the first time Julien had spoken that morning. He seemed so reserved compared to the others.

After we'd all eaten, people gradually disappeared from the table, taking spots outside the cave or inside, setting about their work. I watched them for a bit, not quite sure what to do with myself. Maggie was working miracles again, this time at her urn. Oceane rocked back and forth, scribbling on her notepad. Caden sat cross-legged, staring out to the sea as he whispered lines from a song over and over.

Did they think they were in the current?

Donna passed by, a bowl of water in her hands.

'Don't you have work today?' I asked her.

'Oh, I packed my job in,' Donna replied breezily as she placed it on the table.

'You did *what*?'

She smiled slightly. 'We don't need money here. Why deal with the stress? I'm so much happier now.'

'What about your house?'

'I own it outright. My grandparents passed it down to me, so it's always there if I need it.'

Lucky you.

'What made you come here?' I asked her.

She shrugged. 'I can't explain it.' But her gaze drifted towards Idris, who was looking out to sea, shirtless.

I raised an eyebrow. 'What does your husband think about it all, especially his child living in a cave?'

'My *ex*-husband.' Donna sighed. 'He's not happy about it. But he has no choice.'

'How do you mean?'

Donna shrugged. 'A story to tell another time.' She cocked her head, examining my face. 'You say *living in a cave* like it's a negative thing. Do you see anything negative?' she asked, sweeping her hand around her. 'This is a child's dream.'

'For now, while it's warm. What about the winter?'

Donna smiled. 'Idris will figure it out.'

'What *is* it about him?' I asked, looking at Idris again. 'Everyone here seems so *enthralled* by him. It has to go beyond looks.'

'And you're not enthralled?' Donna asked me, scrutinising my face.

Was I enthralled? Maybe, a little bit.

'It's more than his looks and you know it, Selma. He's not like anyone else we know! You saw him saving that boy.' She leaned forward, grasping my hand. 'You see what I see, what *all* of us do.' I looked down at our conjoined hands in surprise.

144

Donna was usually so timid and distant, now she was gripping my hand so hard it hurt. 'There's a lot you'll learn here, *especially* about yourself.'

She held my gaze then released my hands, placing some dishes in the bowl. 'Good luck getting into the current. It might not happen today, but it *will* happen,' she said with certainty. 'Best to start here, inside the cave. Caves are ideal for getting into the current. That's why Idris chose it. The air in caves is incredibly pure because of elevated levels of humidity, and there are no allergens either. In fact, I read in some documents at the hospital that people stayed at the hotel above us so they could come to use this cave to cure respiratory illnesses.'

'Donna's right,' Idris said. I hadn't even noticed him walk over. 'Caves offer the ideal environment for getting into the current. The sea too,' he added, gesturing towards the waves. 'Anita will tell you how the wonders of yoga and reiki can improve by the sea. And think back to ancient times, how man would be drawn to caves for living.'

I'd noticed a couple of passers-by had gathered outside the cave, listening to Idris.

'Isn't that because there was nowhere else to shelter from the rain?' I asked, crossing my arms.

Idris laughed. 'Just *one* of the reasons.'

'How do you know all this?' a man watching him asked.

Idris sat on a rock, smiling. 'Please, sit,' he said. The couple looked at each other, shrugged, then sat before him. Others walking by slowed down to listen. One young girl headed over too, joining the couple. It amazed me to see how people were drawn to him.

'I lived with a great healer, many years ago,' he explained. 'He was a wise man, truly gifted. There were several of us, all living in a commune. It was there I came up with the process of getting into the current and everything else you see here.'

'Whereabouts was the commune?' I asked.

'We didn't focus on location,' he replied mysteriously.

I resisted rolling my eyes.

As Idris started talking about getting in the current, I walked to the back of the cave, pulling out my notepad. After about an hour, Idris walked in and set about painting nearby. The sound of his paintbrush soothed me into a gentle rhythm as I wrote. It was hard to focus at first, distracted by the sight of him painting, his eyes sometimes darting over to me, his fingers rubbing at the pigment of my curves as he did so. It was only when he headed outside, perching on a chalk rock with a cup of tea to talk to a growing circle of strangers gathered around him, that I was able to really focus. Before I knew it, my pen was tracing words on paper. It was only when I felt a tap on my shoulder that I stopped.

I'd filled pages and pages – more than I had in months!

Another tap. I looked up, blinking as if seeing light for the first time. It was Julien, a frown on his face.

'Your husband's here.'

Chapter Thirteen

Selma

Kent, UK
28 July 1991

Mike was standing outside the cave wearing jeans and a T-shirt, sweating in the growing heat. Behind him, a fisherman looped a line out into the waves, his dog running in and out of the froth, barking as it wagged its tail.

'So you did come here,' Mike said, shaking his head in disbelief as I walked towards him.

'You're the one who told me to leave,' I reminded him.

'Yeah, maybe to go stay with a friend or in a hotel. But here,' he said, looking at the cave. 'With *him*?' he added, flinging his hand towards Idris who was showing a teenage girl one of his paintings at the front of the cave. 'You're thirty-eight, Selma, not eighteen.'

'Why does it matter how old I am?'

'It's *embarrassing*. They'll all be talking about you, your little school-gate friends.'

'They're not my friends.'

'No, not any more after your little outburst last night.'

I clenched my jaw. I didn't want to think about that.

'Where's Becky?' I asked Mike.

'At Greg and Julie's. You should have seen Greg's face when I told him you'd left.'

'*You* told me to leave!' I said again.

'Then come back. It was an argument.'

I frowned. Should I go back? Was this completely and utterly crazy, living in a cave with a bunch of strangers?

But then I thought of all I'd written.

'No,' I said firmly. 'Not now. I just need some space. Think of it like a writing retreat or something.'

Mike laughed. 'A holiday a mile from your home? In a fucking cave with a man who thinks he's Christ?'

'I *need* this, Mike!'

Idris looked up at the sound of my voice.

Mike shook his head bitterly. '*Me me me.* It's always about you. What about what I need? What Becky needs?'

I raked my hands through my hair, feeling grains of sand on my fingertips. 'I know this looks selfish to you, but I promise you it isn't. If anything, I'm *doing* this for Becky. For us as a family. Because if I don't . . .' I paused.

Mike crossed his arms. 'Go on, say it. What will happen?'

'You know what will happen,' I said softly.

He looked me up and down in disgust. 'You call yourself a

mother but you're not. You can't handle it, Selma. You've never been able to. You're too bloody selfish to be a parent.'

I pursed my lips together. 'That's so unfair. It's just a couple of days. I'm on leave anyway for the next two weeks.'

'Yes, to look after Becky while she's on her summer holidays!' Mike retorted. He pointed his finger at me. 'I won't have you coming back, messing with our kid's emotions. Use these next two days to make some hard decisions, Selma. When I see you again, I want a hundred per cent or nothing, all right?'

I sighed. He was acting like a child. 'Fine.'

Mike peered over at Idris, curling his lip. Then he stormed off.

As he left the beach, all the fight went out of me. I sank down onto the sand and wrapped my arms around my knees as I looked out to sea. Had I made a terrible mistake coming here? Seeing Mike, hearing the anger in his voice, brought it home to me. Maybe this *did* make me a terrible mum.

After a while, I heard the soft pad of bare feet on sand. Idris sat beside me, adopting my pose as well: arms around his knees, face out to sea. We sat together silently, watching the waves until eventually our breathing matched.

In out, in out, in out.

It somehow drove the torment away, made me calm. He turned towards me, softly touching my arm.

'It will figure itself out,' he said. 'For now, stay, be *you*. The answers will come in their time.'

Then he got up and walked away.

'What if they don't?' I called after him.

'They will,' he said without turning.

* * *

For the rest of the day, I wrote. By the time dinner was served, I'd filled half my notepad.

'You were right about the cave,' I said as I fell into step with Donna. 'I've written loads.'

'What did I tell you? So, did you enter the current?'

I shot her a cynical look. 'I wouldn't go that far.'

We sat at the table and I took in the feast Donna had created: pesto pasta and chunks of brown bread, slices of chicken and beef to stir in. I had barely noticed my hunger as I'd written but now my tummy rumbled, my mouth watering at the sight of the food. Everyone started piling it onto their plates, buzzing from their day's work.

'Good day?' Idris asked me.

'Great,' I replied. 'Wrote more than I have in a while.'

His face lit up. 'You don't know how happy that makes me. This calls for a celebration.' He pulled out a bottle of gin with a flourish.

'You got gin!' I said.

He smiled and everyone cheered. 'To Selma,' he declared.

'To Selma!' they all shouted.

He opened the bottle and sloshed some into a cup. 'In honour of Selma, tonight we will all be her.'

I frowned. 'What do you mean?'

'It's a ritual we do for each new person who joins us,' Oceane said.

'That means we will drink nothing but gin tonight, Selma's favourite drink,' Idris said as he walked around the table, pouring gin into everyone's cups, 'and we will all paint our lips red,' he added, gesturing towards Oceane who was holding a red lipstick up in the air triumphantly.

'That's my lipstick!' I said.

'You left it in the bathroom. Finders keepers!' Oceane replied with a cheeky grin.

She slathered some on her lips and I tried to hide my irritation. I hated other people using my lipstick. I took an urgent sip of gin.

Just relax, I told myself.

My lipstick was passed around and, by the time it got to Caden and Julien, I was actually laughing as they applied it. Then it got to Idris, and everyone grew silent as they watched him slick it onto his full lips before he pouted.

'Beautiful,' Anita said, biting her lip. 'I've always loved a pretty boy.'

Caden put his hand to his heart, fluttering his eyelashes. 'Me too. I think I'm in love.'

Everyone laughed.

After we had finished our food, we went out onto the beach. My head felt dizzy from all the drink I'd had, full to the brim with this new experience too. It *was* like a writing retreat. With a strange bunch, granted, but fun nonetheless.

'It's amazing here, isn't it?' Anita said as we sat down by the fire.

'It's certainly interesting. I'm beginning to see why so many people are drawn here.'

'Like moths to a flame,' Anita said. 'Helps that Idris is easy on the eye too,' she added, her eyes boring into mine. 'Don't you think?'

'It's undeniable.'

'So you're attracted to him?'

I laughed. 'I didn't say that! It's like looking at a beautiful painting, purely aesthetic. What about you, what's your story?' I asked, desperate to change the subject. Truth was, I *was* finding myself drawn to Idris. It was impossible not to be. He was so gorgeous to look at, the glances he gave me every now and again turning my belly to fire.

'Oh it's not that exciting,' Anita replied. 'I still teach yoga, still rent a flat. I guess I was just getting fed up with how depressing things are. I've lost half the class with the recession – people just can't afford luxuries like yoga. Gym membership is down. Each day I go into work, everyone's looking miserable, worried they'll lose their job. And then this,' she said, looking around her with a smile. 'No talk of numbers, of money. Just fun and creativity. It makes a refreshing change, doesn't it?'

'I suppose it does.' I took another sip of gin. It was so nice to drink without having to worry about the pain of dealing with the early wake-up call from Becky the next morning while nursing a hangover.

I felt that guilt again. Maybe I should have gone back to see her today, to explain things? But I just couldn't bring myself to. Tomorrow. I'd go tomorrow.

'You only moved to Queensbay last year, right?' I said.

'Yep,' Anita said, taking a sip of her drink too. 'I had to apply for a new job, had a sleazy boss to deal with.'

'Ergh, I hate that. One of my husband's work friends is like that. Very touchy feely, always staring at my tits, even tried to ask me out. And that's after his wife just had a baby.'

'Scumbag,' Anita said, nostrils flared. 'Men, hey?' Her face lightened as she noticed Idris strolling over. 'Not all of them are bad though,' she murmured.

'Mind if I talk to Selma?' he asked her when he got to us.

Anita smiled and stood up. 'Sure, no problem.'

'Your husband seemed angry earlier,' Idris said with a frown when she left.

I laughed bitterly. 'Ironic considering *he* threw *me* out.'

'It's hard for some people to understand what we do here. Half the time it's shame that they're not brave enough to do the same. It highlights what's missing in their lives, holds a mirror up to them.'

'That's interesting,' I said, watching as a cloud passed over the moon. 'It's something I'm writing about actually. A man who escapes to the winter woods to find peace. But in the end, society can't help but infringe.'

Idris nodded thoughtfully. 'I like the sound of that.' He paused a moment then scooped up some sand, letting it fall between his fingers. 'My mother liked to write.'

'She did?'

He nodded. 'You remind me of her. She had dark hair like you, was beautiful, so very talented. She knew it too. I mean that in a good way,' he added quickly. 'You need to recognise your talent to pursue a career in writing, otherwise why do it?'

'True. Was she published?'

'No. But she tried.'

I wanted to ask him more: where he came from, what he did before this. But something in his eyes told me not to. He picked up a stick and drew a circle in the sand.

'As a boy, I'd escape to the beach. I would go to the sand and draw with my fingers. Early mornings were the best, the sand damp enough from the high tide for me to make distinctive indents. I'd spend hours doing it. Sometimes, people would walk by. Many would do their best to avoid ruining my creations. But others didn't even notice them there, they were so caught up in themselves. They'd trample all over them, ruining them all.'

'Some people! How did that make you feel?'

He smiled. 'I'd just start over again. I've never been one to get angry, or upset even.' His brow creased as he continued drawing a pattern in the sand. 'But then one day, a boy came along. He was a few years older than me, a teenager. And I sensed from a long way off he was a very angry boy. He stopped to watch what I was doing. I remained calm, just continued tracing patterns in the sand. Then he started kicking at the sand, scrubbing away all my drawings, every last one.'

I shook my head. 'Little shit. What did you do?'

'I thanked him – said I'd been planning to do that before going home for lunch anyway and he'd saved me a job.'

I raised an eyebrow. 'I would have been a lot less polite.'

Idris smiled to himself, swirling his finger in the sand, drawing an eye, a nose.

'What happened?' I asked.

'Saying that to him angered him even more. He jumped up and down on my hand, broke my fingers, told me I'd never draw again.'

'Jesus. That is one messed-up kid.'

Idris shrugged. 'Maybe. There will always be people who try to stop us. But we continue. We thrive, regardless.' He continued drawing in the sand in silence as I watched him. When he finally stopped, he'd created a detailed sand drawing of a young boy. 'But you know who the worst culprits are?'

'Let me guess. Ourselves?'

He swept the boy's face away and nodded. 'That's the thing with you, Selma. You *know*.' He tapped his head. 'You're not like the others. I don't feel like you're learning from me. I feel like I'm learning from you.'

'You keep saying that. It makes me feel old!'

'You should take yourself more seriously. Have more confidence in your actions. You're brave, Selma, you just don't know it.' Then he got up and walked away.

I peered up in the direction of my house and suddenly felt a soaring clarity. Idris was right, I needed to have more confidence in my actions. I kept saying Mike threw me out but, the truth was, I *wanted* to leave. I didn't want to leave Becky, of course, but I did want to leave the marriage. I was sure of it in that moment. The life and vitality I felt there, at that cave, was shining a light on the darkness of my normal life. Becky and my writing were the only bright spots. But everything else – Mike, my job, my so-called friends – they were all grey to me. This cave, these people, *Idris* . . . it felt like an explosion of colour.

And the writing! I'd done so much of it. I couldn't bear the thought of leaving that behind.

If I couldn't bear the thought of leaving, what did that mean? Could I really stay here, in this cave?

I looked at the others, most of them so naive, idealistic. But they were creating, they were happy. Wasn't that what counted? Not the rituals or the current, but the smiles on their faces and the work they produced. It was simple.

And that was what I craved: a simple life.

I caught Idris's eye as he watched me from the cave.

Was I brave enough to leave my old life behind?

I looked down at the drawing Idris had scrubbed away. All that remained was one eye that seemed to stare right into my soul.

Chapter Fourteen

Becky

Granada, Spain
19 June 2018

The straps of Becky's rucksack dig uncomfortably into her sunburnt shoulders as she climbs the hills above Granada. She'd arrived that morning in Spain, nervous as she'd been engulfed by the stifling heat while stepping off the plane. Speaking to her dad had helped make her mind up about coming to find her sister, but that didn't make it any less scary. One article in the *National Geographic* was flakey evidence. Yet it was all she had, despite doing some further research over the past few days. She had to start somewhere, didn't she? As her dad had said, she'd only regret it otherwise.

Despite this, the sight of her dogs looking sorrowful as she'd waved goodbye to them in David's garden the evening before had triggered an uneasy feeling. *Was* she doing the right thing? David had seemed worried when she'd told him, and she could understand why. Travelling alone, on what could turn out to be a wild goose chase. When she'd popped into the veterinary practice to let Kay know, her colleague had been delighted: 'Good on you!' she'd said. 'I admire you. You're brave, it's wonderful.'

'Will you be okay without me?' Becky had asked. 'I was planning to be back in work by now.'

'Your mother died less than two weeks ago, sweetheart. I had a whole month off when my dear ma passed away. Take all the time you want.'

Now, as Becky stares up at the labyrinth of white buildings set into the cliffs above her, she feels slight hope. Kay is right, she *is* being brave. And she might be meeting her sister soon!

That means she might see Idris too, which is a thought that doesn't appeal quite as much.

She looks at her guide book. *The gypsy caves of Sacromonte*, it reads, *a place popular with tourists because of its flamenco dancing and gypsy guitar players.*

She continues walking up the hill, the strum of the guitars growing louder along with the chatter of people. White buildings surround a plaza: shops, museums, cafés all built into caves on the side of the hills. It's pretty, starch white against blue skies. Tourists mill about, peering into the caves and taking photos. Becky pauses, looking back down towards Granada, the views breath-taking. She can see why Idris might have fled here, the beauty of it all. But it is also so busy, so touristy, a contrast to the informal cave community he'd set up in Kent.

A mother and daughter walk past, the mother frail, the daughter supporting her. Are they holidaying together? Becky can't help but wonder if she would have done the same if things had been different with her mum.

In fact, maybe she'd be travelling with her sister right now if she'd known about her.

Becky buys a cool drink then strolls towards the back of the crowd, watching as typically handsome Spanish men in white shirts play music, tourists clapping along to the beat. The music epitomises Spanish holidays in the sun, bringing back memories of the holiday Becky's dad treated her to a couple of months after they moved to Busby-on-Sea, which had felt like a kind of consolation prize for not having her mum around. Instead, it had made her even more achingly aware of her mum's absence as she sat across from her quiet, contemplative father at mealtimes, a contrast to her mum's constant chatter and vibrancy.

Becky sighs and notices some stray dogs loitering in an alleyway. Mixed breeds, one lean and golden, the other small and black. She can't help but gravitate towards them, reaching into her bag to see if she has any dog treats in there. They peer up when they see her, a small black terrier baring its teeth and growling.

'I'd keep away from that one,' a British voice with a Birmingham accent says. 'Looks vicious.'

Becky turns to see a man leaning against the wall, tall with short black dreadlocks, his nose pierced with a green jewel. He is wearing loose Bermuda shorts to his knees, a white T-shirt with a black tweed necklace around his neck, a stone hanging from it.

'It'll be fine,' she murmurs as she steps closer to the dogs. 'Just letting me know who's boss.' She gently places the treats she's found in her bag on the floor and the dogs slowly pad forward, the small black terrier still growling.

'My mate had a Jack Russell that looked like that little one,' the man says. 'Had one eye, looked cute as anything. Nearly bit my arm off when I tried to stroke it though.'

'That's terriers for you,' Becky says. 'Just takes them a while to trust people.'

The terrier takes one of the treats, chewing it thoughtfully. The other dog watches it, as though waiting for a signal. When the terrier takes another, the large dog leaps forward, gulping most of the treats up. The terrier slowly approaches Becky, wagging its tail. She leans down, softly stroking his ears.

'We have a dog whisperer in our midst,' the man says with a raised eyebrow.

'No, just a vet.'

'Cool. Where you from?'

'Sussex. You?'

'Can't you tell from the accent?'

'The Midlands?'

The man nods. He steps forward, putting his hand out. 'Kai.'

Becky shakes it. 'Becky.'

'Picking up strays again, Kai?' a smiling woman says. She's wearing jeans and a T-shirt with two avocados on it, beneath it the words 'Let's avocuddle'. Next to her is a stocky man with the same light hair as the woman.

'Becky, meet Hannah and Ed. Ed and Hannah, meet Becky. She's a vet!'

'Hello!' Hannah says, smiling at Becky. 'You here alone?'

Becky nods. It makes her think of her mum suddenly, like she should be here with her, searching for the child she lost as a newborn.

'We're about to get a drink,' Kai says. 'Want to join us?'

She looks at her watch to see it's nearly five. 'I need to go check out the caves. Thanks for the invite though.'

'Another cave lover!' Hannah declares.

'You a speleologist, like us?' Ed asks.

'I don't even know what a speleologist is,' Becky replies.

'We study caves,' Kai explains. 'I guess you could describe us as cavers with the science bit added.'

'That's really interesting.' Becky peers towards the caves lining the street. 'Do you know a lot about the caves here?'

'More than most,' Kai replies.

Becky pulls out the copy of *National Geographic* that she found in her mum's office. 'Do you recognise this cave?' she asks, pointing to the small cave pictured behind the group.

Kai takes the magazine, staring at it. Then he shakes his head. 'You're in the wrong place.'

Disappointment floods through Becky. 'But these are the Sacromonte caves, right? Please don't tell me I've come all this way for nothing.'

He laughs. 'Don't panic. There are other caves – up there, beyond the fence.' He points further up the hills towards a line of fence. 'This is where the gypsy community live, where all the tourists flock. But up there, that's where real life happens.'

Hannah nods. 'That's where we're heading after we have a drink.'

'Are you working up there then?' Becky asks.

They shake their heads. 'This is pleasure,' Kai says.

'We love caves so much, we decide to have holidays in them,' Ed adds as Hannah smiles. 'Lots of different people live up there. People passing through. Others who've found their homes

161

there. They keep away from the tourist trail. Not many people know the caves are up there.'

Becky looks at the fence, at the bushy land, the sun a sharp yellow beyond it. That would make more sense, wouldn't it? Idris holed up there with his daughter. She feels a thrill of excitement and trepidation at the thought she might be moments away from seeing the man her mum had an affair with . . . and the sister she never knew.

'Well, I'll see you up there,' she says, going to march up the hill.

'Wait,' Kai says, gently grabbing her hand and stopping her. 'They can be a bit funny about people just turning up and poking their noses in.'

'But isn't that what you're all about to do?' Becky replies.

'My cousin lives there so we're staying with him,' Kai explains.

Becky sighs. 'Oh, I see.'

'You can come with us if you want?' Kai says. 'But first you need to join us for a drink, just to make sure you're not a serial cave killer.'

She looks at the three of them, their friendly faces, sunburnt and happy. She had imagined doing this alone, a solitary search. But maybe she needs help after all? She shrugs.

'Sure. I can't promise anything about the serial killer side though.'

They end up in a small café set into a cave, sitting around a table topped with red and white patched cloth. Hannah orders them coffee and cake in Spanish, and they all arrive in colourful china, the cakes' thick triangle wedges topped with what looks like jam.

'*Piononos*,' Hannah explains. 'A Granada speciality.'

Becky takes a bite, cinnamon and lemon filling her mouth. 'Delicious,' she says between mouthfuls.

'My favourite part is the rum in this cake,' Kai says with a wink. 'So what brings you here then?' he asks Becky. 'I get the impression this isn't just a holiday for you. You have a determined look on your face.'

'Like when Kai sees a new headlamp's come on the market,' Ed adds with a wry smile. They all laugh.

Becky looks at each of their eager faces. What's the harm in telling them?

'I'm trying to find my sister,' she says, the word *sister* sounding foreign on her tongue. 'I think she might have been brought here when she was a baby.'

She suddenly imagines her mum forlorn in the cave, arms empty, tears falling down her cheeks, unable to report Idris in case social services found out. Did it really happen like that?

She feels tears flood to her eyes and looks down at her food, coughing slightly. She notices Kai watching her with pity.

'You've never met your sister?' Hannah asks Becky softly.

'It's a long story,' Becky says, looking back up with a smile. 'I just think she might have lived here at some point. Remember the little girl in the photo I showed you? It could be her, she'd be about the right age.' She shrugs, taking a sip of her strong coffee. 'It's a bit of a wild goose chase but I need to feel like I've tried.'

'Absolutely,' Kai says. 'You'll only regret it otherwise.'

They all look up towards the caves above and Becky takes a deep breath. She hopes she'll find her sister. She really does.

* * *

After eating, the four of them head up the hill. The views are spectacular, the sun still hot on their necks, the sound of crickets muffling their ears.

Kai is clearly the joker, pretending at one point to trip and slip off the cliff, sending the three of them rushing towards the edge to see him standing on a large ledge below. It's also clear Hannah and Ed are an item, just subtle hints in the way Ed puts his hand on Hannah's back to guide her towards the fence; how she looks up and smiles at him occasionally. Becky surprises herself by suddenly yearning to be here with someone, to have a partner to lean on. She's had boyfriends over the past few years but nothing as serious as her first big relationship, just the odd fling at veterinary college or awkward dates with friends of friends, even a vet who'd worked at the practice for a few weeks as a locum. Problem is, she enjoys her own company too much . . . and the company of her dogs. It's hard for a man to match up to the tranquillity and independence of her life. They tend to bring in too much drama, too much neediness. She likes the little world she's created for herself, just her and the dogs. But she does yearn for male companionship sometimes and she does want children, eventually. She keeps telling herself she's still young, but she's been saying that for years now.

At least she isn't here completely alone. She's walking in Granada with three strangers she met just an hour ago, searching for a sister she's never known. She shakes her head. Unbelievable. What would her mum think? Becky smiles to herself. She'd like it. Not just the fact Becky was trying to find her sister. But also the *adventure* of it; the impulsiveness.

The smile slips from Becky's face. She isn't doing this to

impress her mum. She is doing it for *her*, to find her sister. She shrugs her rucksack up, legs aching under the weight. As she reaches the fence, Kai puts his hand out, helping her over some rocks.

'Well, this could be it,' he says. 'You might be meeting your sister soon.'

'Maybe.'

They walk beyond the fence and a little further up until the cave dwellings come into view. Many have doors, some with structures built out from the mountains with colourfully painted tin roofs. The smell of delicious food being cooked fills the air, reggae music coming from a stereo in the distance mingling with laughter and talking, dogs barking, even the sound of a child playing. It sits in contrast to the touristy gypsy caves below, these caves more colourful and jaunty, ad-hoc and messy.

'This is real living,' Kai says, hands on his hips as he takes it all in. 'Not living set out to impress tourists.'

Becky thinks of her sister being here as a child. It wouldn't be how Becky would have liked to live, but it looks comfortable enough.

'Yep,' Ed replies with a satisfied grin. 'What's not to love? Reggae music. No tourists.'

'And caves!' Hannah adds.

Becky can't imagine living like this. It feels too claustrophobic. Even the cave where her mum lived, with all its vastness, would feel too much, people living on top of each other.

They all walk up to the first row of caves. A young woman is sitting outside the first one, smoking a cigarette and reading a book. Above her bright blue door hangs colourful bunting. The sweet smell of something cooking drifts out towards them, the tinkle of soft music.

The woman peers up when she sees them. 'No tourists,' she says, her voice heavily accented. Becky guesses Italian.

'It's okay,' Kai says. 'I know Dean.'

The woman's face relaxes. 'Ah, sorry. We just don't like people coming to watch us like we are animals in a zoo. Up there,' she says, jutting her chin towards a line of caves two rows above them.

Kai, Ed and Hannah go to walk up the path but Becky stays where she is. 'You coming?' Kai asks.

'I'll find you,' she replies. She takes a moment to stare up at the caves. If her sister is here, chances are she'll meet her soon . . . and Idris. How will she know it's her? Will she look like Becky? Like their mum?

Or like Idris?

She pulls her mum's copy of *National Geographic* out and approaches the woman. 'I'm looking for someone,' she says, pointing to the photo of Idris and the little girl. 'Maybe you can help?'

The Italian woman shakes her head as she notices the date. 'I've only been here two years. You need to find Julien. That's him there,' she says, gesturing to a tall black man in the photo. 'He's been here the longest, he knows everyone. He lives there.'

Becky follows the direction the woman's pointing towards the top of the mountain to see a solitary cave as its peak.

'He gets a bit confused so don't be surprised if he says something strange. It's not his fault. We think it's probably Alzheimer's but he doesn't want to see a doctor. His decision.' The woman shrugs and continues reading her book.

Becky thanks her then continues up the path, past more caves, including one with charred insides, as though it's been set on fire. People are going about their daily lives: cooking on small barbecues or makeshift kitchens, drinking beer as they listen to music, reading and laughing. She tries to recognise anyone who might look like her sister among them, Idris too, but nobody does.

At the next row of caves, she sees Kai in the distance, hugging a man with a head of curly dark hair.

'This is Dean,' he says to Becky when she approaches them. 'Dean, this is Becky.'

'Welcome to the best views in Andalusia,' Dean says, sweeping his hands towards the spectacular scene sprawling beyond them, tree-clad hills tapering down towards the pretty white buildings of Granada. Behind him is a decent-sized cave, bigger than the others she's seen, neat and sparse with a small single bed and a good amount of floor space. There's even a small kitchen and, to Becky's surprise, a light which is brightening the darker parts of the cave. Hannah and Ed are unloading their backpacks beneath it, taking quick sips of their water as they look up at the cave with smiles on their faces.

'I was only expecting three visitors, but I can squeeze an extra in,' Dean says, looking at Becky.

'Oh no, it's fine,' she says. 'I'm staying in Granada.'

'Sure?' Dean asks. 'Won't often have the chance to sleep in a cave overnight.'

Becky gets a flash of her mum then, lying dead in her arms with her eyes staring up at the cave's roof.

Becky blinks the image away then nods. 'I'm sure.'

'You guys hungry?' Dean asks, gesturing towards his tiny kitchen.

'We just ate,' Hannah says.

Dean smiles. 'Time for beer then!'

He goes to a fridge and opens it.

'So you have electricity here?' Becky asks as she takes the beer he hands her.

'Yep, all rigged up. Pretty sophisticated set-up,' Dean replies.

Was her mum's cave like that? She can't remember.

'So I hear you're looking for your sister?' Dean says.

Becky nods and pulls a magazine out, showing the photo to Dean, gesturing to the blurry photo of the man she thinks is Idris and the little girl.

Dean studies it and nods. 'I wasn't there then but yeah, I know about that dude,' he says, pointing to Idris. 'Idris, right?'

So it is him.

'Is he still here?' she asks.

Dean shakes his head. 'Nope.' The disappointment Becky feels is almost crushing. Her little sister, just a few years old by then, wouldn't have stayed if Idris left. 'Like I said,' Dean continues, 'I wasn't here when he was. But I've heard of him from Julien and some others. Unmistakable with that long hair, right?'

'What about the girl?' Kai asks.

'There were a few people with him,' Dean says. 'He had this cult leader act going on apparently, thought he'd found the meaning of life. They still follow some of what he preached up there,' he says, peering up at the top caves. 'He was here five years, made quite an impression. Something spooked him though so he left.'

Becky frowns. 'What spooked him?'

Dean shrugs. 'No idea, it's just what Julien told people.'

'Maybe your sister stayed on?' Hannah says to Becky, putting her hand on her shoulder and giving her a sympathetic smile.

'She would have only been five,' Becky says.

'Which would put her in her twenties now?' Dean asks. Becky nods. 'I don't know every single person here, quite a few at the top keep themselves to themselves. There *are* a few girls in their twenties with light hair like yours and your sister's though. Would be worth you going up there, looking around. A couple may have taken her in, that's the kind of thing people do here. Tell them you know me if they ask. If you have no luck, ask Julien. He's been here the longest.'

'Yes, the girl at the first cave mentioned him,' Becky says.

'He's a bit odd,' Dean says. 'But then I guess we all are around here,' he adds with a quirk of the eyebrow.

'I'll come with you to talk to him,' Kai says.

'No, I'm fine alone.' Becky realises her voice sounds hard as she says that. She smiles and softens it. 'Thank you anyway.'

Then she heads up the hill, determined.

Chapter Fifteen

Becky

Granada, Spain
19 June 2018

In the distance, the slowly setting sun makes the sky blush as a deep mournful tune is played on a flute nearby. As Becky gets to the higher caves, she feels a different vibe, more insular . . . more serious. People talk in low voices, stopping when they see her approach. Others seem deep into whatever it is they're doing: one woman sits at the edge of the cliff, rocking back and forth as she writes. Another weaves a basket, seemingly in her own world. Becky searches for someone who looks like the girl from the article in their faces but many of them have dark hair and eyes.

'Do you know this girl?' she asks each person she crosses. They all shake their heads and her disappointment mounts. Her sister must have left with Idris.

She pauses before she gets to the very top cave. It sits like a small ramshackle castle at the peak of a mountain. When she draws closer, she sees an old man standing outside, whittling a figure out of wood with a small Stanley knife.

It's Julien; she recognises him from the article. His greying beard is tangled and down to his chest and there are wrinkles around his brown eyes which are narrowed as they observe her. She thinks of how the Italian girl and Dean had described him. She needs to be patient, gentle. Her grandfather had Alzheimer's, she remembers how confused he would get, angry too sometimes.

He stops abruptly when he sees Becky.

'I'm Becky,' she says walking up to him with her hand out. 'Becky Rhys.'

'Thought I recognised you.' He places his knife on the table next to him. His movements are slow, laboured. He must be in his seventies. He takes her hand in his rough one.

'What do you mean, recognised?' she asks him, her hand still in his.

'Your mum,' he says. 'You have her face.'

Becky takes a deep breath. 'I'm really sorry to say she passed away a couple of weeks ago.'

His face whitens.

'Here, sit down,' she says, taking him into the cave and helping him sit in a chair. He looks ahead of him for a while, clearly shocked.

Eventually, he looks up at Becky. 'Who did it?' he asks.

It sends a chill through Becky. But then she remembers how confused he must get.

'Nobody did anything,' she says gently. 'It was cancer.'

The old man's shoulders relax. 'Oh. Well, that's a shame. I liked her. Let's light a candle for her.'

He gets a wax candle from a box full of them, lighting it with trembling fingers. The spark lights and the cave is illuminated. Becky looks around her. It's smaller than Dean's, with a roll-out bed, a small kitchen and table, two battered armchairs . . . and a wall full of paintings: people's faces, stars and moons, solitary eyes staring out at them.

Are these Idris's paintings? They look just like them.

Becky's own eyes alight on a small painting in the corner of the cave of a woman kneeling down, her long dark hair trailing down her back, the sun above her. It's her mum. She walks up to it, puts her fingers against the face. She looks so sad.

'What brings you here?' Julien asks, gesturing to the other armchair.

She sits, feels old springs creak beneath her thighs. 'I'm looking for my sister. She would have been very young when she was here.'

Julien frowns, as though he's grappling with a memory. Then he nods. 'Yes, yes, the baby. Solar.'

Solar. So that was her sister's name.

'When Idris left this place, did he take her with him?' she asks Julien.

He nods again. Disappointment threads through Becky. So she definitely wouldn't be meeting her sister today.

'Where did they go?' she asks.

'Italy.' He frowns. 'Or was it Slovenia? No, France . . . I think.'

Becky's heart goes out to him. He's very confused.

'Are those Idris's paintings?' she asks Julien.

'Yes, this was once Idris's cave. He said I could take it over when they left.'

'Why didn't you go with him?'

'I fell in love.' His face softens as he looks at a photo of a woman with long red plaited hair. It seems to have been taken many years ago.

'Is she still here?' Becky asks gently.

He shakes his head sadly. 'She was older than me. Was taken last year.'

Becky leans over, squeezing his hand. 'I'm sorry.'

He shrugs. 'Such is life.'

'Why did Idris leave?' Becky asks delicately. 'Dean mentioned something about him running from something, someone?'

Julien blinks and looks down at his tea. 'He never said. But I know he had enemies in the UK. People didn't like him, didn't *understand* him, didn't understand *all* of us. They accused him of taking their families away, their wives.'

Becky thinks of that summer, how the fascination for the people living in the cave and Idris in particular soon turned to anger. She heard it in the muttering at the café whenever her dad took her there. The funny looks people gave her mum when they met up. The articles in the papers she caught glimpses of. And her own dad's anger too of course.

'You think someone was after Idris?' Becky asks.

Julien shrugs. 'Maybe. Or maybe he was just paranoid. He wasn't the same after we left the UK and your mum.' He suddenly smiles. 'He loved your mum. Never seen a love as strong as that.'

'Then why did he take my sister away from her?' Becky asks, a trace of frustration in her voice.

'Life's a mystery.' A bell rings and Julien's face lights up. 'Feasting!' he declares. He stands up. 'Come on. Don't want to be late.'

'Feasting?'

'It was your mum's favourite part of the day.'

Curious, Becky follows him to a large cave with a huge table dominating it. It's the biggest cave Becky has seen here, stretching across about fifty metres. Delicious smells waft from a small kitchen, a woman with a long grey plait down her back stirring what looks like fish stew in a pot as a man with an extravagant moustache pours red wine into a large carafe.

Hanging from the ceiling are faded paper flowers and more of Idris's paintings adorn the walls, these ones of people eating. People are sitting around the table, chatting away. Becky assumes it must be a type of dining area for the people who dwell in the caves up there.

The woman at the stove turns and smiles at Becky. 'Who do we have here then?' She has an Italian accent, like the girl from the first cave.

Becky explains who her mum was and the woman's face lights up. 'How wonderful. I never met your mother but have heard all about her.'

'She's no longer with us,' Julien says sadly.

The table grows quiet.

'I'm sorry,' the Italian woman says, placing her hand on Becky's shoulder and looking her in the eye.

'Thank you,' Becky replies, not sure what else to say. They all seem rather intense.

'Will you join us for dinner?' the man with the moustache asks.

'No, it's fine, I'd better head back to my hotel.'

'Hotel food?' the woman declares. 'Pfft. Come,' she says, walking to the table and patting a spare seat as those around the table smile in encouragement. 'You will sit with us.'

Becky hesitates a moment. Maybe some of these people knew Idris and Solar too? 'Okay, if you're sure?' she asks.

'Of course,' the woman says. 'We have plenty.'

Becky takes the spare seat and smiles at the other people around the table. There are seven of them, ranging from a young skinny girl with a red bob to a deeply tanned older man.

The Italian woman wipes her hands on her red apron. 'I am Berenice and this is my husband Mattia.' She introduces everyone else as her husband sloshes wine into the glasses around the table, including Becky's.

Becky takes a sip of hers. It tastes delicious and fruity. The tanned older man stands and helps Berenice bring the fish stew over, ladling it onto everyone's plates.

'You started already!' a voice says. They all look up to see the Italian girl from the first cave holding a cake, Kai beside her. 'I've brought another guest. This is Kai.'

'All are welcome to the feast!' Mattia declares.

'Feast? Sounds good.' Kai takes the seat across from Becky and winks. 'All going okay?'

'Fine,' she replies. 'You didn't need to come check on me, I wouldn't want you missing out on time with your cousin.'

'Just wanted to make sure you hadn't got attacked by a small black terrier. Anyway, I'm here a whole week, plenty of time to catch up with my cousin.'

She can't help but smile. She's pleased he's here.

'Your friend?' Berenice asks Becky.

'Yes, and Dean's cousin,' Becky replies.

The Italian girl who came with Kai sits next to him, and Berenice shouts something at her in Italian.

The girl flings her hands up in the air. '*Mamma! Abbastanza! Chill!*' She looks at Becky. 'She's angry because I'm late for dinner. Papa's only just started serving!' she adds, giving her mother an exasperated look.

Her parents start arguing, and Becky exchanges a look with Kai.

'Oh don't worry!' the girl says. 'They're always arguing. I'm Carina by the way.'

Becky thinks of her own parents. They didn't really argue much. More brooding silences. There was just one time she overheard her mum losing her temper. It was just before she left for good, and Becky's dad had accused her of being just like the grandmother Becky had never met but only seen photos of. Her mum had exploded with anger. She'd always been touchy about her mum, like the time Becky found a photo of her grandmother in an old shoebox.

'Is that you, Mummy?' she'd asked her mum.

Her mum had snatched the photo away from Becky. 'I'm nothing like her!'

But the truth was, her mum *did* look like her: the same glossy dark hair, full red lips, curves. Like a Hollywood actress, was how her dad would describe her, in the days when they were still together.

'It's cool you're here with your parents,' Kai says to Carina now, Becky's memories dispersing. 'Did you come here together?'

Carina shook her head. 'They came here first, while I was at university. I followed. Luckily, there was a free cave going *far* away from this one.' She gives her mum an affectionate wink and her mother flaps her tea towel at her, smiling. Becky looks at the two of them. If her mum had gone to live in the cave when Becky was older, would Becky have done the same and followed her? She'd had no power as a child to do that. But as a teenager . . .

She shakes her head, taking a sip of wine. Pointless thoughts. And who would want to live in a cave anyway? She's sure it is perfect for everyone here, but not her.

Carina's mother stands at the head of the table, her husband sitting down beside her.

'Tonight, we have new guests,' she says, smiling at everyone. 'So tonight, we shall *be* our guests.'

Becky and Kai frown.

'It's a tradition,' Carina explains. She looks up at her mother. 'We don't know them enough, Mamma.'

'Pah,' her mother says, waving her hand about. She walks to the back of the room, rummaging about in a drawer, then brings back some gem stickers, a long string of blue wool and scissors. 'We will pass this around,' she instructs, 'and each person must cut off some wool and tie their hair up with it like Becky's.' She gestures towards Becky's blue hairband, 'and use this gem as a nose stud, like Kai,' she says.

Carina laughs, shaking her head. 'Inventive, Mamma, very inventive.'

Mother and daughter smile at each other. Becky looks between them. The two women clearly have a fiery relationship, but they somehow make it work. Maybe she would have found a way to make things work with her mum if she'd given it a chance. She'd always thought, even if her mum had stayed, they would have grown apart anyway due to being so different. Her dad had told her that when she'd got upset about her mum not attending her graduation. 'You would never have been close, Becky,' he'd said. 'You're so different.'

But Becky hadn't given their relationship much of a chance, had she? Maybe they *would* have got on.

'Where does this ritual come from?' Kai asks, taking some wool and tying it around his hair.

'There was a man here once, many years ago,' Carina explains. 'His ways were passed from one person to the next.'

'Idris,' Becky says.

Carina nods. 'I would have loved to meet him,' she said dreamily.

'Do you know if anyone else lived here when he did, apart from Julien?' Becky asks.

Berenice shakes her head, smiling affectionately at Julien. 'Just this old man.' He smiles back.

Becky drinks more wine, enjoying how it makes her head swim, easing the disappointment of not finding her sister here. She takes a forkful of the stew, tastes bursting on her tongue: ripe tomatoes, citrus, spices, fish and pasta.

'This is amazing,' she says.

'Thank you,' Berenice says with a smile. 'So where is home for you, Becky?'

'A little village in Sussex,' she replies, suddenly missing her cottage and her dogs.

'And you?' Mattia asks Kai.

'I'm a bit of a nomad,' he replies. 'Travel wherever my job takes me.'

'You will settle one day?' Berenice asks.

'Maybe it'll be here?' her husband adds.

'I wouldn't call this settling,' Becky says.

Berenice frowns. 'Why not? Homes can be discovered by accident, like here many centuries ago. When Granada was recaptured from the Arabs, the Arabs fled but buried their treasures here on the hills on their way, hoping one day they would come back. Their slaves, once free, came to these very hills to dig for the treasure.'

'Legend has it this is how the caves were formed,' Carina adds. 'Holes from the slaves digging here.'

Berenice nods. 'Soon they grew bored of digging . . .'

'And they ended up living in the holes they dug,' Carina says. 'Their caves . . .'

'. . . their homes,' her mother finishes for her.

They both laugh.

Carina smiles. 'I'm so used to my mamma telling me this story, we end up telling it together when guests are here.'

Becky thinks of her own mum's stories, elaborate imaginings about princesses in snowy woods and flying unicorns, told with such drama each night Becky would beg for more. She feels an aching grief in her heart for her mum then and takes yet another slug of wine to bury it away.

As they eat, she learns the people she saw writing and weaving baskets earlier were in what they called 'the current', another ritual passed down by Idris and his followers. She can see why her mum may have been drawn to that, the act of completely immersing herself in her writing, no distractions . . . no needy child.

After they've eaten, they gather all their plates up and pretty

Spanish music is turned on as they drink more. Becky and Kai find a floor cushion just outside the cave, sitting together and watching the caves below.

'This place is great, isn't it?' Kai asks.

'It is. I could see you living here actually.'

'Not you?'

'Nope. Wouldn't feel like home. Plus I wouldn't fit my three dogs in.'

'Three?' Kai asks, laughing. Becky digs her phone out and shows him a photo of the dogs. 'Wow, they are big, gorgeous dogs.'

'Thank you.'

'So what made you decide to become a vet?' Kai asks her.

'There were horses behind the house I grew up in,' she says. 'I became a little obsessed with them. I guess it came from that.'

As she says that, an image comes to her. A brown and white dog. The sound of waves. A cave in the distance. And Idris, his hand on her shoulder, blood on his fingertips.

She shakes the memory away. Where did that come from?

'What about you?' she asks Kai. 'How did you get into caving?'

Kai takes a sip of his wine, licking his full lips. 'My dad's Jamaican. He grew up near the Gourie Cave, the longest cave in Jamaica. He'd always talk about it, make up stories about it. He brought me this amazing book about caves and I read it every night, the same pages over and over.'

Becky remembers her mum giving her a book on caving. It had been just after she left the house for the first time. Becky had treasured it. But when it became clear her mum wasn't coming back, she'd torn it to pieces.

'When Dad earned enough money,' Kai continues, 'he took me,

my mum and all my sisters back to Jamaica when I was ten. First chance he got he took me to the cave. No turning back after that.'

'*All* your sisters?'

He smiles. 'Yeah. I have five of them.'

Becky laughs. 'Jesus! Do you still go back to Jamaica?'

'Yeah, when I can. Whenever I speak to my dad on the phone, he bangs on about me going to live out there with him.'

'Will you?'

He shrugs. 'I don't know, maybe one day. What about your parents?' he asks. 'How come you only just found out about this sister of yours?'

Becky thinks for a moment about telling him everything. But she barely knows him. So she shrugs. 'Long story.'

Kai sprawls his long legs out. 'We have all evening.'

'Maybe another time.'

'I hope there is another time,' Kai says, smiling. 'Don't want you disappearing into nowhere after we leave Spain.'

Becky smiles back at him. 'I might give you my email address.'

'*Might.*' He sighs. 'Cruel, dangling a carrot like that.'

Becky finds herself smiling some more. It's just an exchange of emails. And there's nothing Kai has said that suggests he's attracted to her. Maybe that's what she likes so much, how *friendly* he is without trying to hit on her.

Hannah, Ed and Dean appear from the path then. Kai jumps up and gives them high fives. The rest of the evening descends into drunken fun, but Becky feels as though she's watching from inside a bubble. She wraps her arms around herself, staring out at the setting sun and yearning for the warmth of her dogs by her feet.

After a while, she notices Berenice walk outside, picking up a flute and playing a sorrowful tune to the moon above.

So it was her who'd been playing that beautiful music earlier.

Becky goes out to her, watching her until she finishes playing. It makes her think of her mum, of those sad last moments in the cave with her, and her eyes fill with tears.

'You play beautifully,' she tells Berenice after.

'Thank you.'

Becky leans against a small wall that's been created from stones. 'It's lovely here,' she says.

'It is, isn't it?'

They both survey the town for a few moments, silent as they take in the flickering lights against twilight skies, the glimpses of white caves below and the distant sound of flamenco music and cheering tourists.

'Do you visit the gypsy caves much?' Becky asks Berenice.

'Sometimes. But I prefer it here.' She turns to Becky, looking her in the eye. 'Did you live with Idris and your mother?'

Becky shakes her head. 'My mum and I had a . . . difficult relationship. She left when I was eight.'

Berenice is quiet for a few moments then she smiles sadly. 'Yes, I left Carina's father once.'

Becky looks at her in surprise.

'It was when Carina was at university,' she explains. 'I left Mattia to come here. I'd spent so long being just a mother, I needed to get away. I have four children, you see, three of them are still in Italy. It is hard, often *thankless* work.' She looks Becky in the eye. 'Your mother may have felt the same.'

'But she only had me.'

182

'Still difficult. You'll see when you have children.' She looks back out over the city again. 'It was good to be free, to live in a cave with another woman, something I'd never done before since I was with my mamma.'

'Another woman?'

Berenice laughs. 'Not what you think! Just a friend, a free spirit. Then my husband came to find me. I still remember him walking up there with his suitcase,' she says, gesturing towards the winding path. 'He said to me, "I know you still love me. So I've come to live with you."' She laughs a beautiful laugh. 'I was happy to see him. It was a moment of madness for me. But it ended up being the best thing that ever happened to us.'

Becky imagines her dad doing the same. How different would her childhood have been?

'Dean told me about your quest,' Berenice says. 'My friend was here when Idris was.'

Becky peers around her. 'Is she still here?'

Berenice shakes her head. 'She has gone back to France. Come, I want to show you something.'

She starts walking down the path and Becky follows her until they reach the charred cave she'd seen when she first arrived. They stop at the entrance.

'My friend told me there was a fire here,' Berenice explains. 'It was where Idris stored his paints. See, he'd built a gate across it,' she adds, gesturing towards nails drilled into the sides. 'One night, my friend says they all woke to see flames in the sky. She found Idris here, crying as he looked into the cave, watching as all of his paints and brushes turned to ash. The next day, they all left. But not before he painted *that* over the charred walls.'

She points towards a large face, one side white, one side black. Next to the face is a solitary eye.

'*Mal de Ojo,*' Berenice says, pointing to the eye. 'The evil eye. Julien often talks of someone Idris was running from. My friend tells me, when Idris left with his followers, the child with them was wearing an amulet bracelet with the same evil eye on it to ward off danger.'

'That would have been my sister,' Becky says. 'Do you know where they went when they left?'

Berenice nods. 'My friend told me one of the followers, Darja, would often talk of the Postojna caves in Slovenia where she grew up.'

Hadn't Julien mentioned Slovenia?

'The day of the fire,' Berenice continues, 'Idris declared that was where they would all go next. My friend decided to stay but the others went, including the child. If you are searching for your sister, then that might be where you need to go.'

Becky looks back at the evil eye, its whiteness stark against the blue. If Idris had given Solar a bracelet with it on, did he think *she* was in danger too?

There is only one way to find out. Becky has to go to Slovenia.

Chapter Sixteen

Selma

Kent, UK
30 July 1991

I stood outside my house, feeling sunburnt and windswept. It was like I'd been on a gap year, touring every corner of the earth. And yet I'd been gone just two days. In my bag, my notepad pulsed, all the pages filled to bursting after another day of writing. I couldn't believe how prolific the cave had made me! But that wasn't what was important that day. Becky was.

And so was Mike and what I was preparing to say to him.

I put the key in the lock and let myself in. The TV was on, familiar clattering sounds from the kitchen ringing out.

'Hello?' I called out.

'Mummy!' Becky ran down the hallway and bulldozed into my stomach as Mike looked on from the kitchen, brow knitted. 'Mummy, mummy, mummy!' Becky repeated.

'Oh darling.' A rush of emotions ran through me, right at the top of them guilt. When I wrote, hours turned into seconds so it had seemed as though I'd spent barely any time apart from Becky, but I could see as I looked down into her pretty little face it had felt much longer to her.

'I missed you, Mummy,' Becky said. 'Where have you *been*?'

'Just a little holiday,' I said, stroking her blonde hair back from her face.

She grabbed my hand and pulled me towards her dollhouse. 'Play with me, Mummy, play with me! Daddy got me new bedroom furniture for it.'

'Let me go chat to Daddy for a second.'

Becky's face fell and, for a moment, I thought about just returning, going back to my normal life, just so I didn't have to see her so disappointed. But then I remembered how happy I'd been the past two days. A happy mum means a happy child. It might take time, but eventually Becky would reap the rewards.

'Can we talk?' I asked Mike with a renewed determination.

He nodded, face expressionless, and I followed him to the kitchen.

He picked up a knife and started to angrily chop up a cucumber. 'You look tanned.'

'It's been hot.'

'I haven't noticed, been too busy being a single dad.'

'Oh Mike, it's been two days.'

He stopped chopping and turned to look at me, blue eyes flashing with anger. 'Two days when I didn't have a clue if you'd be coming back or not! It's your two weeks to look after Becky, for Christ's sake. I had to book time off at the last minute, you know how my boss is about that kind of thing, especially with the way things are at work at the moment with all the threat of redundancies!'

I looked down at the floor, not sure what to say.

He took a deep breath. 'Look, I'm sorry, I promised I wouldn't do this.' He walked towards me suddenly and took my hand in his. I could see the sense of panic on his face, as if he knew what was about to happen. It made me feel even worse.

'I'm *pleased* you're back,' he said. 'You got it out of your system, didn't you? Now we can get on with things. In fact, how about we get Greg and Julie to look after Becky tonight and go out, just the two of us?'

I shook my head, sadness filling me. 'No, Mike.'

'Fine. If you want to stay in, we can do that. I'll cook us pasta.'

'I mean, I'm not coming back.'

Mike stepped away from me, shocked. 'Are you fucking kidding me?'

'You said a hundred per cent or nothing. I can't give this marriage a hundred per cent, I just can't! I haven't been able to for a while. Neither have you,' I added gently.

He took deep shuddery breaths. 'So you're going back *there*?'

'Yes.'

'But I thought—' He put his hands to his face then pulled them away again. 'So this is it? You're moving out?'

'I think so.'

'You *think* so? Make up your fucking mind, Selma!' He paced up and down the kitchen. 'Jesus, what have I done wrong? Is it the writing? I've been good to you, let you reduce your hours to write, taken Becky out on Sundays when your deadline approached. And all for a paltry few hundred pounds.' He stopped pacing, looking me in the eye. 'Or is it him, that man? Are you fucking him? Is that what I need to do to stop you from flinching whenever I touch you, dye my hair and grow it?'

I felt my cheeks burn with humiliation. 'No, of course I'm not sleeping with him! Don't be ridiculous. I just can't live this life any more,' I said, feeling strangely tranquil despite the momentous nature of the occasion.

'You mean you can't be a mum and a wife?'

'How can you say that? I'll never stop being a mum.'

Mike held my gaze then crossed his arms. 'Life doesn't work like this, Selma. Especially family life. You can't just go live in a cave when it takes your fancy. What about work? Please tell me you'll be going to work.'

I hadn't really thought about that. 'I suppose I'll have to.'

'She supposes she has to,' Mike mimicked me with a bitter laugh. 'Listen to yourself! We have a mortgage to pay. We'd all love to escape the rat race. And Jesus Christ, you've achieved that better than most, doing your little hobby two days a week. But oh no, that's not enough for you. *We're* not enough for you.'

Little hobby. He'd never understood, not like the others in the cave had.

Not like *Idris* did.

I thought of what Idris had said to me the evening before. *You should take yourself more seriously. Have more confidence in your actions.*

'It's clear whatever I say won't make you understand,' I said calmly. I took a deep breath. 'The fact remains, our marriage is over.'

There, better said like that. Quick, painless, like pulling off a plaster. Why draw it out? I was being kind to Mike doing it this way. He might not see that now but, eventually, he'd be grateful.

Mike's face flickered with pain.

'This can't come as too much of a surprise,' I quickly said. 'You must have been able to tell how much I've been struggling, Mike?'

'Yes, and I told you to go to the bloody doctor to get some more anti-depressants but you never did, did you? I thought things had got better after the problems you had after having Becky. But it's all just come back again.'

'It's not like that! Those were baby blues. I – it's just writer's block, it's been getting me down.'

'Maybe we're making excuses when none are needed. Maybe it's just the way you are, Selma.' He paused, his gaze hardening. 'Maybe you're just like your mother.'

I looked at him in shock. He *knew* that was the worst possible thing to say to me.

'I'm nothing like her,' I hissed, trying to remain calm. I would *not* let him wind me up.

'Really? Ignoring your child, leaving your husband. Selfish, cruel. Becky will probably end up bitter and messed up just like you because of her mother.'

'How fucking dare you?' I screamed.

Becky came running into the room. 'Mummy? What's wrong?'

'I'm just telling your mum she's selfish like your grandmother,' Mike spat.

I took some deep breaths to calm myself. I was *not* like my mother and I was going to prove that by calming down.

'Mummy?' Becky said in a trembly voice.

I turned to her. 'I'm fine, darling, I just stubbed my foot. Clumsy like your grandmother, that's all Daddy meant. Let Daddy and me talk for a few moments then I'll come play.'

Becky hesitated, looking between us both.

'Go on,' I gently urged her.

She frowned then walked out.

'Nice lie,' Mike said when she was gone. 'But then you've always been good at that.'

'I need to see Becky properly,' I said, ignoring him. I hadn't expected him to turn bitter like that. I just had to rise above it, put Becky first. 'I'd like to take her to the cave. Just for a few days, make it like a little holiday for her. Isn't that what the school holidays are for? Then we can figure out how we divide her time between us.'

'No way,' Mike said, shaking his head. 'No way is she staying in that cave with those people.'

'*Those people*? Mike, they're good, decent people.'

He laughed. 'You've clearly been brainwashed. They're all nutters. You should hear what people are saying about them at work. And now they'll all be talking about you too.'

I sighed. 'That's ridiculous, nobody's making me do anything. This is all on me and you know it.'

We held each other's gaze then he shook his head again. 'Absolutely not. Becky is *not* sleeping in a cave.'

'It's safe, it's warm, there's food and another child for her to play with.'

'I said *no*,' he shouted.

Becky looked up from her dollhouse in the other room.

'It's okay, darling,' I called out. 'I'll be out in a moment.' I turned back to Mike, heart thumping. 'You need to stop losing your temper in front of her.'

'I'm not the only one.'

'Okay, we both need to. Look,' I said quietly, 'she's my daughter too. You have no right to keep her from me. We've *got* to put her first, Mike, not your hurt feelings.'

Mike took a deep breath then he closed his eyes. 'Fine, just one day and *not* at that bloody cave. There are plenty of things you can do around here without taking her there.'

I thought about protesting again but realised there was no use. So I just nodded. How would Mike know if I took Becky to the cave anyway?

'I want her back by six tonight,' he said.

'Eight,' I replied. I'd love Becky to experience feasting at the cave. We'd even got a little bell to announce when dinner was ready.

'No, absolutely not,' Mike replied. 'Six. You can put her to bed here then we can sit down and talk when she's asleep.'

'Talk?'

'You can't just walk out and not make arrangements, Selma. There's bills to pay, schedules to discuss. Jesus,' he said, pacing up and down as he slid his hand over his head. 'I can't believe it's come to this.'

'This is hard for me too, Mike.'

'No, it's not Selma. As long as you're writing, you'll be fine.' Then he walked away.

Five minutes later, I was walking out of the house with Becky. I turned once to see Mike watching from the window, face drawn, and got a flashback to my own father, his face the same as he walked down the path with his suitcase when I was the same age as Becky.

I shook my head, making the memory disappear. I wasn't like my mother, throwing her husband out in the night so a new man could move in a few weeks later, the first of many. This was different, *so* different.

I looked down at Becky. 'We are going to have *so* much fun!'

It wasn't long before we approached the cave. Idris was by the sea, helping Donna's son Tom fish in the shallow waters. He looked up when I was near, and I couldn't help it, my tummy trembled. He strolled over, giving me a joyous look.

'This must be Becky,' he said, waving at her. She stared at him, her mouth open. She'd probably heard about the man with the long white hair at school. I felt a strange shimmer of pride. It felt like I was walking her into a fantasy book. 'I'm showing Tom how to fish,' Idris said, crouching down in front of Becky so he was at her level. 'Will you join us with your mummy?'

Becky peered up at me with big eyes then nodded. 'Okay.'

We walked towards Tom. The water was calm and the palest of blues, rippling beneath the relentless sun. I settled down on the sand and watched through squinting eyes as Idris showed Becky how to fish with a tiny red fishing net. Every now and again, Becky peered around at me, smiling. I felt the warmth of contentment. This was a good move. If only Mike could understand. Maybe if he came here, he could see it through my eyes. I looked towards the cave, watching people going about their usual business, ceramic plates being moulded, poetry being written, the tinkling of a new tune and the smell of a delicious new sauce being concocted by Donna. Despite how difficult it was to tell Mike the truth, mainly it felt wonderful to be so *free*.

I peered back at Becky who was yelping with joy as a fish flip-flopped around in her net. Now I just needed Becky to be here with me permanently, not just for a few hours.

'Look, Mummy, I caught a big one!' Becky said, looking at me proudly.

'Clever girl!' I exclaimed. 'What are you going to do with it?'

'Eat it for dinner?' Becky said, shrugging.

I crawled towards Becky on the sand and grabbed her, euphoria filling me.

'Then I'm going to have you for pudding.' I pretended to gobble her up as Tom and Idris laughed, Becky giggling in delight. As we did that, the fish escaped, wiggling out into the ocean and swimming away.

Over the rest of the day, Becky played on the beach with Tom as I sat against my favoured rock, its warmth seeping into my back as I scribbled on my notepad. I'd never been able to write for more than five minutes with Becky around. It was as if my notepad was a magnet for Becky's attention. But here, with the beach as her playground, a new friend to run riot with, Becky was content.

'Wine?' I peered up to see Julien standing over me with a bottle and an empty glass. 'I know it's not gin but it's crisp and it's cold.'

I smiled at him. 'Wine would be grand, thank you.'

'Mind if I join you? That rock looks inviting.'

'Of course! I was just about to finish anyway.' I shuffled up as he sat next to me, pouring me some wine and handing it over. It was a surprise to have him join me. Of all the people here, Julien had kept himself most distant from me, quietly watching from afar. I'd been starting to take it personally.

'Your daughter looks like she's enjoying herself,' he commented, looking over at Becky who was now building an intricate network of sand tunnels.

'What child doesn't on a day like this?'

He smiled. 'True. Wait until the tide goes out and she gets to feast her eyes on all the starfish and shells.' He looked down at my notepad. 'How's the writing going?'

'Flowing,' I said with a contented sigh. 'I've never been so fired up about something.'

'That's what this place does to you.'

'I saw you whittling some wood earlier. How's that going?'

'Same. Pretty amazing.' He squinted up at the setting sun with his brown eyes. 'God, I wished I'd discovered this place months ago. I'd have come and buried my head here. But then I guess Idris wouldn't have been here.'

We both peered towards Idris, who was out in the sea up to his waist, still and staring into the distance. The sun was making his wet back shimmer.

'He looks like a god,' I murmured. Julien raised an eyebrow at me. 'Well, he does, doesn't he?' I said, laughing.

'I suppose he does have a touch of the Jesus about him.'

I examined Julien's face. 'Why did you come here?'

He sighed. 'My business went into administration.'

'I'm so sorry. What sort of business was it?'

'Solicitor's firm. Small but thriving . . . until the recession hit anyway. The final nail in the coffin? Seeing my ex-wife swanning

194

around and flashing a huge engagement ring. Oh yeah, I forgot to add she left me as soon as the money stopped coming in.' He looked down at the sand, grabbing large fistfuls of it. 'It got so bad, I nearly took my life.'

'Jesus,' I whispered.

He looked up at me sharply. 'Please don't say anything. I've only told a handful of people that.'

'Of course I won't.'

Julien's face lightened. 'But then I saw a man save a boy and I thought, "If he can save that boy, he can save me too."'

'Has he?'

'Yes,' Julien said simply.

'And yet it's been less than two weeks.'

'Time, it's just a number.' He smiled, eyes dancing.

I smiled back. 'Down with the numbers.'

We laughed, clinking our glasses together. Julien leaned back, taking a sip of his wine. 'So what about you? Has Idris saved you?'

I looked down at the grains of sand on my tanned bare feet, the chipped pink of my toenails. 'In a way, I suppose. I guess I've found myself again. Found my *writing*. This place,' I said, looking around me, 'the impact it has on my creativity. I've never known anything like it.'

'I get it. So what about your daughter?' he said, looking towards Becky. 'Will she stay?'

'I want her to. But my husband has other ideas.'

'Donna managed it.'

'Her husband is a bully.'

'And yours isn't? Bullies come in all shapes and sizes, you know.'

I thought of how angry Mike had been. Maybe Julien was right?

In the distance, Julien's little Jack Russell was limping towards us, tail wagging in between her legs as she held up her paw.

'What have you done to yourself, girl?' Julien soothed, stroking her furry little head.

'Aw!' Becky said, running over and stroking the dog. 'What's her name?'

'Mojo,' Julien replied. He leaned down to look at the dog's paw. It yelped loudly as he touched it. 'Looks like she's torn her claw, probably getting caught up in the bushes again.'

'Oh no, poor puppy,' Becky said, pouting.

Idris strolled over. 'Mojo okay?' he asked Julien.

'Injured her paw.'

Idris looked towards Donna. 'Donna, will you get the first aid kit?'

She jumped up and ran into the cave. I noticed how she was like a little soldier around Idris, following his every command. Donna returned a moment later with a green case in her hands and laid it on the beach, kneeling down as others came over.

'You'll have to restrain Mojo,' Idris said to Julien. 'We have to get it off so a new one can grow back. It'll bleed.'

Julien nodded and gently grabbed hold of his dog. Idris got a nail clipper out and started trying to clip the nail off but the dog squirmed.

'It's okay,' Becky said in her sweet soft voice, leaning close to the dog's furry ear. It looked up at her and she started singing a lullaby, making it calm.

Idris and I looked at each other in surprise.

'My daughter, the dog whisperer,' I said. 'Who knew?'

'Well then Becky, it looks like you have the special touch,' Idris said. 'Here, take this,' he added, handing her a gauze from the first aid kit.

'I don't know what to do with it,' Becky said, looking worried.

Idris looked her in the eye. 'I trust you. When I clip the nail off, it will bleed, a lot. I hope you don't mind a bit of blood?' Becky shook her head. 'I want you to quickly cover the area with the gauze and press hard to stem the blood.'

'Okay,' Becky said.

'What if the dog bites her?' I asked, suddenly worried.

'She won't,' Idris said. 'There are certain people that have a way with animals. Your daughter is one of them. Ready?' Idris said to Becky.

Becky nodded. Idris quickly cut the nail off, the dog yelping, and Becky pressed the gauze to the dog's nail as blood seeped up, starting to sing again to calm her. After a while, the bleeding stopped. Idris nodded at Julien and Julien let Mojo go. The sweet little dog slumped onto Becky, licking her hand.

'She likes me,' Becky said.

Idris nodded. 'You're a natural, Becky. I believe you've just found your calling in life.'

'What's a calling?' Becky asked.

'The thing you're meant to do. You'll work with animals, I can sense it.'

'You mean a vet?' Becky asked.

Idris nodded. Becky peered up at her mum. 'Mummy, I want to be a vet!'

I looked at her in surprise. Becky had never expressed a desire to be a vet before, just a princess or pirate.

'You'd make a wonderful vet, darling,' I said.

Becky leaned against me as the dog fell asleep on her lap. The rest of the group dispersed and it was just mother and daughter, sitting on the beach in the late afternoon light, watching gulls swoop for fish in the sea.

'I want to be here forever,' Becky said wistfully.

'Me too,' I replied. My heart soared but then I felt the watch ticking in my pocket, reminding me we had precious little time left before I had to march Becky home to an angry Mike.

When dinner was served, indicating it was six thirty and past the time I was due to drop Becky off, I ignored the warning voice in my head. Mike couldn't dictate when and where I could see my own child!

But then I saw a familiar figure striding down the beach.

'Look, it's Daddy!' Becky said.

I looked at his face. Mike was fuming.

Chapter Seventeen

Selma

Kent, UK
30 July 1991

Becky jumped up and waved to her dad, then suddenly stopped. 'Oh. I shouldn't have done that. It's a secret, right?'

'It's okay,' I said, faking a smile. I'd asked her earlier to say we went to the café. 'I think we've been busted anyway.'

Becky jumped up, running to her dad. He leaned down to cuddle her, glaring at me over her head.

'I had such fun!' I heard Becky exclaim as they walked over to me. 'I went fishing and swimming really far out, further than I've ever been! Oh, and I saved a dog's paw, and it didn't even bite me even though Mummy said it might.'

Wow, that'll go down well.

'Before you say anything, I didn't plan on coming here,' I lied. 'We were swimming and then Becky saw the cave and ran to it before I could stop her.' Becky looked at me, frowning at the lie.

But she didn't say anything. 'We were about to leave. It's just that this dog got injured and—'

'The dog that bites?' Mike asked sarcastically.

I laughed nervously. 'That dog wouldn't harm a fly. I was just being over-cautious.'

'Right, yes, that's what you are Selma, always so cautious. Letting our daughter swim out to sea, tend to injured dogs. Taking her to the cave I begged you not to.' He looked into the cave, shaking his head at the empty wine glasses on the table. 'Yes, very cautious indeed.'

Becky looked between us, a confused expression on her face.

'It's just half an hour, Mike!' I said.

'Thirty minutes longer then we agreed! And you brought her to this bloody place!' He looked towards Oceane and Caden who were drunkenly swinging each other around. 'I won't have her being here, among these people. It's not right for a child.' He paused, face going very cold. 'I clearly can't trust you. This puts me in a very difficult position.'

I felt panic build inside. What did he mean by that?

'Mike, let's talk about this sensibly,' I said, putting my hand out to him.

He stepped away from me, shaking his head. 'I can't rely on you to be sensible. Come on, Becky.' He grabbed Becky's hand but she resisted him, trying to pull away.

'I like it here, Daddy!' she exclaimed.

'See!' I said, going after him and taking Becky's other hand, anger surging through me. 'Becky likes being here. You can't stop me from seeing her, from bringing her here!'

'Can't I?' I could see the look on Mike's face, a steely determination. It scared me.

'Don't you threaten me!' I said in a low voice.

'Ow, you're hurting me, Mummy and Daddy!'

I looked down at Becky, her arms outstretched, one wrist clutched by each parent. I dropped Becky's arm, tears filling my eyes.

'Say goodbye to your mum,' Mike said.

'I want to stay,' Becky replied, wrapping her arms around my waist and pressing her face into my tummy. I stroked my daughter's hair, blinking back tears as I looked at Mike.

'I'm her *mum*,' I said to him. 'I won't let you stop me seeing her.'

'You might not have a choice in the matter.'

'And you might not either,' I spat back. 'You can't watch her twenty-four hours a day, can you?'

His eyes widened. 'What do you mean by that?'

I looked down at Becky, trying to contain my anger. 'Go to Daddy, darling. Mummy will see you very soon.' I gave her a hug then gently pushed her towards Mike. Becky started crying and I had to turn away, stifling a sob.

'Why can't you just come back with us?' Becky shouted at me as Mike pulled her away.

I pursed my lips together, still unable to look at her. 'Mummy can't. She just can't.'

It wasn't until they left the beach that I turned, watching as they disappeared across the road. Then I sank down onto the sand and sobbed.

I stayed like that for a while, not even going to join the others for the feasting, my appetite gone. Nobody approached me, knowing as they always seemed to that I needed to be alone. I was shaking with rage. How *dare* Mike say all that? I was Becky's mum, for God's sake!

I picked up a fistful of sand, flinging it into the distance.

'You okay?'

I looked up to see Idris approaching.

'No, not really. Mike—'

He put his hand up. 'No need to tell me. All that matters is now. I want you to do something for me. Go into the sea.'

I frowned, peering out at the growing darkness and slippery rocks that spread out between me and the frothing waves. 'Now?'

'Yes, now.'

'My swimsuit's drying in the cave.'

'No need for it. Go in your clothes.' He smiled. 'Trust me. I'll be with you.' He stood, kicking his flip-flops off. I hesitated a moment then I did the same. He took my hand and led me over the rocks, the seaweed squelching beneath the soft skin of my feet. Sometimes, I trod on broken shells, their jagged edges cutting into my feet. But Idris encouraged me along, telling me to blank out the pain and focus on the sea ahead instead.

When we stepped into the waves, I saw blood shimmer around my feet. But I ignored it, putting one foot in front of the other, the splash of the water echoing in the tranquil silence of the low tide. As we got further in, my top and long skirt grew heavy, making it hard to walk. But I continued until the waves were to my chest, my breath shallow.

Idris made me stop, his hands on my shoulders as he looked at me. 'Close your eyes and feel the weight of your clothes, how they drag you down.'

I closed my eyes, felt my floral skirt bubble up around me, my sodden vest heavy against my skin.

'Now think of all that has passed between you and your husband this evening, this week, this month, this year. All the years. All the weight of the years, the dark thoughts, the negative vibes. Feel them all weighing you down.'

I took in a deep breath, my mind going back in time: first my argument with Mike, then my strange numbness recently, those difficult few months after Becky was born. And then my mother, tongue like acid, words ballooning around me like the skirt I was wearing now, so heavy my feet were sinking into the sand below. I thought of the other dark times I'd experienced, times long forgotten. How I would feel a black cloud descending over me and the see-saw between intense anxiety and strange numbness. Even my teachers had noticed and I'd been referred to a counsellor. The counsellor had tried to blame it on my mother. Yes, my mother's words took my depression to a whole new level. Made me feel even more unworthy. But it was more than that, wasn't it?

'Now open your eyes,' Idris said. I did as he asked, looking into his beautiful face in the dying light, heavy now with the weight of his gaze as his eyes travelled over me. 'Take your clothes off. I won't look, I'll turn my back to you. Take every scrap off.'

I laughed. 'Now this is where I *definitely* say no.'

He smiled back. 'Selma, I adore your cynicism, I really do. It's what makes you unique. But I think sometimes it can hold you back. I need you to trust me, just as you did when I showed you the cave. It'll be worth it, really.' Then he turned away.

I hesitated a moment then a thrill ran through me.

What the hell?

I pulled my vest off, unhooking my bra, sighing as I always did at the feel of my breasts being free of pinching wires. Then I leaned down, clutching onto Idris's strong arm for balance as I pulled my skirt off, then my knickers. With each item that was removed, I felt lighter, freer. I watched my clothes float away, my skirt a bed of flowers in the sea.

'I'm going back now to get you a towel,' Idris said, still not turning. 'I'll be waiting for you on the shore. Stay here for a few moments, take it in.'

I closed my eyes, smelling the salty air, hearing the ripple of the waves. He was right, the lightness I felt was overwhelming.

After a while, I opened my eyes to see Idris standing in the shallow waves, holding up a towel. He was watching me but I didn't care, I walked towards him without covering myself. It somehow seemed completely natural and the way he looked at me as I approached, so different from the way other men savoured my curves like they were food.

When I got to him, his eyes were on mine. He wrapped the towel around my shoulders, covering my nakedness, and I felt desire stir in the pit of my stomach at the proximity of him.

He leaned in close to me. 'How do you feel?' he whispered in my ear.

'Like I was gliding.'

He smiled. 'Now you know how it feels to walk on water.'

I tried to call Mike the next day from a phone box in town. I didn't want things left as they were. When there was no answer, I turned up at the house, but I could see that the lights were off and there was no car outside. Maybe that was a good thing – it would give him some time to calm down. I vowed to arrange a meet-up the next day and buried myself in my writing instead. It was another beautiful day, swathes of blue sky with wispy threads of cloud. The cave provided a cool respite from the heat and, as I began to write, aware of everyone else around me working on their creative pieces, my mind began to enter a strange rhythm, matching the swish of Idris's paintbrush and the ebb of the waves outside. It was different from how I'd felt before. Instead of everything disappearing, the noises and the smells around me built into a crescendo, adding to the sound of my pen on paper, encouraging me along. And as it did so, I felt myself rocking slightly to the music in my mind, my heart soaring with each word I wrote.

When I reached the end of a particularly intense scene, I gasped, as though coming up for air. Sounds separated, became normal again: the chitter chatter of Donna and Julien outside, the yelp of Caden and Oceane splashing about in the water, the swish of Idris's brush and the whir of Maggie's clay wheel.

'I told you you'd do it.'

I looked up to see Idris smiling down at me. 'Do what?' I asked.

'The current. You were in the current, I can tell. You can't deny it.'

I looked at him dubiously. 'I'm not sure about being in the *current*. I think it's just being here with no distractions.'

'Always the cynic,' Idris said, smiling.

'You wouldn't have me any other way.' We held each other's gaze, his eyes dropping briefly to my lips then up again.

Then Donna ran over, leaning down to catch her breath.

'Everything okay?' Idris asked her, stepping from his ladder, a look of concern on his face.

'There's someone outside for Selma.'

I frowned. 'Not Mike again?'

'No, someone else,' she replied. 'He's in a suit, looks rather serious. Come see.'

I rose and followed Donna outside, heart thumping. There was a man standing on the beach, looking very uncomfortable in a grey suit.

'Selma Rhys?' he asked in a grave voice.

'Yes,' I answered.

He held an envelope out to me. 'You've been served with an emergency residence order.' Then he walked off.

'I don't understand,' I shouted after him, hand trembling as I looked down at the letter, Idris putting his hand on my shoulder as everyone gathered around us.

Julien put his hand out. 'Looks like legal documents. Do you want me to translate?'

I nodded. He opened the letter, his eyes running over it. Then he sighed. 'Your husband has sought orders for Becky to live with him permanently. He's prohibiting you from removing her from his care save for agreed supervised contacts. There will be a hearing in about a week.'

I looked up at Idris. 'Mike wants to take Becky from me!'

He shook his head, face flashing with anger. 'We won't let that happen.'

I looked towards where my house was, suddenly yearning to hold my daughter in my arms. Anger replaced fear.

'You're right, he will *not* take my Becky away from me, I'll make sure of that.'

'*We'll* make sure of that,' Idris said, taking my hand as the others gathered close around us, nodding. 'You're not alone in this, Selma,' he said, squeezing my hand. 'You'll never feel alone again.'

Chapter Eighteen

Becky

Postojna caves, Slovenia
26 June 2018

Becky sits alone on the bus, peering out of the window as she takes in the beautiful Slovenian scenery: the rows of lush green trees lining the hills around her, the pretty rivers sauntering through those hills, clear water sparkling beneath the afternoon sun. She catches sight of a couple walking by with their dog, a puppy giddy with excitement as it dances around its owners' legs. Becky thinks of her own dogs at home. She'd spent a couple of days with them, booking more time off work. It coincided with her thirty-fifth birthday. She hadn't really celebrated it. It didn't seem right, with her mother's death still so raw. Instead, she'd had lunch in the garden with David, who had handed her a small birthday card with three lurchers running through fields on the front. He was more quiet than usual, watching her with hooded eyes. Sometimes he would open his mouth and then close it, without uttering a word. She could see he didn't know how to deal with her grief, but she didn't mind. She preferred silence to stifling condolences like she'd received at work.

She gets out her phone, scrolling through photos of the dogs. Then she catches sight of a photo of Kai with Hannah and Ed, one of the selfies he'd emailed from their remaining weeks in the Spanish caves. They'd swapped emails when they'd parted ways, Kai insisting she keep him posted with 'The Sister Quest' as he called it. She smiles to herself as she takes in his wide, all-encompassing smile.

The bus slows down, approaching a long white building overlooking the river. 'Right, Mum,' she whispers to herself. 'Let's see what information this visit brings us.'

It's very possible that nothing could come of this, she knows that. But Berenice seemed so sure her friend had told her Idris had gone to Slovenia . . . and that he was led there by a woman who worked as a guide for these very caves. Becky had emailed the caves when she'd got home a few days ago, but she hadn't received an answer. When she'd called them, the woman there had spoken in broken English. In the end, Becky ran out of patience and booked a flight out. Her inheritance would be coming through soon and she knew her mum would approve of her spending it on something like this. She had to give it her best shot, didn't she?

She follows the other tourists to the white building, breathing in the fresh clean air as she peers up at the pine trees. There's a different feel here in Slovenia. Spain was hot and dusty and loud. It's more peaceful here, more green and serene.

She heads towards the information desk, finding a man and woman behind it.

'This is a long shot, but there used to be a lady who worked here about twenty years ago, someone called Darja?' she says, using the information Berenice gave her in Spain.

The man shrugs. 'I wouldn't know, it's too long ago for me.'

The woman with him leans forward, looking at Becky over trendy black-rimmed glasses. 'You mean Darja Krajnc?'

'I don't know her surname,' Becky confesses.

'Maybe it's my friend's mother,' the woman says. 'She still works here sometimes.'

'Do you have her contact details? I think she knew my sister and I'm trying to track her down. I'd love to talk to her if possible.'

'I'll call her,' the woman says.

'Mention Idris. If it's the right Darja, she'll know him,' Becky quickly adds.

The woman nods then makes the call, tapping her fingers on the counter as she waits while it rings. Someone answers and the woman says something in Slovenian then puts the phone down, smiling.

'She will be here in twenty minutes. She sounded *very* excited.'

Becky smiles back. 'Great.' But she can't help but feel some trepidation. She hadn't found her sister in Spain, who was to say she would find her here?

While she waits, she wanders over to the entrance of the cave, peering in. She was expecting it to be dark inside so is surprised when she finds an ultra-modern interior, a long train lining a tunnel. Did Idris and Solar really live in that cave? She sits on a nearby bench, looking into the tunnel and trying to wrap her head around the possibility.

Close to twenty minutes later, a tall woman in her fifties approaches with a long quick stride and striking features. The guides point Becky out and the woman strides towards her.

'I'm Darja,' she says, putting her hand out.

Becky shakes it. 'Becky. Thank you *so* much for coming out so quickly.'

'No problem, I don't live far.' Darja sits beside her, eyes sparkling. 'You know Idris? Have you seen him?'

Becky shakes her head. 'No, sorry.'

Darja's shoulders slump.

'I should explain,' Becky says. 'My mum knew him.' She tells Darja her mum's name.

'I see,' Darja says. 'Idris talked of her often. How is she?'

She takes a deep breath. 'She passed away recently.' It still hurts so much to say it, it doesn't feel real.

Darja puts her hand on her arm. 'I'm so sorry. Come, let's get some tea. That's what you British people like, no?' she asks, gesturing to a small café nearby.

'I'd like that.' They find a table in the corner of the café, and Darja goes to get them drinks. A few moments later, she brings back tea and two slabs of cake which look like brown and yellow versions of arctic roll.

'*Potica*,' Darja explains. 'Absolutely delicious.'

Becky takes a bite, enjoying the nutty honey taste. 'Thank you, it *is* delicious.'

But Darja doesn't take a bite of her *potica*, just leans forward and looks into Becky's eyes. 'So did your mother say she's seen Idris in the past twenty years or so?'

Becky shakes her head. 'No, she didn't.'

Darja leans back against her chair, raking her fingers through her short dark hair.

'What's wrong?' Becky asks her.

'He disappeared a few months after we came here. Just . . . disappeared. I woke one day to find him and Solar gone. He was always looking over his shoulder, scared of someone. I think in the end he realised they'd be better off going somewhere alone.'

Becky's heart starts thumping loudly in her ears. 'So he definitely left here too with Solar?'

'Yes.'

Becky sighs. She just couldn't get a grasp on the two of them.

'Are you okay?' Darja asks.

'I think Solar's my sister, that's why I'm here. I'm trying to find her.'

'Ah, that confirms who her mother was then. I guessed as much but Idris didn't like to talk about it. The past must be left behind us, that's what the Children of the Current always say.'

'Children of the Current?'

'That's what we all call ourselves.'

Becky raises an eyebrow. It sounds so weird to her. She always knew them as the 'cave dwellers', as the local paper had christened the group.

'Looks like my path has run cold then,' she says.

'Fear not! Caden might be able to shed some light on their whereabouts tomorrow.'

'Caden. That name rings a bell.'

'He lived at the cave with us. He liked playing on the guitar.'

Becky gets a fleeting memory of a skinny man with sunburnt cheeks and scruffy hair. 'Why might he know more?'

'He's a genealogist now, can trace family trees. He told me he would try to track Idris down. He'll be here tomorrow for my daughter's wedding.'

Becky smiles. 'How lovely. Congratulations.' Becky takes a sip of tea, weighing up her options. 'Do you think he could fit in a quick chat with me before the wedding?'

'Why not come to the wedding?'

Becky shakes her head. 'Oh no, I couldn't impose.'

Darja leans forward and grabs Becky's hand. 'Please, my daughter would be delighted, especially if you are Solar's sister. They used to play with each other, right in the cave here,' she says, peering through into the cave.

Becky hesitates. To be able to meet someone who knew Solar so well, to properly chat to them. 'If you're sure?'

'I wouldn't have invited you if I wasn't.'

Becky looks into the caves, the reality of it all suddenly hitting her. Usually right now, she'd be grabbing a quick sandwich before her next appointment, doing a quick check of her emails. But here she was, in a country she'd never visited before, having just accepted an invite to a random wedding to find out more about her sister!

She takes a deep breath and turns back to Darja. 'So you really did stay here with Idris then. How did you manage that?'

'There are secret caves. If you know them well enough, like me, it's easy to hide away in them, just like Idris and I did.' Her brow wrinkles slightly.

'You were in love with him,' Becky says softly.

Darja nods. 'When he disappeared without saying a word, I was heartbroken.' She seems to gather herself and shrugs. 'Just a middle-aged woman reminiscing about old loves. Do you want to see where we all lived?'

'I'd love to.'

She looks at her watch. 'It'll be lunch soon. Tours stop so the guides can have a break. We'll go then so we're not distracted by tourists.'

When the guides leave for lunch, Darja leads Becky through to the ultra-modern train, sitting at the front as Darja takes the controls.

'Hold tight!' Darja calls over her shoulder.

The train judders then zooms through a narrow dark tunnel as Becky grabs even harder onto the railings in front of her. They pass walls made from yellow limestone, stunning rock stalagmites and stalactites hanging from the vast ceilings like art suspended in time, and Becky regards it all open-mouthed.

After a while, the train slows down as they reach a vast cavern.

'This is where we get off,' Darja says. She helps Becky down and leads her through a series of caverns as Becky looks around her, smiling. It's vast and beautiful, the smell of damp clogging her nostrils, the cold air making her pull on her hoodie. Eventually, they come to a cavern with an aquarium in the middle.

'What's here?' Becky asks.

'Our lovely little olm fish,' Darja says, smiling affectionately.

'Oh yes, I've read about those.'

'Want to have a quick look?'

'Yes please!'

They walk towards the glass chambers and Becky peers inside, fascinated, at the tiny tubular fish with their clawed legs which glide inside the chambers.

an area to Becky's left. 'She used to press her little face right up against it, like a comfort blanket.'

Becky walks over and crouches down. The ground dips slightly here, the moonlight above casting silver shadows over it. Becky imagines a five-year-old girl sleeping here.

Her sister.

She places her cheek against the cool wall and closes her eyes. 'Where are you?' she whispers.

When she opens her eyes, she gasps.

A face is staring at her, one side white, the other black.

Chapter Nineteen

Becky

Postojna caves, Slovenia
26 June 2018

'Don't worry!' Darja says as Becky jumps up, staring at the face. 'It's just one of Idris's paintings.'

Becky puts her hand to her chest. 'I thought it was a person.'

Darja smiles. 'It *is* rather spooky. I think that's why the owners kept it. It adds to the atmosphere for the events they hold here now. All the others were washed off.'

Becky walks over to the painting. 'I've seen this before, in Idris's cave in Spain. Why would he draw something like this?'

'I always wondered if it was the person he was running from.'

'Yes, Julien mentioned he always seemed to be looking over his shoulder. Do you have any idea who it might have been?'

Darja shakes her head. 'He never said specifically. I know there were people who hated him back in the UK though, especially the families of the Children of the Current, some who even accused him of using us for money.'

'Yes, I remember that anger, even though I was young. He clearly had a few enemies.'

Darja sighs. 'Idris was a complex man, but he was a *good* man. You need to know that.'

Becky turns to her. 'Then why did he take Solar away from my mum?'

'I don't know but he would have had his reasons.' Darja looks at her watch. 'We must return to the train now. Sorry it was a fleeting visit.'

'That's fine, it was good to see the place.'

'You'll be able to talk to Caden tomorrow. Hopefully he will have dug some information up.'

'Fingers crossed.' Becky takes one last look around her, her eyes alighting on the painting, then follows Darja back to the train.

The next morning, Becky smooths down the one dress she'd brought with her as she waits alone in Darja's living room. It's a sky-blue knee-length wrap dress, more casual than smart. She hadn't planned on attending a wedding while there. She peers around her at Darja's house. It's large and modern, sitting in a row of other duplicate houses, all arranged in a neat line, the mountains as their backdrop. She bites her lip, unsure what to do with herself, standing in the middle of a virtual stranger's living room, about to attend the wedding of a person she hasn't met yet. Then she hears the sound of giggles from upstairs. The bride and her sister? It makes Becky relax slightly. They sound fun.

Darja walks in then with an elderly woman who's wearing a

beautiful cornflower-blue dress. She looks like Darja with dark hair in a bun, blue eyes. Becky also notices her hands are gnarled and she flinches every now and again, as though in pain.

'Ah, this is the British girl,' the elderly woman says.

'This is my mother,' Darja explains. 'She lives with us.'

'Yes, my darling girl looks after me,' the old lady says, smiling up at her daughter.

Guilt floods through Becky as she thinks of her mum suffering in silence all those months. If Becky had known, would she have given up everything to care for her, despite their estrangement?

Yes, of course she would have.

More laughter echoes out from above. Darja smiles. 'They're very excited.'

'I bet they are,' Becky says. 'How long before they need to leave?'

'Jurij should be here soon,' Darja says, peering at the clock nervously.

Becky frowns. 'Jurij?'

'The groom,' Darja's mother explains.

Becky raises an eyebrow. 'The groom taking the bride to the ceremony? That's certainly different from how we do it in the UK.'

Darja laughs. 'There are lot of things that are different here! He'll have quite a journey on the way. His friends will have set up a wooden obstacle for him in the road. He will need to pay them to get through, or he will have to saw through it. Knowing Jurij, he will choose the latter so we may be waiting some time!'

'Is that a tradition?' Becky asks.

'Yes. It's died out but Alenka and Jurij like their traditions. You know they're going to live in a cabin in the woods after this?'

Becky smiles. 'Sounds perfect.'

The old woman's face darkens. 'Those two young girls still have romantic notions left over from their time in the cave. Can you imagine taking your children to live in a cave?'

Darja rolls her eyes. 'Not now, *Mati*.'

A car beeps outside. Darja helps the frail woman up and they all walk into the hallway to see a pretty girl wearing a wispy green dress, her dark hair up.

'This is my oldest daughter, Branka,' Darja says.

Branka goes to Becky and kisses her on both cheeks. 'I love that you are here. I will speak English *perfect* after. And my sister Alenka is *so* excited you are here too.'

'I feel a bit bad imposing on your sister's special day,' Becky says.

'Don't be silly!' Branka says. 'We are all Daughters of the Current.'

Darja's mother shakes her head vehemently. 'Nonsense.'

Becky smiles. She likes this old woman.

Branka turns to her grandmother. 'Come on, *Babica*! It is your turn!'

Darja and Branka lead the woman towards the door as Becky watches them all with fascination. What *were* they planning? Behind her, she hears a giggle. She turns to see a tall woman in her twenties peeking around the corner, wearing a beautiful dress made from white silk and chiffon. That must be Alenka, the bride. She's so beautiful, so young and giddy with excitement in her stunning dress.

Becky thinks of her own parents' wedding day. She'd seen the photos and had re-examined them after her mum left, trying to detect the sadness in her eyes and the answers to why it fell apart after all those years. But then her mum had always been an expert at concealing her emotions so she looked just like any other beautiful beaming bride. If Becky had been there though, would she have sensed the unhappiness and frustration boiling beneath the surface as she had in those later years?

As she thinks that, the bride winks at Becky then puts her finger to her mouth before moving out of sight, a huge smile on her face. *No faking there*, Becky thinks.

Becky turns back to the front door as two young men enter wearing suits. In their hands are a veil, a bouquet of roses and long white shawl. They hand the items to Darja and Branka, who quickly dress Darja's mother up in it all. Then a tall man with a deep tan and muscular arms walks in. The groom? He smiles knowingly as he looks at Darja's mother then says something in Slovenian.

'He's saying his bride looks beautiful,' Branka explains for Becky, gesturing to her grandmother and winking. 'They're trying to trick him into thinking *Babica* is the bride.'

The groom leans over, going in to kiss his 'bride'. Then he hesitates, saying something in Slovenian.

'Oh no, he has guessed!' Branka declares in a whisper. 'Now his friends will demand payment so he can see the *real* bride.'

Money is exchanged and the groom is finally led towards the real bride. When Alenka steps out, her groom stops dead, eyes widening. She bites her lip shyly as her sister leads her towards him. Becky notices the tears in Branka's eyes, the way she looks at her younger sister with such love and pride. She thinks of Solar. Is she married? And if so, had she wished her sister had been there to witness her exchanging of vows? Did she even *know* she had a sister?

Becky feels a sudden stab of anger at her mum. If Solar was married, she'd denied Becky the opportunity to be there at her little's sister wedding, as Branka was about to be at *her* sister's wedding. Or was it really her mum's fault? Idris had taken Solar after all, or so her mum had told her. But then her mum was a master of lies and deceit like the game played out at this very wedding.

She feels guilty thinking that and suppresses a frustrated scream. There are so many confusing emotions when it comes to her mum. She suddenly yearns for her dad's calm. Everything is simple with him.

As the others fuss over getting the bride into the car, Becky slips away, making a quick call.

Her dad picks up instantly. 'Everything okay, love?' he asks.

'Just needed to hear your voice.'

'*Is* everything okay, Becky?' he asks again, voice filled with worry.

'Of course. I just – I guess I'm feeling a little lonely out here, that's all.'

'Well, I'm here now, aren't I? Not physically but you can hear my old voice. Any luck?'

'Not yet. But I'm hoping to chat to someone else who lived in the caves. I'll keep you posted.'

There's laughter in the background.

'Where on earth are you?' her dad asks.

'I'm at a wedding. The bride and her sister are *rather* excited.'

Her dad is quiet.

'Dad?' Becky asks.

'I imagine you're thinking about what it would be like to see your own sister get married?' he asks.

Becky smiles. 'You know me so well, Dad.'

'Maybe you'll get a chance, Becky. Or maybe she'll get a chance to see *you* married.'

She sighs. 'I have to find her first.'

'You sound tired.'

'I am. I really need to get some new information soon otherwise I'm coming home.'

'Maybe that's a good idea anyway, Becky. You've tried so hard, visited two countries! If the trail runs cold, it runs cold. You can look back and say you did all you could. And I can look back and think how proud I am you tried.'

Becky nods. 'You're right.'

But as she looks towards the giggling sisters, Branka trying her best to shove her sister's wedding dress into the small car, she longs more than ever to find her own sister.

A few hours later, Becky finds herself surrounded by well-dressed Slovenian wedding guests in the gardens of the pretty hotel where the wedding is being held. She looks down at her wrap dress again. She feels even more out of place now. She'd felt the same watching the ceremony. It was beautiful, the love between the bride and groom obvious. But it had made her suddenly yearn for the same, not just for the romance of it, but the companionship.

Becky takes a sip of her wine, peering at her watch. She's desperate to talk to Caden, see if he knows where Solar might be. But there are so many men here, how will she know which one he is? The bride strolls over then, cheeks flushed from champagne.

'Congratulations,' Becky says. 'You really look stunning. I hope you don't mind me gatecrashing.'

'Hardly gatecrashing!' Alenka says, touching Becky's arm. 'Your sister and I were very close when we were little.'

'What was she like?'

Alenka's face lights up. 'Yes, she was such fun. I was only six but I still remember how wild she was!'

'Wild?'

'Yes! There was a lot of freedom for us as children when we lived in the caves.' She frowns slightly. 'But there were still dangers, lots of chances to get lost, to fall, to eat something we shouldn't. Our parents kept a close eye on us. But Idris was always too busy, too wrapped up in what he was trying to achieve to truly watch Solar. She even slept out on the mountains alone one night when it was particularly warm, can you imagine? At six!'

Becky matches her frown. 'That's not good,' she says, feeling protective over the sister she's never met.

Alenka sighs. 'Yes, not good. Mother tried to keep an eye on her, but it was out of her control when Idris eventually left with Solar. It took her a while to get over that. Not just the fact Idris was gone, but also how worried she was for the child, especially when I told her about the strange pictures Solar used to draw.'

'What pictures?'

Alenka takes a gulp of her champagne, shaking her head. 'Picture after picture of an evil-looking person, like a witch or wizard with jagged teeth. She used to tell me it was the person with the evil eyes who was trying to get all of us. It gave me nightmares! Of course, Mother told me it was nonsense but then we all knew Idris was running from someone. Maybe there really *was* an evil person?'

Becky thinks of the painting she saw the day before. Who *was* this person Idris was running from?

'Caden!' Alenka suddenly calls out.

Becky follows her gaze to see a short slim man with a dark beard wearing a trendy brown suit approaching.

'Come,' Alenka says, beckoning Caden over. He pulls a chair out and joins them, smiling at Becky. 'This is the woman I was telling you about, Caden,' Alenka explains as she stands up. 'Can I leave you both to it? I have about ten million guests to greet!'

'Of course!' Becky says.

Caden puts his hand out to Becky as Alenka walks off. 'Good to meet you. I liked your mum, very much. I was sorry to hear she passed away.'

'Thank you. I've still not quite got over it,' Becky says.

'Of course you haven't. It has only been a matter of weeks.'

They're silent for a few moments then Becky remembers why she's here. 'Darja tells me you lived in the caves here too for a while?'

He nods. 'It feels like such a long time ago now. I liked Spain best – it was like a permanent holiday. Lots of Sangria and pretty Spanish girls.' Becky raises an eyebrow and he laughs. 'But those days are long behind me. I have three kids now! I'm pleased I got it out of my system though, was a good way to cure heartache.'

'You had your heart broken?'

He sighs. 'Yeah, by a girl called Oceane. She lived at the caves too, with her mum, Donna. I went to school with her, followed her there. She left the group before we went to Spain, and I've not heard from her since. It's such a shame as she would have loved Spain. Not here though,' he adds with a frown. 'There was just a different vibe here. Everyone was less carefree, Idris was on edge. I was starting to realise how much I'd missed out on.'

226

'Like what?'

'Like university.'

'You've done pretty well for myself.'

'I was able to catch up after I returned to the UK when Idris and Solar left. Thank God for the Open University. I did a history degree there part-time while I worked at a museum, I wouldn't have been able to get my current job without it. For all of the fun that came with living in caves, it's not very practical for studying. And I've always had a curious mind.'

Becky wonders what it would have been like if she'd lived in the cave with her mum. Would she have become a vet? But then she'd come to that late, like Caden. Maybe she would have.

'Darja said Idris left without a word,' she says.

Caden nods. 'I remember the morning we woke to find them gone very well,' he says with a sigh. 'Donna in particular was devastated. She and Idris were very close. We haven't seen nor heard from him since.' Caden takes a sip of his wine.

'I only got a chance to chat to Darja briefly but she said she asked you to try to track Idris down?'

'That's right. No luck with him but I found some information about Solar.' He places his glass on the table and pulls a print-out from his pocket, handing it to Becky. She unfolds it to find it's an article in Russian, dated March 2015. With it is a photo of a young woman holding up a trophy, smiling. Beneath it, among all the Russian words, Becky sees a familiar word: *Solar.*

'Not a very Russian name,' Caden says. 'I stumbled upon it when searching for caves around the world. I knew Idris had a penchant for them, thought it feasible he'd head to one. I remembered him talking about how he was fed up of dry caves and yearned for ice.' His brow creases. 'Something about wanting to recreate the atmosphere from a book he read once, snow and forests.'

'My mum's book.' Though I hadn't read any of them, I knew what they were about. My mum would often talk of her works-in-progress when we met up during the years we were in contact. It was one of the only subjects she seemed comfortable talking about when we were together. It was like she thought her writing connected us somehow, when instead I saw it as the thing that had driven her to leave me to go and live in a cave.

Caden nods. 'Ah. Of course. Anyway, among those caves was the Kungar Ice Caves in Russia. I came across this article when doing a search for the caves plus the keywords *British artist*. Solar, but no mention of Idris.'

Becky scrutinises the photo. She's light-haired, pretty . . . looks happy. 'Do you know what the article says?'

'I got it translated,' Caden replies. 'Solar won an award for an art piece she did. It says she's British and lives near the caves with her Russian husband. Another interesting thing. It said in the article she was inspired by the Kungar Ice Caves, where she spent a lot of her time.'

'You think she and Idris lived there?'

Caden smiles. 'That's the other thing I found.'

He hands another print-out to her. It's Idris's signature painting: a menacing black and white face. 'This is from an online photo a caver took in one of the off-bounds caverns.'

Becky thinks of a young Solar being alone in that ice cave with Idris, fearful of whoever it was he was running from. Becky looks at the photo again. She *seemed* happy now though, settled with her husband, not scared.

Becky's heart starts thumping against her chest. 'The article about her was from three years ago. Do you think she still lives in Russia, in the same area?'

'No idea,' Caden replies. 'I tried to track her down as it's a pretty distinctive name, but the trail ran cold. Maybe she's moved since then?'

Should Becky go to Russia? Or was it one step too far? How long could this goose chase continue? And anyway, maybe Solar didn't *want* some woman turning up insisting she was her sister?

Or maybe she'd love it.

There was only one way to find out.

Becky takes a deep determined breath. 'Looks like I'm going to Russia.'

Caden frowns. 'You'll fly out there?'

'I have to. I don't want to regret not trying everything. Even if I go visit the cave she lived in as a child, I can feel like I'm close to her.' She shakes her head. 'God, I sound sentimental.'

'No, I get it. I have a sister. You can't escape the bond, even when you hardly see them. Having said that,' he adds with a frown, 'if you want to visit the cavern where Idris's painting was found, you might struggle. It was found in one of the caverns not open to the public. You won't get in without someone who works there.'

Becky thinks about it. 'Or a caver?'

Caden shrugs. 'That might work.'

She smiles. 'I know just the person.'

Chapter Twenty

Selma

Kent, UK
5 August 1991

A few days after receiving the order from Mike, I found myself walking into a small courtroom. It felt alien to me after my time in the cave. It was so bland in comparison, so lifeless. Mike too, in his grey suit: loose because he'd lost weight. It gave me a hint of guilt to see him like that, but then I remembered how it felt to have that cold stark emergency residency order handed over to me. He wasn't even giving me a chance to share equal time with our daughter. He wanted her all to himself, citing concerns I might whisk her away. I was still kicking myself about that stupid threat I'd made about him not being able to watch Becky all the time. No doubt he'd latched onto that and thought I'd kidnap her. My own daughter!

Mike's solicitor glanced up as I walked past. I recognised him as one of Mike's football buddies. His eyes widened as he took me in. I looked down at myself. Had I really changed that much in just a couple of weeks? I took in the brownness of my wrists against the white of my blouse, felt the length of my dark hair against my bare arms. The blouse felt itchy against my skin, it seemed so long since I was out of summer dresses. But I'd left my hair down, something I wouldn't have done normally if going to court.

Looser hair. Darker skin. A deeper happiness? Despite that awful morning when I received the order from Mike, the past two weeks had been relatively calm. Idris had convinced me there wasn't much I could do and he was right. So I'd thrown myself into writing, writing almost a third of the novel in just two weeks! It gave me a thrill just thinking about it as I stood in that courtroom. I *knew* it was special and then Mike wouldn't have a leg to stand on if I got a big book deal!

I took the seat adjacent to Mike and his solicitor. Mike coughed, taking a sip of water as he glanced at me over his glass. I smiled at him. I wouldn't stoop to his level. He frowned and turned away.

The judge entered and proceedings began. It was nothing new at first, just a confirmation of the residency order and whether it should be maintained. I felt a flicker of hope, but then Mike's solicitor mentioned about me threatening to take Becky that night, as witnessed and confirmed by Becky herself. I was shocked at that. Why hadn't Becky just lied? Surely she was old enough to know what impact this would have; that it might mean her not seeing her mum.

Then it was my solicitor's turn. I liked her. Julien had recommended her and she was surprisingly young, maybe in her mid-twenties, with a permanent smile on her face. She'd loved the cave when she'd visited to go through things with me and that made me warm to her too, especially her informal manner. But as she stood up now, a steely look appeared in her eyes and I could see she was a different person in court.

Good. I wanted Mike to learn his lesson.

'My client strenuously denies threatening to abduct her own daughter,' my solicitor said, 'and as the only witness is a very confused eight-year-old child, she's surprised this has even had to come to court.'

Mike looked over in surprise. 'You *did* say that, Selma, and you bloody well know it!' he shouted out.

The judge looked at him sharply and Mike's solicitor put a soft hand on his client's arm. Mike continued glaring at me. I decided to just smile back and that seemed to wind him up even more.

Good. I wanted him to look bad in front of the judge. It was disgusting what he was trying to do, drive me and my daughter apart.

'My client simply wants to come to a suitable arrangement whereby she shares joint custody of her daughter with her husband,' my solicitor continued, 'ideally agreed via mediation, in her daughter's best interests. She's shocked and saddened it has escalated to a situation which could lead to her not seeing her daughter at all.'

The judge looked at Mike. 'This seems like a sensible option to me. Can we agree to set up a mediation session?'

'No,' Mike said. 'She threatened to take our child away!'

'I didn't,' I said simply. 'I swear I didn't.'

'Well, I refuse to mediate,' Mike said, crossing his arms. 'You don't know my wife like I do. It's impossible to believe a word she says.'

The judge sighed. 'I have read all the documents and heard the evidence, and I tend to agree with Mrs Rhys's solicitor that she does *not* pose an abduction risk.'

Mike shook his head in disbelief. I felt like punching the air but restrained myself.

'However,' the judge added, looking at me, 'I am concerned, if you were to be granted joint custody of your child, that your current living conditions might not be suitable. So, while mediation and prearranged visits between mother and daughter take place, which I insist on,' he said, raising an eyebrow at Mike, 'I will be asking social services to produce a welfare report on both parties' living conditions which will be heard at another court hearing in twelve weeks. But until that report is produced, there will be no overnight stays in the cave, Mrs Rhys. Do you understand?' I reluctantly nodded, trying to hide my disappointment. 'Right, let's move onto arranging visitations during this interim period.'

Mike's jaw was tight as his solicitor whispered in his ear. Then Mike sighed and nodded. Over the next ten minutes, they agreed Becky would meet with me three days a week at pre-agreed venues. It wasn't ideal but it was something.

As I walked back to the cave later, I felt energised. Mike was trying to make it as difficult as possible but the courts were clearly seeing sense. Still, I was annoyed it had come to this. If Mike had only kept his mouth shut, we could have come to an arrangement without Becky having to be caught up in all this drama. And Mike was always saying *I* was the dramatic one! Wasn't he the one who'd thrown me out then served me with an emergency order? If anyone was tearing their family apart, it was him.

As I approached the cave, I was surprised to see nobody was outside. It was nearly six, and usually people would be gathering by the fire before dinner. I was expecting the tinkle of Caden's guitar, laughter from Oceane, the clinking of glasses.

But there was nothing.

I frowned, hurrying towards the cave. But as I stepped in, I felt an amazing energy in the air, so intense it made me stop in my tracks. Everyone was sitting at the large table, hands linked, eyes closed, even young Tom. And at the head of them, Idris, his face serene.

When he opened his eyes, he looked right into mine. I felt my stomach tilt.

'She's back,' he said. Everyone else opened their eyes too, stretching and smiling.

'What were you doing?' I asked, sitting down as Donna got up to pour me some gin.

'We were focusing our currents on you,' Idris explained. 'On trying to ensure your court session was successful.'

I smiled. Yes, it was all a bit woo-woo. But it *was* sweet of them. So I bit back my usual cynical response. 'Thank you,' I said instead. 'I think it worked.'

Oceane's eyes lit up. 'What happened?'

'Mike lost it,' I said, taking the gin Donna handed me with thanks. 'Got really angry. The judge was *not* impressed.'

'Yes!' Tom said, punching the air.

Everyone laughed.

'So what now?' Idris asked.

I turned to him. 'Social services are doing a report which they'll present in twelve weeks. In the meantime, I can see Becky three days a week.' I sighed. 'But she can't stay here.'

Idris frowned. 'That's a shame.'

'Does that mean social services will come here?' Donna asked, suddenly looking anxious as she peered at Tom.

Idris put a hand on her arm. 'It will be fine.'

Donna's face relaxed. 'Yes, it will,' she said, suddenly soothed and relaxed, almost as though hypnotised.

'I know this is a lot for you all to deal with,' I said, sighing. 'It won't be nice having strangers poking about the place you consider your home.'

'*Our* home,' Anita said, smiling at me.

'But it is necessary,' Idris said, voice firm. 'We are family now, *all* of us.'

'The Children of the Current,' Donna said with a smile.

I frowned. 'The Children of the Current?'

'It came to me while I was in the current earlier,' Idris explained. 'That's what we will call ourselves.'

'Okay, just don't tell social services that,' I said with a nervous laugh. 'They'll think we're a cult and no way will Becky be able to stay.'

Maggie rolled her eyes. 'Cult? Honestly. You know I heard some bored housewives gossiping about us when I went to the shops earlier? Apparently, we're going to hole up in this cave and poison each other so we can enter a special heaven made of caves.'

Everyone laughed. But as I watched Donna staring adoringly up at Idris, I wondered if there was some truth to the cult element for some of the group. Then I shook my head. If there was, it wasn't Idris's fault, it was Donna's. She just wanted to latch onto someone, *something*.

'Okay, I have an idea,' Idris said, clapping his hands. Everyone went quiet. 'I think we should all focus our energies on making the cave as child-friendly as it can be before the visit from social services. I'm going to ask everyone to temporarily put their individual projects on hold.' Everyone smiled but I noticed Donna was frowning. 'I believe, if all of us work together, we can make the cave a child's paradise for Becky, for *any* child who lives here.'

'Are you sure?' I asked. 'I don't want to take everyone away from their work.'

'Of course!' Idris said as everyone nodded . . . apart from Donna.

'You don't know how much that means to me, Idris.' I impulsively threw my arms around his neck. The scent of him overwhelmed me, the feel of him too, so close, his soft hair on my lips. 'Thank you,' I whispered in his ear. 'Thank you so much for doing this for me.'

He looked down at me, his face heavy with emotion.

Everyone around us started filtering away as though they sensed we needed this time alone.

'Thank you,' I said. 'Thank you thank you thank you.'

'You keep saying that,' he said, laughing. 'But I've done nothing.'

'You've done *everything*. This place has! I've written words of a novel I didn't think would see the light of day.' I paused, trying to find the words. 'This place has *liberated* me. All my life has felt like a waiting room. But now you've arrived, *I've* arrived.'

'What if I've been the one who's been waiting?' Idris murmured. 'What if *you're* the one who arrived for me?'

His eyes dipped to my lips and I felt my heartbeat match

the thump of the waves nearby. Suddenly, I knew I could kiss him right in that moment. Maybe it was the gin I'd quickly slugged down. Maybe it was the comfort of having everyone rooting for me. Or maybe it was the pure chemical reaction of being so close to him? The need to press my lips against his overwhelmed me and I didn't care if anyone saw. They didn't conform to society's normal rules anyway, that's what they always banged on about.

I stood on tiptoes and Idris moved his lips towards mine . . .

'Idris, can we talk?' Donna was standing by him, tugging at his arm. I wasn't even aware she'd come back.

He turned to her with a smile. 'Of course.'

I felt a sense of frustration bubble inside. He was so quick to pander to the others, even when we were having a moment.

'How can I help?' he asked Donna.

'Can we talk alone?' Donna asked, looking at me.

I raised an eyebrow.

'If that's what you want,' Idris said. 'Come.'

I watched as they walked further into the cave, trying to contain my annoyance. Donna was jealous, I could tell. God knows I'd seen it enough before, that green-eyed monster. They both bent their heads low, Donna frowning as Idris listened patiently. Then he put his hand on Donna's shoulder and looked her in the eye, saying something. She sighed then nodded, heading to the table and sitting down.

Idris came back.

'What was that about?' I asked.

'She's just concerned people might be resentful that they're having to take time away from their individual projects to help you,' Idris replied. 'But when I explained how this would benefit Tom too, she agreed.'

I looked at Donna, who was watching us with a furrowed brow. 'Doesn't look like she agrees.'

Idris sighed. 'It's hard for her, Selma. She likes you but she can see how close we've got.'

I looked at him in surprise. He was saying it, just like that.

'I suppose she sees herself as my right-hand woman,' he continued. 'But she needs to learn I don't favour one person over the other.'

I tried to hide my disappointment. Maybe I'd imagined the connection between us?

Later that afternoon, I lay on my belly on the sand sipping gin, my pen moving over the pages of my notepad, filling them with new scenes and ideas. Caden strummed on his guitar as Oceane danced, the sunlight flickering over her bare tanned legs. In the distance, the sun shone above the sea, painting the tips of the waves gold.

I peered down at Mojo, who was stretched out beside me. She'd taken a liking to me, following me all over the cave and settling down next to me wherever I sat. Maybe it was because of Becky.

Becky.

I peered down the beach. How was my little girl? I wished she was here. My house seemed a world away, the town too. It was as if we were on an island set apart from the rest of the world. And yet people passed all the time when the tide was low, locals taking their evening or morning strolls, tourists checking out the cave as more and more people grew curious about the 'cave dwellers', as we were beginning to be called. And now I was one of them. In fact, right at that moment, there were two young men sitting apart from us all, watching. What did they think when they saw me? That I was a mum and housewife desperate for a change? Or an author on the cusp of something great?

I preferred the latter.

After a while, Anita strolled over to them.

'Getting ready to take photos of the sunset?' she asked, gesturing to the camera around one of their necks.

'Yep,' the man with the camera replied, smiling.

'Why don't you come join us?' she asked them.

'All are welcome!' Idris called over.

The two men smiled, following Anita towards where I was sitting. One of them – the man without the camera – had dark hair to his chin and a goofy smile, and the one with the camera was lanky with pockmarked skin.

Anita passed them the bottle. The man with the camera took a swig but the other man shook his head. 'I'm Nic,' he said. 'This is Ollie.'

Anita and I introduced ourselves. 'Ah, the local author,' Nic said. 'I thought I recognised you from an article I read about your book coming out.'

'Oh, it was a tiny article,' I said.

'Are you living here?' Nic asked me.

The question made me dumbstruck for a few moments. I supposed I was now. 'Yes,' I said.

He raised an eyebrow. 'In a *cave*?'

'I know. It sounds mad, right?' I replied. 'I was cynical too at first but it's wonderful, really.'

'What's so special about this place then?' Nic asked. 'Why a *cave*?'

'The atmosphere in the cave is conducive to getting into the current,' Anita replied matter-of-factly. The two men exchanged looks and I saw it from their point of view. It *did* sound odd.

Nic tilted his head, curious. 'Tell us more.'

As Anita explained what we did at the cave – not just getting into the current but the feasting, the welcoming rituals – the men listened, enraptured.

'She's a pretty good saleswoman, isn't she?' I said as Anita got up to get more drinks. 'Has she convinced you to stay?'

Nic laughed. 'I don't think so. It's a bit Shirley Valentine, don't you think?' He looked at Idris, wiggling his eyebrows.

I felt myself bristle. 'It's not like that,' I said firmly. 'See that man over there?' I pointed at Julien. 'He lost his business, his wife. In fact, he was on the verge of committing suicide, then he saw Idris save that boy. It stopped him from taking his own life and now he lives here. I wouldn't call that a *bit Shirley Valentine*, would you?'

Nic thought about it for a few moments. 'Wow. That's quite something.'

I hesitated. I probably shouldn't have told this stranger about something Julien had told me in confidence. But who was he going to tell? And wasn't it important people knew just how influential Idris truly was?

'Yes,' I said with a smile. 'Well maybe this *place* is quite something.'

'It's certainly been enlightening,' Nic said, stretching as he stood. 'But we better head back.'

'You're not staying?' Anita said, back now with two beers.

'Tempting,' Nic said as he eyed the beers, 'but I have work to do.'

'Maybe we'll see you both again?' she asked.

'Yeah, maybe,' Nic replied, smirking. Then they walked away.

'I bet they come back tomorrow,' Anita said with a smile.

I shrugged. 'I don't know. I think they were just curious.'

'You started curious and look where you ended up. I think Idris would like more people here. Wine?' Anita asked me, holding up a bottle of wine she had tucked under her arm.

'I think I've had enough.'

Anita laughed. 'Me too. Maybe I should stop, I have classes all day tomorrow.'

'Then you should definitely stop drinking!'

'You are *very* wise,' Anita said, giving me a quick impromptu cuddle. 'I like you, Selma. I think we'll be great friends.'

I smiled at her. I usually felt a bit awkward about displays of affection like that, but there was something about this place that was smoothing the rough edges of me.

I tried to focus on that over the coming days. I wasn't seeing Becky until the weekend so it was tough. To distract myself, I threw myself into getting the cave up to scratch for the social services visit. Even Donna seemed to have got over her initial strangeness, helping me to create an indoor play area, painting the shelves of a bookcase we'd found at a local charity shop different colours and lining it with colourful books. Idris painted the walls around it with all sorts of animals: tigers and kangaroos, soaring exotic birds and fish. The kitchen area was improved with rat- and weather-proof cupboards. And Julien talked a plumber friend into lending us some equipment to make a more sophisticated toilet than the camping one we had.

When I wasn't working on the cave, I wrote on the beach, one day to the next presenting bluer skies, the sea breeze a welcome respite from the growing heat. Sometimes I paused from my writing, simply watching the goings-on of the cave. I especially liked to watch Idris painting the new furniture Julien had made, his tanned arms sweeping back and forth, his hair, wavy from the sea salt, tied in a bun at the base of his neck.

As I slept at night, I was increasingly aware of Idris sleeping a few metres away. He slept with no covers on, just some shorts, hands behind his head, looking up at the ceiling as though he could see stories dancing up in those rocks. I snuck occasional glances at him and once or twice caught him watching me, returning my gaze with no words.

Had I really imagined the spark between us both, in the way he looked at me? I thought of that moment we'd shared a few nights ago, before Donna had ruined things. There hadn't been a moment like that since, as the group were too busy doing the cave up. But I *wanted* there to be.

Did Idris?

Or maybe he was that way with everyone. More crowds gathered to watch him paint and talk over those few days, mainly teenagers drawn there, bored during the summer holidays and fascinated by the bohemian group gathered in the cave. People seemed enraptured by Idris's talk of getting 'into the current', some visitors even claiming to have achieved it themselves. Some people stayed overnight too, usually disappearing by the morning. It became a retreat of sorts. Even I had taken to doing readings from my work in progress, offering aspiring writers tips for getting published when I'd finished for the day, gathering a regular daily crowd who popped by on their way back from work to listen to me. It made me feel valuable, significant. Idris and I were becoming quite a team.

By the time the weekend arrived, it was time to meet up with Becky in the seafront café. At first, I thought Mike and Becky wouldn't turn up, but then I saw them approaching from the road in the distance. I smoothed my hair down, suddenly nervous. I wanted things to be as normal as possible for Becky but, the fact was, Mike and I were fighting for her, both desperate to present ourselves as the perfect parents. I could see it in the way Mike was dressed, smarter than usual in chinos and a white T-shirt. When they got to me, Becky seemed hesitant to come to me initially, Mike avoiding my gaze as he stubbornly crossed his arms.

'Come on then, say hello!' I said, opening my arms to my daughter.

Becky took a step towards me then smiled, jogging the rest of the way and throwing herself into my arms. I felt a surge of relief. The thought she might not have wanted to be cuddled by me would have thrown me into a spin of negativity. But of *course* she'd be confused, reluctant at first. As long as she quickly got over that and was in my arms, all would be fine.

'Here, I got you something,' I said, excitedly pulling out a book I'd found in one of the local charity shops about caves.

Mike rolled his eyes.

'Thanks!' Becky said.

'I'll see you here at six then, Mike?' I said in as bright a voice as I could muster.

Mike's jaw twitched, his hands clenching and unclenching as he struggled to contain his anger. He leaned down and gave Becky a quick peck on the cheek.

'I've booked more time off work by the way,' he said, hardly able to look at me. 'It's something we'll need to discuss, how we approach things like the half-terms.'

'Oh, I see. So I'm not an abduction risk any more, am I?'

Becky frowned and I inwardly kicked myself. I'd promised myself I wouldn't stoop to Mike's level.

'You have a good solicitor, that's all I'm going to say,' Mike countered. He went to walk off then he paused, turning back to me. 'Exactly how *are* you paying for your solicitor by the way? You haven't touched our savings so I presume you have some money hidden away somewhere.'

I paused. The truth was, I had a small savings account I hadn't told Mike about. It was my only form of financial independence. Maybe in the back of my mind, I'd known the day would come when I'd need it. It wasn't much, just a few thousand pounds, but the solicitor fees were already draining a chunk of it and soon it would run out. The salary I'd get paid in a few days would quickly get sucked up with bills. The thought of work made me sick. I'd managed to delay my return until the week after next, calling my boss from a payphone in town to explain what had happened with me and Mike, but the idea of returning filled me with doom. I needed to talk to Mike about selling the house, I'd be free of any financial ties then. Maybe I wouldn't *need* a job until I got another publishing deal if that was the case. The thought was just too tempting.

'Selma?' Mike pushed.

'Oh, it's just numbers, Mike,' I heard myself saying. 'Why is everyone so fixated on numbers?'

He laughed. 'Do you realise how you sound?'

I felt a blush working its way over my cheeks. He was right. What *did* I sound like?

'I just *mean*,' I quickly said, 'we should wait until we're alone to discuss all this.'

'Agreed,' Mike replied curtly. Then he walked off.

'Now, how are you, my darling?' I asked, turning back to my daughter. 'I have missed you *so* much!'

'I've missed you too, Mummy. Why aren't you at home? I don't understand.'

I sighed. I knew this conversation had to happen eventually. I'd begged Mike that we both sit down and tell her but he'd refused, saying that I'd made the decision to leave for good, so I had to be the one to deliver the news.

'What has Daddy told you?' I asked Becky.

'That you're on a writing holiday.' Becky folded her arms. 'I hate your stupid writing.'

'It's not that, darling,' I said softly. 'Mummy's moved out.'

Becky frowned. 'You're not living with me any more?'

'Well, I'd *like* us to live together, in the cave. But Daddy wants you to sleep in the house every night. We both love you *so* much, we want you all the time, you see.'

'So that's why you're fighting? You're fighting over *me*?'

My stomach clenched with sadness. It wouldn't have to be as painful as this if Mike would only bloody let Becky stay at the cave some nights! I watched Mike rush across the road in the distance. A bus approached and I imagined it speeding up, hitting him. All my problems would be solved then, wouldn't they? Becky could live with me in the cave forever.

I put my hand to my temple. What was I thinking? I took in a deep breath.

'We're not really fighting,' I said to Becky. 'I just want you to live with me, and Daddy wants you to live with him. But the problem is, Daddy and I don't want to live with each other any more.'

'Why?' Becky whined.

'Adults are complicated. It's hard to explain. You'll understand when you're older.' I leaned forward, clutching onto my daughter's small hand. 'All you need to know is I love you, more than you know. So, what shall we eat? I'm thinking we should start with pudding.'

Becky crossed her arms, sulkily staring out of the window. 'Not hungry.'

I sighed. This wasn't going to be easy.

'Becky!' two little voices shouted out.

I turned to see Gym Bunny Cynthia walk into the café, her twins rushing towards Becky. Cynthia raised an eyebrow when she caught sight of me.

'Look what I got,' one of the twins said when she got to the table, showing Becky a colourful tape recorder with a microphone attached.

'Wow,' Becky said. 'A Rockin' Robot. Can I have one, Mummy?'

'Of course,' I said. 'I'll bring one next time we meet.'

'They're expensive for what they are,' Cynthia said. 'Might be a bit of a stretch for you now you don't have Mike's income to support you.' She pursed her lips slightly, suppressing a smile. So the word was already out about Mike and I splitting up.

I flicked my sunglasses onto my head, yawning. 'I can afford to buy my child a toy, Cynthia. Anyway, you don't need toys and money to have fun.'

'Oh yes,' Cynthia said. 'Numbers are so passé, aren't they? Watches too from what I heard,' she added, looking at my watch-free wrist. 'Getting into the current is *so* much better than all that, isn't it? Especially when the current you're getting into has piercing green eyes and a fit bod?'

I frowned. How did she know all that? Idris only talked about the current with outsiders, not the watch stuff.

'Oh, nice photo by the way,' Cynthia said, getting a newspaper out of her bag and slamming it onto the table. '*Hot* off the press.'

It was the local newspaper, the *Queensbay Chronicle*. On the front page was a photo of Anita and I sitting on the beach, drinking. The headline above read *Inside Scoop on the Cave Dwelling Cult!* Then beneath it, the byline: *Words by Nic Carey, photos by Ollie Robertson.*

The men Anita and I had been talking to a few days before.

'Why are you in the paper, Mummy?' Becky asked, peering at it.

I tried to compose my face but I could feel the hot burning blush creep over my skin. 'It's nothing,' I said, turning it over so I didn't have to look at the article.

'Your mummy's a cavewoman!' one of the twins said, giggling. Becky frowned as other people in the café peered over at us.

Damn it, why had I talked to those men?

'It's a real shame, you know,' Cynthia said with a dramatic sigh. 'These two used to love playing in those caves but now they're too scared.'

'That's ridiculous. Children are always welcome to play in the cave,' I said. 'It's perfectly safe.'

Two women nearby raised cynical eyebrows and I felt my blush deepen.

'Easy to say in this weather,' Cynthia said in a loud voice so everybody could hear. 'But after a few days of heavy rain, you'll be changing your minds.' People nodded. 'And what about the winter?' Cynthia continued, on a roll now. 'It'll be awful. Must be damp too, even in the summer. It's no place for a child to be.'

I felt anger leap inside me. 'Why? Because there's no TV screen to stick your kid in front of?' I shot back, looking pointedly at the handheld game device one of her twins was holding. 'No plastic toys to keep them quiet? Just because this isn't *your* life doesn't mean it's not the *right* life.'

'Mummy,' Becky pleaded in a little voice. But I wasn't going to let Cynthia get away with this.

'Yeah, you keep telling yourself that, love,' an older man sitting at the next table shouted over. 'I guarantee it'll be a different story in a few weeks and I for one can't wait to see it all fall down around your ears. Bloody cults!'

Cynthia suppressed a giggle and I imagined going up to her and smacking her in the face. But instead I stood up and smiled serenely.

'I think we'll get lunch elsewhere. Come on, Becky.' Becky hesitantly got up and I marched her outside. 'Have a lovely day being ignorant and bloody boring!' I shouted over my shoulder, barely containing my rage.

'You have a fab day being a crazy hippy, Selma!' Cynthia shot back in an equally faux cheery voice. 'And see you on Saturday, Becky darling!'

'Saturday?' I said to Becky as I strode out with her. 'What's happening on Saturday?'

'Cynthia's coming to our house for a playdate.'

I took several deep breaths to calm myself. A *playdate*? Funny how Mike had suddenly become Father of the Year. And with Cynthia, of all people. He knew I hated her.

As we walked down the street, I noticed people watching me and whispering, and I thought of that article.

What was Idris going to say?

Chapter Twenty-One

Selma

Queensbay, Kent
10 August 1991

I got my answer a few hours later when I returned to the cave. Everyone but Anita was gathered around the table, the newspaper lying on its surface.

My stomach sank. 'Hi,' I said, taking a seat. 'So you've seen it?'

'How could we miss it?' Maggie hissed. 'I noticed it while shopping in town.'

'I haven't had a chance to read it yet,' I replied, swallowing nervously. 'What does it say?'

Maggie shoved the newspaper towards me as Idris avoided my gaze. Did he know I'd talked to the journalist? Anita wasn't here yet so she wouldn't have had a chance to tell anyone what had happened.

I started reading the article.

Several people have taken to living in one of the caves on

Queensbay, it began, *led by a mysterious figure called Idris who saved a local boy from drowning. One of these men is Julien Sinclair, former owner of one of the largest solicitor firms in Kent. A source from the cave claims Mr Sinclair, who recently fell on hard times after the firm went into administration, was on the verge of committing suicide before he was 'saved' by the cult. Residents have expressed concerns about the cave dwellers, especially the enigmatic Idris, with one concerned mother, Cynthia Hoffman, labelling him a threat to the peace of the town during a recent council meeting.*

I shook my head. No wonder she was so proud of the article.

'How the hell did they find all this out?' Caden asked.

I felt my chest constrict.

'I've only told a few people here about my suicide attempt,' Julien said. 'It can only be someone in this group,' he added, face clouding over.

'You were talking to two men the other night, weren't you Selma?' Donna asked me.

All eyes turned to me. 'Only briefly,' I said, trying to keep my voice steady. 'I didn't pay much notice, to be honest. Anita did most of the talking.'

'Maybe Anita said something to them?' Oceane suggested.

'I don't like promises being broken,' Idris said, face very serious. 'It's key to me that we can all trust each other.'

I looked down at my hands, my heart thumping. Why did I open my fat mouth about Julien to complete strangers?

'Selma, *did* Anita say something?' Idris asked me. 'You don't need to protect her, you know. We're all about honesty here, she knows that.'

I swallowed, peering at the article then away again. If Idris

251

learnt I'd betrayed Julien's trust, he'd tell me to leave, I could see it in his eyes. And what then? Where would I go? Mike wouldn't have me back, not that I'd want to go back to him. I'd end up in a tiny soulless flat in town, back to working full-time, all my hopes of finishing my novel shot to pieces.

It was me or Anita.

'Yes,' I whispered.

'Excuse me?' Idris asked.

'Yes, it was Anita who told them,' I said in a louder voice.

Julien shook his head in disgust.

'I was writing, so I wasn't paying much attention,' I quickly said. 'But I did hear her mention Julien . . . and what happened.'

'Where is she?' Maggie asked.

'She's teaching,' Oceane replied, brow knitted. 'She'll be back after dinner. Her last class finishes at eight.'

The atmosphere over dinner was awkward, everyone eating silently, the words in that article rebounding between us. More people seemed to be walking by the cave too, even wading through the high tide in wellies to get a look at us, the 'crazy cave dwellers' as I heard one of them shout out. And it was all my fault! If only I'd kept my mouth shut.

When Anita walked up the beach as the sun began to set, she had a huge smile on her face, making me feel even worse. She noticed everyone looking solemn at the table and her smile faltered.

'What's going on, guys?' Anita asked.

Idris stood, holding the newspaper up. 'You were talking to two men the other night, right?'

Anita frowned. 'What two men?'

'One of them had a big camera,' Maggie said, voice hard.

'Oh, those two men. I hardly remember, I was so drunk.' Anita gave a nervous laugh. 'What's wrong?'

'They were journalists,' Julien said.

Her face dropped. 'Shit. Did they write something?'

'You could say that,' Julien replied.

She took the paper off Idris and scoured it, eyes widening when she got to the bit about Julien. She went up to Julien, looking him in the eye.

'There is no *way* I'd tell them that, Julien. You *know* I wouldn't!' She turned to me. 'You were there the whole time, Selma. We didn't say anything about Julien, did we? They must have heard it from someone else.'

I couldn't look at her. I felt awful but what choice did I have?

'Selma *told* us, Anita,' Oceane said with a sigh. 'Don't lie.'

Anita looked at me in shock.

'I'm sorry, Anita, I did hear you,' I said, voice trembling.

'I wouldn't,' Anita said, shaking her head. 'You must have heard wrong.'

'You *were* drunk,' Oceane said softly. 'Maybe you just don't remember?'

'I'd remember that. Selma,' Anita said, walking over and crouching down in front of me as I sat at the table. 'You were talking to them as much as I was!'

'I was writing, you know that,' I said, making myself look her in the eye.

Her face hardened, her hands clasping painfully onto my fists. 'You're lying. Why are you lying?'

'Anita, come on . . .' Idris went to help her back up but she shoved him away, still glaring at me.

'You're lying to cover your back.'

'No, you're lying to cover yours,' I replied calmly. The lie was out now, no point trying to capture it back.

Anita looked at me in shock. She put her hand on my shoulder, looking me in the eye. The force of it caused my flimsy chair to tip backwards. Idris grabbed it before it fell, steadying me.

'You okay?' he asked as the chair legs slammed back onto the ground.

'Fine,' I replied in a shaky voice as I looked at Anita in shock.

'We can't accept behaviour like this here,' Idris said to Anita, his voice firm. 'Not just the indiscretion, but also what you just did to Selma. We do *not* condone violence.'

'What?' Anita said, eyes wide with surprise. 'I just put my hand on her shoulder, that wasn't *violence*! That chair's been ready to break for days.'

'You shoved her, Anita,' Oceane said, crossing her arms and looking Anita up and down.

'I didn't!'

'Pack your stuff,' Idris said firmly. 'And leave, right now.'

'I can't believe you're all doing this to me.' She looked at everyone imploringly but they avoided her gaze. A sense of determination crossed her face and she folded her arms, glaring at Idris. 'You can't tell me to go. You don't *own* this cave.'

'Actually, I do,' Idris said.

We all looked at him in surprise.

'Now go, get out,' Idris said, showing a spark of anger on his handsome face.

Donna stood next to Idris, putting her hands on her hips. 'We don't want you here.'

'Yeah, go away!' Tom said, sticking his tongue out at Anita.

'Just go, Anita,' Caden said quietly.

'Yes,' Julien said with a sigh. 'I think your time here is over.'

The others nodded in agreement, Idris's protective hand still on my shoulder. Guilt surged through me but I reminded myself it was a matter of survival. This place was my life now.

Donna caught the look on my face and frowned.

Anita's eyes settled on me. I could see they were resigned now, not angry.

Resigned and disappointed.

'I can't believe you're doing this,' Anita said to me. 'I actually thought we could be friends, but clearly I got you all wrong.'

I felt a trickle of remorse but stood my ground, staring her down. Anita blinked then turned on her heel and fled down the beach, leaving her belongings behind. I looked at Idris. He'd said he owned the cave. Had he just lied to make Anita leave? I was about to ask him but then he clapped his hands to get everyone's attention and the moment was lost.

'I know that seemed tough,' Idris said when she was out of earshot, 'but someone with that kind of vibe isn't good for us. It will only interfere with the current. Now she's gone, I guarantee we will all be more creative than ever.'

Everyone nodded and I tried my best to shroud my guilt.

'And while we're all gathered together,' Idris said, 'I have something I'd like us all to do. Remember I asked you all to remove your watches when you came here?' He looked at my pocket. I frowned. How did he know? 'Can you go retrieve them for me?'

We all exchanged curious glances then went off to gather our

255

watches. When we returned, we all stood around the fire Idris had lit, its flames reflected in our eyes.

'I understand this might be difficult for some,' he said. 'But it's a symbolic gesture, a signal we've all entered a deeper phase of our time here.'

'You're going to ask us to burn our watches, aren't you?' I asked him.

He nodded, holding my gaze. 'We need this, Selma. A commitment to what we've achieved here. What happened with Anita, it has shaken us. But as I stand here, looking at how we've supported each other in the face of her lies, it proves to me more than ever how strong we are together. And I want to mark that with a symbolic gesture, a true, clear rejection of numbers, the same numbers the people owning this newspaper are obsessed with,' he added, gesturing angrily towards the newspaper. 'Publishing scandalous rubbish to increase their circulation figures, and in turn generate more money. So now is the time to take that step, truly turn your back on numbers by burning your watches.'

'I can't,' I said, shaking my head. 'It's all I have of my mother's. The only thing she left to me after she passed away.'

He tilted his head. 'Tell me about your mother.'

I thought of my mother's cold gaze, her beautifully painted lips and the curve of her black hair over her forehead.

'There's not much to say.'

'*Tell* me.' His eyes bored into mine.

'She was . . . cold. Distant.' I swallowed, feeling my cheeks turn hot. I rarely talked about this. 'I – I spent my childhood yearning for her approval.'

'And this watch,' Idris said, gesturing to the delicate gold watch. 'It reminds you of her?'

'Yes,' I whispered.

'It reminds you of how cold she was? How distant?'

I frowned and suddenly felt the weight of it in my hands, the hard, cold metal. I peered up at Idris and we held each other's gaze.

'Then why do you keep it?' he asked.

I nodded. He was right. I walked to the fire and threw the watch in, captivated as sparks flew and it started to melt in the flames.

'She told me it was real gold,' I said, laughing bitterly to myself. 'Gold doesn't burn like that. She lied to me.'

Idris nodded. 'She betrayed you again. Her last lie. And now it's gone forever.'

I watched it sizzle and burn. Then I thought of Anita's face when she realised I'd betrayed *her* and felt sick to my stomach. As the watch disappeared, I promised myself I would start over, a phoenix from the flames.

No more lies. Just truth.

Chapter Twenty-Two

Selma

Kent, UK
11 August 1991

In all the drama of the past few days, I almost forgot I had to return to work on the Monday. But the evening before, it hit me like a sledgehammer. I couldn't see any way around it though. If I stopped working, the impact on my chances of getting joint custody of Becky would be diminished – my solicitor had said it herself.

'Back to work tomorrow then?' Donna asked over dinner that night.

I sighed. 'Yep.'

'We'll miss you,' Idris said softly. 'You don't *need* to go in, you know.'

'We've had this discussion before, remember?' I said with a wry smile. 'You all might hate numbers, hell, I hate them too. But the fact is, I have a mortgage to contribute to. Plus not having a job won't go down well with social services.'

'It's just proof of an income they want,' Julien said. 'What about your book royalties?'

'They're only paid twice a year,' I replied, playing with the soup Donna had made for us. 'That won't be regular enough for social services. Plus there's the mortgage still to pay.'

'But your royalties must be a decent whack,' Donna said. 'What with you being a bestseller and all.'

'I'm not a bestseller,' I said, my cheeks flushing.

Donna frowned. 'But that's what the other mums at school told me.'

I *may* have told a few of the school-gate mums my book had hit the charts. 'It was just a few days,' I quickly said.

'Why are you talking about numbers, Donna?' Idris said. 'You know we don't do that.'

Donna looked wounded. 'Sorry.'

I smiled at him, pleased for the support. I took a deep breath, looking towards the town where my office was. In just thirteen hours, I'd be back at my desk, writing copy I hated as people gossiped worthless nonsense around me.

I clenched my fists beneath the table, pressing them into my legs.

'Did you know,' Idris said softly, 'two thirds of many people's lives are spent working in an office? Many of those people hate their jobs, yet they call that *life*.' He looked at everyone around the table who had stopped eating and were listening intently. 'If you open the dictionary, life is defined as *organisms that are not dead and inorganic*.'

Great. I didn't need a sermon about how rubbish the nine-to-five rat race was when I had no choice but to face it. I loved being in the cave, it was doing wonders for my writing, but sometimes the naivety of the group astounded me.

Idris got up and walked outside, leaning down and picking something up from amongst the seaweed and shells left behind by the tide. When he returned, he had a red starfish in his hand, its legs bent out of shape.

'This is dead. But in life, it moved and it changed, like the current.'

He stood behind me, and placed the dead starfish by my plate.

I raised an eyebrow. 'Gee. Thanks for that, Idris.'

He didn't smile like he usually did when I said something like that. 'Are you moved by your job, Selma? Like you are by the current? Or are you dead when you're there, like this starfish?'

I stared at the hopeless starfish, my jaw tightening. Then I looked up, seeing the way everyone was looking at me like they felt sorry for me. It infuriated me how naive they were!

But it also infuriated me that I had to return to normal life the next day.

I flung the starfish to the ground and stood up. 'How many times do I need to say it? I have no choice.' I took a deep breath, suddenly feeling horribly wary. 'I'm going to bed.'

Then I walked to my bed, feeling Idris's eyes on me.

I barely slept that night and woke early, getting ready for work in silence. As I stepped out of the cave into the morning sun, I yanked at the collar of my blouse. It felt like I was wearing someone else's uniform, the wrong size, starchy, unfamiliar. It was like being back in court again. I'd been so used to my long flowing skirts and soft tops with flip-flops lately.

'Packed your lunch?' Caden called out to me.

'Ha ha,' I said.

'Have a good day!' Oceane shouted out, waving.

'Yeah right,' I grumbled back. I took a deep breath and headed towards town. When I walked into the office a few minutes later, the receptionist greeted me with wide eyes.

'Wow, you look tanned!' he said.

'Yep, the summer has a way of doing that to humans!'

I carried on until I got to the main office, stopping at the glass doors. I could see them all in there, *machines* as Idris would call them, faces lit up by the synthetic glare of their screens, circles under their eyes, fingers tapping to the dullest of tunes. They all looked so grey, so *dead* like that starfish.

But that was life. *Real* life – not the refined bubble of life the cave dwellers lived in. I held Becky's face strong in my mind and took a deep breath, walking in.

Monica caught sight of me and looked over at a colleague, frantically gesturing towards me. Everyone else stared up at her as I walked through the office, my head held high.

Jesus, their lives really must be dull if they found a new tan this exciting.

'Selma!' Monica called out as she passed, causing more people to raise their heads. 'Welcome back!'

'Thanks!' I said without looking at her, waving my hand in the air.

Just keep walking, I told myself. *Just eight hours and it'll be over for the day. You can get back to the cave, drink gin and forget about this godforsaken place.*

I got to my desk and sat down, leaning my head on the heel

of my hand as I waited for my computer to turn on. I looked up and peered out at the summer sun in the distance, imagining it warming my skin as Idris painted nearby. I tried to focus on that instead of the shadows that sat in angles over me in the reality of this office. I imagined the smell of salt, paint oils and oranges in contrast to the synthetic office stench of coffee, printer ink and air freshener. I imagined a breakfast of fish caught by Idris instead of the dry croissant I'd bought myself on the way in. And then nightfall, guitar music and the flames of a fire, Idris's green eyes on mine.

Not long . . .

'Ah, she's back.' I looked up to see Matthew swinging his bag onto the table and sitting down, his chair bouncing. 'Monica cornered me in the kitchen after that article was printed,' he said in a low voice. 'Seriously, that woman has no space boundaries.'

'You lucky man,' I replied with a raised eyebrow. 'All your dreams coming true.'

He gave me a disgusted look. 'Please don't put that image in my mind. Oh God, here she comes,' he said, quickly putting his headphones on and pretending to type.

'So,' Monica said, sitting on my table as I resisted the urge to shove her off, 'is it true you're living in the cave with all those people?'

'Yep,' I said, logging into my computer.

'What does *Mike* think?' Monica asked.

'I don't need his permission to be there.'

'So Becky's with you?'

'She's visited.'

262

Monica frowned. 'I see. So what's he like then – Idris? Did he mention the bottle of wine I left him?'

More people were walking over, desperate for information about the mysterious cave dwellers.

'He's fine,' I said. 'Look, I have a lot of work to do. Maybe I'll see you in the kitchen later?' I added, having no intention whatsoever of stepping foot in that gossip pit.

Monica frowned. 'Okay. But can you please tell everyone he's not a kiddie fiddler? He saved my son for God's sake! I keep telling everyone not to believe the rumours, but you live with him so you can tell them yourself.'

'For God's sake,' I hissed.

'Yeah, like he's shagging that blonde kid who never wears a bra,' the man from accounts shouted over.

I shot him a look of disgust. 'No, he bloody isn't. He wouldn't go near Oceane.'

'Oceane?' Matthew said, taking his earphones off. 'My little brother was at school with her last year. Apparently, she's been telling her friends she and Idris have a thing going on.'

I looked at him incredulously. 'What?'

He put his hands up. 'Don't shoot the messenger.'

'But she has a boyfriend,' I said.

'Since when has that stopped you hippy types?' the man from accounts piped up.

'All I know is that she's seventeen,' Matthew said, brow creased. 'Just a kid really. If it is true . . .' His voice trailed off.

I stood up, grabbing my bag. 'I can't be here. Tell Daphne I have a tummy bug.'

'*Another* one?' Monica said, shooting me a cynical look. 'You've had an awful lot of those this year.'

'Fine, tell her I quit instead. Haven't used that excuse yet, have I?' I shoved away from my desk and walked out.

It was just rumours about Idris and Oceane. Surely it was just rumours? But as I drew closer to the cave, anger twisted and turned inside me.

What if it wasn't?

Even worse, when I got there, the first people I saw were Idris and Oceane who were at the edge of the waves, peering down at some fish.

Had the naivety of the people who lived in the cave infected me? Was I seeing Idris through rose-tinted glasses; seeing the man I *wanted* him to be? What if he'd been taking me for a fool all this time, making me believe he felt something for me? Taking Oceane for a fool too, a naive seventeen-year-old?

Oceane let out a giggle as Idris twirled her around. Had he slept with her already? That silly lithe teenager. That would make sense, a kid like Oceane falling for his charms. But me? Nearly forty, a writer and a mum. What a fool I'd been! What a fool to think *he'd* be attracted to *me.* I thought of the dimples on my thighs, the stretch marks on my stomach. How, when released from my bra, my breasts sagged down slightly now, bumping against the top of my stomach.

So why did he look at me the way he did?

I thought of my mother then. There was this one time when I was about ten, when she'd been acting unusually kind: cuddling me lots, buying me pretty dresses. I'd dared to hope she might have changed. But it wasn't long before I realised why she was acting like this – there was a potential new boyfriend on the scene, a rich one left with three kids to care for after his wife died. My mother had seen the pound signs, pretty dresses and parties, and the man had clearly seen a new mother for his unruly children, which was ironic considering she was barely able to care for her own daughter, let alone three new kids. But my mother was astute enough to know the way to impress the man was to weave a lie and show him what a wonderful mother she was. It didn't last long. My mother soon realised what a handful the kids would be. As soon as her ambitious plans to snare him fled, the affection she'd feigned for me did too. I'd cried, asking for the 'nice mummy' to come back.

'Oh you're so naive, Selma,' my mother had said. 'It was just an act, didn't you know? You know I hate cuddles and all that fuss.'

Was Idris the same, just putting on an act? Tears pricked my eyes at the thought then I shook my head, clenching my fists. How ridiculous, to react like this! Nothing had happened between me and Idris anyway!

Over dinner I barely talked, just shrugging when people asked about work. I avoided making eye contact with Idris, but could feel his stare. After, I walked along the beach in the dark, not wanting to be around them . . . *especially* Idris and Oceane. After a while, I heard footsteps behind me. I turned to see it was Idris.

'Mind if I join you?' he asked.

Another shrug.

'You're in turmoil,' he said, looking sideways at me. 'Did someone say something to upset you at work?' He seemed so concerned, his green eyes searching my face.

I took a deep breath. 'Oceane's been telling her friends she has a thing going on with you.'

Idris's hands dropped from my shoulders. There was a look in his face that made me hesitate.

'She's seventeen, Idris!'

'It's just a number.'

I closed my eyes, pinching my nose. 'So something *is* going on between you both?'

'No! You need to stop listening to people. Just know the truth in your heart.' He put his hands on my shoulders again. 'You know if a tree—'

'I don't want one of your bloody adages, Idris,' I said, shoving his hands away. 'I just don't want to be lied to. I thought you were more than the sex-mad cult leader people have been making you out to be, but maybe they were right all along?'

His face hardened. 'There were no *lies*, Selma. Nothing is going on with Oceane and me. And anyway, you're hardly the person to complain about lies, are you?'

I glared at him, my face turning hot. Then I strode down the beach away from him. 'Don't follow me!' I shouted over my shoulder.

I eventually ended up in the cave Idris had shown me that first day we met, peering up at the outlines of the stone birds and bats hanging from the ceiling as I thought of my mother, beautiful face frozen like stone, eyes hard.

'You can hardly talk of *my* lies, Selma,' I remembered her hissing at me once, 'when you're the queen of deception.'

Maybe I'd been lying to myself about this whole thing at the cave, about Idris? What was it that the old man at the café had said? *I for one can't wait to see it all fall down around your ears.*

Maybe that was what was happening now? The newspaper article, the revelations about Idris and Oceane. Even if he was telling the truth and they were all lies, that was what people thought. Add to that the fact I'd walked out on my job and I might lose custody of Becky . . .

The horrible reality of it suddenly hit me. What had I *done*?

I squeezed my eyes shut, tears sliding down my cheeks.

'Selma.' I looked up into the darkness to see Idris entering the cave. 'Can I join you?'

I didn't say anything but he walked in anyway, his shadow spreading across the cave, making him seem like a giant. He sat down next to me, his shoulder close to mine. We both looked up at the frozen birds.

'Maybe I've been frozen here all this time,' I said, wiping my tears away angrily. 'In a stupid naive little bubble, lying to myself about the cave, about *you*, just so I had an excuse to get away from my marriage.'

He looked wounded.

'I think it's time I go back home,' I added.

He looked down at his hands, a frown puckering his tanned forehead. 'The night I saved the boy, I saw you first. Among all the crowds, I saw *you*. Your sadness, your complexity.' He looked up at me, eyes deep in mine. 'Now I see your wings unfurling and the idea of you leaving, just as it's all about to take flight, it kills me.' He took my hand, our fingers lightly touching. 'I feel my wings unfurling with you and it hurts. I *know* how much it hurts as it's so new to us. I'm sorry if I hurt you just now, Selma. I really am. It won't happen again, I promise. And there is *nothing* going on between me and Oceane.' He took a deep breath, his thumb caressing my hand. 'There's only one person I desire and I think you know who that person is.'

I felt my breath quickening, ripples of feeling building inside as I looked at him.

'We're both so afraid to take the leap,' he said. 'But isn't it time we jumped that final hurdle together?'

I swallowed. That was my problem. I was always so scared. I should have left Mike years ago. I should have told my mother to go fuck herself earlier, left home way before I was eighteen. I should have written a novel when I had more time, at university. I should have, I could have, but I always left everything too late. Just like coming to this cave, running away from a life that made me miserable at a time when my daughter needed me most, not when I should have done it – years ago.

And what of Idris? Was that another opportunity I was about to let slip through my fingers?

I put my fingertips to his face, felt the soft bristles of his blond beard. Then I glided my fingers towards his neck, gently curving my hand around the back as I kept my eyes in his.

His long hair brushed against my knuckles and I sighed.

'I've been trying to fight this,' he said in a low voice as he put his hand to my face too. 'I was worried how it would look, being attracted to someone in the group. But I can't resist any more.'

He leaned towards me, pressing his lips against mine, his arm circling my waist and pulling me close, both of us growing more and more frantic, our fingers in each other's hair.

I felt something release inside me then. Something I hadn't felt for a long time. With Mike, I always felt a calmness, a sense of coming home. But with Idris, I felt untethered, unravelled, heart thumping to an uneven rhythm, every fibre in my body frantic to get as close to him as possible.

He pushed me against the cool stone of the rock and I felt him hard against my thigh as I lifted my leg up, hands moving down to his buttocks as I pressed myself against him.

Then I suddenly became conscious of my lumps and bumps.

'Why me?' I asked. 'You could choose anyone.'

'The way you write,' he replied in a whisper. 'The words you choose say a million things about you. Your strength and leadership. Your beauty,' he added, tangling a lock of my hair around his finger. 'Your cynicism,' he added with a smile.

We were both breathing hard, pressing into each other, one heart thumping against the other. The ebb and flow of the waves outside seemed to match that rhythm, the silver ripples cast by the moon in sync too.

I leaned my head back, felt his lips on my neck, trailing down to my collar bone and under the top of my blouse, his thumb nudging the silk material of my bra aside and circling my nipple. I groaned, sensation throbbing within me as I ran my hands over his taut muscles.

He turned onto his back, bringing me with him so I lay above him, my legs either side of his waist. I leaned down, dipping my tongue into his mouth as he groaned against my lips. Our kisses grew more urgent, more intense, barely noticing as rain started thundering down outside, the wind picking up.

Idris hitched the bottom of my skirt up, fingers finding the wetness beneath my silk knickers. I slipped my hand beneath the waistband of his shorts, felt him hard in my palm. Thunder roared outside, the waves now frantic as I pushed Idris's shorts down and guided him between my legs, eyes still in his.

Then I lowered myself onto him.

'Oh God,' he moaned, seeming more human now, less godlike.

I moved up and down on top of him, bending over to kiss him, my fingers running through his long sandy hair as he thrust his hips up, deeper within me, making me cry out.

As I arched my head back, I thought I saw two eyes blinking at us in the darkness. But the next time I looked, they were gone.

Chapter Twenty-Three

Becky

Birmingham, UK
30 June 2018

'I guess this is a bit different from your little village in Sussex?'
Kai asks as he and Becky walk up the busy street where he grew
up, just outside the main centre of Birmingham. Bustling shops
line the road, people enjoying their Saturday morning errands.
People pass the red-brick buildings in colourful saris and
swaying dreadlocks, a multicultural hotspot. This is very different
from Becky's little village. It feels so vibrant, so full of energy . . .
just like Kai.

She'd called him when she'd touched down in the UK. She'd
wanted to broach the subject of him coming to Russia with her
to try to find her sister and explore the cave where Idris's painting
had been found. As she'd been flying into Birmingham airport
– it was the cheapest flight she could find from Slovenia – he'd
suggested they meet up in the town. She'd been hesitant at first.

But then she'd thought *why not?* She'd flown back a day early anyway and David wasn't expecting her home yet. Plus she was intrigued to see where Kai lived.

And now here she is. A group of teenagers pass, looking her up and down. She smiles at them, resisting the urge to pull her bag close to her. Just because they are teenagers wearing hoods doesn't mean they'll steal her bag.

'Yeah, you might want to zip that bag of yours up,' Kai says to her in a low voice. 'I love it around here but there are a few – how shall I put it? – troubled youths hanging around. I know because I was one of them once,' he adds with a sigh. 'Anyway, we live just up the street. You'll love them all. It'll freak you out at first, there are a *lot* of them. But trust me, you'll soon feel at home.'

Becky stops walking. 'Them? What do you mean?'

'My family!'

'But I thought we were going to your house?'

'We are. I live with my mum.'

Becky can't help but laugh. 'How old are you?'

He shoots her a look. 'Thirty-three. And so what? I travel so much there's no point getting anywhere myself yet. Plus my mum cooks a damn good curry goat.'

Becky swallows, suddenly nervous. Hadn't Kai said he had *five* sisters?

'They know I'm not your . . .' She lets her voice trail off.

He laughs. 'Girlfriend? Of course. They won't believe it but who cares? Come on, I'm starving.'

Becky takes a deep breath and follows him for a few more minutes until they get to a quieter end of the street, a line of red-brick houses with bay windows. He swings the gate to one of them open and walks towards a red front door. Before they even reach the door, Becky can smell the mouth-watering cooking.

'Breathe it in,' Kai says, wafting his hand to his nose and closing his eyes as he inhales. 'It's a thing of beauty.'

'Smells amazing.'

He lets them in and a cacophony of noise hits Becky: girls arguing, pop music being played, the bash of pots and pans and, above it all, the sharp loud shout of a woman.

'Keep your pipes down, child. Kai's lady will be here any minute.'

'Lady?' Becky says, raising an eyebrow.

'I told you, Mum won't accept it.'

'Kai!' A girl of about ten comes hurtling down the hallway, throwing herself into Kai's arms. She's tiny and beautiful with black hair tied into tight braids.

'This is Tashel, my niece,' Kai says, swinging her around as she giggles. Two women appear at the end of the hallway then, both in their twenties and identical apart from their dress senses, one dressed conservatively in a smart black dress, the other in ripped jeans and a low-cut red top.

'The twins,' Kai says, disentangling himself from his niece and giving the two women a high five. 'Janique and Chrisette, Tashel's long-suffering mum.'

Tashel crosses her arms and gives him a faux angry look.

'Hello, Becky, welcome to the madhouse,' the smartly dressed sister says. 'So good our big bro's found himself a lady.'

'I hate to break the news but we're just friends,' Becky says.

'But Mum said . . .' The other twin sighs, shaking her head. 'Why does she think every woman you meet is your future wife, Kai?'

273

'It's hope,' the other twin says, 'desperate hope her oldest son will settle down.'

'Never!' Kai declares.

They all laugh.

'Come through,' Kai says, jostling past his sisters and going into the kitchen. It's a long galley kitchen looking out onto a neat garden. Sitting at a round table is a couple in their thirties, another one of Kai's many sisters, Becky presumes. At the hob is an older woman with braided grey hair down her back and a beautiful long patterned dress. She turns when Becky enters and her face lights up.

'Becky!' She jogs forward and pulls her into a hug then holds her at arm's length, examining her. 'Nice and curvy, good. Kai doesn't like them stick thin.'

'Mum!' Kai says, exasperated. 'We're just friends.'

She ignores him. 'So, has my boy been behaving?'

'I don't really know,' Becky says. 'I've not been with him much.'

Kai's mum whacks him with a wooden spoon. 'Take her out more!'

Kai opens his mouth to protest but his sister shakes her head. 'Don't waste your breath – she's in denial.' She smiles at Becky. 'I'm Pheebie, this is my husband, Antwan.'

Becky waves at them. 'I'm Becky.'

'Where are Chanese and Thea?' Kai asks.

Becky takes a deep breath. All these names to remember, all the hustle and bustle of family life, she just isn't used to it.

'Dining room,' his mum declares. 'Lunch ready in five minutes. Get out of my kitchen, all of you! It's getting too damn hot in here.'

Kai rolls his eyes and leads Becky out, but his mum stops him. 'Not our guest. Stay, Becky.'

'Mum, don't grill her,' Kai says with a sigh. 'She really is just a friend.'

'I know, I know. I just like to get to know my guests without all of you harping in my ear.'

Kai shrugs at Becky and she smiles. 'It's fine, maybe I'll get an early taste of the curry. It smells *delicious*.'

Kai's mum winks at him. 'I like her already.'

The others leave the room, the sound of the TV turning on in the next room.

'Can I help?' Becky asks.

Kai's mum shakes her head. 'No, sit,' she replies, gesturing to the table.

Becky does as she is told and sits down, looking around the kitchen. It's a modern room with wooden tops and colourful blue units. Spices hang from a rack, various bottles of oils and more lining the sides. It's clearly the hub of the house and Kai's mum is in her element in there.

'Kai tells me you're searching for your sister?' she asks Becky as she stirs the curry.

Becky nods. 'I think I've tracked her down in Russia.'

Kai's mum raises her eyebrow. 'Russia? Always thought it looked like a strange place. Will you go?'

'I hope so.'

She nods. 'Good. Family's important. You want children of your own?'

'One day, I hope.'

'Better hurry up, you're not young.'

Becky laughs. She ought to be insulted but she likes Kai's mum's refreshing honesty. 'Just thirty-five, it's not so old.'

The woman waves her spoon up and down, gesturing to Becky's tummy. 'Those little eggs will be shrivelling soon and then what?'

'I'm sure I'll be fine, I have my dogs.'

'Dogs, pah! Dogs won't run you ragged and ruin your beautiful new kitchen, will they?' she says, gesturing to a burn ring on her wooden surfaces.

'You want to bet?' Becky replies.

They smile at each other.

'So you and my son, just friends?' Kai's mum asks.

'Absolutely.'

She looks at Becky sideways as she pours some sauce into a huge pan. 'You have a man?'

'Not right now.'

'Ever had one?'

'One serious relationship when I was a teenager.'

'What happened?'

Becky sighs. She's not sure how she feels being quizzed like this. Half of her likes it, the other half feels a bit overwhelmed.

'He left me out of the blue ten years later. I never really knew why.'

The woman turns around and smiles sadly. 'Now I understand.'

'Understand what?'

'Why you and Kai have connected. You know he was engaged to be married last year?'

'I had no idea. What happened?'

'He will tell you all in his own time.' She takes her apron off and sits across from Becky, taking her hand. 'Your mother died not long ago?'

Becky nods, looking down at their conjoined hands as she tries to contain her sadness. It hits her sometimes, like a sledgehammer to the core. She's barely stopped for breath since she's started searching for her sister, so she hasn't had much time to properly process the grief.

Hasn't *allowed* herself much time.

'Kai says you were with her when she went,' Kai's mum says softly. 'That's a luxury. I was thousands of miles away. Hold that in your heart.'

Becky smiles sadly. 'I do. Does it get any easier?'

Kai's mum shakes her head. 'Not really. And the moment you think it has, it comes at you like a wave out of nowhere again. Especially milestones, you know? When my youngest was born, just after my mum passed, I thought how sad it would be she would never know her grandmother.'

Becky thinks of her own grandmother, seen only in photos bitterly shoved back into boxes by her mum.

'Did you know yours?' Kai's mum asks, as though sensing her thoughts.

'No, my mum never saw her. They had a difficult relationship. She used to be a singer.'

'Oh yes?' Kai's mum says.

Becky nods. She remembers the rare times her mum talked about her grandmother, of how she always told her having a child had derailed her career.

She remembers her mum imitating her grandmother. 'I was destined to be the next Patsy Cline. The Brunette Patsy Cline, my manager once called me. Then *you* came along.'

Her mum was a mistake, so she was constantly told. Becky had overheard her dad telling Cynthia about it once during a playdate when she was a child, how her mum's poor relationship with her own mother could be detrimental to her relationship with Becky. He told Cynthia that Becky's grandmother had met her first husband while singing at a nightclub in Margate. He was a manager at the local Dreamland theme park and she had been impressed at first, seeing him in his smart suit and hat. After an impoverished childhood, Becky's grandmother yearned to never have to worry about money as her parents had.

But by the time she was pregnant and she'd married him, it transpired that the man behind the smart suit and hat was riddled with debt and would never be able to guarantee her a good life. Selma's mother had eventually kicked him out when her main – her *only* – reason for being with him gone. As money dwindled, they'd had to downsize, ending up living in a tiny flat in Margate, the same flat her grandmother lived her later years in, only once or twice living somewhere with one of her many ex-husbands during short-lived and tempestuous marriages.

Becky had visited the flat in Margate once, long ago sold. It sat above a fish and chip shop a five-minute walk from Margate's main promenade. She remembers standing outside, peering up and imagining her mother up there as a child, the smell of chips and vinegar floating up, the shouts of drunk tourists outside on the streets. It couldn't have been easy, but at least she'd had her mother with her until she left when she went to university, unlike

Becky who'd lost her mum at eight. Or so it felt. Would it have been better if Becky's mum had been without her mother from eight? From what she could glean from the way her parents talked about her grandmother, it couldn't have been pleasant living with her. Maybe that was why her mum was the way she was. But then plenty of people had difficult childhoods, didn't they?

'Want a taste?' Kai's mum asks, getting back up and going to the pot.

Becky shakes the memories away. 'Yes please.'

She scoops up a spoonful and brings it over to Becky. Spices and herbs and the most succulent goat's meat hits her tongue as she sips from the wooden spoon.

'Incredible,' Becky says.

Kai's mum smiles. 'Good. Let's set the table then, shall we?'

Twenty minutes later, Becky is sitting at a packed table with Kai's mum, sisters, their partners and his sweet little niece. It's a clatter of chatter, words machine-gunned out between mouthfuls of his mum's amazing stew. They're all fascinated by her job as a vet, laughing and flinching as she tells them stories, and Kai fills them all in on his latest cave adventures. His other two sisters are the youngest, in their early twenties, one with her short hair dyed red and a piercing in her nose, the other glamorous in bright pink lipstick. They're each so different but all as lovely as each other, and Becky can see why Kai is so natural and fun.

As she watches them all interact, she imagines things being different with her mum. Maybe she would have had more children if she hadn't have left for that cave? Or if Becky's dad had been more relaxed about it all, Becky could have shared her mum's life, spending half her time in the cave with her sister, growing up around the noise and fun of a community.

But more than anything, Becky feels a loss at having no real female influence in her life. Kai moans about his sisters taking up the bathrooms and filling the house with the stench of perfume and hairspray, but Becky craved that as a child. Some noise, some clatter, even someone to argue with. It was always just so calm and clean with her dad.

'Want to go outside? The sun's out, we can talk all things Russia,' Kai says quietly after they've eaten their succulent delicious sweet potato pudding. She can see in his blue eyes he can sense her contemplation.

'Yeah, sure. That'd be good.'

She says her thanks then follows Kai outside as the sisters exchange raised eyebrows. It seems that, no matter how much they deny it, his family are convinced they're an item. Becky allows herself for a moment to imagine it to be true. Coming here for the weekend, sitting on that big corner sofa with his sisters and watching a girly film. Learning his mum's recipes. Huddling up in the very swing chair they're heading to now, looking up at the stars as they talk into the night.

She feels her cheeks flush. What is *wrong* with her?

'So how was Slovenia?' Kai says as they both sit down, the swing chair creaking under their weight. Next door, a raucous barbecue is taking place, men whooping as girls laugh. On the other side, a woman nurses her screaming baby.

'Interesting,' Becky says. 'The caves are beautiful.'

He shakes his head. 'I'm so jealous, I've never been.'

'Ha, I have one cave up on you.'

He playfully narrows his eyes at her. 'So tell me what you learnt then.'

She tells him everything: about the cavern where Idris and Solar lived, the way they just suddenly left, then the photo of Idris's painting in the Russian cave, and the article Caden found about Solar. She hands the article to Kai and he looks at the photo.

'I guess if Idris likes caves, the Kungar Ice Caves would appeal,' Kai says. 'But to *live* there? Especially with a kid. They'd be freezing.'

'Maybe he had no choice. I keep hearing from people he was running from someone, was *scared*.' She thinks of the burnt-out cave in Spain, the scary paintings Solar drew. Who was after him and why?

'I talked to that Julien guy a bit after you left Spain actually,' Kai says. 'He said the same to me, about Idris being scared of someone. You're not worried about your sister though, are you?' he says, looking down at the article. 'She seems have survived her childhood unscathed judging by the photo.'

'But what about Idris? Nobody can track him down, not even someone like Caden who's trained to trace family members.'

'Solar will probably know.'

Becky nods.

'Hey, I got some other good photos from Spain,' Kai says, pulling his phone from his pocket. 'I didn't want to bombard your inbox with all my photos from the trips so I didn't send them all.'

They lean close as he scrolls through them. Many are of that evening in the caves, Becky beaming out in some, her face red from the wine. A few were taken after she left too, including some of Julien sitting outside his cave as he whittled his wooden figurines.

'These are good,' Becky says. 'Choose the right filter and you'll be an Instagram star in no time.'

Kai laughs. 'Hashtag no filter all the way, baby!'

But Becky doesn't laugh back. She's noticed something in one of the photos from inside Julien's cave during daylight. She can see paintings she hadn't seen before, including one of a building she recognises: the old abandoned hotel her mum bought. She can tell it's that hotel because of the big oak tree that dominates the background.

She zooms in closer. In the painting is a boy, standing on the cliff edge. Behind him, peering out from a window in the hotel, is a face: one half white, the other half black.

The scary face Idris and Solar drew.

Becky shivers, quickly handing the phone back.

'What's up?' Kai asks.

'That face again,' she says, pointing to it. 'But this time, it's in the hotel Mum lived in.'

'The one you own now?'

Becky nods. 'Thing is, it was abandoned for years before Mum bought it. It certainly wasn't open when I lived in the town as a kid.'

'It could be something from Idris's past.' Kai goes to the browser on his phone. 'What was the hotel called again?'

'The Bay Hotel.'

He quirks an eyebrow. 'Original. Okay, let me see if I can find anything on it.' He types the name in as Becky looks over his shoulder and a series of results appear, many of them related to a similarly named hotel in Australia. But a couple are from pages dedicated to the history of the town that Becky grew up in. Kai clicks on it and they both read a small paragraph with a photo of the hotel when it was open. She realises her mum had pretty much restored it to how it once was with its white board exterior and glossy windows.

The Bay Hotel was opened in the year 1900 to a fanfare, particularly popular with people in ill health seeking to benefit from the cave spa beneath it. It dominated the tourist scene for most of the 1900s until the owners put it up for sale in 1975.

'Idris only arrived in the town in 1991, which is when Mum first left,' Becky says.

'Did he? Or maybe he grew up in the area?'

Becky frowns. 'Maybe.'

'Hey, Kai!' a voice calls out.

They both look up to see a woman peering at him over next door's fence. She's pretty with large oval brown eyes and black hair in a wavy bob. Becky notices a change in Kai's face when he sees the woman. His jaw clenches and he nods stiffly.

'Hey, Tara.'

'Who's this then?' Tara asks as she stares at Becky.

'Becky, meet Tara,' Kai says with a sigh. 'Tara, meet Becky.'

'You should come over some time, Kai baby, catch up over a beer,' Tara says, lifting her bottle up.

'I don't think so, Tara,' Kai replies.

She pouts. 'Aw, don't be like that.'

'You're drunk.'

She raises an eyebrow. 'And you clearly need to be. Nice to meet you, Becky,' she says, giving Becky a look that suggests she really isn't pleased to meet her. Then she disappears.

'That was . . . interesting,' Becky says when Tara is out of earshot.

'Always is when it comes to Tara.'

'She a friend?'

Kai shakes his head. 'Not any more. Used to be. Used to be a lot more than that, too.'

'Like your fiancée?' Becky asks gently, thinking of what Kai's mum told her.

'Yeah, something like that,' Kai replies, leaning back and squinting up at the blue skies. She examines his dark smooth skin, the nose gem twinkling in the afternoon light.

'I had a *something like that* once as well.'

He looks at her sideway, one eye closed. 'Oh yeah?'

'His name was Gus.'

'That's some name.'

Becky smiles. 'He was some guy. Or so I thought anyway. I was fourteen, a bit lonely. He was lonely too I guess. He'd just moved from the States. We bonded over books. Wasn't long before we were living in each other's pockets.'

'Sounds like me and Tara. I was sixteen. Except it wasn't books with her, more like beer.'

They laugh.

'So what happened with this Gus dude?' Kai asks.

Becky sighs. 'I wrapped myself up in him, used him as my security blanket. I wouldn't admit it at the time, but I was missing my mum like hell. It worked for a while, things felt good. But he was a bit controlling. I'd always been interested in science, in animals especially. But Gus convinced me to pursue history instead of "soulless science" as he called it.'

Kai rolls his eyes. 'Not sure I like this Gus.'

Becky smiles. 'So I focused on history, following Gus to college and then university, getting a job at a local historic society after, even getting a little flat by the sea in Busby-on-Sea where I moved with my dad. I was so sure we'd always be together.'

Kai nods. 'I hear ya. Same with Tara. It was just the way it was. Kai and Tara. Tara and Kai. Until I discovered Tara preferred it to be Tara and Zane.'

'Zane?'

'My best friend. Found them doing some horizontal dancing on a bench in town last year.'

Becky puts her hand on his arm. 'A bench? God, I'm sorry, Kai.'

He frowns slightly. 'Best thing that ever happened to me. Better to have found out *before* we got married. That holiday in Spain?' he says. 'Hannah and Ed dragged me out there to take my mind off the fact I'd have been getting married that week if I hadn't caught Tara doing the dirty last year.'

'They're good friends.'

He smiles. 'They are. Anyway, here I am talking all about me. What happened with the science basher, Gus?'

Becky sighs. 'He just told me out of the blue he didn't love me any more. We were having dinner, watching some programme. And he turned to me and said it. "I can't do this any more, Becky. I'm not in love with you."'

Kai flinched. 'Ouch.'

'Yep. He moved out the next day. But it's like you say, better it happened before kids and marriage . . . I know first-hand how it feels to watch your parents separate. Plus, I'd never have become a vet if he hadn't left. I'd still be working for that society, archiving photos of old garages.'

'Why become a vet then? You mentioned some horses behind your house but that was when you were a kid.'

Becky smiles to herself. 'Gus's grandmother passed away and left her dog to him. He turned up at my new flat a year after he dumped me, asking me if I wanted the dog because he was going to give it away.'

Kai looks at her incredulously. 'No way!'

Becky laughs. 'Yes way. I took the poor thing in, how could I not? He was gorgeous, a three-legged staffie called Rupert. But boy, did he have health problems! I was in the vets a lot. It made me realise just how much I'd love to be the person treating Rupert rather than the one standing there, nodding.' She frowns. 'Truth was, the seed was planted way before that. I always blame it on the horses behind our house, but now I remember that it all started when I visited my mum at the cave for the first time. A dog got hurt and I helped and . . . and I remember Idris telling me I'd be a vet one day. I've never liked to attribute it to him but the truth is, that's when the obsession started for me. He made me believe it was my destiny. Anyway,' Becky says with a sigh, 'two years of adult classes to get those science A Levels I always wanted, and five years of training later, I finally qualified! All thanks to Idris . . .'

'He sounds like quite something.'

'I guess he was, to pull all those people in.'

'Must be complicated emotions though. Your mum had an affair with him, got pregnant.'

Becky shrugs. 'It wasn't really an affair. Mum and Dad had split up when she lived in the cave really.'

'What do you think you'd say if you met him?'

Becky plays with the hem of her shorts. 'Why did you take my sister . . . and where is she?'

Kai puts his hand on her arm. 'You'll find her.'

'I hope so.' She looks him in the eye. 'You going to help me by coming to Russia?'

As she says that, she realises she desperately wants him to. Not just to help her get access to the cave but for his company too. His smile. His jokes and his support.

He pretends to think about it. Then he shoots her his huge smile. 'Hell yeah!'

As they high five, Becky glances at Kai's phone which is sitting on his knee, still open to the page about the old hotel.

How is it all connected?

Chapter Twenty-Four

Selma

Kent, UK
13 August 1991

The morning after Idris and I made love, I woke in his arms to the sun rising, the old abandoned hotel looming over us. It was so warm and dry after the initial burst of rain, we'd emerged from the small cave to sleep on the beach in the middle of the night, our hair a tangled wet mess in the sand.

I felt as though I was in a dream. Sex with Mike had been mechanical for so long. It wasn't his fault. I'd closed myself to him, to any sexual feelings. Not intentionally. It was just the way I felt. But the night I'd spent with Idris, the way he made me feel . . . all those old feelings of passion I once enjoyed in the past were back.

'You look like a double-headed mermaid,' a voice said from above.

I looked up to see Oceane smiling down at us. I realised then how foolish I'd been to think Idris and Oceane were sleeping with each other. She'd hardly react to seeing us like this if they were.

'It's beautiful,' the young girl added. 'Coffee?'

Idris opened his eyes and smiled. 'The magic word.'

Oceane skipped into the cave and I sat up, looking around me. Everyone was going about their business, seemingly unbothered by the fact Idris and I had clearly spent the night together. It carried on like that throughout the day, as though we'd been together since the start. He held my hand, kissed the nape of my neck and it confirmed what I knew in my heart: I really *was* the only person he'd been intimate with here.

That night, we went back to the small cave with the frozen birds – *our* cave now – and made love again.

'Try to get into the current,' Idris whispered as I moved up and down on top of him, his back against the cool wall, legs out in front of him. 'Look into my eyes, find the current.'

I did as he asked, even though half of me didn't believe in the so-called 'current', focusing my mind and feeling on the place where we both joined. Soon, nothing else existed, just that core between us, him inside me as we moved against each other. Whether it was the current or not, I'd never felt anything like it.

After, we lay together on a blanket we'd brought in with us, looking up at the frozen animals.

'Is that the tantric sex Sting and his wife talk about?' I joked.

'That's all talk. This is *real*.' He tucked a strand of hair behind my ear. 'How are you feeling about the social services visit in a few weeks?'

I'd received a letter that morning to say the visit would be in a month's time. I sighed. 'Nervous.'

'You're a great mother, that's all they need to see.'

'I don't know. I've always found it difficult, this mothering business.'

'How so?'

I thought about it. 'When Becky was born, I struggled.'

'Baby blues?'

I nodded. 'That's what the doctor said. At times, I felt so detached, like I was watching life from inside a bubble. But then the paranoid thoughts came, I grew overprotective of her, wouldn't let anyone hold her. And . . .' I paused.

Idris tilted my chin up, looking into my eyes. 'You know you can tell me anything.'

'I started imagining the most awful things happening to Becky. Terrible violent things by other people, or by accident. The thoughts in my mind were so graphic, like a TV playing over and over. I even wrote some of them down.' I closed my eyes. 'Mike found the notepad.'

Idris pulled me close, softly kissing the top of my head.

'We argued. And . . . and I thought he was going to take her away. I even thought the postman was a social worker in disguise, completely irrational as Mike had only just read the notepad. So when he was on the phone to my doctor to make an appointment for me, I left with Becky. I just walked out.'

I sat up, drawing the blanket to my chin as I stared into the darkness. I'd never told anyone this, apart from Mike of course.

'Do you know what?' I continued. 'I hardly remember doing it. It was just a blur.' Tears filled my eyes. 'Mike was frantic. Becky was fine, of course. But still, it was bad of me to just walk out with her like that.'

'Not bad,' Idris said, putting his hand on my knee. 'You did the right thing, getting away, clearing your head.'

'Mike didn't see it like that. I returned the next day and he was *so* angry. Only promising to go to the doctor for some anti-depressants stopped him calling social services.' I twisted the tweed of the blanket between my fingers.

Idris frowned, trailing his finger down my bare arm. 'Did it feel like you were running away again when you came here?'

I frowned. 'At first, yes. Those old feelings were coming back. The numbness anyway.' I smiled up at him. 'But now it feels different. It feels like I'm coming home.'

Idris leaned up and pressed his lips against mine. 'Good. I don't want this to be transient for you.'

'It isn't.'

Idris was quiet for a few moments. 'You should talk to Donna actually. She confided in me about something – not quite what you went through, but similar. It might be useful for you both to talk things through.'

'I don't need to talk things through.'

'Really?' Idris asked me. 'You haven't been in the current as much with your writing, apart from just now,' he added with a raised eyebrow.

'I've had a lot on my mind.'

'Exactly. Emotional blockages are often caused by deep-seated issues from the past. You need to cleanse yourself. Talking is good.' He leaned close to me. 'I really think you should talk to Donna.'

I sighed. I'd always closed myself off to talking to other women about stuff like that, thought it was a bit crass . . . a bit *pedestrian*.

But maybe Idris was right. Maybe it was time I started opening up a bit.

'Fine, if that's what you think is best for me, Mister philosopher-stroke-therapist.'

'I *always* know what's best. Like right now.' He dipped his head under the blanket as I giggled.

That night, we sat around the fire with the others, drinking and chatting like we always did. But it felt different this time, the two of us wrapped up in each other as if it had been like that forever.

When Donna walked into the cave, Idris nudged me. I got up and followed to find her at the sink, her back to me.

'Hey you,' I said.

Donna jumped, putting her hand to her chest. 'You scared me.'

I laughed. 'I didn't realise my ninja skills were quite so refined.'

Donna didn't laugh back. She'd grown more sullen with me lately.

'Tea? My head's hurting so I decided to stop with the wine tonight.'

'Good idea.'

We were silent as Donna made tea, boiling a tin kettle on the camper hob. When it was ready, she brought it over and I took a sip, welcoming its warmth.

'It feels a bit colder tonight,' Donna commented.

'It does.'

'Nervous about the social services visit?'

'Idris asked the same earlier. I guess I am.' I repeated what I'd said to Idris about my skills as a mother . . . and the way I'd struggled after Becky was born. 'Idris mentioned you went through something similar when you had Tom?'

Donna frowned.

'I didn't mean to pry,' I quickly added. 'He didn't spill any details. Just said it might be good for us to talk. In fact, he seemed quite insistent on it.'

Donna followed my gaze towards Idris. 'I did something,' she eventually said. 'Before I moved to Queensbay a few years ago. It was all about protecting Oceane.' She watched her daughter dancing outside. 'Ironically, one of the consequences meant I didn't get to see her for a while; she had to go live with her dad, which was far from ideal. If I'd known . . .' She shook her head, as though shaking the memory away. 'But what does it matter? We're together now, here, in this beautiful place. And so are you . . . especially now you're with Idris.'

I didn't push her for more information about what had happened. She needed to tell me in her own time.

'We are happy. I suppose it took me by surprise, took *both* of us by surprise.'

'It did for me too,' Donna said. 'I didn't think he'd be your type, to be honest. Nor you his . . .'

I frowned. 'Because I'm older than him? I know there were rumours about him and younger girls,' I said, looking towards her daughter.

Donna followed my gaze. 'What rumours?'

I inwardly kicked myself. 'It's all lies.'

'*What* rumours?' Donna asked again.

'The stupid rumours circulating about him and Oceane.'

Donna's frown deepened. 'Oceane?'

I grimaced. I leaned over, grasping her hand. 'Donna, come on. You know it's all lies, right?'

Donna took in a deep breath and smiled. 'Of course. I'm just being a mama bear. I hope it works well with you both anyway.' She stood, face darkening as she looked out at Idris. 'I'm going to do some cleaning. Let Tom know I'm inside, will you? And make sure he doesn't go in that smaller cave at the end, the one with all those frozen animals? He likes playing in there but I noticed some crumbling rock last time I went in. I tried to talk to Idris about it but he said it's fine. Maybe you can have a word?'

'I'll try.'

Donna threw me a tight smile and walked out.

Over the next month, we all doubled our efforts to get the cave clean and in a fit state for the social services visit.

'It's all coming together,' Oceane said as she sat next to me the day before the visit, surveying the cave.

I smiled. 'It is, isn't it?'

'I haven't had a chance to talk to you much since you came here,' she said, hugging her knees to her chest. 'You know, I knew from that day we talked by the cave that you'd live here one day.'

'*Did* you now?'

'Yep. I'm pretty wise for a teenager.'

'You seem it. Are you happy here?'

She laughed. 'Of *course* I am!'

'But shouldn't you be going to nightclubs and hanging out with your friends at college?'

'I tried that,' she said with a sigh. 'But it always felt so synthetic. *This* feels right.'

'So what's your plan? You write poetry. Do you want to get it published?'

'Why does there always have to be a plan? I have my family here, and I'm doing what I love.'

'But it can't last forever.'

'Can't it? And anyway, even if it doesn't, there are other caves in other countries.'

I smiled. 'Ah, so you *do* have plans. A bit of travelling will do you good. I wish I had at your age.'

'What's stopping you now?'

I looked out towards the sea. What *was* stopping me now?

Oceane stood up, stretching. 'I'm going shopping for some women's stuff. Need anything? Gin, chocolate . . . sanitary towels?' she added with a laugh.

I frowned. When was the last time I'd had my period?

'What's wrong?' she asked.

'Nothing,' I quickly said, panic fluttering its wings inside me.

When Oceane headed down the beach, I hurried to the water's edge, taking in a deep gasp of salty air.

Think, Selma. Think!

What was the date? Becky was returning to school in a week, so that would make it the seventh of September.

When *was* the last time I got my period? I remembered it being just after I'd arrived at the cave as I'd needed to go into town to get some sanitary towels. That was nearly two months ago! My breath started to quicken. I was never this late . . . except when I was pregnant with Becky.

No.

We'd been careful! Idris had used condoms. Apart from that first night in the small cave . . .

I put my hand to my stomach then quickly snatched it away. It would be awful. The worst possible thing to happen. Becky was all I'd ever wanted, no other children. How could I have been so bloody stupid?

'Calm down,' I hissed at myself. Maybe I wasn't pregnant. Maybe I was getting worried about nothing. I tried to explain it away: maybe it was just the change of routine which was making my periods late. Or simply having all that sex with Idris. God knows I wasn't used to it with Mike. That would surely have an effect on someone's body?

Like get them pregnant, a small voice in my head said.

One way or another, I needed to know.

Later that day, I headed into town to buy a test, going into the bathroom of a busy pub to take it. As I sat on the toilet seat staring at the small screen, waiting for it to change colour, I thought my heart might hammer right out of my chest.

I watched as a line started to appear.

'Just let it be one line,' I whispered. 'Please let it be one.' But there was another.

I was pregnant.

Chapter Twenty-Five

Selma

Kent, UK
7 September 1991

As I walked back to the cave, my mind was in turmoil. I thought of Idris. Maybe it wasn't so bad? A part of him was growing inside me. His blond mixed with my dark. His idealism with my cynicism. What kind of child would we produce?

But then other thoughts crept in, such as memories of Becky's newborn days: the blinding exhaustion, the crowding away of anything but the baby. No writing. No going out. No 'me' time. And then there were the dark thoughts too, the slumping into an abyss of sadness.

Would it happen all over again?

I crunched my fist softly into my stomach. At least I'd had a roof over my head then: four walls, maternity pay, a husband. But now? How could I deal with a newborn in a *cave*? And what about social services? This could ruin my chances of getting joint custody of Becky. Another cross to put on my report.

No, I couldn't allow that. It was early enough to do something about it. It could be as though it had never happened. Idris wouldn't even have to know.

I thought of my mother then and that time she was hidden up in bed for a week, the word 'abortion' whispered by her friend. I really was getting more and more like her.

'No!' I snapped to myself, curling my hands into fists. I couldn't.

That night, I lay awake the whole night. Idris sensed my unrest, waking up too. We were sharing a bed now, a double mattress at the back of the cave. We slept with our arms wrapped around each other, something I wasn't used to. Mike and I often slept back to back, contact rare, both starting if skin touched skin. But it was so different with Idris.

Would it stay like that if we had children? Or would the magic wear off?

'It'll be fine,' he whispered in my ear, his arms around my waist.

I froze. Did he somehow know?

'Social services will love you,' he added, voice sleepy. 'It'll work itself out.'

I relaxed against him. I'd almost forgotten about the visit from social services in the shock of everything that had happened that day.

It'll work itself out, I told myself.

The next morning, we woke to shouts.

I untangled myself from Idris's arms and sat up. Donna was standing outside the cave, looking up at it in distress.

'Idris,' I said, jogging his arm as I jumped out of bed.

He sat up, rubbing his eyes. 'What's wrong?'

'I don't know. Donna's upset about something.'

We both walked to the front of the cave as the others woke. Then I froze. Graffitied across its entrance was the word 'THIEF'.

'Jesus Christ,' I said, raking my fingers through my hair. 'Social services are due this morning.'

'It's not just that.' Donna pointed towards her beach garden. All the plants had been uprooted, the supporting sticks pulled out and snapped in half. The cushions around the fire had been shredded too; someone had even emptied their bowels there.

I instinctively put my hand to my tummy, stroking it.

I noticed Idris wasn't moving, just staring at all the destruction, face white. I'd never seen him like that.

'It'll be fine,' I said, softly stroking his arm. 'We have time to clear it up before social services get here.'

He seemed to snap out of it, eyes blinking. 'Social services.' He walked into the cave, clapping his hands. Those who weren't already awake woke with a start.

'Right everyone, we have a job to do,' he shouted. 'Someone has graffitied the cave and we need to get it cleaned up before social services arrive at ten.'

Over the next hour, we all worked together to clear the mess up. Soon Donna's little beach garden was even starting to resemble its old self, but the writing graffitied on the wall was still there, despite being scrubbed. It had faded, but was still obvious. Idris looked up at it with hooded eyes.

'Who do you think did this?' I asked him in a low voice. 'And what could they possibly think we stole?'

'Just kids,' he said. But he still looked worried.

An hour later, a man and woman walked down the beach towards the cave. The social workers.

'Hello,' I said, wrapping my cardigan around myself and putting my hand out. It was silly, I wasn't showing at all. But somehow, I felt the need to protect my stomach from view.

They both smiled, shaking my hand. 'You're Selma Rhys, I take it?' the woman asked.

I nodded. 'Please, come in,' I said, leading them to the cave. Their eyes flickered up to the graffiti. 'That appeared last night,' I quickly explained. 'We've done our best to remove it. Just some silly kids, I imagine.'

The two social workers exchanged a look.

'Would you like a drink? Tea, coffee?' I asked, trying to hide my worry as I led them to the large kitchen table.

'Tea would be good,' the man said.

'Coffee for me,' the woman added.

They both sat down, pulling out some forms.

'We just need to ask you a series of questions,' the woman said. 'Then we'd love for you to show us around.'

'Of course.' I went to the kitchen area, placing the kettle on the small stove. I caught Idris's eye. He was helping Maggie make a large vase. He'd been quiet as he'd helped everyone, deep in thought. It wasn't like him. It unnerved me.

He gave me a reassuring smile. I smiled back.

'So how long have you lived here, Selma?' the woman asked as I gave them their drinks.

'Nearly two months now. Seems like forever though. In a good way, I mean!' I quickly added.

'And why did you come here?' the man asked.

'My husband and I weren't getting on. I met Idris and the rest of the dwellers. It just felt like home. It's difficult to explain. I'm happy here, really happy.' I put my hand to my stomach again. How long would that happiness last?

'And what about Becky?' the woman asked. 'I believe she visited for a few hours not long after you started living here?'

I nodded. 'Yes, she loved it.'

'Can you talk us through what she did here?' the man asked.

I went through Becky's day at the cave, leaving out the part about the dog and the swim out to sea.

'I believe she helped care for an injured dog?' the woman asked, peering towards Julien's dog.

'Oh,' I said with a laugh. 'She likes to tell people that but she just handed us the dressing.'

'She said she pressed the dressing to the dog's leg when we spoke to her.'

'No,' I said, blinking. 'She didn't.' Sure, it was a lie. But it was for a good reason. It was my word against a child's, surely they'd believe me?

'Right,' the man said, scribbling down some notes. 'Can you tell us about your day-to-day routine?'

I went through a typical day, mainly focusing on my writing.

'And what about your job?' the woman asked.

'Oh yes, that's three days a week,' I lied again. I'd been umming and ahhing about what to tell them about that. In the end, I reasoned it wouldn't harm to lie. My solicitor had told me how important a steady job was and I was still on the company's payroll as I was using up my holiday allocation to leave earlier. Officially, I *was* still working for them.

'But the plan is to focus on writing full-time soon,' I quickly added. 'I'm very close to finishing my latest novel and chances are, as a published author, I'll receive a decent advance. In the meantime, I don't need much money here.' I shrugged. 'It's a simple but good way of living.'

'How have relations been with your daughter since you left?' the woman asked.

'Good,' I said. Another embellishment. Truth was, I was finding Becky more and more sulky with each visit we had. She'd even stopped asking me when I was coming home. 'We see each other three to four days a week.'

'What do you do?'

'Oh, lots of things! Swimming, playing on the beach, parks, cinema if it's raining.'

The man looked at his notes. 'I see there have been no overnight stays at hotels as the judge suggested, instead of the two of you sleeping in the cave?'

I paused. I simply hadn't been able to afford it. All the cheap hotels were quickly taken during peak season, the more expensive ones completely out of my budget.

But I didn't want to bring attention to my delicate financial state.

'I felt it would be better not to disrupt her night-time routine,' I said. 'Not until we know for sure how things will go after your report.'

The two social workers nodded. I took a nervous sip of my tea.

'How have you been feeling when you see Becky?' the woman asked.

I frowned. 'I don't really understand the question.'

'Happy? Guilty? Sad? Overprotective?' she said, putting emphasis on the word *overprotective*.

'I see.' I sighed. 'You're referring to what happened when Becky was a baby? I can assure you that's far behind me. I got treatment for it, it was just the baby blues.'

I thought of the baby growing in my tummy again. *Was* it far behind me?

'You left Mike then too, didn't you?' the woman asked. 'When it got too much?'

I crunched my hands into fists. 'It was just one night. And anyway,' I added, feeling panicked about where this questioning was leading, 'it was more about my marriage than Becky.'

'What do you mean?' the woman asked carefully.

I stifled my annoyance at such probing questions. 'Mike – Mike threatened to hurt Becky when she was crying.'

The two social workers exchanged looks. '*Hurt* her?'

'It was just a momentary lapse of judgement,' I quickly added, regretting the lie as soon as it came out of my mouth. 'She *had* been crying a lot.'

'Did you tell anyone at the time about what happened?' the woman asked.

'No,' I said, shaking my head. 'I was worried they'd take Becky away. Look, I shouldn't have mentioned it, it was a small thing really.'

The two social workers exchanged looks again.

'Shall I show you around?' I asked, desperate to get off the subject.

They nodded.

Over the next half an hour, we toured the cave and met its

occupants. Everyone had been so lovely and it all seemed to go well. They'd even smiled when they saw the play area, and I noticed the way the woman hungrily watched Idris stretch up to paint something, his bronzed stomach showing, and felt a strange purr of pride.

'Well, this has certainly been interesting,' the woman said after. 'We've never visited a cave before.'

The man laughed. 'Yep, it's a first.' He peered up at the old hotel above it. 'My aunt and uncle used to stay there when I was kid. Beautiful place when it was in its prime.'

I followed his gaze. 'I used to dream about owning it,' I said, smiling.

'Maybe you will if you get that book deal?' the woman said.

'Maybe. Do you know who owns the hotel now? It's been up for sale for ages.'

'No idea,' the man replied. 'I used to see the former owners around town though, Mr and Mrs Peterson. Mrs Peterson was always so friendly, smiling and happy. They ran the hotel for years but then she committed suicide. I remember even as a kid being shocked. My mum knew her, said she'd had a long struggle with depression.'

'How terrible. I had no idea.' We were all silent. 'So I guess the next step is the court hearing?' I said.

'That's right,' the man replied. 'We'll be compiling our report and will submit it to the courts.'

I took a deep breath. I might be showing by then . . . if I *kept* the baby. Was I really thinking of not keeping it? The thought made me suddenly feel sick. But what option did I have?

'I hope it's clear that I adore my daughter,' I said as I led them out of the cave. 'I didn't leave her, despite what Mike might say. He told me to leave, but he probably didn't tell you that. She's the most important thing in the world to me. I want her to be happy – that's all I've ever wanted, and I truly think she *can* be happy here.'

'Thank you, Selma,' the woman said, shaking my hand. 'We'll get started on the report right away.' Then they walked away.

'How did it go?' Idris asked, strolling over to me.

I smiled, giving him a kiss. 'Good, I think.'

Idris nodded. 'Anyone on the outside might expect something totally different, sleeping bags slung over sandy floors and a bucket for a toilet. But it's so much more than that now. I could see they were impressed.'

'With the cave, yes. But I'm not so sure they were impressed by me. They brought up that incident when Becky was a newborn,' I added, lowering my voice.

'Of course they did! But I saw the way they interacted with you. They believe you to be a good person. I can sense it. I truly think it'll all work out for you.'

I put my hand to my stomach. 'I hope you're right.' I peered up at the sun, using its position in the sky to guess the time. I didn't think I'd ever get used to not wearing a watch. 'I better head into town. I'd like to get something for Becky.'

Idris smiled. 'Good idea. Shall I come with you?'

'No, it's fine, really. I might wander around for a few hours actually, take a break from the writing.'

'Good idea.'

The truth was, I wanted to explore my options. If I were to get an abortion, I needed to know how. There was a family planning

305

clinic just outside Queensbay, a short bus ride away. But when I got to town, I couldn't face getting on the bus. Instead, I sat in the café all afternoon, drinking tea and eating cakes, ignoring the looks people gave me.

After a while, a couple walked in, shaking their brollies from the rain that had started falling.

'I knew this would happen eventually,' I heard the man say, shaking his head. 'Didn't I tell you? That cult would get its comeuppance and now it's happened.'

'What happened?' someone called over.

'Haven't you heard the sirens? One of the caves has collapsed.'

I jumped up, heart thumping. 'What do you mean?'

The man looked me up and down, clearly recognising me as one of the cave dwellers now.

'You better get back there, love,' his wife said. 'The little cave collapsed. People have been injured. *Your* people,' she added.

I ran out of the café, looking up in horror at the darkening sky, which flashed blue with ambulance lights.

Chapter Twenty-Six

Becky

Kungar Ice Caves, Russia
3 July 2018

Becky and Kai reach the Kungar Ice Caves at nightfall. When she'd arrived at the airport a few hours before, it had felt like she'd stepped back in time, taking in the old-fashioned adverts adorning the tops of the walls, glossy-faced women advertising makeup and perfumes. As she'd made her way towards the exit, she'd imagined Idris walking through arrivals with Solar trailing behind him, twenty years before. Maybe he'd have cut his hair to avoid whoever it was he was running from recognising him? Would Solar have looked dirty, neglected, peering around her with fearful eyes?

Now Becky is waiting to go into the cave they may have once lived in. It's a warm evening but, despite this, Becky and Kai are both dressed in thick winter jackets, jeans and gloves, ready for the freezing temperatures inside. Under the moonlight, Becky can make out iron fences lining the foot of the mountains as they walk down a path towards the cave. Pretty benches sit in front of them, the wood painted blue, green and yellow. A blue archway announces the start of the caves. The actual entrance to the caves looks like a small concrete block structure jutting from the hills. She hasn't really seen much of Russia, just a quick taxi ride to her hotel to freshen up, then another taxi ride in the dark.

A man in his thirties with a thick moustache and beard is waiting for them, wearing jeans and a T-shirt.

'Clearly, he's not coming inside,' Becky says, eyeing his attire.

'Nah,' Kai says with a smile. 'Lev's a kind of caretaker here, keeps an eye on the place. He agreed to let us in.'

Becky matches his grin. It's good to have Kai here. He seems to know everyone in the caving world.

Lev laughs as they approach, his blue eyes sparkling. 'You crazy Brits,' he says, shaking his head. 'Visiting the caves in darkness.'

'What's wrong with that?' Becky asks, suddenly alarmed.

'Nothing,' Kai replies. 'Better now than when it's teeming with tourists. Caves are so much more exciting at night anyway.'

Lev hands them both headlamps to put on, then he creaks open the large iron gates to reveal the long, murky entrance – a contrast to the pristine, modern entrance into the Slovenian caves.

'Visitors used to have to crawl into the cave until this was built,' Lev explains with a raised eyebrow. 'So count yourself lucky.'

'I'm used to doing a bit of crawling with my dogs,' Becky replies.

The man laughs. 'What did I say? Crazy Brits. Good luck.'

They step in and he slams the iron gates behind them, the sound rebounding off the narrow corridor. Becky draws closer to Kai, more pleased than ever that he's here with her.

'Where's Hannah and Ed?' Becky asks as they walk down the cave.

The couple had insisted on coming when Kai had told them and Becky was happy with that. The more the merrier.

'We're meeting them inside the first grotto,' Kai explains.

As they walk further into the cave, the temperature drops. Becky pulls the zip of her coat up, breathing in the damp, stony smell. The corridor opens up into a huge cavern and Becky stops in her tracks, open-mouthed as she stares around her. The light from her headlamp illuminates the ice clusters, making them twinkle and shine. White stalactites drape from the ceilings, reminding her of the frozen animals she'd seen hanging in her mum's office.

'Beautiful, right?' Kai says.

'Stunning.'

'This is just one of the grottos. The caves go on for miles. A whole group of people even got lost in here once.'

'That's reassuring to hear,' Becky says, laughing nervously.

There's the sound of talking and footsteps, and Ed and Hannah appear alongside a tall woman with white hair pulled back into a severe bun. She is standing with her feet apart, her arms crossed, surveying the cavern with narrowed eyes. Kai is enveloped by high fives and hugs as Hannah walks over to Becky and surprises her with a hug.

'So cool to see you again,' she says.

'You too.'

Hannah looks around her in awe. 'Isn't it stunning? We were planning on coming here later in the year, but when we heard you guys were making the trip, we thought we'd come along for the ride. I hope that's okay?'

'Of course. I'm pleased you did,' Becky admits.

'Yeah, we speleologists like to travel in packs, like wolves,' Ed says.

'So who's the alpha?' Becky asks.

They all gesture towards the tall woman with them. She puts her hand out to Becky. 'Iskar,' she says in a Russian accent.

'Hi Iskar, I'm Becky.'

She goes to shake Iskar's hand but the Russian woman shakes her head. 'Clench your fist,' she commands.

Becky frowns.

'Go on,' Kai says with a smile. 'She won't bite. Not if you behave anyway.' Everyone laughs.

Becky clenches her fist and Iskar clasps her hand around it, shaking it once before pulling away.

'Our way of saying hello,' Hannah explains. 'You're one of us now.'

'A speleologist?' Becky asks with a raised eyebrow.

'No, just someone mad enough to visit these caves under the cover of night,' Ed says.

'So it really isn't a good idea to visit this cave at night then?' Becky asks, staring into the darkness.

'Are you scared?' Iskar asks her.

'This time a month ago, I was wrestling a pit bull terrier to the ground,' Becky says. 'So no, not scared, just curious.'

Iskar smiles at Kai. 'I like this one.'

'This place is awesome,' Ed says as he strides towards one of the walls and reaches out, touching the freezing surface.

'Yeah, there's something about ice caves,' Kai says, joining him. 'Stuck in a permanent winter.'

310

'Remember to be careful,' Iskar calls out. 'It's slippery in here. Unless you want to marry a prince, I'd advise you step carefully.'

'Marry a prince? That sounds appealing,' Hannah says.

'You have a prince already,' Ed says, shooting her a mock wounded face.

'More like a frog,' Kai jokes.

They all laugh.

'Supposedly a German princess visited the caves in 1914,' Iskar says as she helps Hannah onto a large rock to peer at a stalactite up close. 'She fell and injured her knee. When she left the cave, she married a prince and became Queen of Sweden. Hence the legend.'

'She even left a signature on a boulder here in the caves,' Kai says. 'In fact, it's close to the cavern where Idris's painting was found.'

'Why's that area closed to the public?' Becky asks.

'There's a risk of the roof caving in,' Kai replies. 'Plus the routes in and out are really narrow, makes it difficult to escape when you're in a tight spot.'

'I'm surprised a child as young as your sister was allowed in there,' Iskar says.

'Me too,' Becky says, crouching down to look at one of the larger stalagmites.

Not for the first time, she curses Idris for bringing Solar here. Why on earth take a child to a dangerous cave closed off to the world? Becky thinks of the painting, the gaping mouth. Maybe the person they were running from *was* reason enough?

Becky looks around her, thinking of her little sister down here, arms curled around her knees, mist coming from her mouth as she breathed out the cold air.

'This is *not* a good place for a child to live,' she murmurs to herself.

'Live?' Iskar says in surprise. 'There is no way they'd have lived here. It's too cold.'

'Then why the painting?'

Iskar shrugs. 'They would have visited? Who knows. Come on, we have much to explore. Remember, be careful not to slip and keep close, it's easy to get lost here!'

They follow her out of the grotto and down a new narrow funnel. Everyone looks above them with open mouths at the large ice crystals fringing the ceiling.

'How does it stay so cold in the summer?' Becky asks in awe.

'That's what I love about this place,' Hannah says. 'The permanent freezing nature of the zone means it remains icy.'

Becky reaches up, skimming one with her fingertips. It's freezing to the touch, sharp. Over the next hour, they walk through a labyrinth of grottos. As the cavers take notes and photos, Becky wanders around, trying to imagine her sister and Idris here. The temperatures plummet the deeper they get in, meaning Becky has to pull on her gloves. Iskar's right – there's no way they could have lived here. So why come? Maybe it was just a visit.

'Here we are,' Iskar says, her breath a mist in the icy air. They step into another grotto, smaller than the others, with a tiny lake in the middle. 'This is where the wall painting is, Becky.'

Becky steps into the cave. The ice above forms like large bubbles, gleaming an eerie blue. There's a lake running down the middle of the cave, small and narrow with stony banks around it, large enough for people to sit on. The banks slope down into the water, the walls either side just rock, not ice.

'Where's the painting?' Becky asks.

'There,' Iskar replies, pointing across the length of the cavern.

Kai helps Becky step down onto one of the ledges and they both head to the back, towards one of the flatter walls. Becky stops dead when she sees it, the glaring face staring out at her. It's faded with time but still there, at least six-foot high.

'Creepy,' Kai murmurs.

Becky frowns. It's even worse in the flesh. Was Solar with Idris when he painted it? How terrifying for the little girl.

'The others are going to go on to explore some of the other grottos,' Kai says. 'But I told them you might want to wait here? I'll stay with you.'

She turns to him. 'Don't you want to see the other grottos?'

'It's fine, really. I promise I'll keep out of your way.'

He retreats to the front of the cave as the others leave.

'We'll meet you back at the entrance!' Iskar calls out. 'It's a circular route so we will be coming out another way. You're closer to the entrance here so best to retrace your steps. And remember, no later than midnight!'

Becky sits down at the ledge, wrapping her arms around her knees as she looks at the painting. She stays like that for a while, contemplating it all as Kai walks around the cave, taking photos.

How would her mum feel, knowing her youngest daughter had been in this freezing cave? Sure, it sounds like she couldn't have lived here, but still, Idris had dragged her to a cavern that was out of bounds and painted that awful picture. Why hadn't her mum fought harder to find Solar, to bring her home to safety? Or maybe she had? She'd circled that photo of Idris and Solar in the *National Geographic* after all.

'Shit!' she hears Kai shout out. She turns around just in time to see him sliding down one of the ledges, his leg bending awkwardly as he lands with a thump by the lake's side. He leans forward in agony. 'Ow, ow, ow!' he hisses.

Becky runs over, kneeling beside him. 'Your ankle?'

Kai closes his eyes, clenching his teeth as he nods. 'If the pain's anything to go by.'

'Let me have a look,' she says, gently pulling his trouser leg up and his thick socks down to reveal an ankle that's already swelling.

'It looks bad, doesn't it?' he asks her.

'You'll live,' she says matter-of-factly, dragging his bag over to gently elevate his foot as he bites his fist in pain. 'But best you don't walk on it until we get it looked at.'

He lets out a growl. 'So so stupid!'

'Don't be so hard on yourself. This way, you'll get to marry a prince.'

'I guess there's always a silver lining,' he says with a sigh. 'Though I prefer the sound of a *princess*.' He flinches again, squeezing his eyes shut. 'Treating a wounded man's no different from a wounded pit bull terrier, right?'

Becky raises an eyebrow. 'I find humans complain more.' She sighs. 'Truth is, there's nothing much more I can do here. We ideally need to get you to a hospital, which will be *interesting*,' she says, peering towards the narrow passage they came in from.

'I can try to walk on it,' he says, attempting to get up.

She pushes him back down. 'What did I just say about humans being more hard work than animals?' she scolds. 'You'll need help getting out of here, and I might be strong but I'm not *that* strong.'

She looks towards where the rest of the group disappeared then

314

peers at her watch. Twenty minutes since they left. They'd be taking photos, making notes, so maybe they're not far?

'Right, just stay here,' she says to Kai, standing up.

Kai shakes his head. 'I know what you're thinking. You can't go looking for them, you'll get lost. It's like a labyrinth in these caves! Plus there might be, I don't know, cave monsters or something.'

'I'm a vet, remember? Cave monsters are one of my specialities.'

She grabs her rucksack and places it under his head to make him more comfortable. As she does that, she gets a sudden flashback to placing a pillow beneath her mum's head as she died, helping her sip water through dry, cracked lips. Grief suddenly overwhelms her. She turns away, pleased for the darkness, and gets a bottle of water out, putting it next to Kai.

'Anyway, do you have any better ideas?' She untangles the small pick axe hanging from Kai's rucksack. 'Mind if I borrow this?'

'Blimey, what are you planning to do, burrow a hole out of here? You know that'll take centuries, right?'

'No actually, I was going to axe your foot off.'

He smiles as she walks to the back of the grotto where the ceiling is at its lowest point.

'Be careful. I heard it's a bit slippery!' Kai calls out.

She looks over her shoulder and raises an eyebrow. He shoots her a smile then flinches with pain again. Standing on tiptoes, Becky uses the pick axe to break off some ice. Then she walks back towards Kai with it, wrapping it in her hat before pressing it against his ankle.

'This will help with the pain,' she says.

She leaves it there a few moments as Kai examines her face. 'You're so calm.'

'I've seen a *lot* worse. Right, that'll do for now.' She wraps her belt around the ice pack to keep it in place. 'Ideally, I'd make a splint but this will need to do. Just don't move your leg, okay?'

'Yes, sir!' he replies, giving her a salute.

'Miss will do. Do *not* move, remember?' She jumps up, peering towards the narrow entrance where the group disappeared, trying not to show how nervous she is. The truth is, she might be able to repair broken bones, but navigational skills have never been her strong point. But what choice does she have? There is no way she can support Kai alone in getting out of here.

'I don't like this,' Kai murmurs, brow creased. 'You're not a caver and even cavers get lost in places like this.'

'I'll leave a chocolate trail,' she says, pulling out a packet of chocolate buttons. He raises a cynical eyebrow. 'Look, this is all we've got. So have a little more faith, okay?'

She heads towards the exit.

'Becky!' Kai calls out.

She turns. 'Yep?'

'Just wanted to say you're amazing.' They hold each other's gaze. Then Kai throws her his goofy smile. 'You know, in case you get eaten by a cave monster or something.'

She matches his smile. 'I think there's more chance of *you* succumbing to cave monsters, what with you not being able to run and all.'

He shoots her a thumbs up. 'Gee, thanks for that!'

As she jogs out into the narrow passage, she hears the echo of his laughter. Anyone else might make a big deal of having an injury like his, but Kai's taking it in his stride. She likes that quality in people, no drama, no fuss. She's been told she's like that too, no drama. Her ex Gus told her it was her way of rebelling against her mum's dramas. Maybe he was right?

As she drops a chocolate button on the floor, she wonders what Idris is like. Did he have a penchant for high drama too? And what did that mean for Solar as she grew up with him? Becky remembers feeling like she was at sea with her mum sometimes, calm moments mixed in with the storms.

As she thinks that, her headtorch starts flickering. She slows down and taps it, relieved when it returns to normal. Her phone is in her bag, the same bag Kai's head is resting on, so it isn't like she could use that for light.

She gets to a T-junction to see a dark narrow path leading to the right, a wider and lighter one to the left. The icy ceiling here is like a cracked sheet above her. She'd like to go down the lighter passage, but she remembers Iskar saying the passages leading into the grotto with the princess's inscription were super narrow. So it makes sense they'd have gone down the narrow one. She takes a deep breath then starts jogging down it, the light from her torch bouncing up and down in front of her.

Then it starts flickering again.

She stops jogging, tapping it. But the flickering continues.

'Damn,' she hisses.

She pulls her helmet off to examine it but loses grip due to her thick gloves and it tumbles to the ground, the light from its torch swivelling around the passageway like a strange ice disco ball. Then the light cuts out, plunging Becky into complete darkness.

She feels panic flood her chest. 'It's okay,' she whispers to herself, taking deep breaths. 'You'll be okay.' She slowly crouches down, feeling around the floor for her helmet. She finds it, tapping the torch again.

No luck.

She shakes the hat. Still no luck.

'Useless,' she hisses, putting it back on her head anyway. At least if the ceiling falls down on top of her, that part of her will be protected.

'What next?' she whispers into the darkness.

She could head back to get Kai's torch. It was reasonably light in the grotto for him. But that would mean going back to square one in complete darkness, a good ten minutes or so. She could just plough on – the rest of the group can't be far, surely?

Becky places her hand on the cold bumpy walls and slowly puts one foot in front of the other, feeling her way carefully through the pitch black. But after ten minutes of doing that, she's still no closer to any new turnings or grottos, and the path seems to be getting narrower and narrower, her shoulders scraping the walls either side, her hard hat bumping against the icy ceiling above every now and again, bringing freezing cold shards of ice down over her.

She starts to feel panic bubble inside again. What if she's gone down the wrong passage, and it leads nowhere? She could be walking for hours. The cave system was huge! Kai was right, this *was* a stupid idea.

She stops, gulping in deep breaths.

Then she imagines her mum, right beside her, her hand on her shoulder. 'You'll be fine,' she imagines her saying. 'You've got this, Becks. If you can help a horse give birth to a foal in the middle of a pitch-black field in the dead of winter, you can do this.'

'You're right,' Becky whispers back. 'I can.'

She takes a deep determined breath then continues walking, both hands flat against the walls either side of her, elbows tucked to her side. Just as she's about to give up, she hears the distant sound of voices.

It's the rest of the group!

As she thinks that she feels something in front of her. She reaches her hand out tentatively, feeling wood.

'This is good,' she says to herself. 'Surely this is good?'

She feels upwards, touching more wood. A ladder? She reaches down. Yes, more wooden steps below her too.

'This must lead somewhere, Mum,' she says. She stops, realising what she's saying. Tears prick her eyelashes. Maybe her mum *is* here, watching her, giving her strength, doing all she couldn't do when she lived. She'd always thought her mum was weak, selfish. But she'd gone to live in a cave, given up everything, hadn't she? Wasn't there *some* courage in that? A different kind of courage than Becky could possibly understand, but still. Becky takes in a deep breath, drawing strength from that thought.

Then she lifts her leg, placing her foot carefully on the first rung of the ladder, hand grasping the rung above. She pulls herself up slowly, carefully.

The ladder creaks then sways slightly.

Becky stills, waiting until it stops. When it does, she continues up the ladder until she feels new air on her face. She takes a breath of relief. She can see the outline of a stone boulder above her, so she grabs onto it and hauls herself up. It's still dark, but the darkness has changed in quality and she sees why: there are large white ice crystals above.

She looks ahead into the semi-darkness. It's a small space with wooden planks stretched across narrow caverns. She thinks of what the others said about the passages and grottos around here being unsafe. Should she risk it?

She peers behind her. She's come all this way, hasn't she? And there, in the distance, the sound of voices growing louder. It gives her new resolve. She shouts out, but there's no answer. So she pulls herself up and sits on the ledge, peering down into the abyss. The wooden plank below is cracked in places and it creaks under her weight. No, there's no way she can cross it. She'll need to go back!

She looks up at the vast ceiling in exasperation and something catches her eye: there's an inscription in the stone. She taps her torch again and it flickers on. 'You've *got* to be kidding me, *now* you decide to work?' she says, shaking her head.

She reads the inscription. There are some symbols she can't make out then a date and a name in an alphabet familiar to her.

1914. Louise.

That was it – the princess's inscription Iskar had mentioned!

Then another tiny inscription catches her eye, partially hidden by a protruding piece of rock. She holds onto the wooden pillar for support, crouching down to get a better look.

It has Idris's name on it.

Chapter Twenty-Seven

Becky

Kungar Ice Caves, Russia
3 July 2018

Becky can make out only some vague words. *Idris. Solar.* Then a year: *2001.* There seems to be another name too but it's un-decipherable. She brushes her thumb over the inscription. Maybe Idris had simply brought Solar here to see the inscription. She would have been about nine. A nine-year-old girl would have liked that, seeing a princess's inscription, and making one of her own.

More voices sound out in the distance.

'Iskar!' Becky calls out, her voice booming around the cavern. 'Hannah! Ed!'

Silence.

Then a voice comes back to her. 'Becky?' It's Hannah.

'Kai's hurt his ankle, he can't walk!' she calls back.

'Dork,' she hears Ed mutter. She smiles to herself.

'We have to come back anyway,' Iskar's firm voice shouts. 'The other entrance is closed. Can you find your way back to Kai?'

'I think so,' Becky replies. 'Now my bloody torch is working,' she adds under her breath.

'See you back there,' Iskar says.

'Okay!'

Becky scrambles down and manages to make her way back with less drama now the torch is working. When she returns to the cave, Kai greets her with a raised eyebrow.

'No luck?'

'The path over the cavern was too unstable and I have no caving gear. I managed to call out to them too. They're coming back. Iskar said the other entrance is blocked.'

'Looks like the evening's going well then,' Kai says sarcastically. He reaches into his rucksack, pulling out some biscuits. 'I found these. Might as well keep ourselves occupied while we wait.'

Becky sits down, leaning against the cave wall as she takes one of Kai's biscuits. 'If you told me a week ago I'd be spending the evening in a cave with a speleologist, I wouldn't have believed you.'

'You say it like it's a bad thing.'

She looks around her. 'I guess the company's okay. But the whole cave dwelling thing? Not for me. I prefer fields and countryside.'

'Don't knock it till you've tried it.'

'I have. It's left you with a sprained ankle, maybe even a broken one, and it nearly got me very lost!'

He laughs. 'I don't mind a few broken bones if it means some adventure.'

'I've certainly had some adventures the past couple of weeks.' She pauses, thinking of the inscription. 'I found something interesting in the cave actually.'

'Oh yeah?'

She tells Kai about the inscription Solar and Idris had made.

'Maybe he brought her here to see the princess's inscription then. I doubt they lived here.'

'That's what I'm thinking. There were other words too but I couldn't quite see them. Maybe other Children of the Current members.'

Kai frowns. 'Children of the Current?'

'The name of Idris's cult.'

'You really think it was a cult?'

She takes a bite of her biscuit. 'The way people who knew Idris talked about him certainly makes it sound like he wielded this weird power. Who knows . . .'

'So what next?' Kai asks Becky.

'I'm going to the local library Caden told me about. I might have a better chance of finding records for Solar there. I'll ask around, see if I can track her down. Then I'm going back home,' she adds with a contented sigh.

'You look happy about that.'

'Yeah, all this digging into the past is wearing me down a bit. I need to start looking forward.'

Kai examines her face. 'And what does looking forward mean for you?'

'I don't know really. Work. The dogs.'

'Just you and them?'

'There's more to my life than the dogs, you know! I have my

dad, even if he is a few hundred miles away. I have friends, including the odd speleologist or two,' she adds, jogging her shoulder into his.

'Ah, so we're friends now, are we?'

'Maybe. It depends if you give me your last biscuit.' He hands it to her and she laughs. 'I was only kidding. Here,' she says, snapping it in half and handing him the other piece.

'Okay,' he continues. 'So you have your dad, who lives ages away. You have friends. And you have dogs.' His face turns serious. 'Is that enough for you?'

'Of course it is! God, you sound like my friend Kay. I don't need a man in my life to be happy, you know.'

'I'm not talking about a man! I'm talking about having a deeper connection. You said yourself you didn't get on with your mum. Maybe your search for your sister isn't just about finding someone you're related to. Maybe it's about finding someone you can share your life with – other than those dogs of yours.'

She frowns. Is he right?

They hear voices and both look up to see Iskar jogging in, looking out of breath, Hannah and Ed behind her.

'Why's the other entrance blocked off?' Kai asks.

Iskar shrugs. 'Locked. Lev told me it would be open.'

'What happened to you then, mate?' Ed asks Kai, walking over.

'He slipped on the ice,' Becky explains.

'Finally, he will find his prince!' Hannah says.

'I keep telling you, it's a princess I want!' Kai retorts.

'So how did you manage to get to the princess inscription on your own without getting lost?' Hannah asks Becky.

Becky tells them all about what happened. A big smile spreads over Hannah's face. 'That's amazing. You did that all without a torch?'

'I had no choice,' Becky says.

'Okay, you are *officially* one of us now,' Hannah says.

Becky laughs. 'Near-death experiences make me one of you?'

'That's the beauty of this profession,' Kai says. 'Coming out alive after. We need to celebrate! Any bars around here?'

'*You* need to get that ankle checked out,' Becky says.

'Okay, after that,' Kai replies, shrugging. 'Come on, let's get out of here.'

'That *might* be a bit of a problem,' Iskar says, looking at her watch. 'I told Lev we'd be back out by midnight,' she says. 'It's now past midnight. I know Lev, and he will *not* hang around.'

'When will he come back?' Hannah asks.

Iskar shrugs. 'The first tour starts at eight in the morning.'

'So we're stuck here all night?' Becky asks.

Iskar smiles. 'Looks like it. But don't worry, I have something to keep us warm.' She pulls a large bottle of vodka from her bag and everyone whoops.

Over the next couple of hours, the group huddle in a circle, drinking the vodka and talking. Becky hears stories of their caving exploits and she shares stories from her life as a vet.

'Another sip?' Hannah asks, lifting the bottle up. There's just a third left now and Becky's head is swimming but she doesn't care. She rarely drinks but the past couple of weeks call for some alcohol consumption. She's enjoying the pleasurable burning feeling of the vodka as she drinks it, warming her from the inside out in this freezing place.

'Yep,' she says, taking it and slugging back a mouthful before handing it to Kai, who's lying on the ground and staring up at the icy ceiling in drunken awe.

Becky joins him, her head next to his, feeling a sense of contentment as she stares up at the ice crystals forming a beautiful patchwork above her.

'Maybe it's not so bad here,' she slurs. 'The surreallness of it, the beauty, the feeling. It's like I'm really part of something.'

Kai turns his head to look at her. 'See, I told you you're just looking to connect.'

Becky looks around her at the others. They get on so well, are so natural with each other. In a way, they're their own little cult.

'Did you know,' Kai says as he points up at the stalactites above, 'stalactites grow so slowly that when they break, it takes over a human lifetime for the ice to bond again and recover?'

'I did *not* know that,' she says.

'Each one is different. Individuals, standing alone despite being clustered together,' he continues.

She watches him as he talks. He really is quite attractive. She rolls her eyes. She's had too much vodka, clearly.

'What?' Kai asks, moving awkwardly onto his side so he's facing her.

'Oh, just thinking of how surreal it is, lying in an ice cave with a bunch of strangers.'

His brow creases. 'I'm not a stranger.'

'No, *you're* not. You know what I mean though?'

'Not really. Some relationships can form in just a few moments, others can take years, just like the ice in this stalagmite.'

'Or people don't get the chance to bond at all,' Becky says with a sigh.

'You're thinking of your sister?'

Becky nods. 'My mum too.'

'You've never really forgiven her for leaving you, have you?'

She frowns. 'It's not like that. I'm not bitter.'

'Aren't you?' Kai asks, his eyes probing hers. 'No harm admitting it, Becky. I fell apart when my dad left to go back to Jamaica.'

'How old were you?'

'Fourteen. My hormones were all over the place. I rebelled, my poor mum.' He sighs, shaking his head. 'Fell in with the wrong crowd, got caught up in some trouble. But then this saved me,' he says, gesturing around him. 'Caves. I found something to focus on.'

'And I found romance novels, and then animals. Maybe we're more alike than I thought.'

Kai smiles. 'And we've only known each other, what, about two weeks? I reckon we're one of those fast-forming stalactites.'

They smile at each other. Then there's the sound of clapping.

'Right, time for some fun,' Ed says, standing up. 'One day, Little Johnny visited a cave.' He then sits down and points to Hannah.

Hannah stands. 'Unfortunately, Little Johnny got lost in a grotto in that cave.' She points at Iskar and sits back down.

Becky frowns. 'What are they doing?' she asks Kai.

'The Unfortunately Fortunately game,' Kai explains. 'It's something we do at night if we're all staying together, a little ritual I guess. People take it in turns to tell parts of a story, alternating fortunate and unfortunate events.'

Iskar stands up, the vodka bottle in her hand. 'But *fortunately*, Little Johnny found a bottle of vodka in the cave.'

Iskar points to Kai and he sits up, shrugging as he points to his ankle. 'Unfortunately, Little Johnny slipped on the icy ground because he was a clumsy oaf,' he says with a raised eyebrow, 'and then he dropped the vodka bottle.'

He points to Becky.

'Oh God,' Becky says. 'I've never been a good story-teller.' She thinks of her mum, the award-winning novelist. She'd know how to do this.

She stands up, closing her eyes as she sees her mum's pen working over the pages of her notepad. Then she opens her eyes.

'Fortunately, as the temperatures were sub-zero in the ice cave, the vodka froze so Little Johnny could lick the frozen vodka off the floor.'

Everyone laughs and cheers and she laughs with them, taking a bow and sitting down. As the game continues and they get more drunk and raucous, Becky hugs her knees to her chest, smiling. Was this how her mum felt when she was living in the cave? *Part* of something? Becky has been alone for so long. Even with her patients and David next door, it isn't like this. This is special, the bond these people share, the way they live their lives. And in here, in this cave, it somehow enhances that feeling.

For the first time, Becky is beginning to understand why her mum might have done what she did.

She frowns. But did that justify leaving her daughter behind? What happened when the honeymoon period wore off?

Hannah sits next to her, pulling her phone out. 'I forgot to show this to you in all the excitement hearing about Kai's fall. We saw this in the cavern, and I took a photo of it for you.'

Becky takes her phone to see it's Idris and Solar's inscription.

'Oh yes, I saw this too. Can you email it to me when we're back? Kai has my address.'

'Of course.'

Hannah goes to put it back in her pocket but Becky stops her. 'Wait. Maybe if we zoom in, we can see the other name better?'

'Good idea. I have a sharpening app actually. Let me try.' Hannah messes about with her phone for a few minutes then hands it back to Becky. 'Got it! I am *officially* the queen of forensic photograph investigations.'

Becky takes the phone off Hannah and stares at the other word on the inscription.

Idris, Solar and Oceane were here. 2001.

Oceane. She recognises that name. Wasn't it Caden's ex, the one who left the group before they went to Spain?

'Okay, another game,' Ed says.

Becky reluctantly hands the phone back to Hannah. She could stare at that inscription all night, her mind whirring with the possibilities of how and why Idris, Solar and Oceane had ended up here in this cave.

At eight the next morning, the five of them reappear from the cave. Lev smiles wryly as he holds the iron gate open for them.

'I did tell you I wouldn't hang around,' he says to Iskar. 'My wife would *not* have been happy.'

Becky blinks up at the bright morning, yawning. They'd managed to get a few hours' sleep in the end, huddled up together

329

in the cold, her head on Kai's shoulder. But she still feels as if she's been bulldozed.

Lev frowns at the empty bottle of vodka Iskar is carrying. 'You drank all that inside?' he asks her.

'To keep warm,' Ed says as he yawns.

Lev shakes his head. 'You Brits really are crazy. And I should know, I'm married to one.'

'You never mentioned that your wife is from the UK,' Iskar says.

Lev laughs. 'Perhaps I haven't. And people certainly can't tell from me mentioning her name. Solar sounds more cosmic than British.'

Everyone's mouths drop open. Becky has to take deep breaths to control herself. Tears flood her eyes.

Had she finally found her sister?

Chapter Twenty-Eight

Selma

Kent, UK
8 September 1991

I ran down the beach towards the collapsed cave. There was a crowd gathered around it, police and paramedics being guided by Julien and Maggie to the front. The small entrance was gone, replaced by fallen rock. I put my hand to my mouth. Idris and I had been in there just the morning before.

'What happened?' one of the officers asked.

'We heard screams, then a crashing noise,' Maggie replied, voice trembling.

'How many are in there?' he asked.

'Three, maybe four,' Julien said.

'Is Idris in there?' I asked, leaning down to catch my breath.

He nodded. 'Oceane, Tom and Caden too.'

My stomach sank as I stared into the cave. What if Idris – the father of my baby – was lying in that cave injured . . . or worse, dead?

Suddenly, my thoughts of getting rid of our baby without telling him filled me with horror as I imagined him dying in that cave, not knowing about the child that was growing inside me.

I suddenly felt sick.

'What's going on?' We turned to see Donna running down the beach, shopping bags smashing against her legs.

'The ceiling's collapsed,' I said. 'I'm sorry, Donna – Oceane and Tom are in there.'

Donna let out a gasp, her shopping falling from her hands. Jars smashed, red sauce congealed in the sand, staining it scarlet.

'I told you and Idris how dangerous that bloody cave was,' she screamed at me. 'I fucking told you to talk to him!'

I opened my mouth then closed it. I'd completely forgotten to mention it to Idris.

Donna ran towards the cave but the policemen stopped her.

'We need to call in the fire brigade and some cavers,' one of them said. 'If you go in, you'll only make it worse.'

Over the next half an hour, we watched as men entered with hard hats, shovelling fallen stones out of the way. I tried to comfort Donna but she wouldn't let me near her. I understood. If it was Becky in there, I'd be angry too. I should have mentioned her concerns to Idris, used my influence on him to tell the others not to go in.

As I thought that, Oceane limped out, her arm around a distressed-looking Tom who was hopping on one leg. I caught a glimpse of Tom's bloody leg, a hint of bone protruding. I flinched, turning away.

Donna rushed forward with the paramedics.

'Where's Caden?' Julien asked.

'Is he not here? I thought he'd stormed out after our argument.'

Argument?

'There's someone coming out,' Julien said. Idris appeared from the cave with Caden, who was holding his arm delicately.

I ran to them.

'Idris!' I said as I looked at his dusty shocked face. 'Idris, are you okay?'

He peered towards Tom, who was being treated by the paramedics, crying out in pain. Then at Caden who was being led to another ambulance. Oceane walked over to Caden, trying to comfort him, but he just kept shoving her away, refusing to look at her.

What had happened in that cave before it collapsed?

Oceane looked up, catching Idris's eye. He quickly looked away. Panic flooded my chest.

'What happened in there?' I asked him. He didn't say anything, couldn't look me in the eye. The panic increased. 'Idris, what the hell happened?'

'It's not what you think,' he said, gaze meeting Oceane's again.

I looked between them, humiliation darting through me.

In that moment it became clear to me that they had been sleeping together after all . . . and Caden had caught them in the act in the cave. The same cave where Idris and I made love.

I looked at Idris in disgust and then ran off.

I sat beyond the chalk stacks for what seemed like hours, watching the blue lights of the police cars and ambulances swirling against the white walls.

People walked past, desperate to see all the drama.

'Knew something like this would happen,' I overheard one woman say as she walked by.

'Disaster waiting to happen, that bloody cult,' her friend said.

They were right, had been right all along. The ceiling had literally come crashing down on our heads, letting light come in to highlight what Idris really was: a deceiver, a nobody. Just a man looking for some cheap thrills.

What did that make me? The very middle-aged desperate housewife I was so terrified of becoming?

A couple walked over, peering towards the drama outside the cave.

It was Julie and Greg.

Julie caught sight of me, her face filling with anger. Greg followed his wife's gaze, his face registering surprise then fear. Julie went to walk towards me but Greg grabbed her arm, saying something to her. But she shook her head and strode towards me anyway.

What now?

I slowly stood, stomach turning at the look of anger on my old friend's face.

'I know about the lies you've been telling about Greg,' Julie spat when she got to me, body rigid as she tried to contain her anger. 'That yoga teacher told anyone who'd listen about the lies you told her.'

She was referring to what I'd told Anita about Greg perving over me. *Great.*

'They're not lies, Julie,' I said softly. 'I didn't want you to find out this way, but honestly, I was telling the truth.'

Greg laughed bitterly as he joined his wife. 'Oh come on, Selma. You're a flirt, always have been. Putting yourself on display every chance you can get. And yet I come out the fucking villain, because men always do with women like you, don't they?'

I looked at him, hardly believing my ears. He must have been so desperate to save his marriage that he was twisting the truth. And yet he'd been willing to risk his marriage with his flirtations.

'He's lying,' I said to Julie, my eyes on hers.

Julie laughed. 'That's funny, coming from you. Did you know everyone calls you Tall Story Selma?'

I frowned, wrapping my arms around myself, feeling dwarfed by their remarks.

'All backfired now, hasn't it?' Greg said, pointing towards the collapsed cave. 'The dream's over, Selma.'

'You've torn your family apart for nothing,' Julie added, shaking her head.

For nothing.

Had it really been for nothing? Losing my job, my marriage . . . losing Becky. I thought of Idris and Oceane. All lost for a pack of lies because, let's face it, without the appeal of Idris, would I have really stayed in that cave?

I curled my hands into fists. I couldn't let it be for nothing. I *wouldn't*!

'Accept it, Selma,' Julie said. 'You made a mistake – a mistake that has cost you your daughter. Even more so after the cave collapse. There will be no Children of the Current,' she said, using her fingers for quotation marks, 'and no cave to take Becky to any more. You can't keep running away from your problems, Selma. You're weak.'

'You're wrong,' I said, glaring at her. 'I'm strong. We're *all* strong.' I felt resolve build inside. 'We can get over something like this, you'll see. And when we do Julie, you'll always be welcome to come join us. Especially when you see the real Greg.'

Then I walked away, determination rushing through me.

I *would* prove them all wrong! I wouldn't crumble at the first sign of trouble like my mother did when she was left alone and penniless by her last husband. I'd make this work, no matter what it took.

As I walked towards the cave, movement above caught my eye. I looked up towards the hotel, noticing someone watching me.

Idris.

Why was he up there?

Chapter Twenty-Nine

Selma

Kent, UK
8 September 1991

I quickened my step, taking the rickety path that led up towards the hotel from the beach. The steps were cracked and clogged with weeds, the metal handrail rusted.

When I got to the top, Idris had disappeared. I walked up to the hotel. It looked even more neglected up close with its peeling paint, overgrown grass and cracked windowpanes. I peered in through the cobwebbed windows, noticing a figure slumped over the reception desk inside. It was Idris.

I tried the handle on the front door. To my surprise, it slipped open. I stepped into the reception area, the sound of my feet echoing around the walls. It was dark and smelt of damp.

Idris looked up, his cheeks shining with tears.

'What are you doing up here?' I asked him. 'You need to be down there with the others.'

'I – I can't. It's too much. It's all my fault. What have I done?' Idris let out an anguished cry and put his head in his hands. I looked at him in shock. It was so surreal to see him cry, this man who seemed to be made of stone, a god, indestructible. I felt sorry for him, seeing him like this. But I quickly stifled my pity. He'd brought this on himself.

'Stop this,' I commanded.

He looked up. 'Stop what?'

'This self-pity!' I walked towards the counter, putting my hands on the dusty surface as I glared at him. 'This is no time for weakness, for Christ's sake. Be the man they think you are. They need you now more than ever! We have to show everyone we can get through this.'

'What's the point?' he said. 'It's over. There's no way we'll be allowed to stay in the cave now anyway. It'll be deemed unsafe.'

'Then we fight them! Surely there's something we can do? A bloody hotel wouldn't have been built on a cave that was about to crumble, would it?' I looked towards a closed door behind Idris. 'Is that the office in there? Maybe there are documents, structural engineering stuff.'

I went to walk behind the desk but Idris grabbed my hand. 'Aren't you going to ask me about Oceane?'

'Do I need to?' I countered, my voice showing the first sign of a tremble.

'It happened before I even saved the boy. Not after . . . not when you arrived.'

'Then why the argument in the cave?'

'Just Caden and Oceane having one of their usual dramas. I went in to check on them and Tom must have been drawn in by his sister shouting.'

I shook my head. 'I'm not sure I believe you.'

'It's the truth.'

'Really? Why not tell me that when I confronted you with the rumours a few weeks ago?'

'You asked if something was going on between us. It wasn't then – it had stopped.'

'Oh, stop with that crap!' I shouted, my voice echoing around the walls. 'I've had enough of it. I need the *truth* now. If we're to survive, if the Children of the Current is, I need the truth, every bit of it. Like why are you here, in the hotel? How the hell did you get in?'

Idris sighed. 'I used to live here.'

'In the hotel?'

He nodded. 'My parents owned this place, the cave too. I used to play hide and seek under here,' he said, pointing to the space beneath the reception desk. 'And I'd help my dad pour pints in there,' he added, gesturing to the bar. 'Even helped my mum sort the gardens.'

'Is that why you've been able to stay in the cave? You own it?'

He nodded.

I looked around me, imagining a child running through the hotel's halls, breathing new life into this place, not as a hotel but as a family home for me and Becky . . . and for my new baby too. The Children of the Current could still continue, but I'd have a secure home to bring my children up in . . . and to keep social services at bay if we could move in before the court date in a month or so.

I grabbed a chair and sat on it, rolling it over to Idris so I was sitting in front of him, knee to knee. I took his hands and looked him right in the eye. 'So you actually own this hotel?' I asked him, heart thumping hard against my chest. 'Your family anyway?'

'Not any more, just the cave.'

My heart sank. I let go of his hands.

'After my mother died, my father struggled to run the place.'

'You're a Peterson?' I whispered. He nodded. 'Your mother, she . . .' I said softly.

Idris closed his eyes. 'Yes. She took her own life.'

'I'm sorry. That must have been difficult. Must still be so difficult.'

He nodded, not saying anything.

'So what happened to the hotel?' I asked, looking around me, still so disappointed he no longer owned it.

'Dad met someone – a woman. She moved in to help him then they got married.' His jaw clenched. 'She was awful. The things she made me do while she lazed around. Sweeping floors, cleaning toilets. Even serving bloody food. I was her male Cinderella. I was just thirteen for Christ's sake.' He curled his hands into angry fists. It was good to see the spark back in him, even if he was angry. I'd been worried, seeing him so defeated. I needed him strong now, more than ever. For Becky, for our new child . . . for the Children of the Current so we could prove everyone wrong.

'Dad turned to drink,' he continued. 'It was easy for his new wife to get him to sign the lease over. Funny thing is, the plan was for her to sell it and go off with the money.' He laughed. 'Hasn't been able to sell it though, has she? She refused to budge on the asking price so it's been on the market for nearly twenty years.'

'Then how were you able to stay in the cave?'

'That's one thing that *did* stay in the Peterson family. My mother

340

used to love writing in there, and Dad couldn't bring himself to let it go.'

'And where's your dad now?' I asked softly.

'Drinking his life away in a flat a couple of miles away from here. That's why I came back a couple of months ago, to see him after his friend called to say he was in a bad way. I couldn't face staying in his flat with him and couldn't afford to pay for a hotel. So I broke into this place,' he said, looking around him. 'My old home. What should *still* be my home if it weren't for my step-mother. That's when I saw Oceane. She'd come here some nights with friends to drink, smoke pot.'

'And you slept together?'

He sighed. 'She lied about her age. It was stupid, reckless. I was high. I was mourning, too.'

'Mourning?'

'My dad passed away just before I saved the boy.'

I took in a deep breath. 'I'm so sorry.' I squeezed his hand. He'd experienced such tragedy. 'Where were you before you came back to see your dad?' I asked.

'London. I moved there when I was sixteen; I had to get away. Those street artists you see doing caricatures?' I nodded. 'That was me until a few months ago.'

I thought of all the rumours about him: New Zealand, Australia, the States, even Russia. A rock star. A drug dealer. A millionaire. When all along he'd been selling his art on the streets of London.

'Is that how you managed to live when you first got there?' I asked. 'Selling art?'

He avoided my gaze. 'I had money – money my stepmum thought belonged to her.'

341

'What do you mean?'

'Dad agreed to make his bank account a joint account with her. She drew a few thousand out once to buy a car, left it on the side as she took a phone call. I grabbed it and ran off with it, heard her shouting out at me as I jumped in the taxi I'd called.' He swallows, peering out into the darkness. 'Ever since then, I've been looking over my shoulder. She told me once her family were known criminals and that if I crossed her, I'd never be safe. It made me dislike her even more. Maybe she was a criminal herself and was just with my father for the money?'

I thought of the graffiti scrawled on the cave yesterday.

Thief.

'You think they've caught up with you?' I asked.

He shuddered. 'Maybe.' He peered up at me. 'Not so appealing now, am I? A thief, a street artist, always looking over my shoulder?' He paused a moment then frowned. 'The money wasn't the only thing I stole.'

I sighed. 'What else?'

'All this stuff about the current, numbers, feasts? I got it all from a weekend retreat I went on in Battersea a few years ago.'

'I thought you lived with a healer.'

'I did . . . for two days. At the retreat. It was all his teachings, the current, no watches.'

'Jesus,' I whispered.

'It's over, isn't it?' Idris said. 'All of it is over. The Children of the Current . . . you and me?' He flinched as he said that. 'The dream's over.'

I looked into his eyes. Did I think any differently about him? Of course. But the feelings were still there, somewhere, beneath the disappointment. And what about the Children of the Current? I thought of Greg's mocking eyes as he'd said the same as Idris. *The dream's over, Selma.* And then Julie: *You've torn your family apart for nothing.*

No. Absolutely not. I would *not* let it be for nothing. Idris just needed an incentive to get him back to his old self. And I knew just what that was.

I took his hand and brought it to my belly. 'It's not over, Idris. It's only just the beginning.'

He frowned. 'What do you mean?'

'I'm pregnant.'

His mouth dropped open. 'You're . . .'

I smiled. 'Yes.'

He sunk to his knees and pressed his lips against my belly.

'Now do you understand why you need to stay strong?' I said, stroking his hair as I looked down at him.

He gazed up at me. 'I'm worried I'm too weak, that they'll all see through me now.'

'Not with me by your side. For the sake of our child, we mustn't give up. If we can just hold our dream together, prove to people how safe, how *wonderful* living this way is, the possibilities are endless.'

His green eyes sparkled with new hope. 'You really think that?'

'I do. But not a word to anyone else about what you've just told me, okay?' I said, face serious. 'It will only work if they still look up to you . . . to *us*.'

He kneeled, peering up at me like I was a god. 'What about my stepmother though? What if it is her or her family who vandalised the cave?'

'She's not done anything else, has she?' I said.

He nodded but the frown remained on his face.

When we got back down to the cave, those who remained were gathered around the table, talking. They went quiet when we walked in, hand in hand. Julien went to speak but Idris put his hand up.

'Everything will be okay,' Idris said. 'As long as we remain together and strong, it will be okay. Now, shall we enter the current?'

Everyone looked at each other hesitantly.

'It's out of our hands now,' I said. 'All we can do is what we know. Channel our thoughts onto healing those who have been hurt.'

It felt weird saying that, but the rest of them believed in it so much. If it meant me spouting all of that too for the group to survive, then so be it.

Idris went to sit down at the head of the table and peered up at me. Under the harsh artificial light of the battery-operated lamp we'd placed in the kitchen, I could see the dark circles under his eyes, how pale his usually tanned skin was.

Despite his new resolve, I could see he was crumbling. I needed to take charge.

'Let's start,' I said, pulling a chair up to sit at the head of the table with him.

I woke late the next morning to the sound of heavy rain. The cave was darker than I'd ever seen it during the day, and it smelt different. Damp. Mossy. Rain like a drum of thunder echoing around the cave.

I rose and padded through the cave, past Julien painting his chair and Maggie at her urn. Oceane was in the hospital with her mum and brother, Caden too being treated for his arm injuries.

It was going to take a lot of work to rebuild things but I'd woken with a renewed energy. I was up for the challenge – I *had* to be. I now had a baby growing inside me and a looming court date to determine the fate of my other child. It made me feel even more determined. I had to create a sense of stability for my children. Sure, I could return to a normal life, rent a cheap flat in town. But the money would run out quickly, and I doubted my old boss would take me back considering the way I'd just walked out on my job. And then what? I didn't want to be like my mother, scrabbling around for every penny, relying on men to support her.

Living in the cave gave me freedom from relying like that on money. It gave me the freedom to *write*. For that to continue, I needed people to believe we were strong here, that children could be happy here too.

But what of Idris? Was he up for the challenge? It had concerned me to see him so weak the night before, so easily overwhelmed. He needed to pick himself up, and soon, if we were to prove to everyone the Children of the Current could weather any storm that came our way.

I got ready and found him at the front of the cave, making coffee. His skin took on a different quality in this gloomy morning light, more real. His blond hair looked darker too. I imagined how he would look in winter, wrapped up in fur as he gazed out to a turbulent sea like the character I was writing about.

He saw me approach and walked over, giving me a lingering

kiss. Then he pulled a chair out for me. 'Put your feet up,' he said. 'You need to rest.'

I sat down, smiling up at him. He *did* seem back to his old self. Maybe the fact he was to be a father had sunk in and revitalised him?

'Tea?' he asked me. 'That's better for you than coffee, right?'

'Yes, please.'

'You missed the sunrise,' he said. 'It was beautiful.'

'Not so beautiful now,' I replied, peering out at the clouds.

'Yeah, the clouds started gathering when I walked back down.'

'Down? Where did you go?'

'Up to the hotel.' He smiled. 'I found a recent unopened letter from the council proving this cave's structurally sound. They can't kick us out for health and safety reasons.'

I matched his smile. 'Brilliant!'

'I also got this in town,' he said, pulling out a small grey teddy from his pocket. 'For the baby.'

I took it, pressing it against my cheek. 'It's gorgeous.'

'I got some paint too. That's why I woke when the sun was rising, I wanted to get the exact same colour as the sunrise and found the perfect pigment for it.'

I smiled to myself. He really was back to his old self.

'What are you going to paint?'

'Our child.'

My smile deepened.

'It's going to be a girl,' he continued, voice filled with certainty. 'And her hair will be the colour of the sun rising on a September morning.'

He crouched down to put his hand on my belly and I put my

346

hand over his. His child was growing inside me. This man, this otherworldly person.

'You two look chirpy this morning.' We both looked up to see Donna standing at the entrance. She looked exhausted, her short, dark hair a mess, face creased.

Idris jumped up. 'Donna! How's Tom?'

'I'm surprised you care,' Donna said, her voice shaking. 'All full of smiles and lightness, the both of you. Almost like my son wasn't nearly crushed to death despite me *begging* you to ask everyone to avoid the cave.'

'Donna, be calm,' Idris said, putting his hand on her arm. 'You will only make yourself feel worse.'

She pulled her arm away from him. 'Don't tell me to be calm, Idris! My son's lying in hospital right now with a crushed leg thanks to your selfish naivety and ignorance.'

I stood up. 'We're so sorry, Donna. Idris wasn't to know the cave would collapse from just a few rocks falling.'

'I know Tom will be fine,' Idris said. 'I can *sense* it.'

I nodded. 'We were all in the current last night. You should have seen it, hours and hours we sat around this very table,' I said, desperate not to lose her from the group, especially as she was a midwife. I couldn't risk social services knowing I was pregnant so to have a midwife here would be invaluable. Plus the more people we had, the stronger we were. It seemed so empty in the cave now, just Idris, me, Julien and Maggie.

Donna shook her head in disbelief. 'Jesus Christ, Selma, listen to yourself! You sound just like Idris. Who's the bloody cult leader now? You two need to stop lying to yourselves. The dream's over and it's about time you both did everyone else a favour and

347

accepted it.' She looked me up and down, shaking her head. 'Especially *you*, Selma. The court date will be coming up soon. Go get a flat, for Christ's sake, give yourself half a chance of getting custody of your daughter, won't you?'

I frowned.

'Donna,' Idris said, stepping towards her and putting his hand on her arm. But she shrugged him away and marched to her bed, ignoring anyone else who tried to talk to her, gathering her stuff up then storming back out.

Idris watched her, blinking in shock. Donna had been so consistent in her support of him.

'Why was she so angry?' Julien asked, walking over.

'Grief does that to people,' I quickly explained. 'She needs someone to blame. She'll understand in a few days, when Tom is better. Right, Idris?'

Idris nodded slowly, still in shock.

'*Will* Tom and Caden be better?' Maggie asked. 'Idris, you were there? Were the injuries bad?'

Idris opened his mouth then closed it.

'Of course they will,' I said. 'We just need to keep getting into the current, focusing our thoughts on them.'

Maggie and Julien exchanged doubtful looks, and I felt a sense of panic. We were losing them.

'In fact, we have some news,' I said. 'News that will prove just how much getting into the current works.'

Maggie's eyes lit up. 'You're pregnant?'

I smiled, and Maggie pulled me into a hug as Julien smiled hesitantly.

'What I didn't tell you is, since Becky, I haven't been able to have children,' I lied. 'In fact, I was told by a doctor it was impossible for me to get pregnant again.'

Idris looked at me in surprise.

'But this miracle,' I said, putting my hand to my belly, 'is a sign. You see, I haven't just been focusing on my writing when I've been in the current. I've been focusing on healing my body too. And it worked! There's no other explanation.'

Maggie's smile deepened as Julien patted Idris on the back.

Idris was still frowning. He could see it was a lie. But the important thing was, I needed Maggie and Julien to keep the faith. I needed this new 'miracle' to be like Idris appearing to walk on water that day. Did the fact it was a lie really matter, just as Idris walking on water was an illusion?

'I know it's been a disruptive twenty-four hours,' I said softly. 'But this is proof what we do here works. I suggest we dedicate two hours each evening to getting into a collective current to heal Tom and Caden. What do you think, Idris?'

He continued staring at me.

'Idris?' I repeated.

He snapped out of it, nodding. 'Yes, good idea.'

'It's also worth us taking some walks during the day when you can,' I added. 'Talk to people, spread the word. The cave collapse will have concerned some, putting them off coming here. I think if we can show how *welcoming* we are, it will be a great help. The more people we can get into the current to focus on healing, the more effective it will be.' I ran my hand over my belly. 'Just as it was for me,' I added. I clasped Maggie's hand and smiled at Julien. 'It will all be fine. Life throws us challenges but we can rise to them, right?'

Maggie and Julien nodded, exchanging smiles, and I almost felt sorry for them. But better they were deluded than knew the sad truth. Idris was a fake and I . . . I was a woman desperate to appear strong for the sake of keeping her children. That was all that mattered now. Becky and the child growing inside me.

Over the next few weeks, we settled into our old ways again, despite what had happened in the small cave . . . and despite the fact there were only five of the original group left. Surprisingly, Caden had returned, walking into the cave with his arm in a sling. He was received with joy but I couldn't help but watch the dynamic between him and Idris. *Did* Caden know what had happened in the hotel above between Idris and Oceane?

I was happy though, feeling optimistic about the baby and my chances of winning custody of Becky. I'd had the court date through finally, delayed until the end of November due to the social workers' workloads. It felt like fate was giving me more time.

Becky was still sulky when we spent our days together, but we fell into a routine of sorts, long walks on the beach, lunch at the café. Thanks to it being cooler now, I was able to hide my growing belly from her under jumpers and cardigans. And, more importantly, from Mike when he dropped Becky off for visits.

The novel was going well too. I was on to the last few chapters, more motivated than ever. I needed to make money, to prove to everyone I could support my children financially. I was determined to finish it before the baby was born in May. Maggie had offered to type it up using the skills she'd gained in her life before the cave. I would then edit it and it would be retyped, ready to be sent to my agent in the spring.

Imagine that: a new baby and a new book deal all at the same time.

I didn't think about how the baby would be delivered though. I hadn't even been to the doctors as I was too scared they'd report me to social services. There wasn't one person who didn't know about the 'cult' as we were called by outsiders, and that included the local GPs. I needed Donna back; she'd been a midwife after all. I told myself I'd think about that *after* the court date.

As the days drew in though, conditions in the cave worsened. Rain water spilled into the entrance, and the cave walls iced up when it was cold. We'd installed heaters, powered by the generators Julien had sourced, but it was still freezing. I grew increasingly paranoid about the people that would slink by the cave in the night, even wading through the high tide to get there. Sometimes I'd wake, sure I could see eyes blinking in at me. I thought of Idris's angry stepmother and her family. What if they tried to hurt us?

One day, I tried to broach the idea of putting a gate up of some kind at the front of the cave, but everyone seemed horrified by the idea.

'The whole point is we're open to the elements here,' Maggie said. 'I like it that way.'

'I agree with Maggie,' Idris said. 'Gates would defeat the object of this place.'

I thought about arguing back but I could see they were convinced.

The next day, just as I was about to tackle the last chapter of my novel after breakfast, I returned to my bed to discover pages from my notepad torn and scattered on the floor. I grabbed them and ran to Idris, showing him the scattered pages.

'I just found my notepad like this,' I said. 'Someone must have destroyed it while we were sleeping.'

His face registered surprise. 'The same thing has happened to me.'

Chapter Thirty

Selma

Kent, UK
10 November 1991

Idris walked to his paint area and came back with some paint-brushes that had been snapped in half.

'I woke yesterday to find them like this. I thought it was the dog at first,' he said, peering towards Mojo.

I shook my head. 'Can't be – the breakages are too neat. Who's doing this? Could it be your stepmother?'

Idris peered out towards the rainy beach. 'Maybe. But why sneak in?'

'Mind games.'

He took in a sharp breath. 'Yep, she was a fan of those.'

Over the next few days, other things were destroyed. My pen. Idris's painting apron.

'Whoever's doing this is walking into the cave at night, as we sleep,' I whispered to Idris one morning, rubbing my belly. 'Isn't it time we thought about our security here, especially for the sake of the children?'

'You mean a gate?' he asked. I nodded. 'You know how I feel about that, Selma. Maggie, Caden and Julien too; we're all against it.'

'You own the place!'

'Selma, we can't.'

I folded my arms. 'Yes we can. In fact, if we want to protect our child, we *must*.'

Idris's face flickered with concern. 'Let me think about it.'

A few days later, I woke to the sound of drilling. I sat up as Maggie, Caden and Julien stirred, smiling as I saw Idris drilling at the entrance of the cave.

'What's going on?' Caden asked me.

'Wait and see,' I said, wrapping my dressing gown around my growing belly and walking to the front of the cave as a large shadow spread across the ground, the sound of two men chattering nearby.

'Oh wonderful! Idris is installing an art piece,' Maggie said, clapping her hands.

But then two men appeared with a large black iron gate, its shadow turning the entrance dark.

Julien frowned. 'We said we didn't want this. It's so dark now, so enclosed like a dungeon.' He looked at me. 'Are you doing this to keep people out? Or keep us in?'

I regarded him with surprise. 'That's a ridiculous thing to say, Julien! Idris and I had to make a tough decision to protect us all.'

'I thought you didn't want it either?' Julien asked Idris.

Idris laid his drill down, saying something to the two men, who nodded. Then he walked over to Julien, putting his hand on his friend's shoulder as he sighed.

'I didn't want to tell you this as I was worried about scaring you all,' he added, looking at Maggie and Caden. 'But it looks like I'm going to have to so you understand why this gate is necessary. Selma and I have been been—'

'Receiving death threats,' I finished for him. Idris frowned but I ploughed on. 'Not just aimed at us, but *all* of us.' Maggie's eyes widened. 'It'll probably just be kids,' I quickly added. I didn't want them leaving out of fear. 'But we can't risk it any more.'

'Why didn't you tell us?' Julien asked.

'We didn't want to scare you,' I said softly.

'So letters have been delivered here, to the cave?' Caden asked.

'Outside the cave,' I said. 'Just a couple.'

'What do they say?' Maggie asked.

'That we're not welcome around here, the usual stuff,' I said dismissively.

'Can we see them?' Julien asked, looking cynical.

'I burnt them,' Idris said, snapping out of his surprise. I nodded at him. He understood why we needed to do this.

'Who do you think sent them?' Maggie asked in a small voice as Julien pulled her close.

'Any number of people,' I replied. 'You've seen the looks we get in town!'

'But most of the people I speak to seem so nice, so fascinated with this place,' Maggie said as Julien and Caden nodded.

'To your face they might be,' I said. I noticed Maggie peer outside, brow puckered. Was I laying it on too thick? 'But you're right – many people *are* fascinated by us and want to join us. In fact, maybe having this gate here will allay people's fears about security, meaning more followers will join us?'

Maggie, Caden and Julien exchanged looks.

'Maybe Selma's right?' Maggie said hesitantly.

'Of course she's right,' Idris said. 'Shall we help the men with the gate, Julien and Caden?'

Caden nodded but Julien hesitated. Then he sighed and followed them to the front of the cave, looking over his shoulder at me and frowning.

A couple of weeks later, I walked into the court, pulling my suit jacket down to hide my bump. If it weren't for the fact my time in the cave meant I'd lost weight, I could put it down to eating too much, but now my slim arms and legs stood out against the growing curve of my stomach. How could I be sure Mike wouldn't notice? Everyone else too? I didn't want the authorities to know – not yet anyway.

I glanced over at Mike, who was looking straight ahead. He'd lost even more weight too, was wearing a smart suit, filling it out in all the right ways. He actually looked better, healthier. Behind me, I felt Idris and Maggie's reassuring presences. Caden had stayed back at the cave, trying to practise on his guitar with the arm he wasn't used to. I'd asked Julien to come. He used to be a solicitor after all, but he'd said he'd rather not. He'd been acting off with me ever since I had the gate put in.

Idris gave me a smile. I smiled back. As I turned around, I noticed Mike was watching us both, face stiff with anger.

Then his gaze dropped to my stomach.

I quickly covered it with my bag and took my seat next to my solicitor, shooting her a reassuring smile. I'd talked to her on the phone about the gate a few days ago and she'd agreed it would go down well. She'd seemed optimistic about it all and, in return, made me feel positive too. Once I got this court date out of the way, I could really start planning my life with Becky, and with my new child.

But instead of smiling back at me, my solicitor frowned. 'I've been trying to get hold of you,' she whispered. 'I even came to the cave yesterday but you weren't there.'

'I was with Becky all day. What's wrong?'

'Did you have a chance to read the report?'

'What report?'

'The one from social services.'

'You sent it to me?'

'To your PO Box, I told you we'd get the chance to read it before the hearing, remember?' I thought back to our conversations. Maybe she had mentioned it but, with everything that had been going on, I'd clearly not taken it in.

'I haven't checked my PO Box for days,' I whispered back.

She closed her eyes, pinching the bridge of her nose.

'What did it say?' I asked, panic fluttering inside.

The judge walked in and everyone went quiet.

'What did it say?' I hissed again.

The judge looked at me sharply.

'You'll find out in a minute,' my solicitor said, looking ahead.

I took in a deep breath. This wasn't looking good. I peered behind me at Idris again and he gave me a reassuring smile. Then worry flickered across his face as he noticed my expression. I turned back, trying to calm myself. Maybe it wouldn't be so bad?

The judge said a few introductory words then the female social worker who'd visited the cave took to the stand. I tried to search her face for an indication of what she might say but I couldn't tell.

'We visited the home of Mike Rhys on the seventh of September and spent some time with Becky,' she said, looking down at her notes. 'Mr Rhys clearly provides a secure and loving environment for his daughter, and it was equally clear to me and my colleague that the two share an excellent father and daughter relationship. Mr Rhys has taken steps to change his hours, meaning he is able to pick his daughter up from school on the days she is with him. Becky herself seemed very well and is well cared for under her father's care.'

She took a sip of water and I did the same, trying to control my breathing. I pulled at my suit jacket, blowing my fringe out of my eyes. I always felt so hot now I was pregnant, despite it nearly being December. And now it was even worse, nerves swirling inside at what the report might say.

'Becky misses her mother,' the social worker continued, 'and clearly loves her. During our visit, she asked several times if we'd seen her mother.' I smiled. 'This feeling is replicated by Mrs Rhys,' the social worker continued. 'She clearly has great affection for her child and a desire to see her.'

My smile deepened. Maybe I had nothing to worry about?

'However, Mrs Rhys's actions – leaving the family home to live in a cave – suggest a lack of regard on Mrs Rhys's part when it comes to providing a secure environment for her child.' I put my hand to my stomach. The social worker's eyes flickered to me then down to her notes again. 'We also noted Mrs Rhys talked more about her writing than she did about her daughter, so we have to question her priorities.'

I leaned forward, clutching the railing in front. 'How can you—' My solicitor put her hand gently on my arm, shaking her head. I slumped back and took a deep breath. No wonder she'd looked so worried about the report.

The social worker looked straight ahead, avoiding my gaze. 'We visited Mrs Rhys's residence on the eighth of September. She was living in a large cave dwelling with seven other people at the time including a child. The cave itself is well equipped with a basic but working kitchen and adequate bathroom facilities. It was clean on our visit, and tidy. There was even a dedicated area for children at the back of the cave with books and toys. However, there were clear hazards.'

I tensed.

'While there, we noticed fallen rock and uneven flooring. There were several areas where a child could climb rocks and hurt themselves and, of course, the sea is just a few metres away. Not to mention the damp and lack of security at the front of the cave, allowing anyone to enter whenever the tide is low and the bay isn't cut off.'

'We have a gate now!' I shouted out. 'You told them that, right?' I asked my solicitor. She nodded.

'Regardless,' the social worker continued, 'combined with the recent cave collapse nearby, the security and safety of the dwelling is a real concern for us, especially as there are six other adults living in close proximity to her, some of who have backgrounds which would cause us concern when living in close proximity to a child.'

Mike gripped the bar in front of him, leaning forward and glaring at me. I shook my head, peering behind me at Idris and Maggie. Who could they possibly mean?

'One of these include a woman who spent time in prison for ABH against a minor,' the social worker continued.

I put my hand to my mouth. Did she mean Donna? She said something had happened in her past.

'If you mean Donna,' I shouted out, 'she doesn't even live in the cave any more.'

The judge gave me a sharp look. 'I must ask you to refrain from shouting out in court, Mrs Rhys, otherwise I will have no choice but to have you removed.'

I slumped against my seat, tears sliding down my cheeks. I felt a hand on my shoulder and turned to see Maggie smiling sadly at me.

'And then we have the issue with Mrs Rhys's inability to tell the truth,' the social worker said with a sigh.

Maggie's hand slipped from my shoulder.

'Not only did Mrs Rhys tell us that she was in a secure job when she'd handed her notice in the week before,' the social worker continued, 'she also lied about an incident involving Mr Rhys and her daughter when she was a newborn. She told us Mr Rhys threatened violence to Becky when she was crying.'

I felt my face turn white. I looked over at Mike who was staring ahead with a satisfied smirk on his face.

'However, Mr Rhys was away overnight when the incident she described happened. We believe, combined with other small lies, Mrs Rhys has been fabricating events to win custody of her child.

Therefore, in conclusion, our advice would be that Mr Rhys gets full custody and parental responsibility for Becky with regular visits between Mrs Rhys and her daughter in a pre-agreed venue *away* from the cave.'

'Oh God,' I said, putting my head in my hands. Suddenly, the horror of it dawned on me: I was losing my child! And what about the one growing inside me? Would they be taken away too? I didn't hear the rest of it because I'd sunk into a senseless despair. After a while, my solicitor helped me up and I stumbled over to Idris, falling into his arms as he stroked my hair, Maggie looking on with a frown on her face.

'I don't know why you're crying.' I looked up to see Mike glowering down at me. 'You brought this on yourself, Selma. You chose your writing – chose *him* – over your child,' he said, gesturing at Idris.

'It wasn't about the writing and Idris, for God's sake,' I said. 'I left because I could see no other way of staying sane, of keeping the darkness at bay. I was being stifled. I did it for Becky. You don't know how hard I've worked to build a sanctuary for her in the cave.'

Mike shook his head. 'You never had a chance getting custody of Becky as long as you stayed in that cave. Anyone with half a brain could see that. Anyone apart from the little cult you've got yourself entangled with . . . and yourself, the person who you lie to the most. It's amazing what you can convince yourself of, Selma. You're just like your mother, you know, selfish and deluded. No wonder she lives alone now, rotting away in that little flat in Margate. It'll be the same for you in years to come.'

Then he stormed off.

'I thought your mother was dead?' Idris said.

'She is to me.' I took his hand. 'Can we please just get out of here?'

Chapter Thirty-One

Selma

Kent, UK
25 November 1991

When we got back to the cave after the court hearing, I didn't want to speak to or see anyone. The others seemed to sense it, leaving me alone as I sat under grey skies, a blanket Idris had given me wrapped around my shoulders. In my lap were my notepads, the pages now stuck back in, all of them adding up to a novel just a chapter away from being finished.

It was over. The dream was really over.

I had nothing to offer Becky, nothing to offer the baby I was due to have in a few months. All I had was this – a few notepads of pointless scribbles, scribbles which had cost me my daughter.

I heard the crunch of wet sand behind me and looked up to see Idris approach with a mug of tea in his hands. 'I thought you'd need this,' he said.

'Thank you,' I replied, grateful.

'May I join you?'

I nodded, so he sat on a rock beside me and we both looked out to sea.

'Tell me about your mother,' he said. 'Why did you tell me she'd died?'

'Everything I said about her was true. Apart from the bit about her dying.'

'I see. So she's in Margate?'

I shrugged. 'I presume so. I never see her any more. The last time I saw her, she barely recognised me, she was so drunk.' Idris frowned. 'That's where I really went with Becky all those years ago when I walked out with her. We went to my mother's flat. I was contending with all these emotions after Becky was born.'

I wiped a tear away, taking a sip of tea and sighing. 'I was trying to rationalise my irrational feelings. I needed them to be someone else's fault. So I blamed my mother. By making me feel worthless as a child, she was making me feel worthless as a mother now I was one. Of course, it was down to more than that, I know that now. But still, I wanted to go show Becky to her, show her I *was* good enough to have a daughter . . . show myself too, I guess. It was pointless. She was so drunk, she could barely open her eyes to focus on her granddaughter.'

I looked at the ashy logs from the fire the night before. 'So I stole her watch,' I said with a bitter laugh. 'It was lying on the side. Sounds childish, doesn't it? But I needed something of hers.' My face clouded over. 'Mike's right, I *am* like my mother. I lie, I manipulate . . . and now I've lost my own daughter because of it.'

I started sobbing and Idris stroked my back, but I shoved him away. 'Don't comfort me! I don't deserve it. I've lied to you, so many times! Did you know *I'm* the one who snapped your paint-brushes in half? And all that other stuff too?'

His eyes widened in surprise. 'Why would you do that?'

'It was the only way I could convince you all! You all needed concrete proof of the threat posed by the outside world and I gave it to you. In the long run, it was a *good* thing.' I looked towards the iron bars of the new gate, their dark shadows spread across the cave. I placed my mug down, face tense. 'So there you have it. The truth, for once.'

Idris put his hand over mine again. I didn't push him away this time. 'You and I are so alike, Selma,' he said. 'Mike *was* right about one thing: the people we hurt the most with our lies are ourselves. Especially the lies we tell ourselves. Maybe it's time we stopped doing that. Maybe it's time we accepted the cave isn't the right place to bring up a child.'

'But what else can we do?'

'Find a flat in town? I have a bit of money, enough for a deposit and a couple of months' rent.'

I shuddered at the thought. But I knew he was right. I felt tears prick at my eyes. It was over. My dream was officially over.

Over the next few weeks, we discreetly looked around for local flats, but the ones we could afford simply weren't suitable for a newborn. In fact, the cave felt a safer, more secure option in some cases.

'There's no major hurry,' Idris said after viewing our fifth flat, set above a group of students who were playing music so loud it made the walls throb. 'We still have a few months. We'll definitely find one by the time the baby comes.'

'What about the hotel? Can't we just live up there?' I asked, looking towards it as we walked back to the cave.

'I told you, I have no rights to it, Selma. It'd be classed as squatting and social services really *would* frown upon us then. All I have is the cave.'

I sunk into a silent darkness over the next few days and weeks. The cave became hollow, nights on the beach in front of the fire drinking gin long gone. When Idris expressed concern I told him I was just 'in the current' and needed to focus on finishing my novel. And yes, there was some truth to that. I was writing with a voracity, drawing on my feelings, so very close to the end now. Idris seemed to be in his own world too, painting for many hours of the day. While we still found each other in the darkness at night to gently and quietly make love, there was a new distance between us. Julien, Caden and Maggie seemed to be infected with the mood too, a strange silence falling on our shared feasts as Christmas approached. To add to it all, my weekly meet-ups with Becky had become increasingly difficult, with Becky barely uttering a word, no matter how hard I tried.

Then some light appeared at the end of the tunnel.

'I have some news!' Julien said, jumping onto one of the chalk boulders a week before Christmas.

We all went silent, looking up at him.

'I was going to wait until it all goes through,' he said, 'but what the hell. Turns out my former business partner squirrelled money away without telling me. Not just the company we owned, but others he's been involved in since too. He's been ordered to pay it back, so I'll be coming into some money soon.'

Idris walked over and patted Julien on the back. 'That's awesome.'

'Does this mean you're leaving us?' I asked him.

He jumped down and strolled over, gripping me by the shoulders. 'On the contrary! I have a plan. This might sound controversial, but I think we should think about leaving this cave.'

We all exchanged looks.

'It's wonderful in the summer, but come on, let's admit it,' he said. 'It sucks in the winter. What if we were somewhere where it's warm all year around? Where gypsies dance into the night and the sound of crickets fills the air?'

'Okay, I'm intrigued,' I said, my heart hammering with hope.

Julien's eyes sparkled. 'I've read about this place in Granada where people live in caves. A whole community just like us. Well, I say like us – they haven't been enlightened by Idris and the current yet,' he said, grinning at Idris. 'I could afford to fly us all out there, get provisions, set up in the caves there. I've made inquiries, and some are free to move into right now.'

'You've really thought about this,' Idris said, exchanging an excited look with me.

'Can you imagine bringing your baby up in an endless summer?' Julien said. 'Away from accusing eyes and recriminations? Go forward anew, spread word of the current?'

I felt my heartbeat quicken. Maybe Julien was right? Maybe this *was* the way forward?

But then I thought of Becky. How would I get time with her if I moved to Spain? Maybe Mike would relent to allow a couple of holidays a year to Spain during her half-terms, even if he had to come too. It would mean more quality time with my daughter, wouldn't it?

I looked at Idris, heart thumping like it had once before when I'd walked towards this cave for the first time, on the precipice of change and hope.

'I think this might be the solution to all our problems.'

Idris nodded. 'I think it might,' he said.

On Christmas morning, I met up with Becky in good spirits. I'd booked a special brunch for us at a local restaurant using some of the money Idris had put aside for a deposit on a flat. We wouldn't need it now! He'd even bought me a beautiful structured cardigan which perfectly hid my bump. I promised myself I'd tell Becky I was pregnant at some point. I couldn't keep the fact she had a little brother or sister on the way a secret for much longer, but I didn't want to rock our already fragile relationship.

Becky walked into the hotel with Mike, looking her usual sulky self. She was wearing a red dress, but she looked uncomfortable in it, pulling at the collar. I stood to greet her, her Christmas present on the floor beside me. I hadn't been able to afford much but I'd found a beautiful pink castle in the local charity shop, so tall it was up to my waist! I knew Becky would love it.

'Merry Christmas, Selma,' Mike said when they got to me.

I smiled at him. Part of me still hated him for what he'd done. But what was the point of all the bitterness?

'You too, Mike.' I turned to Becky. 'Don't you look gorgeous! Merry Christmas, darling!'

I kissed Becky's cheek and hugged her, but Becky remained stiff in my arms.

'See you at twelve?' Mike said.

'Absolutely!'

When he left, Becky took the seat across from me.

'Isn't it so Christmassy?' I said, looking around at all the decorations and huge tree. I wondered how Christmas was celebrated in Spain. Would it be hot in the winter? We'd tried to make the cave feel festive but it was growing so damp in there, many of the decorations deteriorated, the tree we'd put outside swept away by a particularly high tide one evening.

We won't have to put up with that for long, I thought in excitement.

'And the tree, isn't it huge?' I said to Becky, desperate to infect her with my festive cheer.

But Becky just shrugged. I took a deep breath. I clearly had a lot of work to do to win her over. We ordered our food and I tried to make conversation, asking Becky about school, her friends, what other plans she had for Christmas. But Becky just answered in monosyllabic sentences.

'Do you want to open your present now?' I asked her when our plates were taken away. 'Your dad will be here soon.'

Becky looked towards the large box, face lighting up slightly. Presents always did the trick! I slid the box towards her and she instantly started pulling the wrapping off. I watched in excitement as the paper fell away to reveal the pink castle.

'Isn't it fab?' I said.

Becky frowned.

'Oh. Do you have one already?' I asked.

Becky sighed, looking up at me. 'Mum, I'm eight. I don't play with dollhouses any more.'

I felt a stab of pain. 'I'm sorry, darling. Let me see if I can take it back.'

'It's fine. I mean, it's not like we see each other much so I guess it's not your fault you didn't know.'

I reached across the table, grabbing her hand. 'Darling, we've seen each other every week! I know it's not ideal but—'

'It doesn't matter anyway,' Becky said, folding her arms and staring into the distance. 'I'm leaving Queensbay soon.'

My heart slammed against my chest. 'What?'

'We're moving to Busby-on-Sea to be near Nanny and Grandad. Dad's going to tell you when he picks me up, because he didn't want to ruin our brunch. But I said you'll be fine with it.' She paused, looking me in the eye. 'Aren't you? I mean, you're so busy with the writing and the cave and stuff anyway.'

'I'm never too busy for you! Your dad can't just move you away without checking with me!' I tried to wrap my head around it. 'When did he make this decision?'

Becky shrugged. I slumped against the chair, heart racing. How could Mike do this to me?

When Mike walked into the restaurant a few moments later, I jumped up, striding towards him.

'What's this about you and Becky moving?' I asked him. 'Aren't you supposed to check with me first?'

'She told you?'

'Yes.'

He sighed. 'That's what I was going to do now – check with you.'

'Then I say no.'

He looked me in the eye. 'It's within a reasonable distance, she'll have her grandparents there to help. There's a great school there. Can't you see what a good move this would be for her?'

'But I have weekly visitation rights!'

'Really?' He crossed his arms. 'How many of those have you missed?'

'I was ill!' And I really was, puking my guts up because of the pregnancy. But how could I tell him that? 'And Becky made her excuses too.'

He looked up at the ceiling. 'Aren't you exhausted with this all, Selma? Can't you just want what's best for our daughter?'

I followed his gaze towards Becky, who was sitting at the table alone, eyes on a new handheld game she'd clearly got from Mike for Christmas.

'Becky and I had a long chat the other week when I ran the plans past her,' Mike said, 'and she *likes* the idea. She wants to make a fresh start. Truth is, she's being bullied at school.'

I frowned. 'Why didn't you tell me?'

'I only found out myself recently.'

'Because of me?'

'Why else?'

I closed my eyes. I used to get bullied myself because of my mum and all the men she used to date. 'Your mum's a whore,' kids would say. 'So that makes *you* a whore.'

'I don't think you know what a toll this has all taken on her, Selma,' Mike continued. 'I think it will be good to get her away from the constant reminder that her mum lives in a cave . . . and not with her.' He put his hand on my shoulder. 'There's a train that runs direct from Queensbay to Busby-on-Sea, just an hour's journey. I'll even pay the fare for your visits and we'll come back once a month so you can spend a whole day with her.'

'But I'm supposed to see her every week,' I said quietly. As I said that, I felt the baby kick. It had started kicking a week ago. It was going to get harder and harder to hide it from Becky and Mike, especially Mike who I was *convinced* would report me to social services if he found out I was pregnant.

'Anyway, we won't be moving until spring. Maybe early summer,' Mike said. 'That's if we *do* move. I won't go if you insist. But I think we need to put Becky first, don't you?'

I felt my shoulders slumping in defeat. Maybe he was right. Maybe this was the best thing to do after all.

'Okay,' I whispered.

As Christmas and the New Year rolled by, I threw myself into revising my novel from the pages Maggie had typed up. I needed to take my mind off Becky moving. I hadn't even told Idris; thinking about it was too painful, let alone talking about it. I also focused on Julien's plans to go to Spain; we were planning to fly out there in the spring, once Julien received his pay-out.

In the meantime, I tried to see Becky when I could, but my belly was growing too big and once I made my first excuse for not meeting up, it was easy to continue, especially when Becky was so silent and moody when we did spend time together. Instead, I went into town every few days to call her under the cover of darkness. But Becky was making her own excuses too: too tired to talk to me, seeing friends, busy with homework. Even Mike seemed saddened by the deteriorating relationship between his wife and daughter. And it sickened me, a good night's sleep now a distant memory as I lay awake, wracked with guilt. I tried to tell myself I had another child to think about now, one I could make a fresh start with, but it was no use. I still yearned for Becky.

I started latching onto the idea of Spain as our only hope to repair our relationship. Maybe Becky could spend the entire summer holidays with me out there?

But when early spring arrived, Julien still hadn't received his pay-out.

'Any news, Julien?' I asked him one particularly freezing day.

Julien avoided my gaze, focusing on the stool he was working on. 'Nothing yet.'

'When do you think the money's coming? It's just that they'll not let me fly soon.' I smiled, gesturing to my huge belly.

Julien sighed. 'Look, it's probably best you don't hang too much on this Spain thing, Selma.'

I paused. 'But it's all we've been talking about. All *you've* been talking about.'

He closed his eyes, taking in a deep breath. Then he opened them again. 'I probably jumped the gun a bit. My solicitor told me it was a sure thing after the last court date and I took that as a yes. But they can't track down the money. There's a chance he spent it all.'

I scrunched my fists together in frustration. 'But we were relying on this!'

Julien raked his hands through his black hair. 'Yeah, I know. But hey, what's stopping you and Idris going to Spain?'

'Money!' I shouted. Maggie, Caden and Idris looked up, shocked. But I was getting desperate. I'd relied on this plan of running away to Spain. Now I had just two months before I was due and yet I was no closer to securing either a safe family home for my baby or the chance of quality time with Becky.

Idris strode over. 'What's going on?'

'We're going to have our baby taken off us, that's what's going on,' I said, biting my nails as I paced back and forth.

'What do you mean?' Idris said.

'Ask him,' I said, flinging my arm towards Julien. 'I can't think about this any more.' Then I stomped into the cave, welcoming its darkness.

It was all ruined. Everything was ruined.

I looked down at my growing baby. What did this mean for my child?

Chapter Thirty-Two

Becky

Kungar Ice Caves, Russia
4 July 2018

Becky and Kai stand outside the cave. They are back again after going to the hospital that morning, where it had been confirmed Kai's ankle was just bruised. In daylight, tourists mill about, the large iron gates open to the vast ice caves. But Becky is standing quietly amongst all the hustle and bustle, thinking about the fact she is finally about to meet the child her mum had given birth to all those years before.

'You okay?' Kai asks.

'I'm fine,' Becky says. She shakes her head. 'No, that's a lie actually. I'm bloody nervous. I haven't been this nervous since my veterinary final exams. No, it's worse than that,' she adds, laughing nervously. 'Or should I say, *better* than that.'

'Totally better!' Kai says with a bright smile on this face. 'This is huge, possibly the most important meeting of your life.'

'That is *not* making me any less nervous, Kai!'

As she says that, Lev approaches with a woman. She has long white hair like Idris's, and is tall and slender. There's a child with her, aged about three or four. They're both wearing summer dresses, sandals, and flowers in their hair.

Becky feels breathless for a moment. Is that her sister . . . and does this mean she has a niece too? They're both so beautiful.

'Well, she looks like Idris from the photos I've seen of him,' Kai whispers.

'She does, doesn't she?' Becky replies, realising her voice is shaking.

'This is Solar,' Lev says when they get to them, his hand on his wife's back. 'And this is Liliya.' He gently pushes the little girl forward, who curtsies at Becky and Kai.

Becky smiles. 'Aren't you beautiful, Liliya?' She peers up at Solar . . . her *sister*. Was she really there, right in front of her? 'Hello, Solar,' she says.

'Hello, Becky.' She has brown eyes, elfin features.

'I've been looking for you everywhere,' Becky says with a nervous laugh.

Solar smiles. 'So I've heard.'

'Can – can we sit?'

'Of course.'

'We'll leave you to it,' Kai says, shooting Becky a smile as he walks off with Lev and Liliya.

The two women stroll to a nearby bench.

'I'm not quite sure where to start,' Becky says, looking into Solar's eyes. She seems nervous, quiet. Maybe Idris was like that, insular, contemplative? Becky never got the chance to properly meet him.

'Then let me start,' Solar says. 'I'm afraid to say I'm not your sister.'

Disappointment crushes Becky. 'But . . . your name. And you lived in the caves with Idris, right? In Spain, Slovenia, visited *this* place with him?' Becky says, looking around her.

'Yes, Idris is my father. But we do not share the same mother.'

Becky thinks of the other name etched onto the wall of the cave.

'Is your mother Oceane?' she asks Solar.

Solar nods. 'Yes.'

'But I thought she was with Caden?'

Solar nods again. 'It happened before Idris met your mother. She ran away when she found out she was pregnant, worried what effect it would have on your mother and Idris. *And* about what my grandmother would say.'

Becky puts her hands over her face, trying to wrap her head around what she's saying. 'I've been on a wild goose chase!'

Solar puts her hand on Becky's shoulder. 'I'm so sorry, Becky. This is why I wanted to tell you myself, to your face, after Lev told me everything you told him this morning.'

'So what about the child my mum gave birth to? Did she even *have* a child?'

'She did. But I'm afraid I don't know much more than that. My mother's on holiday, but I spoke to my grandmother and she confirmed your mother *did* have a baby. She wants to talk to you when you return to the UK. Here's her number – her name's Donna. She said to call any time.' She hands over a piece of paper.

Becky is quiet for a few moments as she looks at it, taking it all in. Then she stands up. 'I appreciate you coming out to meet with me.'

Solar smiles sadly. 'It's a pleasure. If you need to talk, I'm here. As Children of the Current we must stick together.'

Becky looks at the girl she thought was her sister and shakes her head. 'I was never a Child of the Current.' Then she walks away, one question raging in her mind: what happened to the baby her mum gave birth to?

Chapter Thirty-Three

Selma

Kent, UK
13 April 1992

We were all sitting at the table inside, sheltered from the heavy rain. The flames of the fire we'd lit leapt up the walls of the cave, making dark tattoos on everyone's skin. I put my hand to my huge stomach, felt my baby stir inside. I looked over at Idris. He was quiet too, peering at the shadows cast by the large gate. Maggie and Julien were inside, talking in low voices. I had a feeling they might leave soon so it would just be me and Idris.

Would that be so bad?

He noticed me watching him. 'How's the last chapter coming along?'

'I finished it.' I felt numb as I said it. Why did I feel so numb?

His eyes widened. 'Why didn't you tell me?'

'I was going to.'

'We have to celebrate!' He jumped up to tell the others but I grabbed his hand.

'Just us two,' I said. 'Can we do something normal?'

He frowned. 'Normal?'

'Like go out for dinner.'

'Is that what you really want?'

'Yes,' I said, squeezing his hand. 'Don't you think it would be nice to get away for a few hours, just the two of us?'

He nodded. 'Okay. If that's what you want.'

'Thank you,' I said, smiling. I'd found myself *yearning* for normality lately. I'd even started craving the microwave ready meals I used to share with Mike, both silent as we ate and watched something on TV. Not the cave and its gloomy damp walls.

Idris and I found a new restaurant along the beach, in the opposite direction to the town, where no one would recognise us. It sat right on the seafront and served a plethora of seafood. For those three hours, it really felt to me like we were just a normal couple who lived in a normal house with normal jobs. Of course, I noticed the looks we received: Idris with his beautiful long hair and green eyes, me a contrast with my long dark hair and huge belly. But that was fine. Nobody there knew we were from the cave, as far as I knew. We were anonymous . . . and alone. Just the two of us.

But then a familiar face appeared.

'Donna?' I said.

Donna paused as she saw us. She was with a man, his arms covered in tattoos. She said something to him and walked over, staring in surprise at my tummy. I thought of what I'd learned about her in court, ABH against a minor.

'Wow, look at you!' she said. 'I had no idea.'

Idris and I exchanged tense looks.

'Don't worry,' Donna said. 'I won't say anything.' She frowned. 'Are you still in the cave?'

I nodded, wrapping my cardigan around my tummy. Could I really trust Donna not to say anything?

'I presume you've seen a doctor,' Donna said, 'got your birth plan sorted?' She laughed. 'God, listen to me, reverting to my midwifery days.'

I suddenly felt the urge to beg Donna to come back, despite what she'd done. Maggie had been reading up on delivering babies so she could help when the time came, but how could that beat a proper, qualified midwife like Donna?

'She has it all sorted,' Idris said, putting his hand over my stomach. Donna looked at him, frowning. 'How's Tom?' he asked.

Donna sighs. 'Good. But he'll have a permanent limp.'

'I'm so sorry,' Idris murmured.

'And Oceane?' I asked. Idris tensed. I thought about the two of them sometimes, two beautiful people making love. But it had all happened before Idris and I got together, he'd assured me of that.

'I have no idea how Oceane is,' Donna said, face tense. 'She ran away not long after the accident in the cave.'

'Is she okay?' Idris asked, frowning.

'She's fine, sends me postcards. She's travelling with a friend. I have to accept she's eighteen now, I can't watch her every move. You look after yourself, okay?' She took one last look at my stomach, worry flickering on her face, then she walked back to her date.

I returned to the cave in low spirits. The way Donna had looked

381

at me, with such concern, had filled me with worry. She clearly thought my child wasn't in safe hands.

My mood seemed to be reflected back at the cave as Caden lay in his bed, staring up at the ceiling with a gloomy look on his face, a bottle of wine half-finished beside him. Nearby, Maggie and Julien sat quietly at the table, staring sombrely into their teas.

'Cheer up everyone,' Idris said as we walked inside.

'What's there to cheer up about?' Caden slurred. 'I can't play my guitar and this place isn't like it used to be.'

'Then write some songs until your arm heals.'

'Writer's block,' Caden said with a sigh.

'Writer's block, in this place? Selma's finished her novel, you know! What's stopping you writing a song, Caden?'

I looked at him sharply. I hadn't wanted to tell everyone yet.

'Her first one took her five years,' he continued, pouring himself some wine. 'And yet she wrote this one in a matter of months. It's proof that this place,' he said, looking around him in awe, 'can make all of us achieve our dreams.'

He'd been like this the past couple of months. The deeper I sank into darkness, the more he tried to battle his way out of his own darkness with a peppiness that was beginning to annoy me. Any time I mentioned resuming our search for a flat in town, he'd bang on about Spain. When I said we had no money, he said we'd *find* a way to make money.

It was driving me mad, especially as I got heavier and more uncomfortable. I found myself stuck in this numb, still place where every time I tried to think about what would happen when the baby came – hell, what would happen *as* the baby came – I just buried my head deeper into my novel.

But now the novel was finished and I felt *nothing*.

'Dreams? What dreams?' I said, all my frustration suddenly pouring out. 'I'm heavily pregnant with a child who could be taken away from us the moment it's born, and another child who doesn't want to see me!' I pulled the draft of my novel out from my bag, waving it in the air. 'Who knows if the novel's any good either? It'll probably get rejected by my agent, more heartache, more hopelessness. And then what do I have?'

Everyone looked at me in shock. They'd been so used to me being the one to pump them up with enthusiasm. But all the fight was out of me now, the dual disappointments of Becky moving away and Julien's Spanish dreams bursting too much.

'What do you mean, what do you have?' Idris asked. 'You have me, our child.'

I looked at Idris. Love – yes, we had love. But how much of it was real? I'd fallen in love with a version of Idris I now knew wasn't true. No enigmatic rock star with millions. Just a street artist without two pennies to rub together. And *he'd* fallen in love with a lie too. All my lies about my book sales, the way I presented myself when inside I was an insecure mess. Our relationship was built on fabrication after fabrication.

And that *look* in Donna's eyes, the pity . . . the *worry* for my unborn child.

I scraped my chair up and got up, walking out of the cave. I approached the crackling fire outside and stared into it, trying to find some answers. But none came.

'Selma, come on,' Idris said, following me. 'You told me yourself not to give up on the dream, to stop with the self-pity. You're been so down the past couple of months.'

'This isn't about self-pity,' I said. 'We had a chance then. But now it's all just turned to ashes.'

I flicked through the pages of my notepad and stared at it. For so long, I'd dreamed of completing my second novel. And now here it was, heavy in my hands, but I felt nothing. It reminded me of when Becky was born. The excitement and anticipation in the run-up compared to how it felt when I held her in my arms. Numbness. Confusion. Darkness.

'Selma,' Idris said, voice filled with concern. 'What's wrong?'

I turned to look at him over my shoulder, at his beautiful green eyes filled with concern.

He knew, just as Mike had known, when the darkness descended upon me.

'Everything,' I whispered.

Then I threw my novel into the flames, watching as the words I'd slaved over curled in the fire and turned to ash.

'No!' Idris shouted out, shoving me out of the way so he could retrieve the pages from the fire, flinching in pain as the flames bit at his fingertips.

'It's no use,' I shouted. 'It's all over.'

As I said that, I felt my tummy tighten in pain, wetness between my legs. I looked down as waves of pain spread up my back.

'Idris,' I said. He continued scrabbling for my novel. 'Idris!'

He turned to me, scraps of burnt paper in his hands.

'The baby's coming,' I whispered.

Chapter Thirty-Four

Selma

Kent, UK
13 April 1992

Maggie ran outside as I screamed out.

'Is it happening?' she asked, a panicked look on her face.

'Yes, help me get her in,' Idris replied.

They both helped me inside the cave then Maggie ran to her bed, grappling for the midwifery book she'd been reading, knocking a glass to the ground in the process. She put her glasses on then ran to where I was lying.

'Have the contractions started?' she asked, face white with worry.

'Of course they bloody have,' I hissed.

'Right,' Maggie said, flicking through the book with trembling fingers. 'You've caught me on the hop being two weeks early and all. But that's fine, we can do this!'

'It could be hours, couldn't it?' Idris asked.

'Yep,' Maggie said as Julien and Caden hovered in the

background. 'Sometimes. I mean, I had a quick labour with my first. That's unusual though, I think. I *hope*,' she added under her breath.

Idris frowned as he rubbed my belly.

'What do we do?' he asked.

'Keep her comfortable. Julien, can you boil a kettle and get some towels? Blimey, I sound like I'm in *Gone with the Wind* or something.' She laughed hysterically then her laughter trailed off, replaced by another look of fear.

Idris stood up, pacing up and down, raking his fingers through his long hair. 'I need some air,' he said, stopping abruptly. 'I'll – I'll just be outside.' He gave me a quick kiss then jogged outside.

'Where's he going?' I asked, struggling to sit up.

Maggie gave me a reassuring smile. 'Men can be like that.'

'He's scared,' I said.

'Only natural,' Julien shouted over.

'Not of the birth,' I said. 'But of what will happen after, when people find out.' I swallowed. 'When social services find out.'

Maggie squeezed my hand. 'It'll be fine, they won't.'

Over the next twenty minutes, Maggie fussed over me as my contractions started in full earnest.

'Where the fuck is Idris?' I hissed as I pushed Maggie's hand away from my forehead, trying to find his silhouette in the darkness outside. I leaned back as another contraction ripped through me. 'I need some pain relief, *now*!'

'We don't have anything,' Maggie said, voice panicked. 'I – I don't know what to do.'

'This is hopeless,' I cried. 'All so bloody hopeless. What have I done? What have I done?' I let out a low guttural scream as more contractions took over. Maggie helped me get on all fours, and I hung my head down as I breathed in and out.

'Focus on something else other than the pain. One of Idris's paintings!' she said, lifting my skirt.

I looked at the painting Idris had done of our child.

Then I noticed the eyes had been scratched out. Who would *do* that?

His stepmother.

The thought disappeared as quickly as it came as another contraction hit me.

'Please,' I panted. 'Please help me. God help me.' Tears slid down my cheeks and suddenly I thought of Becky's birth when I'd had Mike's hand on my back, words of support whispered in my ear in the warmth of a hospital room. I'd told him to shut up but now I yearned for him, for Becky, for the stable, secure life I once had. It was as though I were on a flimsy ship with a torn sail and rotting wood, violently bobbing on a sea raging with storms.

As my contractions blended into one and I felt my baby start to slide down, the primal truth of the moment took over. I saw the situation with complete clarity; the mistakes I'd made, the lies I'd told myself and others. Lies I thought I'd put a stop to and yet one, the biggest one of all, remained: I couldn't give birth to a child in this cave, despite telling myself I could. And I couldn't bring another child into this world, just as my mother had warned me.

'You're useless, Selma,' she'd once hissed at me. 'God help any child you have.'

I let out a scream as my body took over, pain so intense at the core of me, it took the strength from my knees, making me collapse against Maggie.

Maggie started sobbing. 'I have no idea what to do, Julien.'

As Caden sat on his bed, blinking, Julien paced up and down, reading the book on midwifery. Then he paused, staring at the entrance to the cave.

'Donna!'

In my pain and confusion, I followed his gaze to see Donna rushing over, Idris behind her.

'I'm here now,' Donna said as she clutched onto my hand. 'I'm here.'

The next few hours passed in a blur, with Julien and Maggie pacing up and down as Caden continued watching from his bed, biting his nails. Idris kept right beside me, whispering in my ear, giving me sips of water.

Then Donna's voice. 'The baby's coming.'

Stretching. Tearing. A sharp slice of pain. And then relief, a loud cry and I collapsed against Idris.

I looked down as my baby girl nuzzled at my nipple, her blue eyes so like Becky's, her dark hair like mine, soft and fluffy. She had Idris's nose though, and his beautiful cheekbones. I could see that already.

Donna went to take the baby from me but I resisted, panic flooding through me.

'Just want to check her over,' she said in a soothing voice. 'And let her daddy have a cuddle too,' she added, smiling at Idris.

But I continued clutching my child to my chest. 'Not until you tell me what you did.'

She frowned. 'What do you mean?'

'You went to prison for hurting a minor.'

Julien and Caden looked over in shock. We hadn't told them what had been revealed in court, if it was indeed Donna.

She took a deep shuddery breath. 'It was an accident.'

'Tell me!' I shouted.

'Selma . . .' Idris said in a low voice.

'We're trusting this woman with our newborn, Idris. So I need to know what happened.'

'It's fine,' Donna said. 'Oceane was ten. She was getting bullied. I went into school to talk to her teacher about it. When I came out, she was being held up against the wall by her neck by a girl several years older than her.' Her jaw clenched. 'I ran up, grabbed the girl, twisted her arm behind her back. Her arm broke. I – I used too much force.'

'You were protecting your child,' Idris said.

Donna nodded. 'And now so are you,' she said softly to me. 'I get it. We'd do anything for our children, wouldn't we? We'd do anything to protect them from those who hurt them. But I won't hurt your baby, Selma, trust me.'

I looked into her eyes then I relaxed. 'I'm sorry,' I whispered, sinking back against the mattress. 'I'm just so tired.'

'Of course you are,' Donna said, putting her hands out again.

I hesitated a moment then handed my daughter over, my eyes never leaving Donna as she carried the baby towards a light to check her over.

'She's perfect,' Donna said after, smiling. 'I don't have any scales but feels like a seven-pounder to me, nice and healthy. You ready, Daddy?' Donna asked, holding the baby out to Idris.

Idris looked nervous at first, but when he reached out and his daughter was placed in his arms, I could see by the expression on his face he regarded her as a true miracle.

'She is perfect,' he said.

'Do you have a name?' Maggie asked as she walked over.

Idris looked back at me. 'I'd like us to call her Catherine, after my mother.'

I nodded. 'Catherine. That's perfect.'

The next few days blurred into a long stream of night-time feeds and exhausted daytimes. Donna was living back at the cave now with Tom, keeping a close eye on me and Catherine. She kept telling me I needed to nap when the baby did, but I found it impossible, barely getting any sleep each day, my exhaustion making me irritable with everyone.

It didn't help that each time the gates clanged open, my head would dart up, fear social services were paying an unexpected visit almost paralysing me. We'd kept the secret so far, but how long would that last?

Catherine seemed to notice my nervousness, growing more and more grouchy as the days went by. People offered to look after her for a couple of hours to let me get some rest. Even Julien hovered nearby, making me nervous, especially that dog of his being too close. I wanted to shout at them all: 'She's mine, for God's sake, leave her alone.' I was even tense when Idris held Catherine – what if he dropped her? He wasn't used to babies, I could see it in the awkward way he held her, and my hands itched to have my daughter back.

When Donna and I were alone one day, she pulled up a chair. 'How you doing?' she asked me, exploring my face.

'Wonderful,' I replied, trying to rock Catherine to sleep as she squirmed against me.

'How much sleep are you getting?'

I laughed. 'Sleep? What's that?'

'Are you napping when Catherine is, like I suggested?'

'Yeah, sure,' I lied.

Donna paused a moment. 'You mentioned being worried about social services turning up. Is that still something that plays on your mind? Idris said you've been checking the gate quite a lot, even suggesting installing cameras to keep a watch on the beach outside?'

'It's only natural, isn't it?' I said, staring into my daughter's scrunched-up red face. 'To want to protect my daughter?'

'Of course but . . . I just want to make sure it's not more than that.'

'What do you mean?'

Donna reached into her pocket and placed an A3 leaflet on the table. *Post-natal depression*, it read. *You are not alone.*

'I don't have PND, for God's sake!' I shoved the leaflet away, but not before I saw the checklist of symptoms listed on the front page: *Feeling sad and weepy. Feeling no enjoyment in life. Feeling you can't cope.* Of course there'd been times I felt that way; didn't any new mother? But not to the extent Donna seemed to think.

I peered at Idris who was standing on the beach. What had he been saying about me to Donna?

'I'll leave it here, okay?' Donna said softly. 'Just so you can give it a read. And I'm always here if you need me. You know that, don't you?'

'Sure,' I said, shrugging. Truth was, I was starting to get annoyed with Donna's constant presence and the worried way she watched me. I also didn't like the way she watched Idris. It wasn't like before, that look of adoration. There was something else mixed in with it.

When Donna left, I strode outside to Idris. 'What have you been saying to Donna?'

'What do you mean?'

'She thinks I have post-natal depression. You do realise she'll get onto social services if she continues to think that.'

'Selma,' Idris said, a hint of irritation in his voice, 'you need to stop going on about social services.'

'Are you kidding me? They are *the* biggest threat to us right now. They could take Catherine away just like that,' I said, clicking my fingers. 'Or what if *Donna* wants to take her away? I still find it weird how she came back despite what happened to Tom . . . and what went on between you and her daughter.'

Idris's face tensed. 'That's a ridiculous thing to say, Selma. Why would Donna want to take our child away?'

'Revenge?'

He sighed, raking his fingers through his hair. 'Why are you acting like this?'

'Acting like what?'

He sighed. 'Paranoid. Uptight. It worries me.'

'You're worried I'm not doing a good job?'

He pulled me close and stroked my hair as he looked down at our baby. 'Of course not! You're doing an amazing job.'

On the other side of the cave, Donna watched us. I turned away, pulling my daughter even closer to my chest.

* * *

392

Later that night, when everyone was sleeping, I crept to a small hole at the back of the cave with Catherine sleeping in my arms. Oceane once kept some books in there but it was empty now she was gone. I placed a soft blanket inside then laid Catherine in there.

'Perfect fit,' I whispered.

I looked over my shoulder to check nobody was watching, then hung another blanket from the branches of a plant above. It completely covered the hole . . . and my daughter. If social services came to take her away, if *anyone* came, this would be where I'd put Catherine. I hadn't quite figured out what to do to stop her crying if it came to that – maybe there was a harmless sedative I could find? But at least it was a plan. I wouldn't let anyone take my daughter from me!

I picked her up and took her back to bed with me. As I lay staring at the ceiling, I noticed two eyes blinking at me from the darkness.

It was Donna, always watching.

Chapter Thirty-Five

Becky

Kent, UK
6 July 2018

Becky stands outside the cave waiting to meet Solar's grandmother, Donna. It's strange being back in the UK, back in the town where she grew up. Everything seemed otherworldly in Russia with its vast icy caves and strange language. But here it's achingly familiar. She peers inside towards where her mum had died . . . and possibly where her sister was born all those years before.

What *happened* to that baby?

She looks at her watch. It's past ten now, the time she's due to meet Donna. Becky had called her from Russia and the conversation had been brief, Donna insisting they meet so they could talk face-to-face.

So here she is.

Becky pulls her cardigan off. The clouds are grey above, but the air is cloyingly warm, filled with electricity.

Will there be a storm soon?

As she thinks that, a woman approaches. She's short, walks briskly, her greying hair lifting in the sea breeze. She's wearing a navy blue raincoat and wellies, a coffee in each hand.

'I brought provisions,' she says when she gets to Becky. 'I presume you're Becky?'

Becky nods. 'Thanks for meeting me, Donna.'

'You look like your mum,' Donna says briskly. She hands Becky a cup before reaching into her bag and pulling out two chocolate muffins. 'Fresh out of the oven this morning.'

'Thank you,' Becky says with a smile, taking her muffin. 'They look delicious.'

'Shall we go into the cave?' Donna asks. 'Might be a bit more private in there.'

Becky hesitates. She's not sure how she feels about return-ing to the place her mum died. Then she feels raindrops on her head.

'Well, that decides it,' Donna says in her matter-of-fact voice. 'Come on.'

They walk into the cave, the same cave Becky walked into with her mum over a month ago. She feels like a different person now, but she's not sure *who* that person is. She's still trying to figure it out.

'Shall we sit here?' Donna asks, gesturing to two chalk boulders that sit side by side, one painted red, another blue. 'This is where your mum and I sometimes used to sit, looking out to sea and drinking tea.' She smiles as they sit down. 'Or often it was gin in your mum's case. She loved her gin.'

'Yes, she did, didn't she?'

'So,' Donna says, taking a sip of her coffee and peering sideways at Becky, a nervous look on her face. 'You're looking for your sister?'

Becky nods. 'I thought it was Solar, your Solar.'

Donna sighs. 'I didn't know myself I had a granddaughter until a few years ago. Oceane didn't want me knowing she was pregnant, not with Idris's child. She didn't even tell Idris at first. In her sweet little way, she wanted the best for your mum and Idris.' Donna shakes her head. 'Always so naive, like I once was. Anyway, she stayed with a friend in France, gave birth just before your mum did. She was planning to put Solar up for adoption but then Idris turned up after finding out and she agreed he could take their baby. Years later, she regretted her decision and tracked them down in Russia. They lived there together for many years. Then Idris did his disappearing act again.'

'Where's Idris now?' Becky asks.

'Nobody knows. He just left one day when Solar was twelve. But you're not here to hear all that, are you? You're here to find your lost sister.'

Becky leans forward, eager for information. 'I am.'

'What have you found out so far?' Donna asks, examining Becky's face.

'Nothing. Just that Mum had a baby and you might know what happened.'

Donna nods then reaches into her bag. 'Part of me didn't want to have to do this, but I think I have no choice.'

She pulls out a book, handing it to Becky with a deep shaky breath. 'I think it's time your mum took over from here.'

Becky looks at the book. It's *The Cave* by Thomas Delaney, the book she'd spotted at the little bookshop she'd seen across from her mum's hospital room.

She frowns, looking up at Donna. 'This isn't one of my mum's books.'

'No, but it's her story. She told it to my son Tom a few months before she died.' She smiles with pride. 'He's an author now. He was so inspired by your mum's success, he decided to have a go himself.' Becky thinks of the photo she saw of the man holding the cane at the bookshop.

She turns the novel around, reading the blurb.

In THE CAVE, a gripping novel from author Thomas Delaney, we delve into the world of cults and caves as we follow one woman's journey into a life that spirals quickly out of control.

'I'm still confused,' Becky says. 'It's a novel, a work of fiction.'

'To anyone else, it is,' Donna says. 'But to those in the know, all you'll find in there are facts. Read that and you'll get your mum's full uncensored story, from the day she first laid eyes on Idris to the weeks after she gave birth.' Donna smiles sadly. 'No more lies.'

'How do you know there aren't any more lies?' Becky asks, gripping the book so hard her knuckles turn white.

'I could see it in your mum's eyes when I saw her a few months ago. She gave me an advance copy to read. And when I did, there was one truth I thought she'd never tell in there, confirming every line was fact. The only fabrications are the main characters' names, see?' she adds, pointing to the name on the first page. 'Tom renamed your mum as Selma, instead of her real name, Samantha. Plus she charged the name of this town to Queensbay. That was one of the four things she insisted on.'

'What else did she insist on?' Becky asks.

'That Tom make no reference in his bio or press interviews to his time with Idris and the Children of the Current. She needed to be sure no connection was made to her. She also asked that she write the dedication at the front of the book.'

Becky flicks back through the pages to see the dedication.

To B. No more lies.

'That's you, Becky,' Donna says softly. 'Samantha knew she was dying when I saw her, that it might not be long. She feared you might never get to learn the truth if you refused to see her. This was her way of delivering that truth to you.'

Becky feels tears flood her eyes.

'Shall I leave you to it then?' Donna asks, standing up.

Becky nods, unable to get her words out.

'I'll be in the café if you need me.'

'You don't need to stay,' Becky says.

'You might need me to,' Donna says, looking at the book sadly. As she walks away, Becky opens the novel and begins to read.

Chapter One

It all started when the boy nearly drowned.

Queensbay was experiencing one of those summer evenings where strangers smile at each other as they pass on the street, everyone in awe that the temperature could be that warm in grey old Britain . . .

Chapter Thirty-Six

Selma

Kent, UK
15 May 1992

I checked my face in my little compact mirror, smoothing more concealer under my eyes. I looked ragged, which was no surprise considering I'd given birth just a few weeks before. At least my stomach was more easily covered now, even if it hadn't returned to its previous form.

I peered behind me, looking towards where Catherine was sleeping in Idris's arms as he looked down at her in awe. I had to go see Becky as it was her last day in Queensbay. I *wanted* to see her, of course I did, but this was the first time I'd left Catherine alone. It made me feel sick, frantic even. But I couldn't let Becky down.

I took a deep breath and headed to the café. Becky was waiting at a table with Mike, reading a magazine as Mike talked on a mobile phone. So much for being made redundant. He must have got the promotion he'd always wanted with the move to Busby-on-Sea, a guaranteed work phone part of the package. Social services wouldn't blink an eye if I were still with him. In fact, we'd be ideal parents. But now I was the worst kind of parent according to the authorities, living in a cold, damp cave with no money and an unemployed partner.

I clenched my fists. *Stop the negative thoughts.* The darkness was hovering above, a stormy cloud waiting to burst. I was working hard at keeping it at bay, focusing on my love for my girls. And today was all about Becky. She was growing all the time, taller now and becoming less the little girl I remembered. Sun filtered in through a window, creating the effect of a halo over her head. She looked healthy, fit.

Would Catherine look like that in eight years' time? She wouldn't be afforded the luxuries Becky had: four walls and a secure roof over her head. Three square meals a day. Baby classes. Pre-school. Soft play and regular ice creams. It wasn't just the money. I couldn't have social services knowing about Catherine so we'd have to spend a lot of time hidden away until we got enough money to leave the UK for Spain, and that wasn't looking likely. To make matters worse, Catherine had a little cough, no doubt caused by living in that godforsaken cave.

A woman looked up sharply as I entered. Panic flickered inside. What if it was a social worker spying on me? What if Mike had set me up?

I went to back away but then the woman stood up and walked to the counter, putting an apron on.

She wasn't a social worker, she worked at the café.

Of *course* she wasn't a social worker.

I took a deep breath as I walked forward, making sure my coat was buttoned up over my stomach. Mike frowned when he saw me. Could he sense I'd had a child?

'Hello darling,' I said when I got to Becky.

Becky peered up, a bored expression on her face. 'Hi Mum.'

Mum. She used to call me Mummy.

Mike stood up. 'You look tired, Selma.'

'I've been ill, remember?' I replied, voice trembling slightly. 'That's why I haven't been able to meet up the past few weeks. I didn't want Becky to get it.'

'Are you sure you're okay?' Mike asked, a concerned expression on his face. 'Maybe we should rearrange? We'll be back in a couple of weeks.'

'Yeah, I don't mind,' Becky said, sticking out her chin defiantly.

'No, of course not,' I said. 'I want to see my girl.'

'I'll be sitting outside, making a call,' Mike said. 'I have some work to do so thought I'd do it looking out to sea. Got to make the most of these last hours in Queensbay.' He looked at me sadly then kissed Becky on the forehead before walking out of the café, strolling to a bench just a few metres away.

Why was he staying so close? Didn't he trust me? What if he was spying on me from that bench for social services?

'You're acting weird.' Becky's voice cut through my fears.

I turned to her, forcing a smile. 'Just tired, that's all.'

'You always say that when you're lying.'

I took her cold hands between mine. 'So tell me everything! How was your Easter? Are you excited about moving? I'll plan something fun for when I see you in two weeks, a whole day of it.'

Becky moved her hands out from under mine and dropped

her gaze. 'Easter was all right. We spent most of it with Cynthia and the twins.'

I frowned. 'You seem to be spending a lot of time with them.'

'She has a swimming pool,' Becky said, shrugging. 'Anyway, she's cool.'

I couldn't help but feel a flicker of jealousy. 'I can't stand the woman personally.'

Becky's face hardened. 'I like Cynthia. She's a really good mum.'

I blinked. 'Really? That surprises me.'

'Why?'

'She's always struck me as being a bit competitive, one of those stage mums, you know?' I tried to get the waitress's attention. I needed a coffee.

'At least she cares,' Becky spat.

I looked back at her in surprise. 'What's that supposed to mean?'

Becky crossed her arms and looked away. 'Nothing.'

The waitress came over. 'What can I get you?' she asked.

'We're not ready yet,' I snapped. The waitress gave me a look then walked away. I leaned towards Becky. 'What's *that* supposed to mean?' I repeated.

Becky sighed and turned back to me. 'You're just not much of a mum, you know?'

I flinched back, like Becky had slapped me.

'I mean, when's the last time I saw you?' Becky asked. 'Four months ago or something.'

'Two,' I said. 'I told you, I've been ill!'

'Yeah, you keep saying that. Whatever.'

'What's with this attitude all of a sudden? Where's my little girl gone?'

'Where's my *mum* gone?' Becky shouted.

The café went silent, people looking up from their plates. We both glared at each other. Then Becky pushed her chair away from the table and stood up. Tears started gathering in her eyes.

'You're rubbish! You bloody left us, Mum. Just left us for a hippy and a smelly cave! Mums don't *do* that!'

'I had to,' I said in a quiet voice. 'I – I felt trapped. Not by you, not even by your dad. But me! I was trapped by *me*, by these feelings I get. I *love* you.' I started to sob. 'More than you could ever know. Please believe me, Becky.'

I went to grab her hand but Becky took a step away. 'Dad says you don't really know what love is.' She angrily wiped her tears away. 'I agree with him. You don't think like other people. All the lies you tell . . . I know you've told some to me. Like you being ill, what rubbish. I know you'll just go and have another kid, that's what I heard Cynthia say to Dad. You'll have another kid with Idris and you'll forget about me and you know what? I don't really care, not for me anyway. But what about the poor kid?' She grabbed her backpack, looking down at me with hard eyes. 'That poor kid won't have a chance, at least I get to escape you.' Then she ran out of the café and into her dad's arms.

I stayed where I was, breath a thunder in my ears, my eight-year-old daughter's words echoing in my heart and my soul, over and over. Maybe she was right.

That poor kid won't have a chance.

I didn't return to the cave straight after the incident with Becky. Instead, I walked to a patch of beach where I used to take her when I was on maternity leave. It was in the opposite direction to the cave, ten minutes' walk from the house, in between Queensbay and Margate. It wasn't as busy as the other beaches in the town as the sand wasn't as white, nor as smooth. Instead, there were small rock pools and pebbles. I used to go as a child, my father skimming stones across the waves. It made me happy.

Or at least it used to.

I stepped onto the beach, feeling the familiar crunch of pebbles, imagining Becky wrapped up against my chest, the sight of her blonde hair in wisps as they lifted in the wind. I used to love holding Becky as a baby there, close to my chest in a cold coastal breeze. I used to imagine this beach as mine and Becky's private little world, even telling her we'd get a tent and set up there in the summer. Not that Becky understood, she was so young. But she'd still smile and look up at me with those happy blue eyes of hers.

Why hadn't I fought harder to keep Becky in my world? I'd wanted to escape the wider world, but it shouldn't have been just about me. It should have been wrapped up in Becky as well. If Becky couldn't come, then I shouldn't have gone. Sure, I'd gone to court to fight for her. But after, I'd given up so easily. What mother does that?

'Well this is a surprise.'

I froze. I'd recognise that voice anywhere.

It was my mother.

Chapter Thirty-Seven

Selma

Kent, UK
15 May 1992

My mother looked awful. Her once heart-shaped face was bloated, her complexion blotchy and red. She looked more like eighty than fifty-five. It was a shock to see her like that.

She stumbled towards me and I backed away, blinking. Was I hallucinating?

'I used to come here with you and your dad,' she slurred. 'Is that why you're here too? Do you remember?' She frowned. 'You were young though, just a babe.'

'You're drunk.'

'I'm always drunk.' She laughed, then started spluttering, covering her mouth with her spotted hand. 'Where's my grand-daughter then? You had one, didn't you? I've seen you both looking miserable in that café in Queensbay.'

'You've been to Queensbay?' I asked.

'Why shouldn't I have been? I'm a resident too, you know.'

'Resident? I don't understand.'

She smiled, revealing yellow gapped teeth. 'I own the hotel there.'

I froze.

'You know the one,' she continued. 'The Queensbay Hotel? Not that it's done me much good,' she grumbled.

That was when it dawned on me.

My mother was Idris's stepmother.

'Oh Jesus,' I said, putting my hand to my mouth. 'You married the owner, Mr Peterson.'

'Yes, and that little thief son of his ran off with *my* money.'

Thief.

So my mother was the one who'd scrawled that graffiti on the cave. *She* was the one Idris had been scared of all this time. My mother and her imaginary family.

'He isn't a thief,' I spat. 'You swindled his father out of that money, out of the whole hotel.'

'I didn't,' my mother said, folding her arms and glaring at me. 'He signed it over to me fair and square.'

'I know you,' I said, striding towards her and jabbing my finger at her. 'You would have manipulated him.'

She shrugged. 'Needs must. Don't tell me you wouldn't have done the same?'

I shook my head. 'I wouldn't.'

She laughed a bitter laugh that sent seagulls squawking away. 'I've been watching you, Selma. All set up in that cave, deceiving those fools, pretending you believe all the shit they spout. All in the hope you'd get that hotel off the man they call Idris.' She shook her head. 'I know that kid from when he was this high,' she said, her hand to her chest. 'Snivelling whining, useless little boy. You saw that weakness in him and homed in, just like I did with his father.'

'Rubbish. I don't want the hotel. I didn't even know he'd lived there when I met him.'

'Then what did you want from him?' she asked, cocking her head. 'Why did you leave your family? I might have been a shit mother, let's face it. But I never *left* you, no matter what.' She shook her head in disbelief. 'Now that takes a certain kind of coldness, doesn't it?'

I backed away, shaking my head. 'No.'

'Yes,' my mother said, following me. 'Admit it, Selma, like I've learnt to. Everything we're responsible for turns to crap. Your daughter knows it, your husband does. That's why they're leaving town. Yeah, I overheard someone mentioning it.' She cracked another smile. 'We're two peas in a pod, you and I.'

I stood staring at my mother, speechless.

She was right.

Chapter Thirty-Eight

Selma

Kent, UK
1 June 1992

'Hush little baby, don't you cry, Daddy's gonna buy you a painting brush. If that painting brush don't work . . . Mummy's gonna buy you a pile of books.'

Catherine gurgled, reaching up for my face as I sang. My mother used to sing the original version to me. Dad told me that. There must have been a time she loved me, when I was very young. Like I loved Catherine now, like I loved Becky. But then it turns bitter. Becky's right, I'm not capable of real love.

One of my tears splashed onto my daughter's chubby cheek and I gently wiped it away.

Outside, I saw the flicker of the fire. Julien, Caden and Idris were sitting out there with Donna and Tom, who was scribbling in a notepad I'd let him have. Maggie had finally left a few weeks before, unable to take it any more after some paper flowers she'd made were destroyed in a flood. When Idris told her it was all 'for a reason', she'd exploded, telling him she couldn't cope with living in the cave any more, seeing the very *reason* she'd gone there in the first place – her art – destroyed. I'd met up with her in the café when I'd bumped into her one day while I walked along the beach. She'd told me it suited me, being a new mother. I'd smiled, nodded, pretended I agreed.

I heard Idris laugh. He was in good spirits. The topic of Spain had come up again, Julien and Idris concocting a plan to sell furniture and art from the cave to make enough money to go.

'Just a few months,' Idris had said to me just the night before, 'and we'll have enough money for flights for all of us. We can give our little Catherine the life she deserves and Becky too, when she comes out to visit. No more running.'

But I hadn't listened properly. It was a pipe dream. The fact was, I'd never be able to run from the true threats to my daughters.

Me.

Becky was right, my mother was right. What chance did Catherine have with a mother like me?

I'd been mulling over my options since I'd seen them both. If I handed Catherine to social services, there was a chance she could have a wonderful life with new parents. But what if the right parents couldn't be found for her? What if she stayed in care throughout her childhood, just like my mother had? For some, it worked. But for others, like my mother, it didn't. I couldn't rely on Idris to look after Catherine. He was a loving, doting father, but completely impractical.

So there was only one option left really.

I looked down at my beautiful daughter, kissing her rosebud lips as I stroked her face, breathing in her sweet smell.

'I do love you,' I said in a trembling voice. 'That's why I must do this,' I whispered into her ear. I looked into her eyes. She deserved more than what I could offer her, what the *world* could offer her. It was my fault, being foolish and careless enough to bring her into this world. So now it was up to me to give her peace from it.

'My darling,' I said, sobs beginning to wrack my body now. 'My beautiful sweet Catherine. I love you forever and ever.'

Then I placed the blanket over my dear baby's mouth. She wriggled, making a muffled sound that broke my heart. I closed my eyes, shut myself to what I was feeling, what I was hearing. Instead, I saw Becky as a newborn, the sun above her head, bright and orange. And then my own mother, face expressionless as she looked at me when I was a child.

When it was over, I wrapped my daughter's lifeless body up in a blanket. Then I got up, walking towards the small dent in the wall, placing Catherine gently inside.

'Sweet dreams,' I said. 'You'll be safe now.' I kissed my finger and pressed it against Catherine's tiny face, felt her cheek still warm and full.

Then I placed the blanket down over the hole like I'd planned.

I took a deep shuddering breath. Then I walked from the cave and past the fire and the people surrounding it, completely unnoticed. I could see Idris was still smiling and felt a sudden surge of love for him. I almost ran to him. But then my resolve returned. It was best this way. My family had brought him only heartache. I hadn't told him the truth, that my mother was the woman who'd taken everything from him. Best he didn't know.

When I stepped into the sea, my skirt ballooned up around me, my jumper dragging my arms down. I imagined Idris treading water beside me as I started pulling my clothes off.

All the weight of the years, I imagined him saying as he'd once said before, *the dark thoughts, the negative vibes. No longer will they weigh you down.*

The waves came to my chin now, salt water entering my mouth.

Then strong hands were gripping me under my armpits, long hair silver beneath the moonlight gliding in the sea around me.

'Selma!' I heard Idris shout out. 'What are you doing? Selma, for God's sake.'

I looked up at him, at his beautiful eyes, the same slanted eyes as Catherine's.

'Help me,' I sobbed. 'Our beautiful baby is gone, Idris. Help me.'

Chapter Thirty-Nine

Becky

Kent, UK
6 July 2018

Becky snaps the book shut. It's nearly dark now. She's been in the cave all day, reading this book, her mum's story, skipping sections so she could quickly get to the end.

She closes her eyes, imagining her mum sitting here with Catherine in her arms, the torment of her mind, the words Becky had screamed at her still etched into her thoughts. If she'd only kept her mouth shut in the café that day all those years ago, her sister might still be alive . . .

No, she mustn't think like that. That kind of thinking had been her mum's undoing. Guilt. Lack of self-belief. All compounded by her grandmother's cruelty. But more than that, she was depressed. A deep dark depression that she tried to keep at bay for years by lying to herself. But when the lies fell apart like a pack of cards, those old insecurities and black clouds returned, making her feel she was incapable of even loving her own daughters.

Becky peers towards the back of the cave. She takes in a deep shuddery breath then walks towards the hole her mum had placed Catherine in. It is empty now, of course, no blanket . . . no baby. Becky places her hands inside though, feels the chalk crumble slightly beneath her fingertips. She tries to find the dents left there by her sister. She knows they are long gone now, but she can pretend, can't she?

'Catherine,' she whispers. 'Poor Catherine.'

She peers back at the book, lying on the side. What happened to her sister's little body? Did Idris go back, retrieve her, bury her somewhere? He must have. So in love with her mum, he even covered up his own daughter's death at her hands. And Donna knew – Becky could tell from the look in her eyes as she'd handed the book over to her that morning.

Becky looks at her watch. It's been eight hours. She desperately feels the need to talk to Donna and starts walking towards the café, despite knowing it's unlikely Donna will still be there. But she is. She's been waiting all this time.

She doesn't say anything when Becky sits down across from her.

'You knew, didn't you?' Becky says. 'All this time?'

Donna nods. 'Yes.'

'What happened after Idris saved my mum from drowning?'

Donna takes in a deep breath and looks towards the cave. 'I saw Idris in the sea with your mum. I knew something was up. To be frank, I knew something was up way before that. Your mum was showing all the classic signs of post-natal depression and more on top of that with her paranoia. I had spoken to Idris about taking her to see a doctor I knew – a man I could count on to be discreet. But then she seemed to get better. So I thought that perhaps she had just been suffering with the "baby blues", as so many women do. There are so many hormonal and chemical changes that take place in your body after childbirth – it's entirely normal for women to feel down and depressed at a time they expect to feel happy at having a new baby to look after.' She sighs. 'But I was wrong. It wasn't just "baby blues". I kick myself when I look back. Especially with cases of post-natal psychosis, people often pretend to the world that everything's okay when it's so far from that. I didn't pick up on it though, and the absolute worst happened.'

Tears gather in her brown eyes. 'Anyway, I was waiting for them on the beach. Idris begged me to help carry your mum into the cave. We told the others she'd gone for a swim, got into some difficulty, refused offers of help. When she lay on the bed, she was barely coherent, mumbling something about her beautiful baby and being sorry. We searched everywhere for little Catherine. We were frantic . . .' Donna shakes her head, pursing her lips. 'I knew, I knew deep inside the poor thing was dead.' She puts a fist to her mouth, sobbing. 'Idris found her, in that little hole. I'll never forget the sound I heard from him. It sounds like a cliché but that noise that came from him was inhuman, it really was.'

'Why didn't you go to the police?'

'I wanted to,' Donna says, wiping more tears away. 'But Idris begged me not to. He said he'd take care of little Catherine if I took care of your mum. I never asked what he did with her body. Idris said he never wanted to talk about it again so we didn't.'

Becky leans back in her chair, feeling a mixture of sadness and exhaustion. 'What happened to Mum after?'

'That doctor I mentioned? He agreed to take your mum in, and not to say a word to the police. Your mum was in that hospital for eight months, getting treated.' She smiles slightly. 'Enough time to write a bestseller.'

Becky thinks back to that time. Her mum had sent her letters – short ones in that pretty writing of hers – saying she'd gone away to a writing retreat. Becky had resented that but was used to pretending like she didn't care by then. When they saw each other again, a whole year later on Becky's tenth birthday, her mum was like a different person. Very quiet, her usual vibrancy gone. Becky put it down to the fact her grandmother had passed away a few weeks before. But now she knows it wasn't her grandmother's death that had made Becky's mum so withdrawn . . . it was Catherine's death.

Her novel, which Becky now knows she wrote while in hospital, garnered a huge publishing deal and news was just breaking about it when she met up with Becky that day. She'd even given Becky a cheque for five hundred pounds, the first of many that would be handed over with each meet-up. Becky had saved the cheques up, eventually using them to pay for her veterinary course.

'It was so difficult for Idris,' Donna says. 'He changed after that.'

'You don't know where he is now?'

Donna shakes her head. 'I like the idea of him coming back here and taking back the house he lived in with his mum and dad. But that hasn't happened, so I imagine he's living in a cave in Mauritius or something.' She laughs. 'Yes, I like that idea. Even with him knocking my daughter up, he was good to her in those months they spent in Russia, caring for Solar. But the demons obviously caught up with him and he felt he couldn't stay. He was always looking over his shoulder. I just wish I knew then what I knew now, the person he was running from was a cruel, drunk woman who couldn't really do him any harm.'

'But my grandmother did do him harm though, didn't she?' Becky says. 'The way she treated Mum must have had an influence on her state of mind, and played a role in what she eventually did. I must have played a role in that too, the way I was with her the last time I saw her before I moved to Busby-on-Sea,' she adds in a whisper.

Donna grasps her hand. 'You can't blame yourself. We can't even blame your grandmother. Your mum was ill, very ill. Anyway, now you know it all, the whole tragic story. Makes you realise just how close you need to hold the ones you love, doesn't it?'

Becky thinks of her dogs, of David, of her friends and her patients too.

But before all of that, she surprises herself as she thinks of Kai.

After Donna and Becky say goodbye, Becky walks back to her car, pausing as she passes the local bookstore. There's a poster of her mum in the window, lit candles surrounding a small display of her novels. Behind the poster is another display of books – the very book she's just read by Donna's son, Tom. Next to it is a sign: 'Summer late night opening.'

She impulsively goes into the store and gathers up all her mum's books, taking them to the counter. She'd never owned one, let alone read them. Too painful. But now, for the first time, she thinks she can.

'Did you know her?' the shop assistant asks as she notices Becky staring at the photo of her mum.

'No,' Becky replies. 'I didn't know her at all.'

When she drives home an hour later, it's starting to really rain, thunder rumbling across the sky. Thoughts are swirling in her head, anger and sadness and grief crashing together like the storm outside. Her mum *killed* her own daughter, Becky's only sister. Of course, she's read about post-natal psychosis and knows how serious it can be – how it can alter someone. But it's still so hard to wrap her head around. It will take a long time to digest.

As she approaches her little cottage, relief pours through her at the very sight of it. She's finally home. She gets out and runs through the pounding rain to David's cottage first, smiling at the sound of her dogs' manic barks as she presses the doorbell. Everything with them is so simple. You feed them. You love them. They love you back. No question.

'Shush now, you crazy lot,' she hears David shouting from the other side. A door slams then the front door opens.

'You're a bit late,' David says, smiling at her. 'Your plane got in this morning – I was worried.'

'I had something to do first. Sorry, I should have called.'

'So how did your trip to Russia go?'

She grimaces. 'Long story.'

He examines her face. 'Want to talk about it?'

'I'm not sure. I think I just want to go to bed.'

'At least come in for a quick cuppa? You're soaking!'

She thinks of what Donna said about holding people close. And she can't contest the fact that her T-shirt and jeans are wet through. Perhaps a cup of tea would be a good idea after all.

'Sure, why not? How have you been anyway?' she asks as she follows David inside.

'Oh, you know, the usual aches and pains.' He looks at her sideways. 'You?'

'I'm fine, just tired and desperate to return to normality now.'

'The dogs have missed you. Prepare yourself.' He opens the doors and the dogs come charging out, whining and jumping up to lick Becky's face.

'I've missed you all so much, you don't even know,' she says, kneeling on the floor and greeting each of them. She buries her face in their fur, all the emotions from the past few days soaring through her.

David puts his hand on her shoulder. 'You're not really okay, are you?' he asks her, handing her a towel to dry off her hair and face. Becky's mascara is smudged under her eyes, and she can see David isn't sure if she's been crying or if it's the result of her waiting on his doorstep in the rain.

'It's a long, and rather painful story,' she replies, standing back up.

'Come on,' David says, walking to the kitchen. 'Let's get you that cuppa and you can tell me all about it.'

They walk into the kitchen, the dogs dancing around their legs as Becky sits at the table and stares out at the familiar scenes from David's window. The calm surroundings used to make her so happy, so content, but she feels a new restlessness now. This quest to find her sister has changed something within her.

David flicks the kettle on and Summer puts her head in Becky's lap. She strokes her nose, murmuring to her.

'So what did you discover?' David asks.

'You better brace yourself.'

'I'm ready,' he says, his back to her as he reaches to the top of the cupboard for some teabags.

'There's not really an easy way to say this. My sister . . . she's dead.'

David stops, and places his hands on the kitchen counter in front of him. Becky sees his shoulders slump.

'And worst of all,' she says, voice trembling, 'my mum killed her. She killed her own daughter, David. A baby! She's a murderer.'

David doesn't say anything.

'David?'

He slowly turns and Becky sees there are tears running down his cheeks. 'Your mother wasn't a murderer, Becky. She was ill. You mustn't blame her. *I* didn't.'

'You didn't—'

'I didn't blame her. I loved her. I understood . . .'

'But I don't understand . . .'

'Becky, I'm Idris.'

Chapter Forty

Becky

Kent, UK
6 July 2018

'*You're* Idris?' Becky says, shaking her head in disbelief, her mind spinning from all this betrayal as she pushes away from the table and stands up. Of all the people she thought she could trust, David – *Idris* – has always been one of them, the opposite to her mum. And yet he was even worse!

'Please Becky, sit down,' Idris says, gesturing to the chair.

She shakes her head, crossing her arms. 'I'm fine standing, thanks.'

He sighs, rubbing at his chin. 'I hope you don't mind if I do then. My legs aren't quite as they once were.' He sits down with a heavy sigh.

'So?' Becky asks, her voice trembling.

'Your mother contacted me four years ago, when she first got her diagnosis. She saw me in the background of a photo featured in a review of the bar I worked at.'

Becky thinks of the *National Geographic* magazine. So her mum had been looking for Idris.

'She called the bar,' he says. 'I wasn't there but she left a message, telling me she needed to speak to me urgently. It was a shock. I tried to call her back but there was no answer. So I headed straight to her house above the cave. That's when she told me she was dying.' He sighs. 'Her doctor couldn't say how long she'd have, they were looking into treatments. But she was preparing herself for the worst.' He holds Becky's gaze. 'She asked me to watch over you.'

'She couldn't do it herself?'

'She thought you hated her, that you'd push her away. So she asked me, the one man she could trust to keep an eye on her first child. I had, after all, protected the darkest secret she had.'

'And you did her bidding, just like that?' Becky says, clicking her fingers.

Idris smiles. 'I always have, Becky. I loved her. I loved her in a way that's hard to explain.'

'Sounds unhealthy.'

He nods. 'It was. Anyway, we started talking over the fence.' He shrugs. 'Things went from there. In many ways, you're so unlike your mother. But in others, you're just the same.'

'I'm nothing like her. For starters, I'm not a liar.'

'You don't lie like your mother did, that's true.'

'Don't lie like *you*,' Becky says, raising her voice.

'Yes,' Idris says, nodding. 'Both of us were damaged, messed up, experts at weaving stories. Your mother with her novels, me with my life.'

421

Becky gives him a hard look. He pushes a mug of tea towards Becky but she ignores it. 'You lied to me too. All this time you've been living next door to me, and yet you didn't even tell me my mother was *dying*. I could have made amends with her earlier. I could have had more time with her!' Becky realises her hands are clenched into fists. But she is so frustrated! Everything seems such a waste: all those lost years with her mother, the past month chasing a ghost.

'Your mother begged me not to tell you she was dying,' Idris said. 'It wasn't my right to interfere!'

'Is that why you didn't tell me my sister had passed away too, you didn't want to interfere? Instead, you just watched as I trekked around Europe searching for her?'

He closes his eyes, shaking his head. 'I wanted to tell you, so many times. But it wasn't just a case of telling you your sister had passed away.' He opens his eyes, tears making them shine. 'You'd ask *how*. It was too much to explain. Too painful,' he added, voice trembling. 'Has it really been a waste though? I knew taking this journey would be good for you. I could see it was more about just finding Catherine. It was about finding yourself too.'

Becky rolls her eyes. 'Don't use me as an excuse for your cowardliness. The truth is, you chickened out of telling me.'

His jaw clenches. 'Yes, that was part of it,' Idris admitted.

'Just like you've been chickening out of showing people the real you. Not just me but everyone. Inventing a name. A persona. I presume Idris isn't your real name? That David is?'

He nodded. 'It wasn't intentional,' he said, looking down at his lined hands. 'It all started because I saved a boy from drowning. Some people thought I even walked on water.' He shakes his head,

422

laughing slightly. 'Ridiculous really. I overheard people talking – they were fascinated by me. I'd never really had that before. I was a good-looking lad back then so I attracted attention from that point of view, but not for my actions. The way it made me feel, it was *addictive*.'

His green eyes are watery and have faded with age, but Becky can still see a sparkle.

'It was a chance to start again, become the man I so wanted to be. I created a new persona to match what they thought I was. A new name too. Schoolchildren started gathering around the cave when I painted. They thought I was cool. You have to understand, I was a kid who was never popular at school. I was skinny and odd-looking. Before my mum died, I'd spend my evenings and weekends helping out in the hotel so there was no social life for me, I had no friends. Then when my mum died, I went into myself even more. Other kids called me weird, a loser. They bullied me because my mother took her life. To have these popular, good-looking teenagers looking at me in awe all those years later, the same type of teenagers who'd ignored me at school, was *thrilling*.' He scratches at the table with his nail, sighing. 'I started to believe my own hype.'

'What about the people who followed you though – how did you feel about deceiving them?'

'I really thought I was doing good, Becky,' he says, his lined face sincere. 'It didn't feel like a deception to me. You need to understand that year was a tough year here in the UK. We were in the middle of a recession; the economy was collapsing, people were losing their jobs. They needed something to believe in, and I offered them that.'

'But it was all a lie.'

He sighs. 'Yes, and the person I lied to most was myself, even convincing myself I was the man they thought me to be. Fact is, I was an unpopular kid who struggled academically, had no friends and got thrown out of his own house. No wonder I wanted people to see the opposite of that. Your mother wasn't much different, a neglected girl wanting attention.'

'And she certainly got it. She saw right through you really, didn't she?'

He nods. 'Right from the start, I think. She wasn't like the others. Her focus was on the writing. She saw the cave, saw me, as a way to finish her book.'

'Not me though. That's why she left me.'

'You mustn't hate her, Becky.'

'Have you *read* this?' Becky says, taking the novel out and slamming it onto the table. 'How can I *not* hate her? How can *you* not hate her? She killed your baby.'

David flinches and she can see the memories ravish him, making his whole face sag with sadness.

Becky sighs, taking the chair across from him. 'I'm trying to be angry at you. But to have gone through that.' She shakes her head. 'I can't imagine . . .'

He puts his elbows on the table and rests his head in his hands. 'I knew something was wrong with your mother. Donna certainly did. But I suppose I was lying to myself again, pretending it wasn't as bad as it was. When I saw her in the sea that night I knew it had gone too far, but I didn't have a clue *just* how far.' He takes a sip of his tea, holding the cup with shaky hands. 'I thought we'd return to the cave to find Catherine crying her little eyes out.' He squeezes his own eyes shut, as if he's trying to block the memories. 'But your mother kept saying sorry, over and over. And I knew, I just knew . . .'

His voice breaks and he's sobbing now, wiping the tears away with his wrinkled fingers. Becky wants to reach for him, comfort him, but she's still so angry and confused.

'The silence when we got back to the cave was chilling. Catherine was tiny but, boy, did she have some lungs on her when she cried.' He smiles slightly then his face darkens. 'Donna and I searched for her, all over. When I saw the blanket hanging from those branches, I knew I'd find my daughter in there.' He shakes his head, face filled with such intense sadness. 'It just looked like she was sleeping when I found her. She still had colour in her cheeks, felt warm. But I knew.' He hangs his head.

Becky can't help it, she goes to her old neighbour, the father of her sister, her mum's great love, putting her arms around him. He sobs into her shoulder as the dogs crowd around, close but unobtrusive, sensing the solemnity of the occasion.

'I took her to the hotel above the cave,' he continues. 'I buried her beneath the oak tree my mother so adored. Years later, I discovered your mother inherited the hotel when your grandmother died, and that brought a smile to my face, knowing Catherine would be with her.'

'When did you find out my grandmother was your stepmother?'

'When she died and I read the obituary in the local paper. "Mother to author, Samantha Rhys."'

'But how can you not hate my mum for what she did?' Becky asks him.

425

'I could never hate her. I do hate the darkness that took over her and made her do what she did though.'

'You didn't stay with her. You left.'

He nods. 'I couldn't look at her afterwards. It was too painful, and I knew she needed help. The last time I saw her before I left the cave, she was being driven away by the doctor Donna had found. We didn't really say a proper goodbye – she wasn't herself then anyway.'

'And then you went to see Oceane?'

He nods. 'She'd written to tell me she'd had a baby and was giving it up for adoption. I couldn't let that happen; Solar was mine.'

'Then why did you leave them all those years later when Oceane came to Russia?'

'I have my own darkness to run from too, Becky. I didn't think I deserved happiness like that. That's why I did stupid things like set fire to my paints in Spain.' He rakes his fingers through his now-short silver hair. 'I suppose I was restless too. I travelled, ended up in Ireland, managing a bar for many years. Then I get that call from your mother.

'We met at the café by the cave,' Idris says, smiling slightly at the memory. 'She was wearing those big sunglasses of hers, drinking gin of course. She was as beautiful as ever. But I saw the sadness in her eyes when she took her sunglasses off briefly. The same sadness I see reflected back at me in the mirror each morning. It was very hard when she told me how ill she was, even after all those years, the thought of her dying . . .' He shakes his head. 'Anyway, she told me she needed me to look over you when she was gone. She'd convinced your old neighbours to move out with a large sum of money.'

Becky remembers how sudden it had seemed, the young couple moving out, no sale sign outside. They'd told Becky they'd got a cash buyer.

'She bought this cottage for you so you could keep an eye on me?' she asks, looking around her.

'Yes. All I had to do was write her a letter each month, detailing how you were.'

Becky's heart clenches.

'Of course, I agreed,' Idris continues. 'At the same meeting, I told her that Catherine was buried in the hotel's garden too. A week later, she moved into the hotel. She hadn't been able to face it before then, despite it being hers.'

'And there you have it,' he says, putting his hands out. 'My story. The best and worst months of my life in that cave with your mother. It's been a long and lonely road without her since.'

'What about Solar?'

He smiles sadly. 'Another thing your mother made me promise was that I would get back in touch with her. I'm not sure she'll want me to though, walking out on her the way I did all those years ago.'

Becky remembers how it felt to hear her mum's voice on the phone a few weeks back, despite her walking out on her. 'She will. You must call her.'

He nods. 'I know. So have I lost you?' he asks.

'Maybe.'

He puts his head in his hands. Becky looks at his frail shoulders, and her heart goes out to him. She gently reaches out and puts her hand on his shoulder. 'You know I have to tell you off, right? How else will you know when you've been naughty?'

He looks up, half a smile on his face. 'I'm not one of your dogs, you know.'

'But you're just as loyal as them,' she admits. 'You *did* sacrifice four years of your life to watch over a stranger, after all.'

'You're not a stranger. You're my daughter's sister. And it hasn't been a sacrifice. These have been some of the best, most restful years of my life . . . even with these lot barking at six in the morning.'

'My family took a lot away from you. Like my grandmother. I presume she's the face you drew?'

He nods. 'The light side of the face represents the woman I first met, beautiful, light and kind. The dark how she quickly changed from that into a black hole of dispassion. It was quite something to see. Your mum thought she was like her mother but she really wasn't. There was too much love inside her . . . especially for you.'

'I wish she was still here.'

'Me too.'

He puts his hand on Becky's and she looks up at him. 'So what do I call you now? David or Idris?'

He thinks about it. 'Idris, please. It's how your mother knew me. How your sister would have known me too . . . if she was still here,' he adds with a sad smile. Then he looks out of the window. 'Ah, he's here.'

'Who's here?'

'I was about to tell you after I made us tea.'

She follows his gaze to see someone walking down her path. Not just someone, but Kai.

'You invited him *here*?' she asks Idris.

428

He shrugs. 'You gave me your keys to check on the house so I popped in yesterday to put some new milk in the fridge. Kai called while I was there, we got chatting and I invited him for dinner.'

'Idris!'

'And actually, come to think of it, he looks a bit like a dog,' Idris adds. 'Maybe a Havanese with those dark dreadlocks and puppy eyes? I can see why you like him so much now.'

Becky looks at Kai through the window as he rings her doorbell and can't help but laugh. 'He really does look like a Havanese, doesn't he? And what's this about *liking* him? We're not an item, you know.'

'Maybe you should be.' Becky rolls her eyes. 'Look, this isn't about me wanting to marry you off,' Idris says, face serious again. 'It's just about not letting those you have a connection with slip through your fingers, okay?'

'Funny, Donna said exactly the same thing.' She sighs and stands up, walking to the door.

'Oh, and before you go,' Idris says, 'I got a letter delivered to me by accident.' He goes over to the side and brings over an envelope.

'That'll be from the estate agent's I'm using to sell the hotel,' she says, recognising the logo stamped on the front. 'Or should I say, your old house.'

Idris frowns. 'You're really selling it?'

'Don't give me that look. It's too big for me!'

'You know your mother turned that place into a sanctuary for other women like her?' Idris says. 'Women who needed to escape themselves, a lot of them suffering from PND like she did. She even let them bring their children.'

Becky thinks of the discarded mugs and unmade beds, the children's toys and swings. And all those women at the funeral too, especially the two who did readings.

'I had no idea,' she says, amazed.

'I think she found that old building's true calling then,' Idris says. 'A sanctuary to help those in need. Might be good for animals in need too – you've always talked about opening an animal sanctuary. You have the perfect-sized building to do so now, plus the money, thanks to your mum.'

She shakes her head. 'Pipe dreams.'

'Your mother had pipe dreams. They turned out pretty good in the end?'

She shoots him a cynical look. 'Did they really?'

'You're not your mother in many ways, Becky. Maybe you can achieve your dreams and keep your family close too?'

He walks over to open the front door and Kai looks up.

'Hey stalker,' Becky says, stepping outside.

Kai throws her a lopsided smile. 'Hey yourself.'

As he says that, the dogs suddenly escape Idris's house, flinging themselves towards Kai, almost knocking him off his feet as they jump up at him.

'Well, if the dogs approve . . .' Idris says from behind Becky.

She watches as Kai succumbs and drops to the floor, letting the dogs jump all over him as he laughs. His laugh is infectious and, before long, Becky and Idris are in stitches too.

'What do you know about the healing properties of caves?' she asks Kai as she shushes the dogs away.

'Why?' Kai asks.

'Just a pipe dream I might want to turn into a reality one day.'

Behind her, Idris's face breaks into a huge smile. 'Fancy going for a drive to check the place out?' she asks Kai. 'We can get fish and chips there and watch the sun set from the cave.'

'If there's a cave to be explored, then hell yeah!'

She goes to her car, opening it and letting the dogs jump in. 'You coming?' she asks Idris.

He hesitates.

'Come on,' she says. 'You came up with the idea!'

He smiles and gets his coat, locking his door and getting into the car too.

Before Becky joins them, she pauses, thinking about the fact this rusty old car of hers contains everything precious in her life – those two unlikely men, and her three crazy dogs. It makes her smile.

Then she peers in the direction of her mum's clifftop house, imagining her standing in the garden, looking out towards the sea.

'Goodbye, Mum,' she whispers.

'Goodbye, Becks,' she imagines her mum replying before putting on her trademark sunglasses, her patterned skirt lifting in the wind as she walks into the hotel with Catherine in her arms.

Author's Note

Hello,

Thank you so much for reading *The Lost Sister*. I adored writing this novel and found myself completely wrapped up in Selma and Becky's worlds. I hope you feel the same too. If you do, please leave a review on the website of the retailer you purchased it from, and also on GoodReads if you're a member – reviews are like gold dust to us writers!

Research trips are like gold dust too, mainly because they force authors to relax every now and again! For this novel, I visited the beautiful Botany Bay area of Broadstairs on the UK's Kent coast. While Queensbay is a fictional town, it's loosely based on Botany Bay. If ever you're in the area, I'd highly recommend a visit! Especially to the lovely Botany Bay Hotel, which inspired the Bay Hotel where Selma spends her final years. It sits right on the cliff, overlooking stunning views. I spent some lovely hours there looking out over those views while writing *The Lost Sister*, eating cream scones and sipping tea (and yes, sometimes wine too!).

So that's it, another one of my novels finished. But the journey doesn't have to stop here. You can visit my website at www.tracy-buchanan.com, where you can find all the ways to contact me: I love hearing from readers. You can also learn all about joining the VIP readers' group I've set up with some other amazing authors, where you can get access to lots of exclusive content, goodies and opportunities to read my next novel in advance for FREE!

Thanks again for reading and I look forward to hearing what you think! Tracy x

Some Thank Yous

Thanks as ever to my agent Caroline Hardman and my editors Rachel Faulkner-Willcocks and Katie Loughnane. You guys are fab readers and big cheerleaders for my writing and I'm always so grateful. Big love to all the Avon team too. You are such a fun and supportive bunch, including the copy-editors and proofreaders.

Speaking of a fun and supportive bunch, I'm particularly grateful for you, my readers! In fact, a handful of you played a role in this novel after I put a call out for people to read an early draft. I got a great response and some wonderful feedback. So thanks to Debbie Lampard, Chris Brown, Liv Facey and Rinku Parmer. Thanks to my friends and family who read early drafts of the novel too, including Angela McCallister, Emma Cash and Amy Jones. And, as ever, Liz Richards, my research trip companion and sounding board.

Thank you also to my stepsister, Kirsty Cooper, who helped with the legal stuff and to Hannah Manning too, the loveliest and funniest vet I know, who helped me get to grips with all things animal-related . . . and inspired the three lurchers in the novel! I would say my dog Bronte helped too but she slept through most of the writing!

It was a special year in 2017 as I was blessed to attend milestone parties for my agent and publishers in the same week, and got to spend time with lots of authors. Such a great bunch! So thanks to you all, too many to mention. A special shout out goes to the members of the Savvy Authors' Snug, a group I set up to support fellow authors.

Finally, thank you to my brilliantly supportive family including my mum, as ever, and my wonderful man, Rob, for his expert DIY and latte-making skills. Thankfully, he is very different from Selma's husband and is a zillion times more supportive of my writing, his pride in it driving me on each day. And always thanks to my daughter Scarlett, who started school while I was in the midst of writing *The Lost Sister*. As I watch her learn to read, it makes me even more determined to be the best writer I can be!

**How far would you go for
the one you love the most?**

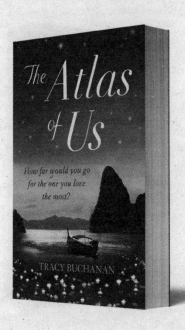

**A stormy love affair. A secret.
A discovery that changes everything . . .**

**Everything you've built
your life on is a lie.**

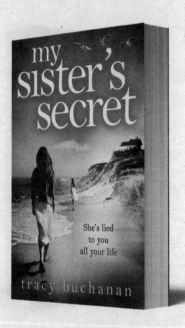

**And no one has been telling the
truth for a very long time . . .**

You'd kill to protect your child . . .
Wouldn't you?

Is murder forgivable, if committed
to save your child's life?

**A girl has gone missing. You've never
met her, but you're to blame . . .**

**When the truth is devastating, how
far will you go to hide it?**